BOOK ONE

A TALE OF RIBBONS & CLAWS

STALE Mate

THE SHIFTER ALLIANCE

R.E.S.

Cover by Miblart.

To the family I've never met, and yet the one that knows me best. Bookstagram community, this one's for you.

Hunters
Witches
Montgomery
House
Berserkers
Mermaids
House Marino
Treasury
Hotel
Witches
Griffiths House
Witches
Addison House
Caroline
Wyverns
Minotaur
Shifter
Alliance
Building
Nephilim
Mermaids
House Durand
Pixies
Mermaids
House Fischer
Mermaids
House Murphy
Witches
Winters House
Firebird
Harpy
Fenrir
Kelpie
Shifter Haven
The Shifter Alliance

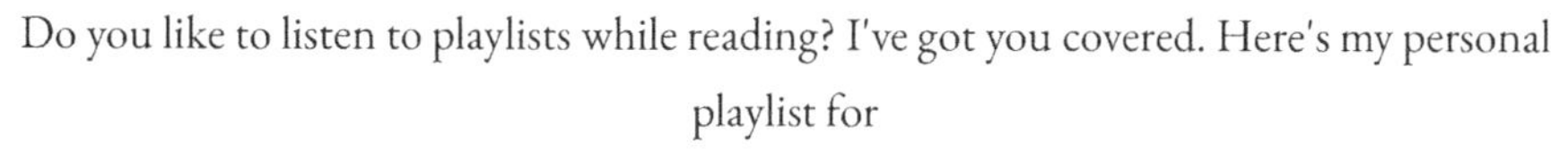

Do you like to listen to playlists while reading? I've got you covered. Here's my personal playlist for

A Tale of Ribbons & Claws: Stale-Mate.

https://open.spotify.com/playlist/1NupYLbKUVwHBwEopEhudZ?si=b081f51f5b7a4bf3

Content Warnings

All of my books are clean reads, but here are some things to note before you begin reading:

- Age gap between love interests (10 years)
- Mention of death of past loved one
- Mention of cancer (past)
- Basic violence (nothing descriptive or graphic)
- No sex
- Kissing that stays sweet and swoony
- Mild innuendos (Ex: 'keep looking at me like that and I'm going to think this is a two way petting zoo where you pet the animals and they pet you back.' No vulgar jokes.)

Note: This book is the first in a trilogy, but by the end of the series, you will get a tied-up story with a happy ending.

Contents

ONE
Caroline

ALL SPIES SHOULD WEAR PINK CONVERSE. Sure, it's a very unorthodox approach to the trade, but let me tell you, it works like a charm. Between my shoes, my white floral-patterned sundress, and the white ribbon tying back half of my temporarily short blonde hair, I was the least suspicious person in the building.

I smiled and waved to the security guard standing by the corridor that held the elevators at the Shifter Alliance Building. Like clockwork, he gave me a nod and a smile, eyeing me with male appreciation before turning his attention back to the lobby. It wasn't his fault, really, that he underestimated me so easily. It was a widely held belief that people couldn't be both pretty and smart—let alone *girly* and smart. Lucky for me, I'd always been a rule breaker.

I hummed cheerily the whole elevator ride to the third floor. My destination in the building often varied, depending on who happened to catch my attention recently. Today it was Luke Payne's turn. He'd been a legislator for the western region of the Shifter Alliance in the U.S. for twelve years. It wasn't until recently that he'd made it onto my radar when he began talking about imposing laws that would prevent Shifters from using magic in public. Not only would it prevent any Fenrir from shifting into their giant wolf forms or Harpy's from sprouting wings, but it would also keep Kelpies from using their magic to save those who were in danger, and Berserkers from being able to calm an active shooter. Not all magic was bad, just like not all humans were good, and I'd gladly ruin the reputation of anyone who tried to prove otherwise.

Smiling, I turned down another hallway, my shoes squeaking ever so slightly against the marble floors. But I didn't mind. I wasn't concerned about being caught now that I'd made it to the correct floor.

Security guards didn't patrol the halls during the day, only watching the entrances and exits in the building. And since I'd taken care of the security cameras on the third floor for the time being, there was no fear of being caught. With that thought in mind, I let my own Shifter magic trail through my body, triggering my shift like someone twirling the wand on a set of blinds. One moment I was blonde, and the next I was back to myself.

Long auburn hair waved down my back, still held in place by the white ribbon, and I picked up a piece and twirled it. I could've changed my entire appearance before sneaking in through the lobby—from my voice to my face—but I had a thing about getting into a building on my own merit and not skating by with the help of magic.

"What do you think Mae? Should I actually dye my hair blonde?" I looked down at my brindle-colored dog, her short brown and black fur patterned like tiger stripes across her body. Daisy Mae was a pure-bred mutt, with a face like a Labrador and a personality that was either Jekyll or Hyde depending on the moment. Not unlike me.

She trotted beside me in her little red service dog vest, a cover to get her into the building. In reality, she was my only weapon. If someone attacked me—which almost never happened because I made a point to appear too innocent to be harmed—then Daisy took care of them.

To get into the building, I had an arsenal of excuses. Today I'd told one of the women in the lobby that I was the Sphynx representative's assistant and that I'd forgotten to take his coat with me to the cleaner's this morning. So, she kindly sent me up to his office on the third floor to retrieve it. This was just one of the many examples why the employees at the Shifter Alliance Building needed severe training. The Sphynx representative was a notoriously no nonsense, intimidating man who'd never employ an assistant. Much less one as bubbly as me. And the receptionist should have known that.

The Shifter Alliance was the governing body that connected humans and Shifters. We coexisted well together for the most part and had since Shifters first made themselves known to humans in the early 1800's. But the Shifter Alliance helped maintain the balance between the races. One representative from each species of Shifter—from Sphinxes that turned into big cats like lions and tigers, to Mermaids who didn't sprout tails, but instead could read minds and grow scales as armor whenever they needed it—had a place on the Shifter Council along with the human mayor. They proposed law changes, discussed relations between humans and Shifters, and ate a bunch of expensive food paid for by the taxpayers.

At this very moment, as I made my way down the hall of private offices, the Shifter Council was meeting in the council chamber on the first floor. I could see them from my vantage point on the third floor, where a glass wall wrapped around the inside of the building, allowing me to watch the proceedings in the council room below. It was why I preferred doing extortion jobs on this floor on council days. I got to scout out my future hits.

All thirteen of the members sat at a ring-shaped table in the large room, drinking fancy coffees and wasting time arguing about petty disagreements. Now, hear me out. I wasn't so jaded that I didn't think some of the Shifter leaders were decent. After all, these weren't just the people who led the Shifters in our area. These thirteen people had been voted in by every Shifter leader in the western region of the U.S. to represent their species. So at least a few of them had to be decent.

"Here we are," I said cheerily, stopping at one of the office doors.

The hall was fairly wide, which meant that the council couldn't see me on this side of the hall, conveniently keeping my identity secret. After two years of pulling these stunts, you'd think they would've beefed up security and that there would be guards patrolling the halls waiting for me. But there weren't. My theory was that Mayor Fitz liked having a vigilante give him information that he'd otherwise have to illegally obtain in order to fire the corrupt individuals who worked here. *I'm basically his very unorthodox, very illegal HR department.*

"And they don't even pay me," I whispered to Daisy as I attached my electronic lock pick to the door handle.

She wagged her dangerous tail—seriously, the thing could take an eye out, I had the bruises to prove it—and followed me into the office once I got it open. While she trotted over to the couch in the corner of the moderately sized office, sniffing a potted Ficus, I went for the computer.

Some part of me probably should've felt bad that I was destroying someone's career—especially given my other magical abilities—but people like Luke Payne were a means to an end for me. Shifters and humans had once lived in peace together, until around the thirteenth century, when a civil war erupted. Both Shifters and humans had refused to get involved, and as a result, two entire species were erased from the planet. We'd kept up that same attitude ever since; if saving yourself means walking over someone else, then stomp, baby, stomp. It was a way of living that I was determined to end.

"Just don't pee on anything," I quietly called out to Daisy as I inserted my USB drive into the computer. "We actually like the mayor."

It only took a few moments for the USB to decode the mayor's password, signing me into his desktop. I uploaded the appropriate document and pulled it over to the very center of the screen where I knew he would notice it. Then, just because I was feeling particularly sassy, I changed the title of the document.

It now read, 'Another cockroach cleaned out of your house. Still waiting on my key to the city.'

"Too snarky?" I looked up at Daisy, who was currently eating the Ficus. "Who am I kidding? Snark is my oxygen; this is as nice as it gets."

"Alright, let's go home, baby girl," I called, and Daisy trotted over, wiggling as I scratched her back. Then I let us out of the office, shutting the door behind me.

TWO

Morgan

"And other than that small debacle, things have been quiet this month," Fitch, the Pixie representative announced, sliding back so far in his chair that he practically disappeared into it.

Stupid though he may be, I managed to feel a slight bit of empathy for the man. The Pixie King had been removed from his position last month thanks to the vigilante who was extorting people in the Shifter Alliance. Leaving Fitch to temporarily take over until the Pixie Princess was able to relocate here. Personally, I had no problem with some of these people losing their jobs thanks to the vigilante's interference. Most of them deserved it.

Unsurprisingly, the entire council managed to get completely off topic in the thirty seconds after Fitch finished his update on the Pixies. Meanwhile, I sat silently—well, mostly silently except for the occasional growl—and watched as everyone at the big ring-shaped table in the council room wasted yet more time. Like clockwork, it happened at every meeting.

Annoyed and unable to pretend otherwise, I rolled my eyes and ran a hand across the stubble on my jaw. *Someone, please put me out of my misery.* Here we sat, twelve Shifters—each of us voted in by the other leaders in our faction to represent our species for the region—all being babysat by a human mayor who was too nice for his own good.

Of the twelve Shifter species, only three actually shifted into animals. There were the Fenrir who turned into giant wolves, Dragons who turned into dragons, Wyverns, who—well, you get the point—and Berserkers who turned into bears. I was the latter.

Everyone else in the room didn't technically 'shift' into anything. Instead, their appearances were altered whenever they used their magic. Each species of Shifter came with their own set of abilities on top of whatever physical changes occurred. The Harpies could sprout wings and control air. Minotaur's could bulk up their bodies to rival The Rock within seconds and were impervious to magic. And Pixies had an affinity for plants that also allowed them to make potions. And yet, for all our combined abilities, we couldn't even manage to get through a simple meeting.

"I'm sorry, Fitch, I'm just a little concerned that you're not seeing the gravity of the situation," Mayor Fitz said, finally interrupting the loud murmur of side conversations.

The ceilings of the council room were high, stretching up to the third floor where a walkway could be seen through glass. Which meant that sounds echoed easily in here. As it were, I would've preferred to sit in the audience seating on the side of the room. At least then I could have stretched out between the theater seats and tried to take a nap while the rest of them bickered. Why we had the extra seating at all, I wasn't really sure. No one could possibly want to watch this pathetic discussion unfold.

We'd been here for an hour and a half already, and we'd only finished the first item on the agenda. Well, almost finished it, since apparently Mayor Fitz wasn't done with the incompetent interim Pixie leader.

Fitch was the Pixie King's nephew, which meant that he was next in line to lead after the King's daughter. Each Shifter species had its own form of choosing its leaders, and Pixies adhered to a monarchy. They only had five kings and queens, one for each region of the U.S. Hopefully the princess would be arriving soon to take over from Fitch, because clearly, he was incompetent and unmotivated. *No wonder he fits in so well on the council.*

"I see the gravity, Mr. Mayor," Fitch defended himself, pushing a nervous hand through his short blonde hair. The Pixie was a small man, and a nervous one. Something I had no patience for in a leader. Do the job or leave the job. That was my philosophy.

"Do you? Because it sounds like all you did to punish the group that was selling Springspell and Blindurtox was to fine them five hundred dollars."

"Yes?" Fitch said uncertainly, obviously unaware of why it was a bad idea to let someone get away with selling *very* illegal potions.

"You are aware that Springspell is an explosion potion that's undetectable until used, making it highly desirable to terrorists? And that Blindurtox is a drug that makes everyone in a ten-foot radius unable to move easily or think rationally, which means that it's essentially a roofie that's also undetectable and can be used even on victims who don't consume any foods or drinks?"

Fitch the Pixie rep just sat there. Dumbly. *Oh, Lord help us all.*

"Would someone please explain to the poor little man that his people aren't just going to get fined if the human police or the Shifter unit catch them selling to the black market again?" Drew, the Firebird leader spoke up. He was reclined lazily in his chair, his auburn hair perfectly disheveled and his model-like face as arrogant as ever. "They'll be thrown in Niffleheim."

Niffleheim was a Shifter prison for the worst of the worst. Basically, a real-life Azkaban. And things like selling highly harmful potions on the black market could get you an express ticket to Niffleheim. Especially if you sold them to someone who used them to harm humans.

"Ah, yes!" The Pixie laughed nervously. "I'll see to it that my punishments are more stringent. But hopefully her highness gets here soon so she can take care of it instead."

"From your lips to God's ears," I grumbled.

Apparently a little too loud.

All eyes turned to me, some accusing, some afraid, but all of them with judgment. I resisted the urge to wiggle in my chair—I wasn't about to show them my discomfort. I couldn't afford to let them see any weaknesses.

And that was the crux of being me: the Berserker Chief. I was hated and feared for the things people believed I'd done, but the moment I stopped being feared, I'd just be hated. Then I'd probably just be dead.

"Clearly, Fitch isn't comfortable doing this job, and it would benefit all of us to have at least one capable person sitting at this table." My gravelly voice carried loudly through the silence as everyone stared at me, but I wouldn't let them think I was intimidated. Better to be feared than to be afraid. "Mayor Fitz, I beg of you to let us move on to the next topic before my head explodes. Clearly, the Pixie reports are going to be a little lacking until the princess gets here. Can't we just accept that and keep these meetings moving?"

The mayor looked down at his stack of papers, seemingly unbothered by my outburst. But just before he bent his head, I could have sworn I saw the edges of a smirk on his face.

Mayor Fitz was young, only in his late twenties or early thirties. Some people thought he got the job only because of his looks—a fair assumption. He was a classically handsome guy, with dark hair that was always perfectly combed, blue eyes and a jawline that I gathered most women appreciated. But I didn't really care how he got in office, because the truth was that he was pretty good at being mayor. Of everyone on the Council, he was the most prepared, the most organized, and the most honest too.

Sad that I liked the human more than my fellow Shifters.

"I'm inclined to agree with Chief Hohlt," Mayor Fitz said after a moment, lifting that Clark Kent face back to me.

"Oh, how surprising," Francine, the Minotaur representative said dryly. Francine was a woman in her late forties with too much time on her hands. She had caramel colored hair that was always in a poofy ponytail, a face that was always set into a sneer, and a mole above her upper lip that I fantasized about her accidentally scraping off the next time she shaved the beard I was convinced she grew. Clearly, we were close friends.

"What's next on the agenda, Mr. Mayor?" Merida, the Witch representative interjected cheerily. She shifted forward in her seat, long black hair sliding across her shoulders, and gave me a warning look.

'What?' I mouthed, offended that I was being wrongfully accused of poor behavior.

Merida titled her head, bright blue eyes unimpressed.

'Fine,' I mouthed again, making sure to roll my eyes this time. But Merida wasn't intimidated, shooting me a knowing smirk. *Terrible friend.* She wasn't wrong though. I had a reputation for being a pain in these meetings, and the reputation *might* have been rightfully earned.

"Ah, yes. Thank you, Merida for getting us back on track," Fitz nodded, returning his attention to his papers. "Next, we need to discuss the proposed law about licenses for selling services performed by Shifter magic. Currently the waiting period between applying for the license and being able to open a business is—"

A hum filled the room as Mayor Fitz's phone began buzzing on the table in front of him. He paused to glance carelessly at it before continuing his explanation, but before he'd said two words, he froze and picked up the phone.

"Mr. Mayor?" Merida asked. "Is everything alright?"

"No," Fitz sighed, rubbing a finger across his forehead. "It looks like the Vigilante has struck again. Someone just accessed my computer."

Mumbles and whispers rumbled through the room like thunder as people turned to whisper theories and gossip. Funny how it only took mere seconds for most people's attention to turn toward me.

There'd never been any evidence to prove that I was really the villain most of them believed me to be. Yet here they were, ready to blame me for another crime I hadn't committed. I'd give it an hour before the rumors spread to the media that the Chief was at it again. But, just like always, I shrugged off the hurt and anger that the thoughts stirred up.

It wasn't the first time they'd blamed me for something I hadn't done. And it wouldn't be the last.

THREE

Caroline

I PRACTICALLY SKIPPED ON MY WAY home from the Shifter Alliance Building, pleased with the work I'd done. Within an hour, I fully expected to hear that legislator Luke Payne was resigning due to personal matters. Personal matters being me and my evidence of the bribes said legislator had accepted from multiple anti Shifter groups over the last nine months.

"All in a good day's work, Dais," I grinned, Daisy trotting happily beside me.

The Shifter Alliance Building was in downtown Shifter Haven, which made my walk to the burger joint on State Street quick and easy. I had Daisy sit outside while I went in to grab the food I'd ordered ahead an hour ago, and she dutifully sat by the door looking deceivingly innocent, while being secretly vicious. Just like her mother.

"Two burgers, two fries, and a vanilla shake," Frank announced as I waltzed up to the bar in the tiny 1950's style restaurant. It was really more of a takeout place, only big enough for three tables and a bar that sported red leather swivel stools and an ad for Frank's famous milkshakes.

"Thanks Frank, you're a life saver," I said with a smile, grabbing the bag and drink he offered.

"I know," the older man said with a cheeky smile. Frank was probably in his early sixties, with a head of snow-white hair and a face that you could tell used to belong to a heartbreaker. To me though, he was an honorary uncle—my favorite since he provided me with food. "Women are constantly throwing themselves at me. Mayors are always trying to give me the key to the city. I'm a regular savior."

"And in uniform," I teased, backing toward the door, and opening it with my backside. "Ugh! Be still, my beating heart."

"Oh, get out of here." He grinned, taking the towel from his shoulder, and whipping it playfully in my direction. "Go be young and cause trouble."

"Will do! And if I get arrested, I'll tell them you told me to do it."

Frank shook his head but didn't deny me another smile before I slipped back out to the street. I paused as I caught sight of a young woman inching toward Daisy, who sat wagging her tail against the side of the dated building.

"Aw, you cute little thing," the woman crooned, quickly reaching out a hand toward Daisy's head. *Oof, wrong move.*

Daisy growled and snipped at the air in warning. The woman—clearly a reasonable person—jumped back with a dramatic screech, clutching her arm to her chest as if she'd been bitten.

"Evil puppy!" she exclaimed in a whiny high-pitched voice that made my ears hurt. "You should be put down!"

Before I could open my mouth to berate her—and possibly throw my shake at her, which would've been a waste of good food—a little kid, maybe four years old, broke away from his parents and ran to Daisy. Without any hesitation, the little boy threw himself at Daisy, wrapping his arms around her neck.

"Puppy!" he shouted. "Cute!"

"Careful, it'll bite you," the mean young woman shouted. But the child didn't heed her warning, too busy laughing as Daisy licked his sweet cherub face.

"Seems sweet to me," the boy's mother said as she and her husband stepped up to watch the boy be assaulted by dog kisses. I considered warning them that Daisy had a penchant for eating her own poop, thus making her kisses a biohazard. But with the way the little boy laughed, I decided not to ruin his fun.

"Just make sure he washes his face," I advised, watching Daisy's tongue wet his cheek again. *Cleaner than a toilet seat, my foot.* The parents nodded, unphased while their child giggled and grinned.

"She loves kids, but she's careful with people," I said, glancing at the petulant woman who was still holding her—*uninjured*—arm. "She has a pretty amazing sense of intuition about who's decent and who's not."

The young woman glared at my cloaked barb before stomped away dramatically. *Well, maybe you should ask before you pet next time, Miss. Prissy Pants.*

After the little boy's parents finally dragged him away, he called out 'Bye doggie' over and over until he'd gone far enough down the block that he couldn't see us anymore.

"Well, aren't you popular today?" I said to Daisy as we headed in the direction of home.

We walked past shoppers and people out for lunch, everyone drinking up the nice spring weather while it lasted. With it only being February, the warmth wasn't guaranteed to stick, and we'd be back to cool days and cloudy skies soon. But for today, it was nice to walk home.

It only took about five minutes to get out of downtown to where a residential street was hidden a few blocks back from the hustle and bustle. My neighborhood was quiet, a few people out pushing their garbage cans onto the street, and a few older ladies weeding in their gardens. The houses were quaint and old, with big windows, wide yards, and blossoming dogwood trees that grew along the sidewalk, shading the pavement.

"Good afternoon, Miss Birch," my elderly neighbor, Mr. Finch, called from across the street.

Daisy barked excitedly at his voice, and I had to bribe her with a fry to stay near me. Mr. Finch—though he wasn't ancient, and he sported his beret with pride—wasn't a young guy, with his stooped back and slower walk. I could only imagine what havoc Daisy could cause if she tried to jump on him.

"And good afternoon to you too, Daisy Mae," he chuckled from beside his mailbox, stuffing envelopes under his arm.

"Good afternoon Mr. Finch," I called back. "How's Mrs. Finch? Still enjoying the preschool?"

"To be honest, I think she likes working with them little kids more than being with me. But I've got plans to seduce her into retirement. It involves me and my beret. *Just* my beret."

"Oh my gosh," I laughed, closing my eyes against *that* picture. "Mr. Finch, you're incorrigible."

"You know, my wife says the same thing!"

"I wonder why," I teased dryly, checking my mail.

"Oh, don't you start getting on my case now. We're partners in crime, remember?"

"Of course, Mr. Finch," I said, keeping my voice serious, though I couldn't suppress a smile. "I'll see you tomorrow."

"See you tomorrow, Caroline," he chuckled before turning back to his house.

We both disappeared up our driveways and I shuffled the food in my hands to unlock my front door.

"Alright, time to eat," I announced as I dropped my small backpack onto the bench by the door.

The click clack of Daisy's nails on the wood floors followed me to the kitchen at the back of the house. I'd just put a plain patty into her dog dish as a job well done for our success today when my phone began to buzz.

"I'm alive, I'm home, I'm unharmed," I pleaded immediately, pressing the phone to my ear. With one hand, I dropped the takeout bag on the round dining room table, slurping unceremoniously on my milkshake.

"Then why didn't you call once you were done with your ridiculous escapade?" my sister complained halfheartedly into my ear. I didn't have to see her to know that she was giving me a look dryer than the Sahara. This was Ariel we were talking about. "I can hear you slurping, so I know you stopped for food before alerting me to your still beating heart."

"Dramatic much?" I complained, though the emotion was empty as I sat and tossed my feet up on a dining chair.

"I'm a Birch, of course I'm dramatic."

I laughed. It was true, our parents had raised us to be unapologetically ourselves. If only they'd known what they were creating.

"Are you playing some kind of fantasy video game?" I could hear instrumental music in the background on Ariel's end.

"Is the sky blue? Does two plus two equal four? Is Aragorn the standard that all men must be held to?"

"...yes?" I guessed, knowing my sister's obsession with *The Lord of the Rings*. Okay, so it was a mutual obsession, but I'd always been more of a Thorin Oakenshield kinda gal myself.

"Exactly!" Ariel exclaimed, ruining my eardrums. "So, in answer to your question, yes, I'm playing a fantasy game, and it's awesome. You know, you could hop online and join me if you weren't so busy trying to destroy the world."

I decided not to respond to the comment, knowing she couldn't understand my vendetta. My sister was normal, human. Sure, she'd had to be careful growing up, making sure her friends never figured out my secret. But she hadn't lived her life *being* the secret. She hadn't grown up always having to be careful to make sure no one saw her move too fast, or noticed her anticipate a need, or alter an emotion. She hadn't had to dilute herself and smother her instincts so she could stay safe. She didn't know what I felt.

I knew that she and my parents both did their best to empathize with me, but they were humans, not Elves. I'd spent my entire life completely alone in my uniqueness, they hadn't.

For three years, I'd lived in Shifter Haven, watching other people suffer some of the same things I had. And while I couldn't change the fact that I was the only one like me, I could help make sure no one else had to feel this way. That no one else was forced to hide because of fear or hatred. So, I'd spent my time plotting and planning. I watched leaders and government officials, and though a few of them had proven to me that humanity still existed, many of them were poster children for depravity.

And if there was one thing I'd learned living life as an extinct species, it was that I could affect the most change from the shadows.

FOUR
Morgan

TODAY WAS A NEW DAY. THE SHIFTER Council was meeting, and the same twelve people all sat around the same table eating expensive pastries and wasting time. But not me.

Because today, I was prepared. I knew that eighty three percent of the vigilante's targets worked on the third floor. I knew that although sneaking in at night would be the more obvious choice, they liked to sneak in during the day. And I knew that the vigilante seemed to prefer pulling heists on council meeting days when they could add insult to injury by pulling off their crime as we all sat drinking coffee and eating scones.

Clever and vindictive. A dangerous combination in a spy.

And now this spy's actions were directly affecting me. Because as I'd predicted, the rumors had begun, claiming that me and my people were behind the heists. That if we went unchecked, we'd take over the whole region. It genuinely baffled me that people were stupid enough to believe such nonsense. But whatever, the world needed Jesus and a whole lot of therapy, not my backhand.

I resisted the urge to whistle as I lurked through the hallways of the Shifter Alliance Building, not wanting to draw attention to myself as I kept my eyes peeled for the culprit. It seemed that so far, the attacker was able get in and out of the building completely unnoticed. *Until today.*

Because today, I was going to catch a spy, and clear my name.

I'd excused myself from the council meeting, claiming a need for the bathroom. Since my reputation was so ugly, no one questioned me—the only perk of being seen as the bad guy. I was making my second lap through the hall when I heard the muted sounds of a keyboard clicking.

I paused, my nerves thrumming, and my Shifter abilities prodding me to be used, begging me to shift. But I stuffed down the urge, locking it up tight where it belonged. I would *not* shift here.No matter how bad I wanted to clear my name.

Silently, I inched further down the hall, following the sound of the keyboard. Up ahead, an office door stood open, the faint blue light of a computer shining against the door. And then I heard...was that someone humming?

Curious now, I peeked inside the open doorway, where someone was crouched over a computer on a desk in the middle of the room. The person's face was shadowed and all I could see was a curtain of dark hair partially held back by a green bow.

A grunt from my left brought my attention to a medium sized dog that was eating a napkin that had been left on an end table. Its large dark eyes stared curiously at me, but it didn't approach. Instead, it continued to eat, its small ears flopped over rather than standing at attention, unconcerned with my presence.

"That ought to do it." The woman's voice snapped my attention away from the dog and back to the computer. "Five years of fraud and money laundering should buy him some decent jail time. And someday maybe I'll get a thank you from this city for cleaning up the trash."

Unsure if she was talking to the dog or to herself, I glanced at the dog, but she just continued to chew on her napkin.

"No, I'm not talking to her." Confused, I whipped my head around and stared at the woman that I couldn't quite see. Then, she turned the computer screen off and the room went dark. "I'm talking to you, Mr. Tall Dark And I'm assuming Handsome over there."

"What?" I stuttered, so taken aback by her brazenness that I forgot my purpose in being there.

"Catch."

Confused and bemused as I was, I almost didn't realize that something was whistling through the air toward me. But at the last moment, my hands reached out and I caught an empty vase just before it could hit me in the chest.

"What the—"

"Thanks, this has been fun," the woman teased, an arrogant lilt to her words as she slid right past me, leaving me standing there like an idiot.

Irritated at my own lack of focus, I dropped the vase and let it shatter, turning to chase the woman and her dog down the hall. Dark hair flying out behind her, she bolted down the halls at a faster pace than I was prepared for, clearly using her Shifter abilities. Unfortunately, as a Berserker, I was strong, but I wasn't fast. I might've been able to catch up if I shifted into bear form, but it wasn't worth it. Nothing was worth that.

So, when she disappeared around a corner and I found the adjoining hallway empty, I gave up, knowing I'd been bested. We all had. Because this woman had been sneaking in and out of the building for months and no one had been able to catch her.

"Yet," I growled. She'd gotten away so far, but now I knew what to expect. And how to beat her.

FIVE

Morgan

I PACED THE LENGTH OF MY OFFICE LIKE I was digging a trench from the double doors to the stained-glass window. If I wasn't careful, the plush rug would have a burn mark through it within the hour from my fuming.

"You act like we're getting evicted," Logan—my best and oldest friend—droned. He sat in an armchair beside a grey couch, his feet tossed carelessly on the coffee table like he didn't have a care. Must be nice.

"We might," I growled, spinning around to pace back the other way.

This room was filled with floor to ceiling bookshelves that contained years, and years' worth of records from past Chief's and all kinds of tomes on history. Yet even with all this advice at my fingertips, I didn't know how we were going to get out of our current predicament.

"You're being dramatic. The Shifter Alliance can do some things, but not that," Logan argued, raising one blonde eyebrow at me.

"They might not need to evict us," I said, swiping a pen from the large oak desk that sat across from the assorted couch and armchairs. I clicked it as I began pacing again, annoyed with my own stress. "If they can show the rest of the Sleuths in the region that I'm unworthy to lead—or worse, convict us of a crime—then I'll not only lose my position as the Berserker representative, but all the progress Berserkers have made in the last decade will be gone. We'll just be the problem children of the Shifter world again."

Logan rolled his blue green eyes at my dramatics and ran a hand through his short blonde hair. He was an easygoing, positive-attitude-only kind of guy through and through. It annoyed the crap out of me.

"Oh, stop being Chicken Little, Morgan Gareth Hohlt. They don't even have any evidence yet. All they have is a suspicion motivated by rumors. It won't result in anything," he said, shrugging his shoulders.

"The agent who came by this morning said that we are officially people of interest in their investigation about the heists." Defeated and yet somehow still angry, I discarded the pen that had quickly begun to annoy me anyway and leaned back against the desk. "She said that given my absence at the last meeting, my track record, and the tactics used, they suspect we may be involved. Which is ridiculous because Berserkers are not known for stealth!"

Logan raised his eyebrows again, tilting his head in a patient way that annoyed me. "I get why you're upset, but you seem...combustible. Why?"

I shook my head, reliving the moment I'd let that girl slip past me. I should've caught her; I shouldn't have been thrown off so easily. "I just don't like that I had the culprit right there in my path and stupidly let her get away."

"Was she cute?" Logan asked, as if this were an important factor.

I glared at him. "I don't know, it was dark. But it doesn't matter! She was fast, and she was clever, and like an idiot, I let her get away. I don't like that I'm being outmaneuvered by someone who's ruining our reputation one heist at a time."

"You say that like we have a reputation to ruin," Logan winked. I remained unimpressed. "Alright, come on sourpuss. What else has you all fit to be tied?"

That was a hard question to answer, because ever since yesterday when I'd almost caught the intruder, I'd felt strange. Like my feelings were...random. Wrong.

"I'm not sure," I admitted, rubbing my chest, "It's like my emotions are off beat. They're being triggered at the wrong moments..."

"You definitely seem a little discombobulated," Logan nodded, watching me carefully. "Maybe you should hit the gym for a while. Get your brain back on track."

I nodded, knowing he was probably right. Working out usually helped me feel more in control of things—which I desperately needed right now.

"Yeah," I sighed, straightening from the desk. "It's not like I've ever been a ray of sunshine anyway. So, I'm a little prickly right now, what else is new?"

"Oh, come on," Logan snorted as he stood. "You may not be a violent person, but you're as prickly as a porcupine. I wouldn't cuddle you for a million bucks."

"Good, because I like being the little spoon and I'm taller than you, so that wouldn't work."

Logan laughed as we left my office, but my smile quickly melted off my face. *Why do I feel so strange?* And what was the woman's goal in targeting people at the Shifter Alliance?

"Only one way to find out."

SIX
Caroline

I GAVE THE GUARD OUTSIDE THE SHIFTER Alliance building my brightest smile, unable to mask my good mood. Although anyone was allowed to enter the building, no one could get past the lobby without a badge. Well, almost no one.

The man in uniform returned my smile and let Daisy and I pass, mistakenly thinking us unthreatening. *He's not the first.* And he certainly wouldn't be the last. I made my way across the marble lobby and stepped up to the front desk, where I made sure to choose the busiest receptionist who had a phone pressed to her ear.

'Bathroom?' I mouthed, dancing in place like I had to pee.

She nodded distractedly and pointed behind her at the small corridor where the elevators were. I smiled gratefully at her, shouldered my backpack a little higher and flipped my auburn hair over my shoulder. I'd opted not to alter my hair with magic today. It'd been a few months since I'd come into the building sporting my natural hair, and since most of these people couldn't remember what they ate for breakfast, there was zero chance they'd remember my hair color.

I followed the sign that said 'Restroom' down the hallway but headed straight for the elevators instead. The guard behind me at the entrance of the corridor was too busy watching the front entrance for 'obvious' threats to notice me sneaking my way upstairs.

I smiled at the security camera in the corner as the elevator went up to the eighth floor. The camera wasn't active, thanks to my feed blocker, but I needed someone to gloat to.

"I don't know if I'll ever be able to retire, Dais," I said aloud, twirling the hem of my periwinkle shirt. It was trimmed with lace and had faint white flowers all over it. And of course, I was sporting a periwinkle blue ribbon in my hair to match. "I don't think anything else will ever be this satisfying."

Today's victim was Bernice Weston. Head accountant for the taxation department, forty-four years old, and a member of the Durand family of Mermaids. They weren't currently the ruling family in the area, but the next person that took over once Queen Chloe either retired or died was expected to be from the Durand family.

Mermaid families weren't comprised of actual relatives, instead they were groups that Mermaids elected to join. Apparently, Bernice was hoping to get Chloe an early retirement by making it look like the queen had been siphoning funds from the Sphinxes for her own projects. I wasn't a fan of Chloe the Mermaid rep myself, but I hated it when people played dirty.

I'd just stepped out of the elevator and onto the eighth floor when someone called out, "Miss, may I help you?"

I turned toward the kind voice of a security guard and gave him my signature 'I'm sorry, I know I shouldn't be here' smile. It wasn't common for guards to be in the halls, though this one was probably on his way somewhere.

"I'm sorry, I know I'm not technically supposed to be in this area," I said, making sure to act much younger than my twenty-two. The guard's expression softened a little, especially when he noted Daisy's service dog vest. "But my dad grabbed my wallet this morning by mistake, and I need to get it back to him. I texted him and he said it's in his office. Since he's in session right now with the rest of the council, I figured I'd grab it without disturbing him. But I can totally go grab him if you want."

"Who's your dad?" the man asked with a healthy dose of skepticism.

Depending on the name I gave him, he'd either agree to go grab a man who would have no idea who I was, or he'd be too terrified to bother.

"Gerard, the Hunter representative."

Hunters were a unique kind of Shifter. Rather than shifting their appearance, they had unique abilities that made them able to defeat other Shifters. There was a kind of Hunter for every kind of Shifter, and each Hunter faction had the opposite abilities of their Shifter counterpart. So, where Mermaids could read minds, Mermaid Hunter's minds were impenetrable, and while Mermaids could conjure scales that protected them, Mermaid Hunters could cut through those scales like butter. So, of all the people on the Shifter food chain, Hunters were probably at the top. Hence my choice for my fake dad.

"Actually," the guard said, a little nervous now that I'd name dropped the Hunter rep, "Let's not disturb the meeting. I'll walk you down to his office."

"Oh, that would be great, thank you!"

We walked in companionable silence, Daisy Mae dutifully trotting beside me. After a few moments, I discretely glanced down at my watch. *He's a minute late.* If the guard's radio didn't go off in the next thirty seconds, I was going to have to use magic on him. Because there was no way I could let him see which office I was really going to.

But then, just as I'd hoped, the guard's radio buzzed with static, and a voice called out for assistance at the reception desk.

"I'd better go check on that," the guard said, looking nervously between me and the hallway ahead.

"Want me to come with you, or wait here?" I said, knowing that the least suspicious attitude to have was a compliant one.

"No...you know the way to your dad's office, right?"

I nodded and smiled, and the security guard, convinced of my innocence, left me to my own devices. Feeling a little cocky, I smirked to myself and continued down the hall to the appropriate office.

"Paul has definitely earned that hundred bucks," I hummed.

Paul was a friend of mine who often helped me with my heists. He was a homeless man who'd made his home near the Alliance Building. And while I knew that he was kind and brilliant, the sad truth was that most people assumed he was either dangerous or not completely lucid based on his appearance. Which he used to his advantage by providing the occasional distraction for me.

Really, I'd told Paul that today's assignment would earn him fifty dollars, but I knew how strapped he'd been this winter, so I was going to give him another fifty whether he liked it or not. He could consider it a work bonus if it made him feel better.

My peppy attitude followed me down the hallway for a few paces...but then it suddenly began to falter. The smile slid off my face and I rubbed at my chest, confused. For the last month, I'd felt off. Like even when I felt happy, I somehow still felt sad or anxious or annoyed. And now, when I was feeling on top of the world and excited about today's job, there was a sense of irritation lurking in my mind. But no matter how hard I tried to focus on my happiness or rub the feeling away like an ache, it still remained.

I was in the middle of trying to weed out that annoyed feeling when suddenly I felt the presence of someone behind me. Close behind me. But even as I tensed my muscles to run, big beefy arms banded around me, locking my arms to my side.

"Finally," a vaguely familiar gravelly male voice said, "You're not an easy woman to catch."

Shocked as I was, my snark came back online fast, followed by my clever instincts.

"How else am I supposed to get your attention?" I teased dryly. Then I swung my head back as hard as I could. Right into his nose. The man's arms loosened slightly as he groaned, but I still couldn't manage to slither away.

"So clearly you have super strength," I grunted, trying my best—and failing—to wiggle free. "That's inconvenient."

"Funny, I was just about to say the same thing about you."

"Oh yeah? How have I inconvenienced you? I'll need to make sure I do it again," I said, smiling sardonically at him over my shoulder.

But the moment my eyes met his, I sensed him go cold with shock.

Kidnapper guy was hot—like, call your mom and tell her to get out the wedding planning book kind of hot. Dark hair waved messily to just below his ears. A bit of scruff highlighted a very sturdy jaw, and dark brows sat low and menacing on his forehead. A faint white scar slashed across his left eyebrow and onto his right cheek, only bringing more attention to his unnerving eyes. Good Lord, those *eyes.* They were a piercing colorless grey that seemed to be raging and calming all at once, and just around the iris was a thin ring of an impossibly bright blue. He was like the long-lost twin of the older, glowed up Milo Ventimiglia. Very *glowed up indeed.*

Kidnapper guy seemed a lot less thrilled to see me than I was to see him though—which was ironic considering that he was the one with the terrifying reputation. *Which, come to think of it, I should probably make sure not to let him take me.*

While big scary bear man—because now having seen his face, I knew that he was the Berserker Chief—seemed overcome with panic and disbelief, I pushed my elbows into his abdomen. This approach proved very effective, and he stumbled back a few steps, letting me go.

"No," he whispered insistently, his shocked expression morphing into a glare, "It can't be."

"Not sure what that means, but Ima go now," I smiled, wiggling my fingers patronizingly at him.

Then I turned and fled, letting my Shifter magic kick in and give me a boost of extra speed. However, I seemed to have underestimated just how dangerous an angry Berserker could be.

Before I'd gone more than a step, my arm was caught in a vice grip. Knowing that I was dealing with someone who possessed super strength, I knew there was no breaking out of it. So instead, I turned, ready to disarm him with my manipulation magic. But he moved faster than I anticipated, pulling out a pre-tied zip tie from his pocket and slipping it over my wrists.

"Seriously?" I exclaimed, too stunned to move for the moment—he'd literally tied me up. *Who does that?* "The least you could've done was buy me dinner first!"

The Berserker Chief—or 'kidnapper guy' as I was henceforth going to call him—stared incredulously down at me, like I'd ruined *his* day. "I'll get you a granola bar on the way home."

I opened my mouth to give him the tongue lashing of his life when a quiet thumping drew my attention to Daisy Mae. Who just sat there on the marble floor. Happily watching her mother be abducted.

"Do Berserkers have animal magic that I don't know about?" I snapped, glaring at Daisy once more before looking up at Kidnapper Guy.

"No," he ground out—clearly a verbose man.

I watched him, silently considering my options. Since I was never going to be able to beat his strength, and he clearly wasn't going to play fair—*stupid zip ties*—I wouldn't play fair either. Leaning close, I put my lips next to his cheek and whispered in his ear. "Careful, Chief, get any more talkative and I'm gonna think you like catching me."

As expected, he went completely still, and I pulled back to watch his expression go slack. Then, I put on my best innocent look and carefully snaked my foot behind him...

And yanked it forward, swiping his foot out from beneath him. He fell to the ground with a thud just like I'd hoped he would. Unfortunately, he still held my wrists...so I fell on top of him.

I groaned, wiggling like a fish as I tried to roll away from him. But before I could get far, he was sitting up and had snatched my calves in his big hands. Then he pulled out another one of those *freaking* pre-tied zip ties and tightened it around my ankles.

"Ow!" I complained, as I struggled to sit up.

"You know, you're a big pain for such a small thing," Kidnapper Guy groaned, rolling his shoulders as he got to his knees.

"Oh, you ain't seen nothing yet, bear man," I smirked, lifting my now conjoined legs, and kicking him in the jaw. Boy was I feeling thankful for all those Pilates videos I'd done.

Kidnapper Guy's head snapped back with a crack, and I let a smug smile fill my face. Now to get out of the zip ties. I looked around for anything I could use to get out of the plastic, but I didn't travel with weapons—just Daisy. And she was currently watching us with a doggy smile on her face.

"Do you have a pocketknife?" I wondered aloud, thinking that someone as manly as him probably kept one on him. And there was really only one way to find out.

Mr. Scary Berserker Chief was busy rubbing his jaw, so he wasn't prepared when I launched myself at him. But with my legs pinned together, it was hard to control how I fell. So I ended up with my face in his pecs. *If he were a woman, this would be very awkward.* But as my hands pressed against a very firm stomach, I realized that it was awkward anyway. *How many abs does this guy have?* So far, I counted four sets.

"Sorry, I just need to borrow something," I mumbled, pushing myself up while he rubbed the back of his head—which had probably hit the marble floor when we fell.

"You're going to need to repeat that," he grumbled, "That was the rustiest 'sorry' I've ever heard. Clearly the word has gone unused for the better part of a decade."

"Oh, stop with the judgy eyes. You don't even know me." Then, because I was in too tight of a pinch now to care about social boundaries, I stuck my zip-tied hands into one of his front pockets, searching for a knife.

"No, I don't!" He squirmed beneath me, batting at my hands. "So, I hardly think you should be feeling me up right now."

"Ugh! You wish!" And he did, because I could sense his attraction...as well as a whole bunch of hostility.

"Stop sticking your hands in places so we can get out of here."

"In what world do you expect me to listen to you?"

Kidnapper Guy snatched my wrists in one hand and held them to his chest as he sat us both up—a very awkward position to be in when you're tied like a pig at a luau.

"Well, you are zip tied on the floor and currently in my possession. So, I hardly think you have a choice," he said matter-of-factly.

I growled.

"Stupid, hot blooded flea bag!" Before I could throw out any other insults though, he shoved a gag between my lips—a *gag!* Who the heck does that??

Undeterred from expressing my emotions, I screamed at him, but my words came out in a string of unintelligible mumbles. Kidnapper Guy wasn't bothered. In fact, his lips turned slightly up at the corners. If I wasn't so ticked, I might've enjoyed the sight of it.

Without saying a word, the guy pulled me to my feet, then cut the zip ties from my hands. Only to pull my arms behind my back and retie them.

'Don't trust me?' I tried to say, but the gag muffled the words.

"Not even a little," he smirked. Then without warning, he grasped my waist and hoisted me up on his shoulders, my head facing his derriere. "Now be a good sack of potatoes and just dangle quietly."

I roared, but the man was unphased, readjusting his grip where it now rested on my thighs.

"Alright, my little spy," he said in that deep baritone voice as he traipsed through the halls, Daisy trotting happily behind us, "Let's get you home."

SEVEN

Caroline

KIDNAPPER GUY DIDN'T EVEN HAVE TO explain himself as he removed me from the Shifter Alliance building like I was a prop on a set. No, thanks to the Berserker Chief's big scary reputation, the security guard at the side door didn't even question it when he told the guard that he 'had this covered'. *Idiots, all of them.* They should fire everyone in the building and just start from scratch. Even having no employees would be better than these morons.

Ten minutes later, I whined through my gag inthe back of an SUV where I'd been *dumped* on my backside.

"Oh, stop complaining," Kidnapper Guy hollered from the front of the car, Daisy sitting passively in the passenger seat.

She hadn't so much as growled the entire time that he was abducting me, simply watching and wagging that freaking tail. And now, the two of them were riding up front like they were on a road trip, and I was the baggage.

"Oh, I'll be your baggage alright," I yelled through the gag as I threw my shoulder into the window, flailing to try and get the attention of the other cars. "Your baggage cart will be overflowing by the time I'm done with you!"

"Sorry, I didn't catch that," he shouted back to me, giving me a dry look via the rearview mirror.

I snarled at him but didn't bother to shout. I was too busy maneuvering myself toward the middle of the car, where I had to do a version of the worm to get myself up over the seats. It was awkward, but I was able to hook my bound legs around the headrests and pull myself over. Unfortunately, with my arms still zip tied behind my back, I ended up with my legs in the middle row of seats, and my top half still in the trunk area.

"A spy who can sneak into a government building, but can't escape an open trunk," Kidnapper Guy taunted me, "Impressive."

"I hate you!" I screamed the words through the cloth in my mouth, but I couldn't see his face to know if he understood them. Regardless, the sentiment was there.

Finally, I managed to flop into the backseat—and banged my head on the door in the process. Groaning, I flopped onto my belly and pulled myself up with my abs, sitting on my knees.

Apparently, my Houdini act had taken longer than I thought, because we were now parked in a garage. The evil flea infested bear man turned in his seat to look at me, and I glared as hard as I could. Maybe, if I tried hard enough, I could manifest heat vision abilities and he'd turn to a pile of ash. *Now there's a fantasy.*

Rather than say something snarky or demeaning like I'd do if I could talk right now, the man just stared at me, studying. He no longer looked so taken aback like he had when we first locked eyes, but he also didn't seem as angry as he had in the Alliance Building. Curious, I focused on his emotions, and was surprised to find that he felt the same curiosity and confusion that I did. *Hm...*

"Listen," he began, plucking the rag from my mouth, "I'm sorry I'm taking you prisoner, but I have no choice."

When I immediately started to scream—I thought it would be the most accurate representation of how I was feeling—he shoved the gag back in and sighed.

"Just when I thought you could be reasoned with."

Then he disappeared, shutting the car door behind him. When he appeared at my door after letting Daisy out, I was ready for him and kicked my feet at his face. Clearly, he was ready too, because he dodged the blow easily, snatching me up by the waist. Once again, he draped me over his shoulder like a wet towel.

As I hung with my head against Kidnapper Guy's back and my arms still tied behind me—it was as uncomfortable as it sounds—I saw Daisy finishing up a Milkbone on the concrete floor. *So, he gives my dog treats but throws me around like a sack of flour. Rude.* Although if I was being honest, it's exactly what I would've done too—treat the dog better than the person.

I tried to get a look at the place as we left the garage, but it was hard to keep flexing my abs so I could look back the way we'd come. And looking ahead proved to be difficult given how *big* the flea bag was. I'd need a surveyor to come and give me a map just so I could find a spot to see around. Come to think of it, I could probably charge women a lot of money for the pleasure. *I'll put it on my list of ways to get revenge.*

As we walked, all I saw were flashes of wood, warm light, and...was that a fur rug on the ground? I thought I was going to throw up once he started up a flight of stairs, but I knew that if I did, it would end up in my hair. And somehow, I doubted that this man would lend some shampoo and conditioner to his captive.

Finally, after some more walking, I was set gently—to my surprise—on the ground.

"Please play nice," Kidnapper Guy pleaded, plucking the gag from my mouth. Then he took a generous—and very wise—step back from where I sat.

I opted not to scream at him—mostly because I was a little distracted taking in my surroundings. He'd deposited me on the floor of a very large bedroom that looked like it belonged in a log cabin. A giant plush bed with a log frame sat against one wall, with a thick rug taking up most of the wood floor. A cold fireplace was set into the wall next to the door, and on the other side of the room were two other doors. One was open and showed off a nice bathroom, while the other I assumed led to a closet.

Wait a second...am I in his *bedroom?* Rumor had it that The Chief was a violent man, but I'd never heard of him being completely depraved. Genuinely freaked out now, I tried and failed to stand, kicking out at him with my tied feet. "Pervert!" I shouted. "You're going to be one sorry, castrated man if you try to touch me again!"

I thought I saw him flinch as I felt a pinch of hurt twinge inside him. But then just like that, the look was gone.

"Stop it," he begged, and since I was still tied up and incapable of moving freely, I couldn't stop him from kneeling in front of me and pressing a hand to my mouth. But I did bite his palm. "Dang it, woman!" he hissed, snatching his hand back. "Would you just listen for a second? I'm not a pervert and I'm not going to hurt you. I brought you here because the heists you've been pulling at the Alliance Building have landed me and my people in some hot water."

"Don't care," I spat at him, unimpressed with his pleas.

I sensed his irritation flash as he pulled a pocketknife from his jeans—*I knew he'd have one*—and flipped it open. With the faint scar across his face, his frustrated expression and those unnerving grey eyes glaring at me, I was honestly a little nervous. Plus, there was his stellar reputation to consider. *I'm totally going to die.*

"Now, just listen for a minute," he insisted, carefully grabbing my wrists, "Please."

Shocked that he even knew the word 'please', I remained silent, letting him cut the zip ties from my hands.

"You've been outing Shifter Alliance employees for bad behavior," he said, moving his knife to the zip ties on my ankles, though his eyes never left mine, "And although I don't have a personal grievance with that—though I am surprised you've left me alone so far—"

"I don't act on unconfirmed rumors," I cut him off. I had a reputation too. I only ever got bad people sacked. And even after all my investigating, I still didn't know if the Berserker Chief was actually bad or not. *Although kidnapping doesn't help his case.*

He stared silently at me for a moment, clearly confused by my decency. Considering that I'd kicked him in the jaw earlier, I figured that was fair.

"I appreciate that," he grumbled. It wasn't quite a thank you, but I'd take it. "But you see, the problem is that I'm now being treated as a person of interest for *your* heists. They're saying that I'm behind it, and we both know that people need very little motivation to think I'm guilty of just about anything. So, I feel it's fairly reasonable that I kidnapped you in order to prevent you from continuing to put me and my people at risk."

I tried hard not to find logic in his argument, but the truth was, I would've done the same thing. The problem though was that I didn't know this man. I only knew rumors about 'The Chief' and 'Mr. Hohlt', and none of them were pretty. Granted, the rumors of his body count could be wrong, dramatized or even made up. And so far, he hadn't hurt me—plus, he'd been kind to my dog—but that was very little to go on when I could easily become the next dead body on the news if I wasn't careful. And if I was wrong about him and the rumors were true, and he was who people said he was, then this was a man I needed to escape. And soon.

"Cool story, bro," I replied, feigning complete calm, waiting for my chance to escape.

Annoyed, Kidnapper Guy snarled and spun away, shoving a hand through his dark hair. Which gave me the perfect opening.

With his back to me and my feet now free, I launched for the door at top speed. Unfortunately, he was kind of in my way. I tried to go around him, but he was ready and when those freaking arms wrapped around me, they might as well have been tree trunks.

I had to give the man a few points in the decent guy column though because he didn't hold me longer or closer than necessary. Instead, he quickly deposited me behind him, stepping up to guard the door.

Annoyed and tired of being manhandled today, I tapped into my Shifter magic. It immediately uncoiled, and I sent it Kidnapper Guy's way. The magic silently tugged at him, pulling at his confusion, worsening it until it made him all but unable to fight me.

Except that when my magic tugged at him, nothing happened.

Instead of going where I wanted, his emotions remained unchanged. I frowned, confused, and tried again. But again, the magic wouldn't affect him—almost like it refused to.

"I don't understand..." I mumbled to myself. "Why can't I..."

Then, realizing the gravity of the situation—that my magic wasn't going to get me out of here—I switched gears. With a battle cry—probably a bad idea since it told him I was coming, but oh well, I was committed now—I threw myself at him. I shoved and pulled at him, even punched at his chest to get him to budge, but he was a tank. He didn't even move a centimeter.

"Okay then," his deep voice boomed as he gently shoved me a few steps back. It shattered my pride to realize that he could've done that with one finger. He'd been placating me by even letting me try to push him. "We'll try this conversation again later when you've had a chance to chill out."

Then he slipped out the door, and the lock clicked a moment later.

"What, you think I'm difficult right now?" I shouted through the door. "You have no idea how difficult I can be, bear man!"

I could've sworn I heard a heavy sigh from the other side of the door. But after a moment, his footsteps carried him away. When I turned back to the room, I leaned against the door, seriously regretting waking up today. My eyes narrowed when I saw that Daisy had found her way to the bed and was now sprawled out on her back—snoring.

"Worst. Weapon. Ever."

She just snored louder.

EIGHT

Morgan

"THIS CAN'T BE HAPPENING," I GROWLED at no one as I entered my office. "I won't allow it."

Which was a stupid thing to say, because I had no choice in the matter. Things like this were chosen divinely—without my input.

"Which is stupid! It's my life," I shouted, slamming my palm against my desk, careful not to dent it. "I should get a choice!"

Truthfully, I shouldn't have been acting so petulant about it. I'd known what was going on for an hour now—since I first saw her face. Yet I couldn't quite control the rage—rage that belonged to *her*. It was part of the deal, being able to sense her emotions. It also explained why I'd been feeling so off for the last month. Being near her in the hall that first time had triggered it and started the process without me even knowing it. *I should've recognized the signs.* After all, I'd been through this before...But I'd never expected to go through it again. I never *wanted* to go through it again.

Ugh! Why did she have to be so young and vibrant? A spy in her fifties would have been so much easier to resist. But this woman? With that long auburn hair that fell in waves to her lower back, and those startling green eyes. The elegant swoop of her nose and all those freckles on her cheeks. I was doomed. She was easily one of the most beautiful women I'd ever seen. Probably the most beautiful other than...

"No," I told myself sternly, gripping the edge of the desk, "We're done with that. Gen was it for me. There will be no one else." No matter what the magic insisted.

"Hey, everything okay?"

I took a breath to compose myself and turned to see Logan and my two brothers standing in the doorway. Each of them wore varying looks of concern. *Great.*

Next to Logan stood Mike, who was the second oldest after me. His expression was the most worried—which checked out. A classic middle kid, he cared the most about making sure everyone was okay all the time. Though the skeptical look in his hazel eyes was new. Between that and Clint's—my youngest brother—raised eyebrow, I gathered that they'd all heard the noise from my arrival with the girl a few minutes ago.

"What did you do?" Clint asked bluntly.

I wanted to shove him and start a wrestling match to release my frustration, but he'd hate me if I ruined his pretty face. He and Mike both were good looking dudes. But while Mike had that sweet puppy vibe with his shaggy, wavy brown hair and broad smile, Clint was all angles and smirks—something he used often to get women's attention. As the baby of the family, Mike and I tended to indulge him and his immature behavior a little too much.

"I have a prisoner," I shrugged, sitting on the couch by the bookshelves. "She's upstairs." Those last words came out in a mumble as I shoved my face into my hands.

"I'm sorry, did you say a prisoner?" Logan taunted, a smile in his voice. I lifted my head to glare at him, but he wasn't intimidated.

Instead, the lot of them all took seats in the armchairs around me, Mike sitting on the other end of the couch. Smart move. Of all of them, he was least likely to tick me off right now.

"Why are you keeping a prisoner?" Clint asked, running a hand through his short brown hair, still looking more judgy than worried.

"She was the one extorting council members," I explained briefly, "I caught her in the act—twice—and decided I'd remove her from the equation."

"You say that like you fired someone," Logan argued, looking at me as though I'd lost it—and I was pretty sure I had. "Dude, you stole a *person*."

"I know!" He didn't have to remind me.

"No need to shout."

"I didn't shout!"

"You did," all three of them said in unison.

Annoyed, angry—thanks to the girl's emotions still swimming around in the back of my mind—and a little scared, I let out a loud sigh and collapsed against the back of the couch. It was weird, having someone else's feelings in my mind after so long of it being just me. But as I sat there, reorienting myself to the experience, I was able to sort out what was her and what was me. Which just showed me how much anger and fear belonged to her.

Fear. Something I never thought I'd have to deal with in this situation—because I never expected to be in this situation again.

"I didn't know what else to do," I said quietly, pretending that the investigation at the Alliance Building was the only thing bothering me. I couldn't tell my brothers or Logan about this thing between me and the prisoner upstairs. They'd be excited for me—supportive even. To them it would be my second chance. But to me, it was a punishment. One that I would do everything I could to outrun.

"I'm sorry, I have to ask this," Mike began cautiously. "Did you try just talking to her before you kidnapped her?"

"Ask me that question again after you've met her," I replied dryly. *Good luck getting her to speak without insulting you or trying to maim you.* That girl was a vengeful, clever little thing.

Logan and Clint chuckled, and all three of the boys exchanged entertained looks. I tried glaring at them to shut them up, but they weren't fazed. *Freaking family.*

"So, she's feisty then," Clint smiled, wagging his eyebrows in his standard 'I've found a new conquest' way.

"No!" I barked, pointing a finger at him. "Evil succubus or not, she's off limits! And if I catch you so much as flirting with her, I'll put peppermint in your face cream." He was allergic to peppermint and obsessed with his own face, so breaking out in hives was a decent level threat. "Plus, she'd probably chew you up and spit you back out anyway."

I knew it wasn't wise to show any kind of possessiveness over the woman, but even though I didn't want anything to do with her, I didn't want my brother to either. None of us could get attached to her. Because the moment this whole investigation was over, I never wanted to see her again.

"Okay," Clint nodded, a look passing between him, Mike, and Logan that I didn't like, "I won't flirt with her."

"What exactly do you plan to do with her though?" Logan asked, watching me in that way where I knew he saw more than I showed. That was the privilege of being a best friend rather than a brother. I hid less from him because he didn't need my protection in the same way. Well, neither did Mike or Clint at twenty-five and twenty-four years old. But that didn't mean I was going to stop being their big brother.

"Keep her until she agrees to stop doing what she's been doing—at least until the Shifter Alliance declares me innocent," I said, rubbing away some of the tension in my forehead. "Then, I don't care what she does."

No one seemed to believe my words, but I didn't care. I had bigger problems now than being accused of some extortion. I had to figure out a way to get that girl upstairs out of my house without letting her ruin my already tattered reputation. Because the longer she was here, the longer the bond had to build. And no matter what happened, I refused to bond with anyone ever again...

Except that I already was bonded. Because the bond didn't care about what I wanted, all it cared was that it had found *her*. And now, I was cursed to sense her every emotion, knowing that this was 'it' my shot at happiness. A happiness that I would eagerly reject—I wasn't about to do this a second time.

No, that girl upstairs—who's rage I could feel still fuming at the back of my mind—would never be the thing that the bond marked her as...

My mate.

NINE
Caroline

DESPITE MY INTENTION TO HATE everything associated with Kidnapper Guy—AKA scary Berserker Chief—I loved his bed.

"I mean, who can blame me with these pillows?" I hummed, burrowing deeper into the covers, one of the many feather pillows scrunched under my head.

Kidnapper Guy still sucked, but boy did he know how to pick out bedding. If I was ever buried alive, and the interior of my casket was as comfy as this bed, I'd die happy.

"Daisy let's get caught more often."

Daisy Mae huffed, shifting next to me in the bed. She was only forty pounds, but she still somehow managed to take up half the mattress. I was just about to shove her off my side when a knock sounded at my door.

"Why?" I whined, tossing back the covers. "Why wake me now? No one came to check on me when I threw a chair at the window last night." It turned out, the thing was bullet proof and didn't open. *Of course.*

"Or when I tried to kick the door down," I continued, walking over to answer the door. "So why bother me now?"

But as I reached for the door handle, I froze.

I didn't have a key; Kidnapper Guy had locked it himself when he left. Which meant that he could open it now if he wanted to. And yet he was knocking. Something about that—and his respect for my personal space and kindness toward my dog—didn't quite add up with the terrifying stories I'd heard about 'The Chief'. A man who was said to have murdered over two dozen gambling den members in his life and somehow gotten away with it every time. *But if he's so evil,* a little voice in my head whispered, *why am I still unharmed?*

"I did hear you last night," came his muffled voice from the other side of the door. His annoyed attitude was clear as day in both his tone and his emotions. *This'll be fun.* "Both with the window and the door. So, since you kept everyone up until two in the morning with your rampage, the least you can do is let me in."

"You have a key," I pointed out, trying to figure out what his game was. Was he trying to con me into trusting him? If so, it'd be a long con—I didn't trust easily. And somehow, I didn't think he'd have the patience for such a thing anyway.

"Listen, you're here against your will, and I get how that makes me the bad guy. But I'm not an evil bad guy. I'm not going to hurt you or trample on your privacy. As my captive, the least I can do is not barge into your room."

I pursed my lips, considering him. "Nice words for a man who's in the position of power here."

"Words and time are all I've got."

The petty part of me insisted that I barricade the door just to be a brat. Or that I open the door—which I assumed he'd now unlocked—and tackle him. But given how many times I'd used that move; he'd probably see it coming now. And the reality was that he *was* the one in a position of power. For now.

"Come in," I finally called out, arms crossed and ready for round two.

I expected him to come prepared with another speech. Demanding that I see reason and relent to not pulling heists at the Alliance Building anymore—which wasn't going to happen. My heists were about more than just than me.

But instead of Kidnapper Guy immediately launching into a sales pitch, a woman barged into the room and latched onto my wrist without a word of explanation. Too late I realized that I recognized her. It was Merida, the Witch representative on the Shifter Council. And her touching me couldn't be a good thing—especially when she did *that.*

Her eyes shifted from blue to gold as she stared at the air in front of me, seeing strands of magic I couldn't see. Her black hair rippled, slowly turning a pearly white, and her skin became almost translucent, her body glowing from the inside out. Witches—like many non-animal Shifters—shifted in conjunction with their magic, alerting you that they were using it. The thing was, I didn't know what kind of magic Merida was using on me.

"Please tell me you're performing a blessing or a charm," I whined, trying to drag my arm away from her. She ignored me, using her free hand to draw patterns in the air, manipulating the magic that only she could see. Kidnapper Guy intervened on her behalf, banding one arm across my chest, and pinning me against him.

"Don't worry, it's just a binding, not a curse," he explained, his breath rustling the hairs at my temple.

Technically, a binding was a type of curse. But depending on what you were being bound to and how, it could be good or bad. Witches had a caveat to their magic; they had to fuel it with their own emotions. So, curses could only be cast from things like anger and hatred, while blessings and charms came from joy and affection. Lucky me that our Witch was brimming with irritation.

"You know, that's not nearly as encouraging as you think it is," I said, trying to wriggle out of his grasp even though I knew it was futile.

"She's protecting us both by binding you. You're not being harmed. This is just a temporary solution until we can figure something out that will make sure I don't get arrested for your crimes."

"Why? You always seem to get off free anyway."

"You don't know me," he growled, his anger seething out of him.

"You're right, I don't. Which is why magically binding me without my consent doesn't do you any favors. You want my cooperation? Earn it."

"Fair enough, but if you want me to trust you enough to let you go, you have to earn it too."

Touché.

"I'm finished," Merida announced with a friendly smile, her hair back to shiny black, and her eyes once again blue. Her irritation was mostly faded now that the magic was done and no longer feeding off it. Now she just seemed curious.

"Thank you, Merida," Kidnapper Guy said, and I noted that he'd never used such a kind tone with me. He also didn't release me, though I wasn't sure how far I'd get if I tried to escape from a Berserker and a Witch.

"It'll last until you release it, and you control the—" Merida paused, glancing at me, "Details." Well, that wasn't sketchy at all.

"Perfect, I owe you one."

Then Merida, with all her regal-esque beauty, glanced at me, a slow smile spreading across her lips. "I'll keep your tab open, Morgan. I think you'll need it." Then she disappeared into the hall, shutting the bedroom door behind her.

We stood there for a few silent moments, both of us filled with varying degrees of irritation and confusion. An ongoing theme in our story so far.

"So, Morgan, huh?" I asked, shattering the quiet.

Morgan jolted behind me, apparently just then realizing that he hadn't let me go yet. Embarrassment and frustration pinged inside him, and he quickly dropped his arm and stepped a few feet away.

I watched him, trying to reconcile his intimidating face with his not so intimidating name. For all the rumors I'd heard about him in the last three years, I'd never heard anyone use his first name. I'd probably come across it when I'd initially done my research on the council and just forgotten it...but I understood now why no one used it. Because something as simple as a first name somehow humanized him—making him harder to hate.

"Yeah," he replied, shifting uncomfortably. "Morgan Hohlt. And you are?"

I thought about ignoring his question, just to spite him. But then I imagined all the insulting nicknames he might've created in his head the way I had for him.

So, I told him the truth. "Caroline." Just not all of it.

He waited a moment for me to continue, and then nodded when he realized one name was all he was getting. "Alright, then. Well, I probably should've introduced myself sooner, but with yesterday being so..."

"Illegal?" I suggested, putting my hands on my hips. "Severely illegal considering that you kidnapped a minor."

Morgan's grey eyes went wide, and he looked me over, searching for signs that I was underage. For a few moments, his panic went through the roof. Then he narrowed his eyes. "You're lying."

"I'm seventeen."

"And I'm an easy going, loveable guy. There, now we've both told a lie."

Both curious and annoyed, I tried to twine my magic around him again like I had yesterday. But when I tried to mold his curiosity, it refused my efforts. *Well, that's useless.*

Angry that he somehow managed to resist my magic, I hissed and spun away. "How long are you going to keep me here?" I demanded, pacing toward the bed and back. Daisy was still sleeping soundly, unconcerned that her mom had just been bound by a Witch. "And what exactly did your Witch friend bind me to? Is she the reason I can sense your feelings, but can't mess with them?"

"What did you say?"

Oh no. You've got to be kidding me! I'd been living my life as one big secret for as long as I could remember. I'd had to forego relationships, never been free to play sports or let anyone see me run in case I moved too fast; always careful not to draw too much attention. Which was why my overall girly aesthetic was helpful—it kept people from taking me seriously. I was a pro at keeping my abilities as a Shifter a secret. So *why* had I just revealed one of those abilities to my *captor?*

"I didn't say anything, flea bag," I scoffed, trying to feign nonchalance.

"You can sense my feelings," he said, almost more to himself than to me. And I paused, sensing the worry inside him. The fear. "And you can get into my head..."

"Well, technically I *should* be able to get in your head. But whatever magic you're blocking me with is keeping me from manipulating you—" I froze, staring into his wide, panicked eyes. "Pretend I didn't say that."

"I don't think I can." And then he took a step toward me. It might've seemed small to him, but those long legs covered a lot of ground.

I took a step back. "Sure, you can! Better yet, let's call your friend back in here and have her curse you to forget me altogether."

"Not a chance. Plus, I don't think a curse would be enough to erase you anyway. You pack quite a punch, Caroline." What could've been construed as a compliment from one lover to another was definitely an insult from Morgan.

"Oh, believe me, I can," I sassed, shoving at his chest. He didn't budge.

He did, however, stare at me with those stupidly gorgeous grey eyes. Studying me, reading me, silently urging my secrets to come forward.

"What are you?" he asked quietly.

For some bizarre reason, his question didn't make me feel nearly as scared as it should have. Instead of all my walls going up and my instincts going on defense, I felt...safe. *What??*

"What is going on?" I exclaimed. "Why aren't I more afraid of you?"

That question seemed to shut bear man up. His nerves flashed, anxiety roiling through him as he took a big step back from me.

"You're probably just sensitive to Berserker magic." He didn't even sound like he believed those words.

Berserkers—along with super strength—had leadership magic. It allowed them to manipulate people, not unlike the way my magic worked. Except that Berserkers only manipulated people into trusting in their leadership and decision making. Which meant that they were usually the leaders in every Weight Watchers group they attended and had no problem commanding a small crowd. But like my magic, their manipulation was a suggestion to someone's emotions, not mind control.

Morgan could have been telling the truth, that his magic was affecting me...except that I could sense his panic, and his flighty attitude. *He's lying.* Question was, why?

"What aren't you telling me?" I asked, noting the way he refused to meet my eyes.

"You first."

Again, with the stalemate. *We're never going to get anywhere with this.*

"Fine, new topic. What did the Witch do to me?" I crossed my arms, giving him a defiant glare—AKA my resting face.

Morgan immediately relaxed. "She bound you to the house."

"*Excuse me?*"

At my shrill tone, Morgan turned for the door, but I latched onto his bicep—*whoa!* That sucker was firm! For a second, I got lost in my head, wondering what his workout routine was like. And wondering if he allowed lurkers.

A fantasy filled my mind where I tested his muscles by putting varying fruits between his forearm and bicep to see if he could squish them. Of course, it'd be a messy process and I'd have to wipe his arm off—

"Caroline?"

I gasped, returning to reality. Where Morgan was staring at me over his shoulder. My hand still on his arm. Squeezing it.

"Oh my gosh," I mumbled, disgusted with myself. Sure, I liked to appreciate a good manly view, but Morgan? Really? *Gross.*

"Were you actually going to say something? Or did you grab me just to squeeze my bicep?" he asked, a slight smirk tugging at the corner of his mouth.

"I wasn't squeezing it. I just didn't know how forceful I'd have to be to get you to stop."

"Uh huh." He looked pointedly down at my hand. Which was *still* holding onto his arm. Oh, *come on!* I immediately let go, taking a step back just to be safe.

"I was just going to say that I can't believe you were going to run away after telling me that I'm magically bound to your house. Kind of a cowardly move, don't you think?"

Morgan just shrugged, sticking his hands in his pockets. "Call me crazy, but I assumed you were going to try to rip my face off again."

Fair enough. "What do you mean when you say I'm bound to the house?"

"Exactly what it sounds like. You can leave your room—so feel free to explore as much as you like—but you can't leave the house. The binding will stop you."

Well, that was inconvenient.

"Unregistered bindings are illegal, you know," I growled, and my anger must have been palpable, because Daisy jumped off the bed and came trotting to my side. Before quickly abandoning me for Morgan. "Do you have animal powers or something? Because she hates adults."

"No," he replied carefully, reaching down to pet her, "She just knows I won't hurt you."

"Is that why she didn't warn me that you were following us in the Alliance Building? Because she trusts you?" I mocked. He just shrugged. "How did you find us in the building anyway? We didn't go to the same floor as last time."

"I waited for you by the elevators. I couldn't see you well from where I stood, but I saw your dog—"

"Daisy Mae," I automatically corrected him.

He nodded, mumbling Daisy's name under his breath. "Then I watched the display above the elevators to see what floor you got off on." Done with his explanation, he straightened and headed for the door.

"So, what am I supposed to do now?" I demanded as he opened the door. "Sit and twiddle my thumbs?"

"If I were you, I'd use this time to think about making a deal with me to stop pulling heists for the time being."

Yeah, that wasn't going to happen. Not when bear man could end up being exactly who everyone said he was—a very bad person to be making deals with. And even if I did agree, there was no way he was going to release me. We both knew that if I got away, he'd never see me again.

"And by the way, you're right. Unregistered bindings are illegal, but who's going to report it?" He smirked, winking at me before he disappeared into the hall.

TEN
Morgan

IT WAS DAISY MAE'S SNORING THAT WOKE me up from my very uncomfortable slumber. I groaned, lifting my head from one of the many open books that laid across my desk. As expected, my neck hurt, and my back ached from awkwardly leaning over all night.

"I'm getting too old for this." As if on cue, a sticky note fell from my face. Then, because I needed more reminding of just what a mess I was, one look into my black computer monitor confirmed that I now had 'Caroline problem' stamped on my cheekbone. But unfortunately, it was so smudged that it looked more like 'Caroline property'.

"That's a bad omen," I grumbled, licking my fingers to scrub the ink from my face.

Like an adult, I'd been avoiding my mate by sleeping in my office for the last two nights. Well, I'd also spent that time looking through every book I owned for some hint about which Shifter Caroline was. Did it really matter if I knew what she was? Not really. She was a prisoner here regardless...but curiosity was a funny thing. Unwanted or not, she was my mate, and I wanted to know who she was.

Which is stupid because you're just going to send her packing anyway. And I was. The moment she was no longer a threat to me or my people, I'd send her on her way and pray we never saw each other again...

Except that we were bonded.

Simple proximity was all it took for a mate bond to show itself. At which time both of us would be revealed to have blue rings around our irises that only the other person could see. The bond also allowed us to sense each other's emotions no matter the distance. A way to try and con us into falling in love. *Not going to happen.*

At first, when Caroline said that she could sense my feelings, I panicked. It seemed more dangerous for her to know about the mate bond than for me to keep it a secret. If she didn't know about it, she'd leave with no problem. But if she knew...*She'd probably kill me just so she wouldn't have to be saddled with it.* Because that was the only way out of a mate bond—death.

Mate bonds only happened to animal shifters because of our hot-blooded nature and tendency to act impulsively when big feelings were involved. It was like a divine, magical sign that showed you who 'the one' was. Mate bonds couldn't create affection or attraction, they just pointed you to the right person.

"Of course, then there's the whole trust part." I rubbed the sleep from my eyes and sat back in my chair, exhausted just thinking about it.

Because we were mated, we both trusted each other more than strangers should. Sharing emotions meant that mates didn't cause each other serious physical harm—we couldn't. When you can feel someone's suffering, you can't stand being the one who caused it. So instinctively, we both felt safe with each other—even if we didn't know why. Which was why Caroline had spilled more about herself to me than she meant to.

Which brings us to the real reason I'd been hiding out in my office for two days. Because Caroline—for all her ribbons and florals and innocent looks—terrified me.

She was too smart, too clever not to eventually realize what the mate bond was. Not to mention that she constantly refused to listen to me—something I was not used to. Every time I tried to reason with her, she just ate the reason and logic up and spit it back out. In my face. *Lovely girl, that Caroline.*

She'd barely come out of her room in the last two days, only sneaking down to get food and then return to her hideout. I'd left her a pair of clothes that Logan's mom had forgotten here the last time she visited, but I hadn't seen Caroline to know if she'd worn them.

My brothers and Logan had kept their distance from her at my request, but that good behavior was bound to expire soon. My family didn't do obedience well. *Maybe that's why Caroline and I butt heads so much.*

"What do you think?" I asked Daisy Mae as she slowly woke and stretched from where she'd been sleeping in an armchair. She'd hung out with me periodically over the last two days, fluctuating between me and her mom. Dogs, ever the intuitive creatures, picked up on things like mate bonds. Which was why Daisy liked me so much. She knew I would always keep her mom safe. Whether I wanted to or not.

"Is there any hope that when I go up there, she won't try to toss a piece of furniture at me?" Daisy jumped down from the chair and trotted over to me, wiggling her entire body as she greeted me. "Yeah, I'm not feeling very hopeful either."

Especially after what I'd learned. I turned again to the book I'd been reading when I fell asleep last night. About the Elves.

Before Shifters had gone public and integrated with humans, we'd been nothing but legends for five hundred years. Ever since the civil war that decimated our numbers and wiped out an entire species.

Up until the 1300's, Elves had been the governing force among Shifters. The light Elves, called Alfar, were our rulers, our kings and queens. The dark Elves, called Nephilim, served as our military. The Elves managed to keep peace amongst Shifters for centuries...until a Berserker killed the Alfar King.

The stories were muddled and embellished, but there were two major beliefs about how that day went down. Some believed that the Berserkers acted out because they were tired of being used as the muscle and fire power to help support the Nephilim. That they killed the king out of vengeance and thus began the war. Others believed that the Berserker Chief in the capital city went to plead with the Alfar King, claiming that the Nephilim General had been using the Chief's people for unsanctioned violence. But the Nephilim General found out about the coup and barged in, attacking the Berserker. When the Alfar King tried to intervene, he stepped in front of the Berserker as he was shifting, and the king was accidentally killed. The Nephilim General, seeing an opportunity, used the king's death to start a war.

Of course, being a Berserker, I believed the second story. But no one would ever really know what happened other than that the war began immediately after the king's death.

Few elves survived the civil war, and the ones that did were tracked down and killed by Hunters. And now the Elves were nothing but a ghost story. A legend kids were taught about in school as a cautionary tale.

Except that this book claimed that Nephilim had the power of speed, and physical manipulation wherein which they could become anyone they wanted in the blink of an eye. They were even the reason people believed in vampires. Because for a long time, Nephilim were known to take the appearance of someone who'd died, leaving people to believe that their loved ones had risen from the dead.

"It doesn't mention reading or manipulating emotions though," I sighed, flipping through the pages even though I'd already read it cover to cover—and taken notes on my hand. I paused, double checking in the monitor to make sure I'd gotten all the ink off my face. The last thing I needed was another thing for Caroline to sass me about.

"Although it's been a thousand years since Elves were known to walk the earth. There's bound to be some missing details." And now it was time to stop procrastinating and go see if my assumptions were right. Standing, I walked around my desk to where Daisy Mae lay in an armchair.

"Pray for me, okay?" I said leaning down to scratch her head. She licked my nose, thumping her tail. "I'm not sure that's going to help me." With Caroline, I doubted anything could help.

I left my office and made my way upstairs—slowly. I wasn't exactly looking forward to this conversation. Thankfully, Caroline's door was open when I got there. So, I didn't have to knock and give her time to find a weapon.

She stood in front of the large window at the end of the room, staring down at the side yard and surrounding forest below. There was a granola bar in her hand and her backpack sat open on the floor beside her. As I watched her, part of me wanted to flee back downstairs, maybe bribe Logan to go babysit her somewhere far away from me until this whole investigation about the heists blew over. But if I asked Logan or my brothers to do that, then they'd know that something was wrong. Then it wouldn't take them long to guess that Caroline was my mate—and immediately begin shipping us. They were incorrigible like that. *Family trait.*

"Is that your real face?" I asked, stepping into the room. Chances were that this wasn't going to go well, so I might as well get it over with.

Caroline didn't turn toward me, but she went incredibly still, and her emotions flared with panic. At first, I thought she might try to run. It would have been pointless, but Caroline was used to running away. I gathered it was how she survived.

"Yes," she finally replied, straightening her shoulders. "I don't shift often."

"You're a Nephilim," I breathed, saying the words out loud for the first time.

"Careful about saying that word where people can hear you!" She hissed, spinning toward me with a threatening look on her face. "Do you have any idea how hard I've fought to stay a secret? You can't just go blurting that word out! I could become a tragic headline on the news just like that." She snapped her fingers, glaring at me.

"If you're so worried about being discovered, then you shouldn't have told me about your magic."

"I didn't mean to," she insisted. "Now stop yelling!"

"I'm not yelling."

She waved a hand, motioning for me to be quiet and walked over to shut the bedroom door. "You do yell," she said, leaning back against it.

I ground my jaw, annoyed at how easily she unraveled me. "I know."

"Wow, bear man knows how to admit that I'm right. I'm surprised you didn't choke on those words," she taunted, smirking at me.

"I was too busy suffocating from your sweet, saccharine personality."

She grunted and rolled her eyes but didn't argue with me. Instead, as the moments passed, she became very interested in the half-eaten granola bar in her hand.

"Your stupid leadership magic made my tongue loose, otherwise I never would have told you about my magic," she said, though I could tell by her lack of genuine nerves that she was fishing for something. She hadn't believed me when I told her that it was the Berserker leadership magic that made her trust me. *But if I deflect long enough, hopefully she'll forget about it.*

"Do you have any other abilities besides enhanced speed, altering your appearance, and the stuff you do with emotions?" I asked, hoping she'd take the bait and change topics.

At first, it didn't seem like she was going to let it go. She stared at me for a moment before she finally sighed and crossed her arms.

"No, that's all of it," she said, expression pleading. "But I need you to keep my identity a secret. I know you don't know me, and I honestly have no idea if I can trust you or not. Because quite frankly, I still can't tell if you're who everyone says you are or not. But regardless, I'm begging you to do this one thing. Because if word gets out that there's a Nephilim in the world, I'll either be caught and put in a cage or dead within a week."

As she spoke, her fear and anxiety reached out to me, prodding my guilt. And some desiccated, forgotten part of me felt empathy for her, but this wasn't just about me. I had people to look out for and protect. And right now, Caroline was a threat to that.

"I don't know what I'm going to do with you yet," I admitted, "Your existence is dangerous, and my people have already had enough backlash from the public."

"So, you're going to rat me out," she snarled, looking ready to lunge.

No. Because the mate bond wasn't going to let me. Even though I had free will in the situation, my ability to sense her emotions made me weak. How could I turn her over to save myself, knowing that I'd be there to feel every horrible moment of her fear and her pain? Plus, I didn't exactly *want* to give the government the only living Nephilim. Who knew what they'd do with her. I just needed to find a way to keep her out of the game so I—and my people by extension—wouldn't be blamed anymore.

"I have a lot to think about," I said, stepping forward to gently push her away from the door.

"Morgan, if you betray me, I *will* make your life a living hell! I don't care what it costs me," she threatened, latching onto my arm—as if she could stop me.

But instead of feeling irritated or annoyed with her for it, I found myself struggling against a smile, enjoying the image of her attacking me—and failing—again. Even if I got nothing else out of this situation, at least Caroline was entertaining.

"I'd expect nothing less." Then I shook off her hand and left the room.

ELEVEN
Caroline

I POUTED IN MY ROOM FOR A GOOD hour after Morgan left, sensing his amusement at my predicament. The jerk. He might not have acted like the psychotic murderer everyone said he was—yet—but he was still a pain in the freaking backside.

"This is God getting even with me, isn't it?" I complained, pacing in front of the large window, practically digging a trench in the floor. Daisy sat on the bed, her brown eyes tracking me, watching me fume. She'd disappeared multiple times throughout the past two days, and I had a suspicion that it was to visit he who shall not be named. *Traitor.* "After a lifetime of being a problem causer and a thorn in everyone's side, God has finally decided to give me a taste of my own medicine." I hated how effective it was.

At the end of the day though, my biggest priority was keeping my secret. So, if Morgan wanted to be a pain, then fine. But I'd do whatever I had to do to make sure he didn't rat me out. I'd spent my whole life protecting my secret from everyone but my family, and I wasn't about to let some flea bag with anger issues ruin it now. No matter what Morgan had planned.

There were varying opinions on Elves. Some hated them because of the oppression they had inflicted on certain Shifters like the Berserkers. Others regretted that they no longer walked the earth because they'd kept the peace between Shifters—something that was much more tenuous these days. But most people would want to get their hands on me not to kill me or worship me, but simply for what I could do for them. My abilities to alter my appearance and sense and manipulate people's emotions were a highly attractive set of magic for a lot of unsavory people.

"But I won't end up in a cage." No matter the cost.

Feeling determined and ready for battle—AKA any interaction with Morgan—I left my room, Daisy following on my heels.

The second story of the house, which could only be called a lodge, consisted of a single hallway with lots of bedrooms similar to mine. There was a bulky log staircase down to the first floor that looked sturdy enough to withstand an earthquake, and I wondered if it was so the Berserkers could go up the stairs in bear form. Although since they were almost a thousand pounds as bears, they'd probably break the furniture.

The stairs let out into a dining room that was connected to the kitchen. Two long wooden dining tables sat in front of the stairs, with two pairs of French doors nearby. One that led to the home gym on the left, and another straight ahead that led to the backyard. I'd explored the whole house in the last two days, but it was always empty except for Morgan, who'd barricaded himself in his office. I wondered if he lived alone here, or if he'd just told the other tenants not to speak to me.

"I don't bite," I mumbled as I stepped into the empty dining room. "Well, not unless provoked, anyway." It was doubtful that anyone could provoke me more than Morgan, and so far I'd only bitten his palm. *So, give me some credit bear man.*

As I stepped further into the room, annoyed that Morgan had locked me in a house with no one to talk to, I thought I heard a faint growl.

"Is that..." Curious, I walked over to the French doors on the other side of the room and looked out at the backyard. It was huge and open, with no real landscaping, just lots of grass. And out there, in the middle of the grass, rolling around like puppies, were three Berserkers. In bear form.

I'd lived in Shifter Haven for three years, and even though there were generally more Shifters in the city than in the small town where I'd grown up, I'd never seen a Berserker in bear form before. It wasn't illegal for animal Shifters to shift in public, but it usually either ended with people screaming or trying to take selfies with them. And with Berserkers being a generally solitary species, they tended not to want a ton of attention.

I watched transfixed as the three bears played, tackling each other on the grass and roaring out their victories. *They're adorable.*

A man stood near the wrestling match, his salt and pepper hair perfectly combed and a casual blazer on his broad shoulders. He also held a clipboard in his arms, marking it occasionally like he was keeping score. The three bears all looked very different, with varying sizes and colors of fur.

The largest one was a black bear, with a body so big that he would've been a whole head taller than me if we stood side by side. The two other bears—one with brown and beige splattered across him like an oil painting, and the other with rust colored fur that glinted in the sunlight—weren't quite as large, but still bigger than a normal grizzly bear.

"Wow." It was an inadequate description, but it was all I could manage. They were magnificent...I kind of wanted to go cuddle them. "What are the chances they'd let me?" I asked as Daisy trotted over to my side after thoroughly sniffing around the kitchen.

Unfortunately, the moment she spotted the bears, she started barking—loudly.

All three bears—and the guy with the clipboard—turned in unison to stare at me. And one by one, their eyes went wide. Varying degrees of surprise, amusement and wariness emanated from them.

The black bear was the first to shift. Within seconds, he'd turned into a broad-shouldered man with a head of wavy dark hair. There was a sweet, authentic way about him as he smiled tentatively at me.

Then the dappled colored bear shifted and a man with blonde hair took its place. He, the man with the clipboard, and the dark-haired man all headed toward the house. The rust-colored bear ambled behind them, not bothering to shift into human form.

"Well, this should be interesting," I mumbled, ushering Daisy toward the kitchen island. "You cannot fight these guys, okay Dais? They're bigger than you and I'm pretty sure they could eat us both as a single afternoon snack."

The three men all made their way into the house, having to open both doors so the bear could fit inside. It was almost comical to see a massive bear standing in the dining room. His largeness made everything look hobbit sized and that somehow made him seem less scary.

"Morgan's going to kill you," the blonde man said to the bear in a sing song voice.

“No, he said he’d kill me if I flirted with her. Not if I showed her what a Berserker is.” To my astonishment, this voice came from the *bear.*

“Wow. I didn’t know you could talk as a bear.” I blurted, immediately grateful for the large white island between us in case I ended up insulting them in the next few minutes. A large possibility considering that I was...me.

“I take it back, Clint,” the blonde man spoke again, sitting on a barstool at the other side of the island. “Stay in bear form. We have some teaching to do.”

“Don’t mess with her, Logan,” the dark-haired man warned, taking a seat in one of the remaining barstools.

“I’m not messing with her, Mike. I’m preparing her for battle.” Logan gave me a friendly smile, his emotions bright and mischievous.

"I think Morgan’s the one that needs preparing,” I retorted, unsure what exactly was going on, but naturally not one to leave a challenge unanswered. The three younger men all laughed, and cat called, but the older man just leaned against the counters on the other side of the room, completely enigmatic.

Now that everyone was in the room, Daisy decided that it was time to do some investigating. Of course, she went for the bear first.

“Daisy, no!” I tried to catch her, but since I was unwilling to tap into my Nephilim speed with others in the room, she got away from me.

“Hey little munchkin,” Clint, the bear, crooned as Daisy sniffed his furry legs and nuzzled her head into his chest like they were pals. “I know, I’m all cuddly now. No, I don’t have any pockets right now, so I don't have any treats for you."

"Wait..." I paused, watching the men, each of whom Daisy went to with ease, licking their hands and accepting butt scratches. “Has she already met you guys?”

“Sure, the little lady likes to trot around looking for handouts early in the morning,” Mike smiled, pushing a hand through his dark hair.

“How’d you get her to like you? She usually hates adults. Wait—is it a bear thing? Because she seems to like Morgan too. And the only way someone could like that man is if under the influence of magic.”

The room went suddenly silent, and everyone seemed keen on avoiding my eyes. Judging by the protectiveness and discomfort emanating from the group, I’d gone a step too far in insulting Morgan.

“Sorry, I didn’t mean to disrespect your Chief,” I defended, picking at my cuticle, “But the guy kidnapped me and insults me in every conversation we have. Granted, I insult him too, but he started it. So, you'll have to forgive me for not being his biggest fan, and for my vengeful plan to drive him completely insane."

The men—and the bear—all exchanged a silent look. Logan and Mike both began to smirk and even Clint gave a bear version of a smile. But it showed so many sharp teeth that it didn't quite give the same impression.

"We can help you with that," Mike nodded readily.

"Wow, you've gone and got Mike involved. I'm shocked! We need to hang out with you more often," Logan teased, lightly shoving Mike's shoulder.

Mike rolled his eyes but took the goading good naturedly. "We should probably introduce ourselves," he said, pointing to each man as he said their name. "That's Logan, Morgan's moronic best friend."

"And proud of it," Logan winked, his attitude friendly rather than flirty.

"That block of granite over there is Morgan's Second, Grey. He's kind of like Morgan's assistant and right-hand man." Mike pointed to the older gentleman who was still holding onto his clipboard. "And the bear is Clint. Morgan and I's baby brother."

"This baby beat you three to two today," Clint bragged, sitting back on his haunches, his big back legs sticking out on either side of his front legs. He looked like a giant, terrifying version of a teddy bear.

"Nice to meet you all," I said, a little mystified but genuinely meaning it. They were already three thousand times better to be around than Morgan. Not that it was hard. "I'm Caroline the captive."

"Suits you," Clint said, smacking one clawed paw on the floor. "Now let's get to the fun stuff. How to annoy Morgan."

"You're going to annoy *me* if you scratch that floor Clint Eugene Hohlt," Grey warned him, his expression not moving a millimeter.

Clint smiled his toothy bear grin and gently patted the wood floor like he was apologizing to it. "Got it, Grey."

"Now lucky for you," Logan said, continuing with the lesson, "You already do a naturally good job of frustrating our dear Chief. I've never seen the man so discombobulated and annoyed before."

"Me neither," Mike agreed. "I personally think it's good for him. He's been too uptight for too long. He needs someone to come in and shake things up."

"Then I'm your girl." I smiled, lifting my hands.

They were all being so friendly that part of me considered trying to talk one of them into helping me find a way around the Witch binding so I could escape. It was unlikely that they'd help me willingly—they clearly loved Morgan. *Can't understand why.* However, if I wanted to, I could manipulate them with no problem since none of them were Chief and thus unaffected by my magic like Morgan was. But I hesitated.

They were all so kind and welcoming...and other than Ariel, I'd never really had friends before. *If they turn out to be sucky people, then I'll manipulate them.* But until then, it felt nice to be included. Even if it was just so they could use me to further irritate Morgan.

Although if that was a pastime these guys enjoyed, then we were going to get along just fine.

"Perfect! Well, the first step to annoying Morgan is talking to him in a calm, peaceful voice." Logan suggested, giddy as he plotted against his best friend. "He *hates* being patronized, so the more you coddle him, the better."

"And he doesn't like people touching his stuff," Mike added, a little less excited than Logan, but he still smiled as he spoke. "He's very particular, so if you can manage to mess up a few small things, it'll drive him nuts."

"Better yet, tell him you think I'm cute. That'll send him through the roof," Clint laughed, his big bear mouth spreading wide and showing off more teeth than I realized bears had. But his laugh abruptly ended when Mike reached out and kicked him in the shoulder.

"We want him to be annoyed," Mike reminded Clint as Clint rubbed his shoulder with one hand and smacked Mike's foot with the other. "Not skin you alive. Caroline, whatever you do, do *not* mention any of us in any romantic way."

"Why?" I asked, watching as all the boys exchanged confused glances.

"Don't know, but Morgan was *not* happy when Clint joked about flirting with you," Logan shrugged. "So, I just overall wouldn't advise bringing us up in any romantic way. Morgan's funny when he's mad, but he's a pain in the backside when he's really ticked."

Noted. None of them were afraid of him, just wanting to avoid dealing with him when he got mad. Yet another piece of Morgan's puzzle that didn't quite fit with the picture the media had painted of him. *Interesting...*

"Anything else? I was going to go talk to him now, so if you have any last suggestions, now's the time," I said, pushing my hair from my face, and wishing desperately that Morgan had supplied me with some decent shampoo and conditioner. All I'd found in my bathroom was a bar of soap and a cheap off brand shampoo that had left my hair feeling stringy and dry. *Ugh, I miss my curling irons.*

"Morgan is all bark," Grey surprisingly interjected, a mischievous twinkle in his eye, "And very little bite. If he's yelling, you're on the right track."

I smiled. "Got it. Well, thank you boys for your advice. Please wish me luck as I go forth into the unknown to request a release and some common sense from the big bad, bear."

The men all gave me shouts of good luck and said that if anyone did any killing, to make sure that Morgan and I both killed each other. That way they wouldn't have to bail one of us out of jail. *Charming boys.* Now if only I could say the same for Morgan.

As I walked down the hall and knocked on Morgan's office doors, I wondered if he'd even answer it. *Probably not if he thinks there's a chance it could be me.* A few moments of silence passed, and I was just considering barging in when the doors swung open.

"What do you want?" Morgan snapped, already glaring at me.

"Now is that any way to treat a lady caller?" I sassed, batting my eyes just because I knew it would annoy him. It worked. He sighed and turned to leave me in the doorway.

"Caroline, I'm exhausted and quite frankly, you take a lot of energy," he said, walking over to a large oak desk and sinking into the chair behind it with a groan. "So, I'll ask again, what do you want?"

I considered him as I walked into the room. Morgan actually *did* look tired. There were slight shadows under his eyes, his hair was a mess, and I was pretty sure he was in the same shirt he'd been wearing when he first kidnapped me. He was the perfect picture of a man pushed to his limits. *Ugh, why does that make me feel bad?*

Because I could feel his exhaustion and his stress, and it humanized him, poking holes into the villainous image I had of him. Not for the first time, I wished I could turn my magic off when I wanted to. Then I wouldn't have to sense everyone's emotions like a hum in the back of my mind all the time. Granted, I seemed to be more attuned to Morgan's feelings than I usually was to anyone else's. *But considering that he's the big, unfortunately attractive roadblock between me and freedom, I get it.*

"Alright, fine. I'll get to the point." I shrugged, setting my hands on the edge of his desk. "I'd like to know how long I'm under house arrest."

Morgan sat back, crossing his arms, a smug knowing look on his face. "Are you going to attack council members once you're free?"

"Of course not. I know what it would mean for the Berserkers."

Morgan shook his head, his lips tugging up a little at one corner—almost a smile but not quiet. "Liar," he challenged. "If I let you go, you'll go back to doing what you've been doing—which I can't allow right now. So, you're staying here until I can figure out what else to do with you."

"I can't stay here forever, Morgan!" I snapped, my sweet demeanor fading in an instant.

"Actually, you can."

I glared, but he just steepled his fingers, that stupid scar giving him a more menacing appearance. He didn't even bother glaring at me now, like I wasn't worth the effort. *Oh, I'll give you something to glare about, Morgan.* All I needed was sixty seconds and one snarky smile.

"You have a bathroom, food and water," he said matter-of-factly, his expression patient. Taunting me. "You can survive here just fine until you're too old and fragile to cause harm."

Irritation clung to me like dog hair, popping up no matter how much I brushed it away. I was trying to maintain the upper hand here, making *him* lose it. Not letting him prod me. *Time to take the boys' advice.* Holding back a smirk, I nonchalantly reached out, taking a pencil from Morgan's pencil holder.

"Your brothers and Logan and Grey all seem to think you need to have some sense knocked into you. And I agree."

Morgan watched me for a moment, his eyebrow twitching as his gaze latched onto the pencil in my hand. I gave it a twirl.

When he suddenly latched his big hand around my wrist and snatched the pencil from my fingers, I knew I was pushing the right buttons. "Stay away from my family. They don't need to be involved in this."

"What makes you think I'll listen to you? Considering that you've been so warm and fuzzy and accommodating toward me," I snarked with a sweet-as-poison smile.

"I'm doing the best I can," he growled, releasing my arm with a shove. "You're the one making this difficult for yourself. If you'd just let go of whatever petty vendetta it is that has you extorting Shifter Alliance employees, then I'd let you go free. But you're too selfish to let it go!"

"*I'm* selfish?" I hissed, leaning further over the desk so he could feel the heat of the hatred in my eyes. "You're the one who kidnapped someone to save your own reputation! Did it ever occur to you that maybe the problem with the Berserkers is you? That if you left, people would stop blaming them for things."

Apparently, those were the wrong words to say. Because suddenly Morgan was on his feet, circling the desk and headed right for me with a fire in his blue ringed eyes. *Bring it on, bear man.* I could do this all day.

He didn't stop until we were toe to toe, but I stood my ground. I wasn't about to let him intimidate me into compliance. "You know nothing about me," he whispered venomously. "You don't know what I've done for my people or how they've suffered. You don't know what kind of leader I am or what pain I've endured. You're just a privilege child playing spy and ruining everything you touch."

"I'm the child? I'm not the one who's judged someone and condemned them to house arrest until I see fit! I'm not the one who's belittling someone else's motivations that you don't know anything about! You don't know me, Morgan. You don't know anything about who I am or why I do what I do. So stop acting like your life and your pain is more important than mine!"

Morgan's anger turned to fury and the heat inside him became a volcano as he let loose a wicked, domineering smile. If I hadn't been fired up and ready to hit him in that moment, I might've swooned. The man looked *good* with a smile. Like Captain America leveling up with new muscles or a character in a video game getting a power boost—this expression had *game.* Too bad I planned to dent his face in the next five minutes.

"Your pain?" he sneered, mocking me. "You're playing vigilante on some romantic notion that you can save the world. You get a few shady people sacked and you think you're the savior of the world. Newsflash, you're not Robin Hood, Caroline. You're just some petulant girl who got offended that one time and decided to use it as your origin story for becoming a superhero. And it's pathetic. Your pain is nothing." He paused, studying me in a way that said he found me lacking. "So what if you had to hide your species your whole life? That's not pain. What *I've* endured, the agony *I* survived is pain. So don't you dare compare us."

I will not cry. I will not cry. I *refused* to give the big fat flea bag the satisfaction of seeing me burst into tears. It didn't matter how deep his words cut, or that the derision in his eyes scraped me raw; made me feel so small and pathetic. I wouldn't show that to him. *I'd rather die.*

"I wouldn't *dream* of comparing us," I snarled, barely keeping the tears from my eyes, resisting the urge to throw something at him. The hurt and anger were like an earthquake shuddering through my body, and it took all of me to keep it under control. "Because I would never do what you've done to me. You see a shred of humanity in me, and you strangle it. You complain that people judge you, judge your people, and yet you've done nothing but condemn me without even knowing me."

The anger in Morgan's eyes dimmed slightly as guilt and doubt clouded around him, replacing the loathing that had been burning inside. *Good. I hope it eats him alive.*

"You're right that my story isn't like yours," I continued, my own fire a raging inferno now, "Because if the rumors are true, you've not only lost a parent, but you watched it happen. My experience isn't so obviously traumatic; I can't sum it up in one sentence for you. But that doesn't mean that my story or my pain aren't valid. Because you have *no idea* what it feels like to be the only one like you in the world. To spend your whole life hiding, always keeping people at arm's length, always terrified that you're going to slip up and get caught. You don't know why I pull these heists or why I don't want to stop. You don't know anything about me, Morgan. So, when you go to sleep tonight, I hope you toss and turn, realizing that while I never questioned whether you had a right to pain, you questioned mine."

While he was standing there, flabbergasted, and filled with confusion and guilt, I poked a finger at his chest. "You don't know everything, Morgan." Then I left him to spiral alone.

TWELVE

Morgan

She was right. I didn't know anything. Which was why I'd spent the last three hours tossing and turning just like she'd told me to. *Idiot*.

Here I'd gone and made a bad situation worse, ensuring that Caroline would hate me forever. Don't get me wrong, the end goal was still to separate us so the mate bond would hopefully fade. But there was the small problem of my feelings...Which seemed to care very much whether or not Caroline hated me. *Ugh, I'm such a hopeless sap.*

And this hopeless sap was losing sleep over the fact that not only was Caroline still mad at me, but she had a right to be. I'd been a jerk, and I didn't even know why. Why had I pushed her so hard? Said so many hurtful things?

Because she pushed you, some part of my brain whispered back, *and you've never been pushed before.*

My brain wasn't wrong. Caroline was so different than what I'd have expected in a mate. So much more reactive and driven than I would've pictured. I could sense her now, somewhere in the house, filled with irritation and frustration. She was still angry with me. *And rightfully so.*

It felt wrong somehow, to sense her this way, but I knew I couldn't make it go away. After all, I'd been through this before.

And that was the crux of the whole thing. Caroline was vastly different from my first wife—and my original mate—Genevieve. Where Gen had been gentle and patient, willing to see past my outer gruffness from the moment we met, Caroline was combative and aggressive, dramatic, and unwilling to budge when she thought she was right. Which, in this case, she was.

But I didn't *want* to sense Caroline's emotions. I didn't want to understand her. To know her better or figure out why we were bonded as mates and what it was that made God decide that we would balance so well together. I didn't want to know any of it, because it all felt like a betrayal to Gen. Like I was cheating on her. *Which is stupid because you know she'd want you to be happy.* In fact, she'd made quite the argument about it on her death bed, determined that I should have a life beyond her. What she hadn't understood was that there *was* no life beyond her. Well, until now...

I growled and flipped onto my back in the king-sized bed, grabbing a random pillow and tossing it as hard as I could. It flew across the room and hit the wall with a smack. And thanks to my Berserker strength, one end of the pillow burst open, allowing little white feathers to float through the air.

I sat up, staring at the mess I'd made, unimpressed with both myself and the thoughts in my mind.

"I don't want a new mate," I growled to no one. Then, a pang of Caroline's irritation made its way to me through the mate bond. "And I don't want to feel her either!"

But I didn't have a choice. Caroline was my mate whether I liked it or not, which meant that I could sense her emotions at any distance. It was like a constant hum in the back of my mind, always there, letting me know how she was doing. Even when I didn't *want* to know. Which was always.

"Especially because she's so dang irritated right now!"

And she was...But as I sat there, paying close attention to every shift in her emotions, her irritation suddenly ballooned into massive anger. Whatever she was doing, she was revved up and ready for war. *That can't be good.*

Anxious and sure that I was the last person she wanted to see, but unable to just set aside my worry because the *freaking bond* made her emotions constantly known to me, I snatched up a discarded shirt and left my room. When I made it down the hall to her room, I found the door open.

Both Daisy and Caroline were nowhere to be found.

My anxiety took a nosedive into panic at the sight of the empty bed, and I took the stairs two at a time. I may not have wanted Caroline as a mate, but that didn't mean I didn't want her on the planet. And if she was in any danger, I'd do anything I could to eliminate it.

As I stepped off the stairs and it into the dining room, I heard the sound of a woman's growls from the other end of the house. Caroline.

Spinning on my heel, I raced down the hall, ready to destroy whatever it was that was upsetting her so much. *Freaking bond.* When I got to the living room, it was dark but for one lamp that was lit in the entryway, where Caroline stood before the double doors. She was ranting to herself in a slew of growls and mumbles as she tossed pillows, remotes, and other various things out the open doors.

"Care?" I called out, my worry decreasing now that I knew she wasn't in danger. Though I did make a point to approach her slowly. *I wouldn't put it past her to bite me.* And not in a fun way.

Caroline spun around, her movements just a little too fast to be normal; one of her Nephilim abilities. Her green eyes were wide with anger as she glared at me, her red hair wild and untamed, and her fingers were balled into fists at her side.

"I can't leave!" She screamed. Then, with no warning, she launched herself at me.

Unprepared to brace against her, Caroline's body knocked us both to the ground, where we struggled in a heap of limbs.

"Stop it," I shouted, carefully pushing her arms away from where she was trying to strangle me. I didn't want to accidentally hurt her with my enhanced strength, but she was a vicious little thing. "Caroline, calm down! You knew you couldn't leave."

"But I thought I could at least go outside," she grunted, shoving my head back onto the ground. Then she latched her fingers onto my hair and pulled. Hard.

I glanced over at Daisy Mae, wondering if she'd get involved, but she just sat there. Thumping her tail, happy to watch, knowing that we wouldn't kill each other thanks to the mate bond. Even when Caroline pushed her knee into my gut, Daisy did nothing, leaving me to end the fight myself. *Such a helpful child you have there, Care.*

"Enough!" I yelled. This time, I grabbed her arms and yanked her against me as I sat up. Then—because I'd be an idiot to trust her—I pinned the appendages to her side. I was not about to have her try and gouge out my eyeballs. The mate bond would keep her from actually removing my eyeballs, but she'd have fun trying. "What is wrong with you? You're down here pacing like a tiger and throwing things like a child!"

"You locked me in the house!" she shouted; her voice just as loud as mine—which was impressive, considering how loudly I yelled.

Frustrated and far too tired for this situation, I sighed and hung my head, trying to think of a way to restrain her without holding her the whole time. Then—because she was Caroline—she started writhing again. And although she was no match for my strength, she was a massive pain in the butt.

Out of patience for the night, I quickly turned and pinned her to the ground, sitting on her thighs and pushing her wrists to the floor beside her. Boy did that tick her off. She snarled and thrashed, fighting me like the devil even though it was useless.

"Stop it, Care."

"Why should I? I'm being held hostage by a monster! I have every right to want to throw you across the room right now," she snapped, her beautiful face drawn into a fierce glare that made her look like the Dark Elf she was.

My grip on her loosened ever so slightly, my chest suddenly tight with hurt. Calling me monster wasn't the first time she'd insulted me...but this time seemed to sting more than the rest. I'd been called ugly things for a long time—monster, beast, murderer, you name it—but hearing those words from *her* and sensing *her* judgement was different. Because she was my mate—because she was 'the one'—I naturally wanted her to think well of me...and it hurt that she didn't.

"Listen," I said, softening my voice. I might be hurt that Care saw me as a villain, but acting like a villain wasn't going to fix it. "I'm sorry I kidnapped you and I'm sorry I'm keeping you prisoner. I need you to know that I hate doing it, Care. I hate being the bad guy, but I don't know what to do with you. If I let you go, you'll just go back to extorting people at the Alliance Building, and me and my people will keep getting blamed. So please, tell me how to fix this so that neither of us gets hurt, and I'll do it."

Then, as if by a miracle, Caroline went completely still. She was still angry, her expression stubborn and her emotions annoyed, but she no longer looked like she wanted to kill me. *Progress. I'll take it.*

"I can't even step outside, Morgan," she bit out, brows pulled low and green eyes shooting fire. "How exactly is that fair?"

"You can go outside," I sighed, "You just have to go with me."

"What?"

"The Witch binding doesn't just bind you to the house. It binds you to either be in the house or be with me. If I leave, you can come, but you can't leave my side unless you're inside this house."

She considered my words, weighing them out, looking for a loophole. Which was exactly why I hadn't wanted her to know how the binding worked. Because she was bound to try and find a way around it. She wouldn't be successful, but I wasn't looking forward to her many attempts to try.

"Why would you—"

Whatever she was going to say was interrupted by the sound of a door squeaking open. Caroline, Daisy Mae and I all whipped our heads around, and watched as someone dressed in black and wearing a ski mask came through the still open front doors.

"What the heck?" Caroline whispered beneath me.

Though I was equally confused, I reacted quickly, my protective instincts pushing me into action. Snarling, I launched to my feet and threw myself at the intruder. Either the person had never seen a Berserker, or they were completely unaware of which house they were breaking into, because they actually attempted to fight me. *Idiot.*

I almost laughed when they punched me in the chin, the blow doing little more than irritating me. When I didn't react to the hit except to glare, the person's eyes went wide, and they took a step back. Smirking, knowing I had the upper hand, I swiped my fist at their face. But they ducked at the last moment and slipped around me.

To go after Caroline.

Care saw the attacker coming though, and she used her Nephilim speed to outmaneuver them. Then, instead of running for safety like I'd hoped she would, she jumped on the intruder's back. *I should've seen that coming.*

I had to give her credit though, because she did a fair amount of damage, banging on the attacker's head with her fists. She let out a loud, wailing warrior cry as Daisy drove her teeth into the person's leg, eliciting a masculine scream.

But just as I made my way toward them to help end the fight, the guy ripped Caroline from his back and threw her to the floor. Daisy growled and renewed her attack on his leg, but he kicked her off, and she squealed, sliding across the room. Caroline groaned from the ground, and her attacker dropped beside her, grabbing her wrists as if to pick her up.

No. Not my mate. Instinct took complete control of my body, and every muscle went taut and ready for battle. A threat against my partner was a threat against me. And I'd never responded to threats well.

I stalked toward the man, my Berserker magic *begging* me to shift into bear form and rip the man to pieces. But I couldn't. Not without hurting Care. And hurting Caroline was guaranteed to completely shatter me—unwanted mate or not. So, I fought against the urge to shift and instead put all my focus into my magical strength.

It only took two strides to reach the man, and as he turned to fend me off, a knife now in his hand, I made my move. I grasped his head with both hands, ignoring the pain as his blade sliced across my forearm, and I flicked my wrists.

And snapped his neck.

He flopped like a ragdoll in my grasp, and I immediately tossed him aside, disgusted with the whole situation. But it was Caroline on the floor that had my full attention.

I knelt next to her, terrified that he'd hurt her. But when she sat up, eyes locked on the attacker's body, I knew that she wasn't in pain. She was horrified. *And she should be.* Any moment now, she was going to look at me and scream. Writhe away from me and name me as the monster I was. Caroline didn't know me. She didn't know that the rumors about me and my body count weren't true. To her, this moment, where I'd managed to kill someone as easily as flicking a penny would only solidify my position as the villain in her mind.

In this moment, when my mate had been under attack, I'd managed to keep my cool enough not to shift, and yet all that would come of it was alienating her more. And as much as I didn't want a second mate—didn't want Caroline to be 'the one'...it didn't change the fact that she was. And like magnets, I was pulled to her, wanting her to think well of me. To trust me. *And now she probably never will.*

When she finally looked at me, I did everything I could not to notice her emotions, not to feel the horror and disgust I knew she'd be feeling. But I felt it anyway. Her worry, her concern...her fear.

"Are you hurt?" she asked, her green eyes frantic as they scanned over me until they fell on my arm. "You are! How bad is it?"

"I'm fine." My voice came out so monotone, so robotically, still waiting for her to freak out.

"No, you're not, let me see." Rising to her knees, she grasped my wrist carefully, the pads of her fingers so gentle that it almost made me cry. I couldn't recall the last time anyone had touched me like this, treated me like *I* was precious and breakable.

What was even more shocking was the worry I felt in her, and the realization that she was worried *for* me. *How is that possible?*

Daisy, having rebounded from being kicked in the chest, trotted over to us with a wagging tail, and licked every inch of our skin that she could reach.

"We'll have a vet come check her over, just in case she has internal injuries," I assured Caroline when she began to cautiously pet Daisy's chest, leaving one hand on my wrist.

Caroline slowly lifted those green eyes, studying me cautiously. The blue rings that rimmed her irises mocked me, reminding me that she'd sensed my rage as I snapped her attacker's neck. She knew just how dangerous I could be. And yet, all she said was, "Thank you."

"Aren't you afraid of me now?" I asked tentatively, not really wanting to know, but unable to take the anxiety of not knowing.

Caroline's expression hovered between confusion and incredulity, and she stared up at me, still holding onto my wrist. Somehow, I thought that might've been on purpose. To prove a point that I otherwise wouldn't believe.

"I was afraid that I might die," she said, and though her touch remained soft, her voice was hard and stubborn, "Afraid that Daisy might get hurt...or that you would."

"You were afraid...for me?" I'd felt her emotions, saw how quickly she moved to make sure I was okay. I knew that she'd been worried about me, but hearing it and feeling it were two different things.

Then, possibly for the first time ever, I sensed empathy in Caroline. It was deep and cool, calming, and safe like a weighted blanket, and I wanted to wrap myself up in it.

"Morgan, you annoy me. You've kidnapped me, argued with me, ignored me, and acted like a caveman in most of our conversations," she said matter-of-factly. "But you also care about my dog and protect me when you don't have to. So of course, I was afraid for you. I don't like you very much, but the world would be a little too easy going without your eternally tense energy buzzing in it."

"So..." I stuttered, not quite sure how to accept her simple summary of me—one that painted me as...not evil. "It doesn't freak you out that I just killed that guy with my bare hands?"

"You saved me, Morgan," she insisted. "The only thing that freaks me out about that is the fact that clearly we both value each other's lives more than we've led the other to believe."

And she was right. Because I valued her life *way* more than I'd expressed. I'd been a jerk because I wanted to defy the mate bond, and in the process, I'd made my mate believe that she meant nothing to me.

I decided then, that the mate bond wasn't my concern anymore. Was it inconvenient? Heck yeah, and I wasn't about to go falling head over heels in love with Caroline either. But I also wasn't willing to keep her at arm's length just to protect myself. *It isn't worth it.* Not when it meant hurting her.

"You called me Care," she said after a few moments of my silence, finally letting go of my arm.

"Sorry, it felt...natural I guess," I shrugged, scooting back to give her space.

"Listen, I'll make you a deal."

I shook my head immediately. Deals with Caroline couldn't be a good idea.

"Relax Mr. Grouchy Bear," she smiled, the expression lighting up her face in a way I'd never seen before. Maybe because this time she wasn't trying to manipulate me with the expression or cloak her words behind it. Instead, she was genuinely entertained. "I was just going to say that if you'll let me call you Mor, then you can keep calling me Care."

"Mor?" I didn't think anyone had ever given me a nickname before. Fitting that it would be Caroline who started it.

"Take it or leave it," she shrugged, "Or I could just keep calling you insulting things like flea bag, overgrown teddy—"

"Fine, you can call me Mor," I agreed quickly, hearing the rest of the group come down the stairs and not wanting any of them to hear the rest of her list. They didn't need any new ideas for how to annoy me.

"Thank you, Mor," Caroline sassed, giving me a sardonic smile.

"You're welcome." I stood, offering her a hand up. "Care."

THIRTEEN

Caroline

I HADN'T REALIZED HOW DISTURBING IT would be to see a dead body. I mean, it wasn't exactly on my bucket list in the first place, but the experience was even more traumatizing than I'd expected.

Part of the problem was the simple fact that a person—it didn't matter that he'd attacked me, he was still a person—had just been murdered. That was traumatizing enough, but then there were also the practical things; the smell, the way the broken neck swelled and bruised, and the way the guy's eyes just *stared* straight ahead.

Somehow, I managed to keep myself from throwing up, but once the smell started to spread and I felt bile rise in my throat, we relocated to Morgan's office.

Dead body now out of sight—and out of smelling range—I silently sipped my tea, thankful for the warm mug in my hands to ground me. When Morgan had demanded that I sit down the moment we got to his office, I was a little irritated. But when he brought me a steaming cup of tea and a fluffy blanket, I thawed like Olaf, the talking snowman in *Frozen*. And like Olaf, who was stupidly obsessed with summer, I was stupidly obsessed with figuring out Mor and his Rubik's cube of a personality.

I watched the Berserker Chief as he paced the length of his office, all wound up and fuming. His hands were balled into fists, and he now sported a bandage on one arm thanks to Logan's mothering. Mor's knife wound from the earlier fight had ended up being relatively shallow and didn't need stitches. *He's lucky it wasn't worse.* We both were.

It didn't escape my notice that the reason there was a dead body in the entryway was because Morgan had chosen to save my life. Something that I wasn't *entirely* sure I deserved considering he was suspected of *my* break-ins. Once again, he was bending the assumptions I'd made about him, and I didn't know how to feel about that.

"Who was he?" Logan asked about our dead attacker. Him, Mike, and Clint had thankfully removed the body—to where, I didn't know, and I didn't *want* to know. So long as I didn't have to see it again, I didn't care.

"He had no identification on his person," Grey explained, standing next to Mor's desk, a cell phone in one hand and his trusty clipboard in the other. "And the phone he carried was a burner phone with only one number dialed, which was disconnected when I tried it. And the attacker's DNA is human."

"So as of now, we have no clues," Clint complained, sitting on the couch beside Mike and Logan. "Great. I guess we can show his picture to some of our contacts and see if we get any hits."

"Even if someone does recognize him, they're unlikely to know who hired him or why," Mike sighed, his bulky frame taking up more than his third of the couch. He was like a pale, blue-eyed Dwayne Johnson. With hair.

"Why would a human be hired to attack you?" Logan asked, blue eyes narrowed as he watched Morgan continue to pace.

"They weren't," Mor answered quickly. Then his eyes turned to me, hard and angry. "They were here for Care."

My first instinct was to be annoyed and tell him that there was no evidence I was the cause of the attack and how dare he insinuate that it was my fault! But then I noted the variations in his emotions. The anger that burned bright and dangerous...and the protectiveness that surrounded it. *Oh.* He wasn't mad *at* me; he was mad *for* me. *Well, that's new.*

"Caroline?" Grey said—I think for third time. *Gosh dang it!* Embarrassed,I turned my attention away from Mor—whom I hadn't realized I was staring at.

"Hm?" I hummed, praying that he hadn't had to say my name more than once to snap me out of my musings.

"Do you have any enemies?" he asked.

I couldn't help it. I laughed.

"What a stupid question! I'm literally under house arrest for the problems I've caused, and you have to ask if I have enemies?" I snorted and glanced at Morgan, but he just sighed and closed his eyes, apparently not entertained. Grey was similarly unimpressed.

But Mike, Clint and Logan laughed. I took that as a win.

"But would any of your enemies want to harm you like this?" Grey clarified calmly, completely enigmatic.

"They don't even know who I am," I said with a shrug. "To them, I'm just the mysterious spy who extorts Alliance employees and gets away with it." My anonymity was thanks to the feed blocker I used on the security cameras and the magic I tapped into to alter my hair. It was the security guards' faults that they didn't recognize my face.

"As far as you know," Mor argued, still pacing like a nerd trying to get a personal best on his Fitbit, "But someone could have figured you out, Care. It only takes one person learning your identity to put you in danger."

Boy did I hate how right he was. Like, I hated his rightness even more than I hated it when people said *The Office* wasn't 'that funny'—and that comment *always* got me revved up.

A knock at the door startled us all, but Morgan wasn't concerned, casually whipping the door open to reveal a woman in her late thirties wearing purple scrubs.

"How is she?" Mor asked with a growl.

The woman, however, wasn't intimidated. "Her tests and scans came back clean," she said. A moment later, another woman in scrubs appeared, barely holding onto a leash as Daisy Mae pulled on the other end.

"Maisy!" I crooned, setting my mug on the coffee table so I could scratch my little croissant-like contorting dog properly. Daisy broke free of her handler and ran straight for me, attempting to give me slobbery dog kisses.

"No, no kisses," I complained, leaning my chin up so she couldn't reach me even as I bent over to pet her. "You eat your own poop. That revokes kissing privileges. Remember what Mommy taught you? We don't kiss, we're cuddle fish."

Daisy quickly got tired of my no kissing rule and left to go beg for attention from everyone else instead. Mike, Clink and Logan all three spoiled her with ear rubs and butt scratches, but when Daisy tried to beg Grey, he just stared down at her like she was an alien creature. She gave up pretty quickly on him and moved on to Morgan, who surprisingly seemed to be her favorite.

"I know, little worm," he crooned, crouching down to rub her belly, "No one wants to kiss you. Life must be rough to be rejected all the time. But in their defense, eating poop before a kiss is just rude."

Part of me wanted to laugh at this exchange, and part of me wanted to stare in awe. While I was torn between the two, the boys had no such issues. Logan chuckled loudly, not even trying to hide his amusement. He even took a picture with his phone to document Morgan's moment of softness. Mike and Clint at least had the good sense to hide their chuckles behind their hands and even Grey cracked out the shadow of a smile.

"What's so funny?" Mor demanded, glaring us all down.

"I think that's the sweetest, most tender I've ever heard you in my life," Logan wheezed, wiping tears from his eyes.

"Oh, shut up," Morgan snarled—though I noted that he gave Daisy one last good scratch before he stood and turned to the veterinarian. "So, was there anything else we should be aware of?" he asked.

"Yes," the woman replied, trying and failing to hide her amusement, a small smile gracing her lips. "Daisy has no internal damage, no lacerations or bruising that we could find. But if she has any vomiting or diarrhea or shows any strange behavior—especially in the next twenty-four hours—go ahead and give us a call."

Morgan thanked the vet and Grey walked the two ladies out, shutting the office door behind him.

"Thank you," I said to Morgan, Daisy now laying in a tight little circle on the carpet, sleeping peacefully. "You didn't have to bring a vet all the way out here, and I can't imagine that it was cheap to make a house call at two in the morning. So, thank you...it means a lot."

When Morgan met my gaze, his expression was blank. He was white noise, completely emotionless. At first, I was offended...but then I felt his empathy and his relief. *'Are you afraid of me now?'* That's what he'd asked me after he killed my attacker. That had been his greatest concern. And judging by the relief that he felt at my gratitude, it still was.

Morgan might not have been my favorite person, but he didn't want me to think poorly of him. And that said a lot.

"You're welcome," he finally replied. No expansion, no smile, no nod. He was completely detached, but now that I'd gotten this little peek into him via my magic, I wasn't fooled. Morgan cared...and I cared that he cared. *Weird.*

When the silence stretched on a little too long, and everyone's eyes were still pinned to Morgan and me, Logan finally spoke up. "Alright, back to the topic at hand. If no one knows who you are, then how would they even know to find you here?"

"Is there any reason someone would attack you, other than your heists at the Alliance Building?" Mike prompted as Grey came back into the room. "Maybe there's another motive behind the attack?"

Without a word, Morgan and I turned to each other. There was indeed another reason that someone might hunt me. A big reason.

The look in Morgan's eyes told me that he was thinking the same thing. The question was though, should we tell the rest of the group about my secret lineage? They didn't even know if I was a human or a Shifter. All they'd been told was about my work as a spy. *Should I tell them the other half of the truth?*

My secret was a big one, but it wasn't as if I was actively being hunted because of my species. People didn't even suspect that any Nephilim would be alive today, let alone know they needed to look for me. So really, the test was in making sure those who did know my identity didn't go telling council members—other than Mor, who already knew.

Unsure what to do, I sent Morgan a questioning look, and he made a point to look at everyone in the room before turning his attention back to me. Then he nodded. *He thinks I can trust them.* When I bit my lip, still uneasy, his expression softened to one of comfort and he inclined his head to me. He was letting me decide how I wanted to handle the situation. He wouldn't tell them if I didn't want him to. *But do I want to tell them?*

So far, I'd felt no reservations about trusting Morgan. Sure, I was annoyed that my instincts so quickly urged me to confide in him, but I never questioned the wisdom in trusting him. I just innately knew that he was safe. That I was safe with him. *And if I trust him, then I trust them too.*

I gave Mor a single nod.

"What Caroline is about to tell you stays in this room," he announced, that deep voice cloaking me in a way the blanket across my knees never could—though I imagined it wrapped around the other's throats like a noose with his threat. "If the Sleuth is ever notified of this information, it'll be from either Caroline or myself, after we've both discussed it. Understood?"

All four of the other men exchanged serious glances, unsure but immediately taking Morgan seriously. How could they not with his expression so threatening?

"Consider it sworn," Clint said, clapping a fist over his chest.

"I swear," Mike added, mimicking Clint's gesture.

Grey and Logan swore similar oaths, tapping their fists to their chests. Then, instead of explaining my situation to the room, Morgan nodded to me and leaned back against his desk, letting me take the lead. *Okay, who is this man and what has he done with the tyrant prison warden?* If I didn't know any better, I'd wonder if a Nephilim was impersonating him. It was unnatural for Mor to be this nice to me. *I don't think I like it.* It felt too close, too friendly and we were anything but friends.

Shaking my head to clear it of the distracting thoughts, I put all my attention on the rest of the group. "I'm not just a spy," I said, deciding to just rip off the band aid, "I'm a Nephilim."

I always thought the expression 'you could hear a pin drop' was an exaggeration, but the silence that followed my announcement was so empty that I could *hear* my pulse thudding and the light bulbs buzzing in the light fixture above us. *Well, this is fun.* Everyone was so overcome with shock and anxiety that they couldn't speak for a few minutes.

"I'm sorry, *what?*" Mike blurted once he found his voice again. Poor guy looked like I'd dumped sticky soda all over his brain's operating system. "The Nephilim are all—you're all...dead."

"I think she knows that, genius," Clint retorted, but there was no snark behind it as he watched me with utter confusion.

"I know, but it's just...I don't get it," Mike continued, a wrinkle appearing between his dark eyebrows. "Elves are extinct. The Berserkers even partnered with the Nephilim to help wipe them out! It caused a war so big that Shifters in general were almost eradicated. Then the Hunters picked off any remaining Elves after the war ended, so how the heck are you here right now?"

"I know, it's a lot to wrap your head around," I said calmly, trying to figure out how to explain it all without making poor Mike's head explode. "But obviously the civil war didn't eradicate the Elves like everyone thought. Someone survived, otherwise I wouldn't be here today. Now, I don't know the details, but the real point is that I'm a Nephilim—the only one I know of—and I've lived my entire life trying not to get caught."

"I can imagine why." Mike rubbed a hand across his shaggy brown waves. "Everyone would either hate you or worship you."

Morgan shot him a warning look, but I didn't mind Mike's candor. I'd rather everyone fully understand the levity of what I was telling them.

"Sorry," he amended, more to Morgan than to me.

"It's okay," I assured him, shooting Morgan a small smile to ease his irritation. "You're right. Some people might think that an Elf should be put back in power since the Alfar managed to maintain peace before the civil war ruined everything. Most people, however, would probably hand me over to the government for a payday. And Lord only knows what they'd do with me. Plus, I'm a Nephilim, one of the bad guys. Anyone coming for me is likely unsavory."

"So then why do you target the Shifter Alliance? Why not just live a normal life where you'd be less noticed?" Logan's question was curious rather than accusing, and I got why he would ask it. No one had ever understood my choice to live like a vigilante. That wasn't about to change now.

"Because some things are more important than my comfort or safety," I said simply, not feeling the need to elaborate. My reasons for how I did things were personal, and as curious and harmless as these boys might be, none of them had earned that level of vulnerability from me yet.

"What's it like?" The question came from Clint, who was watching me with obvious fascination.

"What's what like?" I asked.

"Being the only one," Clint supplied, his tone surprisingly gentle. He knew the weight of the question he was asking, but still he wanted to understand. Sensing the genuineness in all of them as they watched me, I sighed and tried to formulate an answer that would be honest and yet not make me feel emotionally naked.

"Well, it's kind of...lonely. Everyone else belongs to a faction; a Sleuth, a Pack, a Horde. And I'm just...me."

Everyone went quiet, and I sensed the oodles of empathy and compassion rolling my way. I hated how vulnerable it made me feel.

"How do your powers work?" Morgan asked. I glanced up to stare at him, confused at first because he already knew how my powers worked. But then I saw the look in his grey eyes and felt the compassion inside him; a different brand than the one coming from everyone else. *He's changing the subject for my sake.*

And there he went, ruining all my preconceived notions again.

"Well, I can change my appearance with magic, I have heightened speed, and I can sense and manipulate people's emotions," I explained, "With my appearance, I can change anything. My hair, my eyes, my figure, my gender, my voice. I can be anybody, but the caveat is that I can only change into people that I've seen before. With emotions, I can sense what someone's feeling, but not why. And I can influence someone's emotions by sort of tugging their feelings from one emotion into another, but I can't make feelings from nothing."

"So, you can sense what any of us are feeling right now?" Logan said, eyes dancing between Morgan and I.

Mischief, humor, and amusement passed through him. Meanwhile, irritation, anxiety and annoyance flashed in Morgan. *Interesting...*

"I can," I replied, studying both him and Morgan, "And now I'm wondering why you feel so mischievous."

"Okay," Morgan grumbled, apparently not interested in whatever Logan was up to "Show and tell is over—"

"Technically Caroline would need to show us how she uses her powers in order for there to be any show to our show and tell," Clint argued with a sassy smirk.

Morgan was *not* entertained.

"Back on track," he snapped. "Someone is either targeting Care because of her history pulling heists at the Alliance building, or because they somehow know that she's Nephilim. The things we need to find out are how they figured out who she is, and how they knew she was here."

"I have no idea how anyone would know who I am," I said, going along with his change of subject mostly because it was two a.m., and the lack of sleep was starting to get to me. "I'm careful to never leave any clues behind, so there should be nothing that connects me to the heists. And as for how they knew that I would be here, I'm not sure. I use a feed blocker every time I sneak into the Alliance Building, so even when you kidnapped me," Mor had the good sense to seem contrite about that, "The cameras weren't live...Except that you did talk to those security guards when you took me out the side door."

"Oh crap, I did talk to the security guards," he winced, pinching the bridge of his nose. "Which means that even though I didn't tell the security guards that you were the one responsible for the break-ins, whoever the guards told might've put that together themselves. But since it was a human hitman who came for you, and not a team from the

Shifter Unit, that means that the council itself doesn't know about you. An individual had to be the one to hire that hitman."

"Standard protocol for corrupt officials," I nodded nonchalantly.

Morgan glared, unamused.

"Since we don't know who's behind it—and it could be anybody at the Alliance Building—you'll need to stay here. It's not safe for you to leave anytime soon." Then he took a seat at his desk, pulling out a notebook and a pencil like he was making a pros and cons list. I had half a mind to pull a Michael Scott from *The Office* and say 'Pro: you get to share your pros and cons list with the other nerds. Con: you unzip your pants, and you find that there's a calculator down there.' Mor probably wouldn't find it funny though. "We'll start a patrol outside since the security system can't stop people from lurking. And all windows and doors need to remain locked at all times from now on."

"Is that really necessary—"

"And you'll need to stay right next to me any time we go outside," he continued, talking over me. "You can't go far without the Witch binding stopping you, but any distance is a danger when we're in the open like that. Hmm...maybe we should put a tracker on you too. If the attacker realizes that we're bound by the Witch binding, they might kill me so they can take you. In which case, the others will need to be able to find you."

"Treating me like a gem in a case isn't going to stop whoever's after me, Mor," I argued, but he just continued to scribble on his stupid list. "It's just going to make them more determined. What we need to do is find out who it is that's after me. Do some recon, interview people—"

But I may as well have kept my mouth shut, because Morgan just started talking again like I wasn't even there. "Maybe Merida can give you some charms to use when you're attacked next time. I haven't had cause to worry much about our security system before, but I'll have it updated and assign someone to watch it—"

Finally, I'd had it. "*Morgan!*" I shouted, and although my voice wasn't as booming as Mor's when he yelled, mine still managed to be plenty ferocious.

Morgan's head snapped up from the page in his hand, pencil poised to keep writing as his wide eyes studied me.

"I've been alone a long time," I warned him, the little patience I'd found for him in the last hour beginning to fade away, "I know how to survive. I don't need you suffocating me with all your protections. I need you to *listen* to me so we can come up with a plan *together*."

"You sure you know how to survive?" Mor snapped, tossing the pencil onto the desk where it bounced to the floor. The room went silent, everyone watching us shout at each other like children. "Because that guy almost got you this morning, Caroline! And I snatched you in the middle of a hallway. You're a spy, you're not a warrior. That innocent look you play so well might save you from getting arrested, but it can't stop a bullet or a knife. If you keep insisting on being in the middle of the fray, you're going to end up dead. So, stop getting in my way and let me handle this!"

Anger burned and crackled in my chest, my face going hot and my fingers shaking with the need to throttle him. Slowly, I stood from my chair; a hurricane bottled, and let all my hatred show on my face.

"Someday, I really hope you stop pretending you know everything," I hissed, and then Daisy and I fled from the room.

FOURTEEN

Morgan

I didn't see Caroline the rest of the day. Between me holing up in my office, petulant and angry, and her stewing in her bedroom, stubborn and annoyed, we spent the rest of the day ignoring each other. Which of course, really helped our relationship.

By the time the next morning came, I wasn't sure if I should leave my room and risk the wrath of Caroline or stay in here and hide. On the one hand, hiding would help keep our relationship as thin and shallow as possible, but on the other hand, my connection to her through the mate bond made it hard to keep my distance. I could sense her frustration with my rules and feel her chafe against the restrictions I tried to impose. I could even sense her need for revenge, and the purpose it gave her. All of which made it almost impossible to stay away. How could I resist empathizing with someone I understood so deeply?

Answer: I couldn't. At least, not unless I got some major—and permanent—distance between us. And soon.

But almost immediately following that thought, there was a tugging in my chest, a hollow kind of ache. *What is that?* When the feeling deepened, becoming slowly more painful, I realized what it was, having felt it deeply when Gen passed away. *Does the idea of Caroline leaving make me...sad?* No. Couldn't be.

But the pang wouldn't go away, no matter how much I rubbed at the spot. *Dang mate bond.* Trying to convince myself that the feeling was just indigestion, I left my bedroom behind and tromped down the stairs. Hopefully I could make it to my office without any further thoughts of my mate haunting me.

I should've known better.

Laughter met my ears halfway down the stairs and I paused. The loud chuckles of my brothers and Logan came first, but it was the light, clear sound of a woman's voice that had me grasping the railing for balance.

I hadn't heard Caroline laugh before. Kidnapping her and holding her prisoner hadn't exactly given her a lot of reasons to be jovial. I was surprised though, how real this laugh sounded. It wasn't a ruse meant to fool anyone; just a pure, simple sound.

I hated it.

Growling, I made my way down the rest of the stairs to where Mike, Clint, Logan and Grey were all gathered around one of the dining room tables. They laughed as Clint told a story about a first date gone wrong—he had a lot of those—and even Grey smiled as he listened. I wasn't sure I'd ever seen my Second laugh in the entire ten years I'd known him, and even smiles were a rare occurrence.

Then there was Caroline, sitting on the edge of the group, laughing and smiling at all the right moments. As I watched her green eyes dance with happiness, I realized that I'd never seen her happy before. *Probably because I've been such an ass.* I blamed the mate bond. *When in doubt, always blame the bond.*

But as I watched Caroline smile and heard her laugh, I couldn't pretend that her happiness didn't make me happy. And as much as I wanted to blame *that* on the mate bond, I couldn't. Mate bonds only showed you who your best partner was—the one person you were meant to be with given the way the chips had fallen in your life. But the respect I was feeling, the contentment of watching Caroline *enjoy* this moment, that was all me.

It's starting.

The mate bond couldn't create feelings—I knew, because I'd had a mate bond with my first wife—but how could someone *not* catch feelings for 'the one'? The bond was a lighthouse, and once you saw the way home, it was almost impossible not to head straight for it.

For me, Caroline was sunlight, and though I could live without sunlight—had lived without Caroline's specific brand of sunlight up to this point—now that I'd seen it and felt it, how could I walk away from it? How could I go back to darkness when I knew that the light was there?

Suddenly, Care's eyes lifted and latched onto me. Then the smile fell from her lips, and she glared.

Maybe resisting her won't be so hard after all.

Before Caroline could put words to that glare, Daisy rose from her spot beneath the table where she'd been waiting for scraps, and trotted over to me with her tail wagging so hard that it wagged the rest of her body too.

"Hey little lady," I crooned, squatting down to pet her, and narrowly avoiding a kiss to my mouth. "Now what did your mom tell you? You're a cuddle fish, and cuddle fish don't kiss."

Daisy, the determined lady that she was, continued to try to lick me. But once she realized that I wasn't giving her access to my face, she started turning in circles, too excited to stand still. I snickered and turned my attention back to the table. Where Caroline was staring at me.

She wasn't glaring anymore—thankfully. Instead, she was watching me with a confused wrinkle between her eyebrows. Paying more attention to the mate bond, I sensed her frustration...and a bit of reluctant admiration. *Hm...*

"So, you're the key to your mom, are you?" I whispered to Daisy. "That's good to know." But it shouldn't be. Because I shouldn't care if Caroline admired me or not. Except that I did care. A lot. I growled. *Stupid mate bond.*

"Morning bro," Clint called out, just now noticing my presence.

The others likewise greeted me. Except for Caroline.

"Morning," I nodded to her, trying to get a sense for just how rough the day was going to be.

Instead of greeting me back, she just said, "Mind if I talk to you for a minute?"

Well, this'll be fun.

"Sure." I sighed, internally preparing myself for battle as I turned and made my way toward my office. I could've told her I didn't want to talk yet, but why avoid the inevitable? If Mount Caroline was going to blow, we might as well get it over with so I could assess the damage.

I didn't hear her following behind me, but I sensed her irritation closing in. And although I wished I could blame the mate bond for picking up on her body heat, that was just my own bizarre Caroline flavored fascination.

Grumbling to myself about inconveniently attractive house guests, I opened my office door and immediately strode over to my desk, needing to put space—and multiple pieces of furniture—between us.

"So," Caroline hummed, crossing her arms over the T shirt and sweatpants she was currently borrowing from Logan's mom. I'd offered to let her borrow some of my clothes, but she found the idea so disturbing that she actually said 'ew' and insisted that she'd just keep washing her own dress and Logan's mom's clothes. Apparently, I had cooties.

"So?" I parroted, crossing my arms in an effort to keep myself from fidgeting. But then it just looked like I was mirroring her, and I'd read once that people did that when they were attracted to each other. So, I instead fisted my hands in my lap. *Oh my gosh, she's even impacting the way I* sit. *I'm pathetic.*

She didn't reply. Just raised her eyebrows at me. Unsure how to approach the situation, I let myself take note of her emotions again. *Great, she's feeling impatient and annoyed.* I was off to a great start in this conversation.

"What did I do now?" I sighed, exhausted. The drama this woman had brought into my life was really wearing me out.

"'What did you do'?" she repeated incredulously, eyes narrowed and pointed at me like the laser sight on a rifle. "Are you *serious* right now? You need me to parent you, tell you what you did wrong so you can tell me the words you think I want to hear?"

"There can't be a right response to that...is there?" I asked, pretty positive that no matter what I said, she was bound to hate me regardless.

Caroline's lips snapped shut, her nostrils flared, and her anger swayed like a snake, poised and ready to strike.

"You are the most difficult man I have ever met in my life!" she roared, going from zero to one hundred in five seconds. "I can't believe that you could be so obtuse! How can you not understand why I'm angry right now? Forget the fact that you kidnapped me," she shouted, and I had enough sense of shame to blush at the mention of my crime, "But you act like a beast every other conversation! I thought we'd made a little bit of a pact last night, maybe laid down our weapons and ceased this little war we've had going on, but no. You had to go all caveman and boss me around like I'm your prisoner." Then she pointed her finger in my face. "You have to choose, Morgan. Do you want to be the evil warden who tries to control me, or do you want to be the ally who puts his ego aside and gets the job done? Spoiler alert, there's only one right answer, and if you try to control me again, I *will* bite you."

I chuckled in spite of her serious expression, because honestly, I could genuinely imagine Caroline biting me in retribution for trying to control her. *And she probably bites just as hard as a Berserker in bear form.*

So, I thought very carefully before I spoke. Because Caroline might look like a day-dream, but I was no fool. She could turn into a nightmare and rip me to shreds in two minutes if she had half a mind to do it. *Tread carefully Hohlt.*

"You're right," I said tentatively. I was a guy, and guys could be dumb sometimes, but I did know that those two words were *always* the right thing to say. When Caroline's expression softened just a fraction, I jumped on that train and kept talking. "We did have a truce last night, and I ruined it by trying to boss you around—which was stupid, because we both know you can't be bossed."

"Darn right," she muttered, still not quite giving in.

"I don't want to be the villain Caroline, but I need you to understand that your usual MO isn't going to help us get out of this mess." At this, she lowered her eyebrows and puckered her lips into a pout that would rival any three-year-old. I hated how adorable it was. "You make a good spy, Care, but being good at sneaking into places isn't going to keep you alive the next time you get attacked. What you need is physical protection and to stay out of the vengeance game for the time being, which we both agreed on last night."

Care rolled her eyes, though she seemed less annoyed with me and more annoyed with the situation in general. I considered that progress.

"Like you said, it would be stupid for me to try and control you. Plus, I'd rather not get bit," I teased, grateful when the line won a small smile from her. "So, what you do want to do moving forward?"

This seemed to surprise her, her chin pulling back and her eyes roving over me like she wasn't quite convinced that I hadn't lost my mind. I couldn't blame her. It hadn't exactly been my go-to approach so far to ask her what she thought or what she wanted. *My bad.*

"I..." she sighed, stepping back to sit in one of the armchairs in the middle of the room, "I guess I want to work together."

I nodded, not disagreeing, but not convinced that it would work. "We hate each other. Can we work together without tearing each other apart?" More like, could I work with

Caroline without losing the battle of the mate bond and becoming completely enthralled with her?

"Well, we both want the same thing, which at least makes us allies."

"What do we both want?"

Caroline smiled.

"We both want me out of your hair," she shrugged innocently. "And if we solve this whole mystery of my copycat, then I can go back to outing people at the Alliance Building for their bad behavior, and you can go back to...whatever it was you did before I showed up."

I scoffed, simultaneously annoyed and entertained by her bravado.

"I don't know, I'm not sure I can trust you to go back to your vendetta without getting in my way again," I said, all bluster.

"Oh, come on, old man, I wasn't even a blip on your radar until you got blamed for my break-ins."

"*Old man?*" I demanded, genuinely offended considering I had exactly three grey hairs—all of which were Caroline's fault. "I'm only thirty-two."

"Thirty-two huh?" she hummed, looking me up and down, unimpressed. "You're even older than I thought. I pegged you at thirty."

"And I was almost fooled into believing that you were seventeen."

At that, she smirked. "I'm twenty-two, so don't worry, you've kidnapped an adult. A much less severe crime than kidnapping a minor."

I rolled my eyes and prayed that God would help me survive this new somewhat-friendly dynamic. *I'm going to need all the help I can get.*

"Alright, Miss. I'm-So-Full-Of-Sass-That-My-Words-Will-Bite-You-Even-If-I-Don't, how do you propose we work together?" I snarked dryly, getting us back on topic.

"Oh, that's easy," she said. Then she stood and made her way to my desk where she fiddled with the pencil holder by my computer. "We agree not to boss each other around, and then we focus our efforts on figuring out who's after me and who's trying to frame you. Which also means that we should investigate the council since they're one hundred percent the ones behind it."

"Not all of them."

"You're awfully protective of certain council members," she said offhandedly, but I could feel the possessiveness flare up in her, the jealousy.

This time, I let myself not just smile, but laugh as I watched the confusion on her face. She may not understand why she felt so possessive of me, but I did.

She liked me—and not through any gallant efforts on my part. No, it was the natural draw we felt to each other that made her like me. The genuine attraction, the natural interest and the curiosity that came with meeting 'the one'. It also helped that the mate bond allowed her to sense my feelings so acutely, giving her a peek at my reactions to her.

Caroline was just as interested in me as I was in her. And we were both equally annoyed about it.

"Worried that I have romantic interest in Merida?" I taunted, unable to stop tugging on her proverbial pigtails. The reactions she gave were just too fun to watch.

Care glared at me as I removed her hand from my pencil jar. It probably wasn't wise for me to touch her, but I couldn't be at ease with her in my personal space. Where her nearness muddled all my thoughts about distancing us until the mate bond faded. Here, with her face so close and her wrist in my hand, my plans for bachelorhood seemed so shortsighted and silly.

"No." Caroline scoffed, but the carelessness of the response was ruined when I felt her flood with embarrassment. "Why would I be worried about your romantic life? If anything, I feel the need to send Merida a condolences card." Then she slipped her hand from mine.

Whatever spell I'd been under suddenly burst, and the tenseness of the moment fell like confetti, lackluster and unexciting once it hit the ground. I shook my head. *Get it together, Morgan.*

"Of course, you'd do that," I managed to squeeze out, sober enough now to joke.

A smirk pulled at her lips as she took a step back from the desk, her absence bringing a cold but very needed distance between us.

"Absolutely I would," she said, quoting *The Office* with far too much pleasure, "Anyway, now that we've established our reluctant working relationship, I need to ask for a favor. And you can't say no, or I swear I'll start crying, and we both know you'll hate that."

"What do you want?" I whined, picturing her demanding an entire overhaul of the food in my kitchen. My food preferences were very basic and very healthy, and Caroline's...well, I'd spied her putting peanut butter on a Pop-Tart the other day, so it was safe to say we ate very differently.

But instead of demanding an update to our pantry, Caroline's face turned desperate and pleading. "Can I *please* go home and grab some personal things? I've been brushing my teeth with my finger, my hair is in serious need of some conditioner, and although my clothes are clean, I'm tired of having to go without underwear while my only pair is being washed."

I opened my mouth. Then promptly closed it, realizing that all I was going to say was 'why'. Heat crawled up my neck and latched itself onto my cheeks, every inch of me extraordinarily uncomfortable discussing Caroline *not* wearing underwear. *Oh gosh, I hope she's wearing some now!* Wait no! *Abort! Stop thinking about the underwear!*

"Was that last detail absolutely necessary to share?" I managed to ask, my voice a little tight.

Caroline—you guessed it—smirked. Like the freaking devil. "No," she shrugged, "But it was fun."

FIFTEEN

Caroline

"WAIT, *THIS* IS WHERE YOU LIVE?" MORGAN blurted as we drove down my quaint neighborhood street.

"What, did you think I'd live in some abandoned warehouse like a vigilante?"

Morgan shrugged from the driver's seat of his SUV—this time I sat up front like a grown up instead of in the trunk like a sack of groceries. "Kinda. I just never pegged you for conventional."

I didn't argue with him because he wasn't wrong—I *didn't* seem like a conventional person. I didn't seem like the kind of person to choose a neighborhood that was sweet and traditional. Where the houses were from the thirties and most of my neighbors were older. Where every home had flowers in the front yard and personalized mailboxes.

"I guess it makes me feel normal even though I'm not," I admitted, not quite sure why I said it out loud.

Though that wasn't necessarily true. Because I did know why I seemed to have a word vomiting problem in Mor's presence. *I trust him.* Sure, he'd done shady things—kidnapping me hadn't been a fun experience—but he'd also gone out of his way to keep me safe.

Then he killed my attacker and brought me tea. Now, that may not have been a lot to go on as far as handing someone my trust, but it's like those statistics they do. People who hurt animals are ten times more likely than the average person to harm or even kill a human. Or how most serial killers start out by maiming and killing pets and then graduate to people.

Morgan gave me tea and liked my dog. That had to mean something. I mean yeah, he yelled a lot, but it was a frustrated kind of yelling rather than a 'I'm going to turn violent if you don't obey me' kind of yelling. He was a big guy, and with the faint scar on his face, he looked menacing, but so far, I found him to be mostly annoying rather than terrifying. For all the horrible stories I'd heard about him and his alleged murders, he didn't strike fear into my heart. Actually, in a very weird way, he made me feel safe.

"So, which one's yours?" he asked, thankfully interrupting my strange train of thought. I nodded to the third house on the left. "You have a pink front door?" He stared incredulously at my home as he stepped out of the car and onto my driveway.

"Are you really surprised?" I said dryly as I stepped up beside him and pointed to the bow that was now limp in my hair and the dress that hadn't been as comfortable to sleep in as pajamas would've been. The spare change of clothes Morgan had lent me—thank you Logan's mom for leaving some things behind when she had last visited—had been comfortable for the most part, but I wasn't about to be seen in public wearing striped sweatpants and a shirt that said 'spicy mama bear' on it.

"Come to think of it," he said, looking from the door to me, "No, I'm not."

I'd only taken one step toward the house when a friendly voice called out from across the street, and I grimaced.

"Shoot, it's Mr. Finch," I groaned, turning back to Morgan.

"Who?"

"My neighbor. We always talk when we see each other, and he and his wife like to check in and make sure I'm okay."

"Sweet of them," Morgan admitted—reluctantly—as he glanced over my shoulder.

"Got a visitor today, Caroline?" Mr. Finch called out.

I cringed and searched for a reason I could give my elderly neighbor that would explain Morgan's presence. It wasn't as if I'd brought many guys around before—or ever—so this was a very new occurrence for everyone. *Wait...*

I turned wide eyes up at Morgan, considering, and he glared at my scrutiny.

"What?" he demanded.

Oh yeah, this'll work. A slow smirk tugged at my lips, and I took a step closer to him, eyeing him like the arm candy he was about to become. That's when he seemed to catch on.

"Oh no," he said, shaking his head, "Don't you dare—"

"Yeah, this is my boyfriend," I shouted back to Mr. Finch. Then I turned, sliding my arm into Morgan's, and resting my head on his shoulder. "We just came by to grab some of my things since I've been staying with my sister while she recovers from her breakup." Mr. Finch didn't need to know that Ariel's 'breakup' was with her favorite author after said author killed off her favorite character. A breakup is a breakup. "Since he knew the bags would be heavy, my boyfriend kindly offered to help."

"Good man," Mr. Finch nodded as he ambled across the street.

Mr. Finch was spry for an old guy, but I didn't want him to overwork himself. So, I dragged Morgan with me down to the sidewalk, saving the old man the trip.

"Mr. Finch," he introduced himself, sticking his hand out to Morgan.

But Morgan just stood there. Silently. He didn't glare, but I could sense his irritation—hopefully he'd save it for me and not show it to Mr. Finch.

"Morgan," my fake boyfriend finally said, shaking Mr. Finch's hand, and I let out a breath of relief, "Nice to meet you."

"You too," Mr. Finch nodded, sizing Morgan up—which was a tad funny since Morgan was over six feet tall and Mr. Finch had shrunk to my size in his old age. "You treating our girl well?"

Morgan looked down at me, raising one eyebrow as if to say, 'this sweet old man thinks you're innocent enough to be 'their girl'?'. I just smiled harder. *Yes, Morgan, I am their girl. Because other than with you, I'm actually nice to most people.*

"I'm sure I could never truly be as good as she deserves," Morgan replied, his voice smooth and honest, though the look he gave me was full of mirth, "But I try my best to be what she needs."

Touché, Mr. Hohlt.

"I like that," Mr. Finch nodded, his winkled face stretching into a kind smile, "You're a good man, Morgan, and good for our girl Caroline. I can sense it."

Morgan didn't seem to like that part, immediately shifting into an expression of discomfort, a bit of embarrassment and defensiveness bubbling up in him.

"I'm not a Shifter, so I don't have any magic to help me know such things, but I do have experience," Mr. Finch insisted, pointing a finger at us, "And I know what I'm talking about! I know a good match when I feel it—just ask my wife!"

"I believe you," Morgan hurried to say, probably not interested in getting to know any more of my neighbors than he had to. "It's just nice to hear that someone sees the potential in us that I do."

Boy was he good at the fake boyfriend thing. One could almost believe he knew how to function in a romantic relationship. Almost.

"Aw honey, you always say the sweetest things," I teased, giving him a sugary smile.

When Morgan looked down at me, there was a promise of retribution in his eyes. "What can I say? You bring out the romantic in me."

Bull shirt. If I brought out anything in Morgan, it was a need for antacids and a vacation.

"And you bring out the affection in me," I crooned, squeezing his bicep. Okay, so maybe that part was more for me than for our charade.

"And the jealousy," Morgan taunted quietly.

"I wasn't jealous," I hissed, trying not to glare so Mr. Finch would have no reason not to believe our ruse.

"And yet you knew exactly what I was talking about." This time Mor had leaned so close that when he whispered, his breath brushed against my ear. The whole left side of my body went warm with awareness of his presence, and I felt his eyes boring into the side of my head, but I refused to look at him. Refused to let him know that he was affecting me. Mostly because I couldn't figure out *why* he was affecting me. Morgan's nearness shouldn't be a big deal.

Key word: shouldn't.

"Alright, I know when I've overstayed my welcome," Mr. Finch laughed, eyeing Morgan and I with an impish attitude. "You two behave yourselves. Caroline, tell your sister I hope she gets to feeling better." Mr. Finch smiled and patted my arm before turning a threatening look to Morgan. "And Morgan, you take care of our girl! She's one of the good ones and she deserves the best."

I expected Morgan to make a sarcastic comment about what I deserved, but instead, he shook Mr. Finch's hand again and said, "Yes, sir. She does."

For possibly the first time in my life, I was completely speechless. I nodded goodbye to Mr. Finch but was unable to form a single word as the old man toddled back to his house and Mor and I walked up to mine.

"So, you're friends with your elderly neighbors," Morgan mused as I unlocked the front door and led us inside, trying to get my brain back online so I could use words again.

"Mhm," I hummed, switching on the light, and heading down the hall toward my bedroom, my mind closer to speaking capabilities with every step away from his oddly kind comment.

"And you apparently have a sister," he continued, following me as I began to take clothes from my closet and dresser, piling them on the bed.

"Mhm."

"And you really like florals."

I glared at him from where he stood beside my bed, eyeing my floral bedspread and muted lavender wallpaper. So what if my bedroom was girly? *I'm a girl.*

"Did you think I'd be a tom boy?" I quipped, dragging two suitcases from underneath the bed, and slapping them on my bedspread beside my growing pile of clothes.

"No, I guess not." He trailed a finger along the vase of flowers on my nightstand. "It's just strange to see where you live, see how you interact with people that aren't me. People who don't aggravate you to the end of your sanity."

I sighed; hands stilled on the top of my favorite leather jacket as I tried to find the right words.

"You do aggravate me," I acquiesced, and Mor rolled his eyes, grabbing one of my sweaters from the bed and folding it meticulously before setting it in the suitcase, "And apparently you're extraordinarily organized—not that I'm shocked."

"I like control," he shrugged.

"Me too. Which is probably why we butt heads."

"That and the fact that I took you prisoner," he mumbled, and I caught the faintest bit of shame in his emotions.

It was so odd to see him feeling such a vulnerable emotion. Since I'd moved to Shifter Haven three years ago, I'd heard whispers of the Berserker Chief who had a temper that could scorch and self-control that basically didn't exist. Yet here was that same man, carefully folding my clothes in a bedroom decorated with florals. It just didn't add up.

"I'll make you a deal," I said, and his grey eyes flashed up to me.

"Why does it feel like it's a deal I won't want to make?"

"Because you don't trust me," I complained, setting the leather jacket on the bottom of one of the suitcases so it wouldn't get creased.

"Believe me, that's not my problem." The words were said so quietly that I almost didn't hear them.

"Sorry?"

Morgan quickly shook his head, avoiding my eyes again. "Nothing, what deal did you have in mind?"

I eyed him for a moment longer, considering my options and wondering whether or not I should chase down whatever it was that had him changing subjects. In the end, I decided against it. *Progress, Caroline. We're hoping for progress.*

"I'll answer two questions of yours, and you can answer two of mine." I smiled up at him, and this time I made it a genuine one.

He took a moment to study the expression, and I got the sense that he was trying to think of questions I might ask him that he wouldn't want to answer. Fair enough. The questions I had in mind weren't ones I anticipated him to answer happily.

"Deal," he said finally, folding a T shirt, "But we each get one pass."

"Deal."

"You first," he nodded, "Since you seem to have at least one question already picked out."

"Of course, I do," I shrugged, retreating to the bathroom. I grabbed my curling irons from the vanity and shoved my cosmetics into a large makeup bag along with a pouch full of ribbons. I may have been a hunted creature, but this prey didn't pack light. "My first question is why do you have blue rings around your irises when no one else does?"

When he didn't answer after a few beats of silence, I thought maybe he'd left. Leaning my head back into the bedroom, I found him still standing there, holding a pair of jeans in his hand like he'd forgotten they were there.

"Let me guess, pass?" I sighed, returning to the bathroom to grab my toiletries.

"It's because of my position." His words were obviously very carefully chosen, but I was honestly surprised he was answering at all—deal or no deal.

"Position?" I clarified, returning with an armload of products.

He raised his dark eyebrows at my haul, the scar beside his left eye stretching with the movement.

"Got enough toiletries, Care?" He joked, and I pressed my lips together to hold back a smile. Couldn't let him think I actually found him funny.

"No, this is me packing light," I sassed, dropping the whole load into a suitcase.

Morgan laughed and shook his head. It was a nice sound, if not a little rusty from only being used once a year or so.

"What? Does my extravagance bother you?" I teased, arranging the shampoo so it wouldn't pop open during transit.

"Honestly, your extravagance is probably the most endearing thing about you."

I froze, surprised to hear both me and endearing in the same sentence. Was he having an aneurysm?

"I'm confused, did you just compliment me or insult me?"

"I think it was both," he said, scrunching his nose in distaste, "But we'll call it an insult so we can maintain this antagonistic rapport we have going on."

I allowed myself a grin, even if the expression did feel strange directed at Morgan. "Alright, stop trying to distract me. What else were you going to say about your eyes?"

I noted the way Morgan sighed, his shoulders tightening up toward his ears and his hands moving slower as they folded and stacked clothes. He was being cautious, thoughtful.

"Nothing. The blue in them came with the position," he said simply, as though this was answer enough.

"So, they haven't always been that way?"

"No, definitely not."

"Why does becoming Chief change your eye color?" I asked, not convinced that he was giving me the whole truth. "Or was it becoming the Berserker rep for the Shifter Council that made the blue appear?" From what I understood, Morgan was only Chief for a year before the other Chiefs in the western region of the U.S. voted for him to be the rep on the Shifter Council. So which position offered him blue rings in his eyes?

"Um..." he froze, his panic funneling straight over to me, "It wasn't becoming the Berserker rep for the Council that did it, and the blue is a sign. It's magic's way of giving us a guide." These words, for some reason, felt more honest. Less frazzled. "As hot-blooded creatures, we animal shifters tend to overlook reason in favor of emotion. So magic likes to give lighthouses in a way. It shows us what path we should be on, so that we don't make the wrong choice in the heat of the moment."

I'd never heard of such a thing, but I also knew that each species of Shifter had their own secrets that stayed within the faction. Magic that protected you from yourself though? It sounded kind of sweet, which was a little at odds with the scary aesthetic that went along with a species that shifted into super-sized bears.

"So magic is looking out for your people, by giving you blue rings around your irises, so that your people can recognize you as the rightful leader?" I surmised.

"Yeah," he nodded, an amused smile pulling at his lips, "That's right."

"Hm."

"What, you don't buy it?" he said, back to his usual self as he stuffed the last of my tops into the suitcase, all traces of nerves completely gone.

"No, I buy it. I can tell by your emotions that you're not lying. It's just such a thoughtful kind of magic for a species that's so...chaotic."

"That's kind of the point. We can be aggressive and unpredictable when our emotions are high. Like little kids when they go bowling, we need magical bumpers to help us stay out of the gutter," he said, reaching over to my side of the bed and grabbing a stack of pajamas. "Now for my question."

I groaned, rolling my neck. This ought to be fun.

"Alright, hit me with it," I pouted, returning to my closet to pick out my top four favorite pairs of shoes. *Mm...make it five.* I grabbed an extra pair of boots.

Mor eyed the pile in my arms as I returned and generously began to remove them for me, setting them on my already massively stuffed suitcase. "You going to have enough room?"

"No," I said around a pair of workout shoes, "But that's why I also have a carry-on sized suitcase, two duffle bags and a backpack."

He huffed a laugh and shook his head, mumbling something about girls being a species all their own. He wasn't wrong.

He was quiet as we finished with the shoes, and I wondered if he was ever going to ask me his question. When he finally did, it wasn't what I was expecting. "Tell me about your family."

"Is that a question?" I asked, swallowing back my sudden discomfort.

"*Please*, tell me about your family?" He rephrased, staring intently at me.

As far as questions went, it wasn't a bad one. It wasn't crossing any lines and it wasn't inconsiderate, but it still felt too personal. A lot of who I was was wrapped up in my family, and explaining them would give Morgan more insight into me than I'd intended to offer.

Feeling a little uncomfortable with this new level of vulnerability I'd be giving him, I spun around and left the bedroom, heading for the kitchen and hoping a change of scenery would ease my nerves.

"I have a sister," I said as I started opening cupboards and removing all the snacks I thought I might want, hearing Morgan's quiet steps behind me. Speaking of my sister, I needed to call her later. I'd kept her in the loop on my situation at Morgan's via text message, but she was getting antsy without any real answers.

"So, you said." I watched out of the corner of my eye as he took a seat at the small dining table, watching me. "What's she like?"

"A pain," I smiled at him, he mirrored the expression. "She's a massive nerd. Loves superheroes, plays fantasy video games all the time and she likes to dress up for comic con, but she's always too nervous to actually go. She's brilliant too. Clever and witty."

"Family trait," Morgan commented, and I shot him a look.

"She's older than me by eight days, but you'd think she was younger since she's shorter than me."

"Eight days apart..." Morgan interrupted, and I paused, setting a package of Oreos on the counter, "So you're not—"

"Biologically related? No." I glanced at him over my shoulder. "I was adopted when I was a few days old. I was born in the same hospital as my sister, and when my birth parents met my adoptive ones by the nursery, they just decided they liked them...or something..."

I trailed off, returning to my search for snack food with vigor, taking out Wheat Thins, Doritos, Pop-Tarts, anything I thought might help me feel better.

"You know we have food back at my place." I jumped at the nearness of Morgan's voice, turning to find him standing right beside me. He was so close, closer than we'd ever willingly been to each other when we weren't actively fighting—not including our fake relationship ruse in my driveway earlier.

The strange thing was that I didn't feel the need to move away or tell him to back off. The warmth of him close by didn't anger me, and the gentle tone of his voice didn't push me into irritation. Instead, I felt comforted.

"You only have healthy stuff," I pouted quietly in response, risking a glance up at him. "I prefer my food sources to be chemically processed."

"Okay," he shrugged, opening the next cupboard, and taking out a package of strawberry wafers, "I'll just grab anything that I wouldn't eat."

"Perfect."

I gave him a weak smile, and even though he didn't touch me, not to squeeze my arm or my shoulder in that way that friends do to assure each other, Morgan nodded. And in that one gesture, I felt like I'd been added to his team. Antagonistic enemies or not, we weren't on opposite sides now, and that felt much better than I would ever admit out loud.

"Anyway," I continued, pulling a bag from under the sink and stacking my snacks inside, "My birth parents showed up—"

"You don't have to finish, Care," Mor interrupted, shooting me a patient look, something I'd never expected to see pointed in my direction. "I don't want you to feel uncomfortable."

"I'm not." And I wasn't. I wanted to tell him the whole thing. To explain not just where I came from, but why I was like this; so focused and alone.

"Okay." Morgan went back to packing food and I took a deep breath, preparing myself.

"My birth parents showed up at my adoptive parent's house a few days after they met in the hospital," I explained, continuing with the story—a story that I'd never said out loud before. "They explained that they were Elves—that *I* was an Elf. That I wasn't safe and that they thought my adoptive parents could provide a life for me that my birth ones couldn't. They'd watched my adoptive parents, checked in to their backgrounds to make sure they'd be good parents to me. Then they begged them to pretend that I was their child."

"How did your adoptive parents take that?" Morgan prompted, handing me some pretzels.

I held the bag for a moment and watched Mor go back to hunting down more snacks, thankful that he was listening intently enough to ask questions, while giving me space to feel all the things. He knew this was a hard story to tell and he was trying to be supportive. It made me like him more than I'd wanted to.

"They thought it was insane," I laughed quietly, setting the bag in with the rest of the snacks as I thought of my parent's reactions, "My mom was worried that people would know she hadn't given birth to twins, but my birth parents used their manipulation skills to have the hospital change the records. As far as the government knows, my mother bore twins, and I was one of them. After that, my mom cracked quickly," I said, smiling. She'd always had a bleeding heart. "She's such a softie. She couldn't handle the idea of me being in danger, so she convinced my dad to take me in."

"And your birth parents?"

"They never came back. Didn't leave any names or contact information. They were just gone...I'm sure they've passed away now. I don't have proof of it, but I feel it, you know? Deep in my gut." When Morgan nodded, I knew he understood that feeling. The moment when a part of you—a part that had been connected to someone else—just went dark. It was something I hoped neither of us experienced again for a very long time. "I know I'll never get to meet them, but they did give my parents a photo."

"Of them?" Morgan asked, dropping a box of Mac N Cheese into the full grocery bag before taking it from my hands.

I nodded, meeting his gaze.

"But they changed their faces. So, it's not really what they looked like, but it's them that are holding me in the picture." I smiled when I thought of the frame I had stuffed in the bottom of my nightstand, the one I'd spent so many nights staring at, and wondered if I should leave it here or take it with me to Morgan's house.

"That's the important part, right?" he said, and I followed him to the entryway where he set my bulging food bag down. "The fact that they held you. That you have evidence of it, even if it's not their faces in the picture."

I nodded, unable to respond with words just how much that picture had meant to me growing up. Especially knowing that it was all I'd ever have.

"Can I ask you something? It's not a part of the deal. You don't have to answer," he said as he turned toward me, crossing his arms, looking relaxed and patient.

"Sure, why not?"

But then he hesitated, seemingly unsure about this question now that he was going to ask it.

"Why do you have a vendetta against the Council? I mean, I know there are bad Council members, but what made you start your career as a modern-day Robin Hood?"

Ah. *This might take a minute.* Sighing, I leaned back against the front door and prepared myself, wondering if he would see the reason in my plans or not.

"There's two parts to that answer, really," I explained, not shying away from his gaze, the look in his eyes so intent. "For the first part, you have to understand what it was like growing up as a Nephilim. I was blessed in a lot of ways. I had parents who loved me and supported me. I was safe and valued and I had my sister."

"But?" Mor prompted, listening patiently.

I bit my lip. This was the part I didn't like telling. I didn't like to have people think that I was asking for pity. Because I didn't want pity. I just wanted Morgan to understand the headspace I was in, the background for *why* I felt the way I did.

"But it was also hard," I admitted, struggling to maintain eye contact when this level of honesty made me want to tuck tail and run. "I wasn't allowed to tell anyone what I was, which meant that relationships were hard. It's not exactly easy to be friends with someone when you have to hide so much of yourself. So, for most of my life, it was just me and Ariel, my sister. We didn't hang out with a lot of other kids because it got old always having to lie to them. What friends we did have were Ariel's because even though she was keeping my secret and that was hard, she didn't have to pretend to be something else the way I did."

"I always had to be so careful not to accidentally manipulate someone's emotions just in case they noticed," I went on, nervously picking at a seam on my dress. "Careful not to move faster than a human should be able to, and when I was really little, it was hard to keep myself from shifting my appearance on accident. Over time, it was easier to just be someone that people didn't give serious thought to. I'm a natural girly girl, so I wear ribbons and skirts because I like it, but I learned quickly that it made people underestimate me. No one ever suspected I was Nephilim, but I spent my whole life terrified that someday someone would."

When I paused, Morgan was still listening, silent and thoughtful. So far, I didn't detect anything other than empathy and a passive anger that I didn't think was directed at me, so I kept going, in too deep to stop now.

"Then when I was in high school, there was this news report about the Shifter Council. They suspected that the Kelpies were involved in a black market scheme to kidnap Shifters and sell their blood." Since Shifters had magical abilities, some of those abilities could also be used from Shifter blood for things like potions and charms. All of which were highly illegal.

"I remember that," Morgan said, leaning against the wall opposite me, "But the Kelpies were proven innocent."

"Not at first. For months, people thought the suspicions might be true, and how did they react? By completely exiling the Kelpies—who are the most empathetic Shifters in the world since they can feel when people are in danger and sense their fear! But did the public care? No. They harassed the Kelpies, spray painting their cars, throwing bricks in their windows. Kelpie children had to stay home from school because they were getting bullied, and Kelpies ended up having to pretend they were another species so they wouldn't be the victim of a hate crime! What's worse though is that Council members themselves encouraged the public to keep a distance from the Kelpies and be wary of them. A few Council members even got caught harassing Kelpies and they got away with it!"

Morgan's expression darkened and I felt his emotions go heavy, angry and pained.

"I remember," he said quietly, "I wasn't Chief yet, but I wanted to be so I could help."

"I'm sure you would have helped if you could." And I meant it. I knew Morgan well enough now to know that he would've helped the Kelpies if he'd been Chief. Which was exactly why I'd taken up my mantle of vengeance. "And that's why I do what I do. After I got my inheritance from my birth parents when I was eighteen, I spent the year planning for how I could clean out the Shifter Alliance. I didn't want anyone to go through what the Kelpies went through. I didn't want anyone to have to feel afraid or alone—"

"Like you did," he said, finishing the thought for me.

Suddenly I couldn't answer without crying, and I *refused* to cry in front of Morgan, so I just shrugged. I hated growing up as a dirty secret. My parents had done their best, told me I was special, let me use my powers as much as I wanted in the safety of our house...But a child shouldn't have to hide like I did, they shouldn't have to be afraid they'd be found out. Even as an adult now, I shouldn't have to feel that way...but I did.

As much as I hated acknowledging the loneliness that *still* plagued me, it had no such reservations, and it came for me anyway.

"Care," Mor whispered, and in only two strides he'd closed the distance between us, standing close enough for me to feel the heat of him, "I was wrong about you."

I slowly peered up into his handsome, scarred face and was taken aback by the sincerity I found there.

"I'm sorry, can you repeat that?" I replied, too shocked and emotional to make the words snarky.

He offered me a tiny smile.

"I was wrong when I said that your pain didn't matter, that it wasn't enough to qualify," he explained, his words weighted with genuine respect and empathy. "Your pain is valid, Care. So valid. You don't need me to tell you that, but I'm saying it anyway, because it's true. You've survived so much hurt and loneliness, and I can only imagine what that felt like to an adult, let alone to a child. Once you got your inheritance, you could have taken it and moved to an island, forgotten the rest of the world. But instead, you're here, fighting to make things better so that no one has to experience the things that you did—the things you're *still* experiencing. You're a much stronger, braver, and kinder person than I gave you credit for, and I'm so sorry for that. I respect you Care, so much, and I need you to know that."

I realized then that of everyone I'd ever known, Morgan was perhaps the first who could genuinely understand what I felt. He was 'The Chief', the man people whispered about and cowered when they saw him coming. Of everyone, he knew best what it meant to be alone.

I was alone because of fear for myself, and he was alone because of fear from others. *We're a sad, matching set.*

"Thank you," I finally managed to whisper, a little embarrassed by the emotion clogging my throat, "For all of that."

"I meant it," he insisted, reaching out to tug gently on the ribbon in my hair.

"I know."

"Okay, I just want to make sure you know I'm not being nice to you right now. I'm just being honest. That's all."

I smiled, pleased that he was trying to release my stress by lightening the mood.

"So, are we still enemies?" I asked, for once looking at him like an ally instead of an adversary.

He pursed his lips. "Hmm...what about antagonistic coworkers?"

"I like it. We still annoy each other—"

"But we get along well enough to work together."

I smiled. "Deal. Antagonistic coworkers it is."

Morgan's own smile was genuine and unburdened, both of us feeling lighter. Ironic after sharing such a heavy conversation.

I opened my mouth to tease him about getting work uniforms when Morgan's phone started ringing.

"Yeah?" Morgan answered, rolling his eyes at me as he mouthed 'Mike'. I chuckled and waited patiently—look at me, maturing already—for him to finish the conversation.

"Wait, what? That's not possible." His voice was low and commanding, his face turning serious and his emotions pinging with anger and panic. "You're *sure?*" He paused, listening to Mike on the other end. Now I wasn't waiting quite so patiently, wondering what the heck had Morgan so stressed. "Yeah, I'd have to agree...Okay...Thanks Mike."

"What is it?" I asked the second he ended the call.

He shoved his phone in his pocket with a heavy sigh and sent me a look that was full of worry.

"There's been another break-in for blackmail at the Alliance Building."

"*What*? How? That's not possible. I've been with you all day."

"It gets worse. Apparently, there was some Berserker DNA found at the scene."

Well, that's not good.

SIXTEEN

Caroline

"GERARD'S AFFAIR WAS BLASTED ON THE internet an hour ago," Grey said, sitting in one of the armchairs in Morgan's office, his phone in his lap and his eyes glued to the screen. "Apparently, the Hunter representative had a six-month long affair with a family friend four years ago. None of the Hunter factions have commented yet, but many suspect Gerard's wife was aware of the affair."

"That's disgusting," I scoffed, reaching down to scratch Daisy's head, "I would never involve someone's family like that. I may be a spy, but I'm not heartless—and I'm too good to leave DNA at the scene."

"I agree," Mor sighed, reclining in his desk chair, and staring up at the ceiling like a man defeated, "The MO is completely different. You have a pattern of stealing information and then planting it on the mayor's computer so he can do what he sees fit with it. This person just stole information and blasted it. Then they left not just a drop of blood or a single hair behind as DNA, but an entire ball of hair on the keyboard. Whoever it is that's copying you isn't even trying to make it look realistic."

"I'm sorry, did you just say that you agree with me?" I prodded.

Mike smirked as he watched me mess with his big brother, and when Clint leaned over and whispered something to him, I reached out for the pair's emotions. What I found was a boatload of mischief. *What are they up to?* I opened my mouth to ask, but Morgan leaned forward in his chair and interrupted me.

"Yes Caroline, I agree with you. You're a much kinder and more efficient spy than your copycat," he said, his words sounding surprisingly genuine.

I studied him for a moment, wondering if maybe he was having some kind of early midlife crisis. It was the only thing I could think of to explain why he was being randomly nice to me.

"Thank you?" I asked, not sure if I should expect an insult to follow his compliment.

Mike and Clint whispered some more, smiling, and I determined that at some point, I was going to find out whatever it was they were always plotting. Meanwhile, Logan struggled to keep his shoulders from shaking as he chuckled to himself.

"What's so funny?" Morgan snapped, not entertained by any of our reactions.

"Nothing," Logan mumbled, not cowed by Mor's glare, "I just love seeing you two reconciling."

His sincerity was cheapened, however, as he sank into another fit of chuckles. Rolling my eyes, I looked at Grey, hoping he of all people could provide some clarity, but he just raised a greying eyebrow at Mor like he knew a secret.

"Am I missing something?" I shouted, annoyed that I was somehow out of the loop on something that was clearly irritating Morgan. Which was ridiculous because irritating Morgan was my favorite pastime.

"We all are," Morgan said before anyone else managed to answer me, settling his big beefy forearms on the desk like he was ready to rain down judgement. My interest now piqued, I paused. Why hadn't I ever noticed a man's forearms before? Sure, shoulders and abs were lovely, but there was something so innately masculine about the veins in Morgan's forearms. The dark hair that sprinkled along his skin, the angles of his muscles compared to the slimness of my own arms.

I bet he could pick me up with one arm. Not because I was so tiny—I wasn't. I had hips just like Grandma Ethel's to prove it—but because Berserkers had super strength. Honestly, even if Morgan had been only human, I had a feeling that those arms could still lift me easily. *Maybe if I hide all the weights in his home gym, he'll have to start lifting me instead...* I could be interested in fitness if he was my trainer.

"Care?"

I snapped my eyes away from Morgan's arms—blasted things were nothing but trouble. He should really start wearing long sleeved shirts so they wouldn't distract me—and found Morgan watching me, a blush staining his cheeks.

Oh shoot. Did I say that out loud?

"I'll consider wearing long sleeves tomorrow," he rumbled, his voice all rough and low.

I pretended not to notice the way his tone made goosebumps breakout on my arms, focusing solely on my own death via the *major* embarrassment I was feeling. *Why am I allowed to talk?* What was God *thinking* when he gave me a voice? *I'm not adult enough to control my words!*

New plan, change the subject. "I'm sorry, I didn't hear what you said before—"

"About the shirt?" Mor asked, somehow managing to keep a straight face even though I could *feel* his amusement.

"Lord, no! Whatever you said before that."

"Get a little *distracted,* Care Bear?" Clint taunted, using the nickname they'd all begun to call me in the last few days. Annoyed and embarrassed, I grabbed a pencil from Morgan's desk and threw it at him. When Logan and Mike started laughing with him, I threw pencils at them too.

"Enough," Morgan called out, rubbing his forehead when I stuck my tongue out at the boys one last time, "I said that we should be paying attention to the fact that whoever is copying you is clearly doing it to frame the Berserkers. It was Berserker DNA they found in the office."

"So why haven't you been visited by an agent today?" Mike asked, crossing his ankle onto his knee. I didn't miss the way his eyes occasionally darted between Morgan and I, studying us. Those boys were up to something, I just hoped they weren't trying to read into my accidental comments about Morgan's forearms.

"Because Merida deleted the analysis from the lab at the Alliance Building, so they lost their evidence," Morgan explained.

There it was again. Jealousy and possessiveness burned bright in my chest, just like when I met the witch Morgan seemed to never stop talking about, and again when I'd asked him if they were dating. *What is that about?* Why was I so bothered by his interest in someone?

"Merida, huh?" I said casually, unable to stop myself—more proof that God shouldn't have given me a voice. A speaking Caroline was a dangerous thing. She was prone to breaking things, like any illusion that I was mature. "She sure does a lot for you."

This time, when Morgan met my gaze, he didn't bother trying to hide his entertainment. His lips pulled up a little at one side, barely perceptible, and I felt his emotions brighten with humor. There was something else in the middle of it though. A little bit of pleasure. Was he happy that I was jealous?

"Yeah, she does," Morgan replied suggestively, egging me on.

"Maybe she should spread the wealth around, do something for someone else for a change." I tried my best to sound uninvested, but it clearly wasn't convincing, because Morgan's smile expanded, and Logan, Clint and Mike all three began laughing. *Looks like Grey is the only one getting a Christmas gift from me next year.*

"Do you three wanna sport broken noses?" I snapped, spinning in my seat to singe all three of the idiot triplets with my eyes.

Mike, to his credit, did try to stop smiling and swallow his laughter. Clint just perked up at the threat.

"I don't know, would I look tougher if I had a broken nose?" he asked, turning to Mike, his nose up in the air for his brother's scrutiny.

Logan, of course, wasn't even a little remorseful, still shaking with laughter as I glared at him.

"Sorry, Caroline," he huffed between laughs, "It's just...I've never seen this before."

"Seen *what*?" I demanded.

Instead of replying, he just looked past me to Morgan. Confused and annoyed, I glared at my antagonistic coworker, who was still smirking at me like he'd won something.

"I'm not a particularly lazy person, Care," he said, and I could almost swear I saw the blue ring around his irises flash, "If I want something, I get off my butt and go after it. But Merida isn't here, is she?"

"So?" I crossed my arms, being purposefully obtuse. If he was going to be vague, so was I.

"So, if I wanted Merida, she'd either be here now, or I'd be out pursuing her instead of arguing with you."

There seemed to be a veiled message somewhere in that statement, but with the intensity of his stare, I was having a hard time focusing well enough to read between the lines. All I got from it was that he wasn't dating Merida and apparently had no interest in the prospect. Why did that make me so happy? And why was he smiling like he knew it?

I glared harder.

"Did I ask if you were dating the Witch?" I barked, embarrassed, and confused. "No. What you do with your time is your business, I just want to make sure we don't trust the wrong people. Because someone on the Shifter Council is trying to ruin you, and since we have no actual information about who it is, it might be wise to keep everyone on the suspect list."

Morgan nodded, but he wasn't convinced. *Yeah, well, neither am I.* I was honestly surprised my face hadn't gone all Wicked Witch of the West and turned green with jealousy.

"Wise point," Grey interjected, breaking the awkward silence brought on by my outburst.

I nodded to him, grateful that he was feeding into my false bravado even if everyone in the room knew it was all bluster.

"Yeah, fair point," Morgan agreed, his smirk finally disappearing, "We should be careful. I'm not worried about Merida in particular—because she's my *friend*," he added with a pointed look in my direction, "But I can't speak for all the Witches. We'll have to be careful with all the shifter species until we know what we're dealing with. We also need to start investigating Berserkers, because someone got that DNA onto the crime scene—whether it was destroyed or not—which could mean that someone broke into a Berserker's home to get it, or it could be that they snatched it off of someone's coat in town...but there's also a chance that it could be from a Berserker who's working with the culprit."

"But why would your own people work against you like that? You're their Chief." Sure, I'd heard the rumors of the Chief who killed in the shadows and never got caught, but I'd never heard of the Berserkers harboring hatred for their own leader. Morgan wasn't just Chief of his Sleuth, he was the Berserker representative for the entire western region of the U.S. It was a position that all the Chiefs in the area had to vote on, and Morgan had won that vote. *So clearly his people admire him...right?*

No one answered at first, and I couldn't blame them for being hesitant. I'd asked a question that was guaranteed to have an uncomfortable answer. But I couldn't help it. The longer I knew Morgan, the more I struggled to reconcile the image others had of him with the man I actually knew.

"Sometimes people are elected because people love them," Logan said, his tone a little too eerie for my liking, "And sometimes they're elected because people are afraid."

The silence that followed was achingly loud. Part of me regretted having asked the question as everyone suddenly became interested in looking everywhere *but* at me, but the other part of me wasn't sorry. Because ignoring the public's opinion of Morgan hadn't done him any favors so far.

Morgan, unlike the rest of the group, didn't have a sudden fascination with his hands the way the rest of the men in the room did. Instead, he stared straight at me, and I couldn't tell if he was angry with me for bringing the topic up, or only wishing that I'd asked him in private. His expression was inscrutable, his emotions too jumbled to tell.

"Okay," I nodded, willing to table the topic for the moment until I could ask him more in private, "We'll deal with that later. For now, what do we do about the frame job?"

Morgan's shoulders immediately drooped in relief, and he quickly jumped into leadership mode. "Mike, see what you can find online? Clint, and Logan—"

"We'll ask around about the break-ins," Logan nodded, already pulling out his phone.

"And I'll look through our records for potential suspects," Grey added, scribbling something on his clipboard.

"Thank you," Mor sighed, "And I'll go check the gossip line tomorrow."

"Can I come?" Everyone's eyes turned to me, surprised by my question.

"You want to help?" Morgan clarified.

"Common goal, remember? The faster we solve this issue, the faster I don't have to be under house arrest anymore."

Morgan flinched a little at my words, but looked down so quickly that I wondered if I'd seen it wrong.

"Sure, you can help," he stuttered, "Gotta get you back to your vengeance."

I nodded, but the action felt disconnected. Morgan wanted me gone; I wanted me gone.

So why did he seem so off?

SEVENTEEN

Morgan

THE NEXT MORNING, I STAYED IN MY ROOM longer than I normally would have, contemplating my own stupidity. *I might be here a while.* After all, not only had I shown too much emotion in my office last night, but I'd shown it in front of *everyone*. A fact that Logan, Mike and Clint were never going to let me live down.

Caroline may have been blessedly oblivious to some of it, but that would only last for so long. If my unwanted attachment to her continued to grow, she'd eventually feel it through the mate bond. I could suppress my feelings a little bit, but not forever. *But they're not 'feelings'. They're just...thoughts.* Yeah, that was it. I wasn't forming a romantic attachment to my mate; I just had some passing thoughts. Like a blip on the radar.

So then why did her announcement upset me so much?

When she'd mentioned the idea of going back to her life, I felt like I'd been elbowed in the gut. Sure, we'd had the conversation about getting her out of my hair and back to her revenge...but something had shifted when we went to her house to get her things. At least, it had for me.

When I first brought Caroline here, I wanted her gone as soon as possible. The quicker we could be separated, the less chance the mate bond would have to grow. Plus, she annoyed the crap out of me.

Now though...I found that I didn't quite like the notion of her leaving. I also didn't necessarily always like the notion of her company. She frustrated me, pushed my buttons, broke my boundaries and made me more irritable than I'd ever been before. Even still, the thought of her leaving just didn't feel right.

And I didn't want to find out the reason why.

Needing to be free of my whirling thoughts and hoping Logan and my brothers were both gone for the day, I tiptoed out into the hall. I loved my family, but I knew that after last night, there would be no end to their teasing for the way I talked to Caroline. To them, my match of wit with her—where we pushed each other inch by inch, dancing on a cliffs edge to see who fell off first—was just a form of flirtation. Their ribbing was the last thing I wanted to hear right now.

Thankfully, I didn't come upon any of them as I made my way down the hall, slowing when I came to Caroline's open door.

The object of all my frustration was sitting on the ground in front of the floor length mirror that stood in the corner of the room by the bathroom. She had an array of girly products around her. Ribbons, curling irons, makeup. I understood the purpose and process of none of it. Lip gloss was for making kisses sticky, and mascara made girls look like racoons when they cried—which they did *not* like. That was the extent of my knowledge on the subject.

Daisy lay curled up beside her on the carpet, fast asleep as Caroline tied a ribbon in her hair, this one black. She wore pants today, a pair of white jeans with a floral top and a muted pink denim jacket. I wasn't surprised by her outfit choice—we'd already established that Care was girly—but it was different to see her in pants instead of the dress I'd originally kidnapped her in and the ill-fitting set of loungewear we loaned her.

She looked good. Too good. I wasn't particularly talented at picking out the differences between a woman with and without makeup on, but I did know what heavy makeup looked like, and Caroline's wasn't that. She was all dark eyelashes, and pink cheeks with her hair softly curled.

I shook my head, awed by the stark contrast between my first mate and my second. Caroline and Genevieve couldn't have been more different. Where Gen had been laid back and simple, Care was always going and complicated. Genevieve might have packed one small suitcase for a trip, and Caroline had brought two, plus three other bags. And yet both women had shared a mate bond with me. How could I be the common factor between two such different people? Better yet, how could I be *attracted* to two such different people?

Yes, I said 'attraction'. Because you can be attracted to someone and remain otherwise completely unaffected by them. *Not sure that's what's happening, but...*

"I'm curious," I said, announcing my presence as I leaned against the doorjamb, trying to derail my current train of thought, "Why don't you ever change your face? You have the magic to look however you want, right? Why not change it so it's easier to sneak into places?"

She didn't respond at first, carefully tying her bow, half her hair pulled back into a ponytail. I'd noted it when we met, but it bared repeating that she was the most beautiful woman I'd ever seen. Her and Gen. But while Gen had always had a more serious look to her, all dark hair and dark eyes, Caroline was all swoops and angles, brightness and freckles.

"I do use my magic to sneak in," she said, her green eyes finding me in the mirror, "But just on my hair. I could become anyone I wanted to with the help of my magic—even you—but I don't have to. Altering my hair to a new color or style is enough because people don't take me seriously enough to look that hard." She played it off like it wasn't a personal offense, just a fact. But I knew better—I *sensed* it via our bond. "If I was just a pretty girl, they might suspect me as a threat walking into the building, but a girl who wears bows and florals, who likes pink and smiles like she's selling girls scout cookies? They always assume I'm too simple to do anything devious. Innocence is always mistaken for stupidity, and beauty seems to cancel out smarts."

"And that bothers you," I surmised, studying the way her features shifted with her emotions. She hid them well, but the mate bond didn't do dishonesty and she couldn't hide her feelings from me completely. Even if she didn't realize it.

"Of course, it does," she scoffed, standing from the floor. She walked toward me, stopping a few feet away—a distance my body seemed to instinctively want to cross no matter how many times I told myself I didn't want her. "Doesn't it bother you that people look at you and assume you're dangerous? That they hear these horrific rumors of the Berserker Chief who can't control his own people? The Chief who goes around murdering those who work for the gambling dens because he can't manage to bring them down legally? I didn't even know your first name before I came here, because they only call you Mr. Hohlt, or The Chief. They're too scared to even say your name, Morgan. Doesn't that bother you?"

My nostrils flared with my anger, and despite my desire to appear unaffected, I felt my face go hot.

"Why should it? Maybe they're right. Maybe I do kill those gambling den members. Maybe I am a terrible Chief. Maybe I am a monster."

I was bluffing. I hadn't killed a gambling den member since...I shook my head. *Nope, not thinking about it.* But I didn't like this line of conversation now that it'd shifted toward me, and I didn't feel like being honest.

Caroline wasn't put off though, shaking her head and coming closer still. If I reached out just a little, I'd be touching her. But somehow, I felt like if I reached for her, I'd be tainting her right along with me.

"You're not a monster." It wasn't a question. She pinned me with that fiery gaze, daring me to argue with her. "And you and I both know it. I may have believed the rumors before, but after knowing you just a short while," she paused, shaking her head, "I know the truth. You may have the looks of someone who can be beastly, but you're far from a beast, Morgan."

"But you called me a beast, you also called me a monster. And you weren't wrong," I argued, remembering the words because of how much they'd hurt. It hadn't been the first time someone had labeled me that way, but to realize that my *mate* believed it...there was no worse feeling.

Caroline pulled her bottom lip through her teeth and studied my shirt with great concentration. In any other moment, I might've been flooded with attraction at the behavior. I might have even been tempted to imagine myself kissing that lip, but when she looked up at me again, determination in her expression, I only felt raw and insecure.

"I'm going to say this once, so you'd better engrain it into your memory, because it's never happening again," she threatened, completely serious, "But I was...wrong. Gosh I hate saying that word." I smiled as she crinkled her nose in distaste. "You were a little bit of a jerk at first—I mean, you kidnapped me so that doesn't exactly earn you points—but I was also a brat who was putting your people in danger so...I can't say I completely blame you."

I felt a small smirk tugging at my lips and noted it, smiling. But then her expression turned sad.

"I've heard all the rumors about you, Morgan. I was fully aware of your reputation the moment we met, and yet there hasn't been a single moment—not when you kidnapped me or when you yelled or even when you locked me in this room—that I was ever afraid of you. You're not a monster, Morgan. I've never really believed that."

I didn't want to open up or show her something deeper, but she was being vulnerable and something about a vulnerable Caroline pulled out the honesty in me. I blamed the bond.

"It does bother me," I admitted with a whisper, "The way they see me. It's always bothered me."

She was quiet, and I found myself unable to hold her gaze, instead, pointing my attention to Daisy, who was still snoring on the floor.

"Use it," Care said softly, and when she set her hand on my arm, I had no choice but to look at her, "When they look at you with condemnation, use it as motivation to shock them. When people look at me like there's nothing but static in my brain, I use that judgement to fuel me, to find a way to shock them with the truth. That I'm brilliant and remarkably clever."

I smiled at her false arrogance, and she returned the expression.

"When they look at you like you might rip them apart at the slightest provocation, use it to motivate you. Then, when the moment presents itself, shock them with the truth."

"The truth?"

She dropped her hand and took a step back, and suddenly I realized how close we'd been standing. Yet I wasn't bothered by the proximity, instead I was bothered by the gap. Why did it feel so cold?

"That you're not a beast," she said simply.

Her words brought me back to reality, and away from daydream land where I was dangerously close to imagining myself reaching out to touch her. Pulling her into my arms. Testing out the smoothness of her hair. *Wait, what? No.*

"You think I should play off of their assumption that I'm a terrifying monster," I said, struggling to get my brain back on topic, "And then when I've got their attention, just shock them by..."

"Being you." She shrugged. "Be your grouchy and yet generally kind self. Trust me, their surprise will be deliciously satisfying. Plus, it'll hopefully help them realize how stupidly wrong they've been."

It was an interesting approach, and not remarkably far off from what I'd been doing. Except that when people judged me, I got irritated and defensive, arguing—often loudly. What Caroline was talking about was a little different. She wanted me to do the opposite of what those people expected. Prove them wrong. The image of Francine the Minotaur or Drew the Firebird open mouthed and shocked made me curious about just how much fun I could have with this.

"I'll give it a try," I nodded.

"Good," she said, "You should, because I'm right."

I laughed and she grinned, our rapport of antagonistic coworkers returning itself back to normal. *Thank God.*

"You enjoy saying that way too much." I shook my head, awkwardly shoving my hands in my pockets, all my movements stilted because as a thirty-two-year-old widower, my skillset with women was rustier than the boat Logan once bought. To clarify just how bad the boat was—and how pathetic I was by comparison—he took it out on the lake without checking it out thoroughly first, and within fifteen minutes the thing started taking on water. Turned out that a hole had rusted in the bottom. It sank. Just like I was bound to do if I kept spending time with Caroline.

"Not possible," she winked.

Crap, I don't know what to do when a woman winks. Which didn't matter, because Caroline wasn't a woman. Well, obviously she was, but—*Not the point! Change the subject!*

"Anyway, I actually came in here because I need to go make a visit to someone who keeps track of all the Berserker gossip." *Wow, Morgan, great segway. Real smooth.* I cringed. "I'm hoping he might have some information about the frame job at the Alliance building. Since you said last night that you wanted to come check the gossip line, I thought you might want to come."

Her lips spread into a wide, mischievous smile. *Oh no. What have I gotten myself into?*

"Absolutely I do," she said.

"Really? You're referencing *The Office*?" I asked as she patted her leg to wake Daisy, who stretched more like a cat than a dog before coming over to join us.

"What, you're not a fan?"

"I never got past the first episode, but I know the references."

Care froze, staring up at me with complete devastation on her face. It was like I'd admitted to beating puppies in my free time. Which, to clarify, I would *never ever* do. Then Caroline smiled deviously, and I wished I'd lied.

"Oh, we're definitely going to fix that."

"Do I get a say in this?" I asked as we stepped into the hall and she shut the door behind us.

"Of course not."

I shook my head. Why wasn't I surprised?

EIGHTEEN

Morgan

"Why can't we come?"

I rolled my eyes and tried to swallow the urge to shove Clint back until he fell on his backside. He may have been in his bear form, but as Chief I was still stronger than him. He'd go down easy.

The boys—Clint, Mike, Logan and Grey—were enjoying the March sunshine in the backyard, which unfortunately meant that it was impossible for Caroline and I to sneak past them on our way to interview my friend. The backyard was huge—bigger than we really needed considering that Berserkers didn't really ever hang out in crowds big enough to fill the space. It was just grass and shrubs, none of us being much into flowers and no one wanting to have a gardener underfoot just for some color in the yard. Unfortunately, the lack of foliage also meant a lack of an escape route.

"Because Morgan's finally being nice to me and I don't want any of you to spook him out of it," Care whispered loudly.

I glared at her, but she just winked.

Clint, in his bear form, nudged her side, grumbling and she leaned into him, rubbing the top of his rust colored head. Out of nowhere, a flash of jealousy erupted in my chest, and I struggled to tamp it down before Caroline could notice.

When she cocked her head at me curiously, I turned to Logan.

"Any luck with your contacts so far?" It was a brutally obvious subject change, but thankfully my best friend saw my distress and went with it.

"The gossip mill is running like clockwork," Logan shrugged, a glass of iced tea in his hand as he bumped hard into Clint, sending him conveniently a step away from Caroline.

"Hey!" Clint growled, sitting back on his big haunches so he could lift a front paw to rub at his side.

"Did I hit you? Sorry," Logan smirked, "Anyway, as I was saying, there are people occasionally talking smack about you, but it's nothing more than the usual comments." Thankfully, he didn't specify what those comments were. I knew them well enough to never need an explanation, and I definitely didn't want Caroline to realize just how frequently I was faced with people's poor opinion of me. It'd probably result in her giving me another pep talk. "So far, I can't find any leads on any Berserkers who've said anything about wanting to have you removed as Chief. Everyone's too scared to make that kind of move. Sorry, but it's true."

"Don't apologize," I shook my head, "It's not like we didn't expect this. What about you, Mike? Anything?"

Mike stretched his neck where he sat cross legged on the grass, his laptop balanced between his thighs. It was always a little funny to see my middle brother—the biggest of all of us with his broad shoulders and meaty arms and legs—cradling a computer. Next to his large frame, the tech looked like he'd stolen it from a child.

"There's not a lot new in the chat threads," he said, shoving his shaggy, wavy brown hair from his face, "A few comments here and there about the accusations that the Berserkers are involved in the break ins."

"And?" I asked. Mike was the most considerate of us all, and he had a tendency to protect other's feelings. Primarily mine. While I appreciated the sentiment, right now I needed to be prepared, not coddled.

"And some people think we deserve it," he sighed, his blue eyes flashing with annoyance that he had to repeat the comments out loud and thus destroy my 'fragile confidence'. "That *you* deserve it. A few threads online talk about the gambling dens, and how you of all people should have taken care of it...Then some more empathetic people chimed in and said you did the best you could. Altogether, there's nothing particularly threatening or mean enough to make me believe they're behind the frame job."

I nodded. I'd anticipated that it was unlikely the Berserkers would be behind the frame job at the Alliance Building. For one thing, the Sleuth—and all other Sleuths in the state—were afraid of me, so they'd have to be pretty bold to make a move like a frame job. And even if there were a few brave souls, ruining the name of Berserkers wouldn't help our people. It might get rid of me, but in the end, we'd be distrusted even more than we already were.

"What about you?" I barked, turning my attention to Clint. I probably shouldn't have been so abrupt, but I really wanted to finish this topic as quickly as possible.

My baby brother, who'd been licking his paw, flicked his big brown eyes up at me.

"Well," he said in that sing song way he used when he was trying to lighten the mood, "I just got back, and—"

"*Please* tell me you didn't go into town as a bear!"

"Easy, big bro. Don't yell."

"I wasn't—"

"You were," Clint, Logan, Mike *and* Grey all said in unison.

I ground my teeth but said nothing.

"As I was saying," Clint smirked, his lips pulling up to reveal his pointed teeth, "I just got back from meeting with a few people—as a human, so don't get your panties in a wad—and while most of it was completely unhelpful, Sarah did say that she heard there was an open hire for a break-in going around somewhere."

"Where?"

"She didn't know. She heard it through the rumor mill, so it's not corroborated, but it's possible that it was a hired job, which means—"

"That whoever hired it out is too careful to get their own hands dirty," I nodded, "It's unlikely Berserkers are involved at all, but it's highly likely that whoever's doing this has enough of a reputation to need to hire someone else to take care of it, and the means to be able to."

It was essentially what I'd expected, but it really only left me with questions. Why did someone—who had influence and money—frame me? Usually, people who did things like that were from the underbelly of society, like the gambling dens. Then there was the more complicated question. Why did someone attack Caroline at my house? Better yet, how did they know she was even here?

There were one too many strings tethered to this mess, and they weren't tying up. *There's got to be answers somewhere in all of it.*

Caroline was unusually quiet as the boys finished up their reports. I watched her skeptically while Grey announced that he hadn't come up with any new information in his searches through our past complaints from Berserkers. The whole time Care's eyes were on Grey, but her emotions were distracted...compassionate.

I wasn't sure what that meant for me.

Finally, I thanked the team for their research and turned to head through the yard. Daisy, who'd been sunbathing peacefully, leapt up to follow us as Caroline and I entered the forest that surrounded the Berserker house.

We walked in silence through the trees, the sun peeking through the leaves overhead and dappling across us in shades of gold. Birds sang and a breeze rustled the branches above us. It was a peaceful kind of quiet.

"Is that what people really think? That you deserve to be framed because you haven't been able to take down the gambling dens?" Caroline asked quietly.

Or so it *was* peaceful.

"We already went over this," I said, not really interested in being vulnerable again just yet. Wasn't once a day enough?

"Yeah." When she didn't immediately expand, I glanced over at her. She had her lips pursed, her eyes on the ground as she followed my lead through the trees. "But I guess I didn't realize how *frequent* the judgements are."

I shrugged, trying to convey calmness through my emotions. "It's not my favorite part of life, but whatever."

"Whatever?" She parroted, staring up at me, shifting quickly from empathetic to annoyed.

"Yeah," I repeated, "Whatever."

Caroline scoffed and crossed her arms.

Moments went by, but we walked in silence. Daisy sniffed a tree, peed on a patch of grass. Still, Care said nothing. And a silent Caroline—though peaceful as it may look—did not seem like a good thing.

I was starting to feel ominous, my gut clenching at her continued silence and the disapproval swirling inside of her. She was upset, but she was holding it back. Stewing. *That can't be good.*

"Okay, out with it, please," I begged, pulling us both to a stop with a hand on her arm, our destination now only a few yards away. Though she was probably too distracted by her frustration to notice it.

"Out with what?" she goaded me, looking innocent.

"Care, please just tell me why you're upset. I'm not good at reading between the lines."

She seemed to think it over for a moment, glaring at me.

"Fine," she huffed, arms still crossed and her expression haughty, "I just don't get you, Morgan. You say that you don't want to be seen as a beast. That you don't like how people view you."

"I don't," I agreed.

"And I know you well enough now to know that you didn't kill any of those gambling den members they've shown on the news." It wasn't a question. She wasn't asking for confirmation; she believed my innocence without me fighting to prove it.

"I didn't," I confirmed anyway, for some reason needing her to know she was right about me, "I've only ever killed in self-defense."

She nodded, eyeing me carefully.

"So then why do you act like this?" She waved a hand in my general vicinity. "You grumble and growl and yell and you act completely closed off and cold to everyone. You even do it to your own brothers when you're in leadership mode! It'd be fine if you were actually that kind of person, but you're not! You keep presenting this cold, apathetic exterior and then expect other people to see what you're not showing."

"Which is?"

"That you like my annoying, aggressive, kiss-obsessed dog," she smirked. "That you protected me when I was attacked, even though I was the bane of your existence."

"Still are," I grumbled.

She shook her head but smiled ruefully at me. "That you let me bring an obscene amount of luggage to your house even though I know you wanted to say no. That you protect your brothers, and you spend an inordinate amount of time trying to find ways to better serve your people."

I squirmed under her assessment but didn't rebuke her. "You got all that after just two weeks, huh?"

"I got all that and more, Bear Man," she snarked, lightly punching me in the arm, "But what I don't get is why you hide all of that. These people on the internet are making assumptions and that's on them. But you're not correcting them or showing them anything different. I'm just saying that showing a little softness would go a long way."

Sighing, I began walking again, needing less attention on myself for a moment. The trees began to part ahead of us to reveal a clearing where a cabin stood alone amongst the forest. It was small and a little dilapidated, with a wraparound porch and a garden off to the side. A dirt road led off in the other direction, and an old blue car was parked near the bottom of the porch steps.

"I'm not going to admit that you're right," I said, but Caroline bumped my arm, grinning up at me.

"You don't have to," she said. "I can feel it."

I cringed at the reminder that the mate bond went both ways. She could feel my emotions just as starkly as I could feel hers. Right now, that wasn't much of an issue because she assumed that her knowledge of my feeling was thanks to her own magical abilities, but once things shifted... *Wait, 'once things shift'? Why am I thinking of a romantic connection as an inevitable thing?* Just because we were bonded didn't mean we had to fall in love. *But you're already opening up to her. Worried for her safety. Showing her your inner cinnamon roll.*

I growled. *Shut up.*

I was doing none of those things, and my subconscious trying to push me toward it was just my natural instincts pushing me not to be alone. *But I don't have to give in.*

"Fine, then I don't have to say it out loud," I winked.

I didn't give her time to respond, plowing forward into the clearing.

"So, you brought me to a cabin in the woods?" she said dryly as Daisy Mae wandered off a little ways to sniff the new area. "If you wanted to kill me, Mor, there are much easier ways to do it."

"Oh, I know. I've considered many of them," I retorted, leading the way forward.

"How many exactly?"

"Poison, overdose, smothering," I ticked off the options. "But then I realized that I didn't have to go through with any of them, because you're already doing them to yourself."

"Explain." Her eyebrows crinkled as we stepped up onto the porch.

"You poison yourself regularly with the food dye and inhumane chemicals found in your snack foods," I said, holding up one finger, "You're about one Oreo away from overdosing on processed sugar." I held up another finger. "And you sleep with your face down so aggressively on your pillow that I'm not sure how you get any airflow."

Her pink lips pulled up into a smile, and her eyes lit with humor, the blue rings around her green irises tempting me with their promises.

"So then do you keep me stocked with dangerous food because you're hoping I'll die from either poison or from too much consumption of sugar?"

"No, nothing that devious," I shrugged, knocking on the front door of the cabin. "I just like you happy."

Her mouth dropped open, green eyes a little wide. But before she could ask me to expand, the door swung open.

A large bear with honey brown fur that was dappled with grey stood in the doorway, and I could feel the pleasure rolling off of him even without the benefit of powers like Caroline's.

"What are you doing?" I rolled my eyes.

"Oh, don't give me that overconcerned attitude," the old bear growled harmlessly. "I may be old, but I'm not reaching for depends just yet. If you keep acting like I need assistance, I'm going to have no choice but to take you to task. I'll fight you here on this porch and shame you in front of your lady. I mean it, Morgan!"

I was sure he did. And that was the problem.

Caroline began snickering beside me as Mr. Wallace—AKA the big old bear—threatened me, and his eyes shifted to study her. Mr. Wallace wasn't as old as he pretended to be—really, he was only seventy-two. He just liked to act like he was ninety. He'd once been six-foot-four in human form, though now he was closer to six-foot, his frame thin and lean. But his eyes were always filled with mischief.

My father had never been much of a parent to my brothers and I, but Mr. Wallace had gladly filled that gap for us. And when my brothers and I had no one, he took us in. Raised us as his own. He was pretty good at it, except for the cantankerous bits.

"And who is this lovely young lady?" he said, quickly shifting back to human form. Probably so he could more easily whisper embarrassing factoids about me. "And what kind of idiot is she to be hanging around with you?"

Caroline watched with obvious fascination as Mr. Wallace's body morphed from bear to man. The transition was quick and painless, but you could see the bones shrinking, the fur dissipating, and the facial features morphing back into human. Within the span of ten seconds, Mr. Wallace was no longer a bear.

"Technically, I'm the kind who's here against her will," Care teased, shooting me a smirk as she shook Mr. Wallace's hand.

"Against her—Morgan Gareth Hohlt, have you been kidnapping young ladies?" he demanded, looking over at me.

"It's a long story that's best told inside—maybe over a cup of tea." I gave Care a warning look, but it was useless. She wasn't even a little bit contrite.

Wallace motioned for us to follow him inside, and Caroline clapped to get Daisy's attention.

"It's actually not that long of a story," she said, Daisy traipsing into the cabin behind her. "You see, I've had a vendetta against the Shifter Council for years. I mine secrets about people who work at the Alliance building—by breaking into the building. Then I anonymously give those secrets to the mayor so he can have cause to dismiss those people from their positions. But the council started to blame my heists on the Berserkers. Morgan here thought that instead of having a conversation with me about how my revenge was getting him in trouble, he would just kidnap me and put me under house arrest with an illegal binding spell done by his lady witch friend."

I sighed at her jealous mention of Merida, and tried *hard* to hide the pleasure it gave me. The last thing I needed was for Care to realize that I liked it when she got jealous. *Come to think of it, I shouldn't even be thinking about it.*

"But now there's a copycat pretending to be me," she went on, paying me and my emotions no heed, "And planting evidence that makes the Berserkers look guilty. So, Morgan and I have decided to stop hating each other and become antagonistic coworkers so we can catch whoever's behind it all. There," she nodded, looking up at me with a contrived look of innocence, "Did I miss anything?"

"Nope." I gave her a tight-lipped smile laced with sarcasm. "I think you covered it."

Meanwhile, Mr. Wallace stared at us both with his mouth open like a flytrap, completely speechless for the moment.

"Well then," he finally said, closing his mouth, "I think I'd better get started on the tea."

Before he could go far though, Daisy Mae trotted past Caroline to inspect the old man. I watched, curious to see how Care's small but aggressive dog would take to Mr. Wallace. Granted, she liked me, but that was mostly because she sensed the mate bond, and she liked the guys at the house because they fed her table scraps. I wasn't sure how she'd take to a cranky old man.

"Who's this little princess?" Wallace said as he set three cups on the small round dining table that lay on the right side of the room.

The cabin was just as small on the inside as it looked on the outside. The living, dining and kitchen area all shared one space, with the fireplace, couch and chairs on the left, the dining table on the right, and the kitchen at the back. To the right were three doors, one of which I knew led to a bathroom, the other to Mr. Wallace's bedroom, and the third to a spare room that Mike, Clint and I had shared for eight years.

It was just as cramped as it sounded. But I also had a lot of good memories both in that room building forts and in this house being raised by Mr. Wallace.

"Her name is Daisy Mae," Caroline said as she took a step forward, watching Wallace's approach toward Daisy with caution, "But she's not necessarily the friendliest..."

"Nonsense," Wallace chided.

Bending over, he reached out and roughly patted Daisy on the head as though she were some retired Golden Retriever with a pleasant disposition rather than a rabid attack dog who pretended to be sweet—much like Caroline.

Daisy seemed unsure of his affection, curling away from his hand, but he wasn't deterred. He scratched her ears and crooned to her like she was his grandchild.

"That's a sweet girl," he said, and Daisy slowly stepped forward to sniff his legs and hands. "You're such a pretty little lady, aren't you? Just the most beautiful girl in the world—yes you are!"

I tried to smother my chuckle with my hand, but when I caught Caroline snickering too, we both ended up cackling at the new besties.

Daisy Mae and Mr. Wallace didn't care though. They bonded quickly, largely due to the fact that on his trips to the kitchen, Wallace would take a cracker from a package on the counter and offer it to the dog, who was apparently now endeared to him for life.

"Well, now that we're all comfortable, let's get to know each other," he said as he sat at the kitchen table across from Care and I, his eyes filled with mischievous plans.

"I already know you," I pointed out.

"Yes, but Caroline doesn't," he argued, adding more sugar to his tea. "Nor does she probably know the things about you that I do."

"Lord no," I exclaimed, nearly choking on the tea that I was still swallowing, "And we're going to keep it that way."

"And why should we when she's not just any girl, but—"

"A coworker," I interrupted, glaring at Wallace with wide eyes.

Curse the man for knowing me so well! It was no surprise that he'd only needed five minutes to figure out that Caroline was my mate. It was incredibly annoying, however, that he just *assumed* I was excited about it.

"She's my coworker, so we're here to talk about work," I said carefully, watching the annoyance that carried out on Wallace's face. Of course, he'd want me to accept the mate bond without question—he wasn't the one with an unwanted mate. "About the attacks at the Shifter Alliance. That's it."

I felt Caroline's eyes on me and knew she could sense my panic, but I avoided her gaze. There was no way I was giving her a reason to suspect the mate bond. *Especially* not in front of Wallace.

"I think you should let Mr. Wallace tell me at least one embarrassing story in exchange for keeping quiet about whatever it is you don't want him to say," she suggested, that sweet innocent look in her eyes as I turned to her.

It was her fakest expression, I'd learned. Caroline was made up of snark and sass and a little girl's impish impulse to push every boundary given to her. I could picture her as a kid, any time her mom said not to touch something, little Caroline probably walked right up to that very thing and touched it as slowly as possible. Holding her mom's gaze the whole time. *Great, now I'm picturing little Caroline, who's absolutely adorable.* And it only made adult Caroline that much more endearing. Which was the opposite of what I was trying to do.

I opened my mouth to tell her to stop prodding me, when she raised one well-groomed eyebrow.

"One story, Mor," she whispered, "And I won't ask about whatever it is you're hiding."

I growled, low and deep in my chest. Some people didn't think growling was a legitimate way to describe the sound, but that's because they'd never heard the deep throaty rumble that I seemed to be prone to do in Caroline's presence.

"Fine." I rolled my eyes, turning accusing eyes to Wallace. Who was looking unabashedly entertained. "One story."

"Oh, which one to choose," Wallace said in a sing song voice, lifting his tea to his lips, Daisy Mae was now curled up on the chair next to him, and he reached out to pat her head. She sighed contentedly, blissfully uninvolved in this ridiculous conversation. *That makes one of us.*

"Pick one that tells me something about Mor that I wouldn't know otherwise," Care suggested, offering a genuine smile this time.

Wallace's eyes flicked from Caroline to me, picking up on her usage of the nickname she'd come up with. No one had ever called me Mor before her, and I couldn't say that I wanted anyone to start. I had nothing against the name, I just didn't want to share it with anyone else...

Forget I said that.

"Alright then," Wallace hummed, a smirk pulling at his wrinkled lips. "How about the time that he had a crush on the Phillips girl?"

I groaned and sat back in my seat, covering my face with my hand as if that could save me from this mortifying experience. "Why?"

"Because obviously Wallace thinks I should hear it," Caroline snarked and I lifted one finger from my face to glare at her coy smile. "Go on Wallace, please. I'd love to hear about a young Morgan in puppy love."

"We call it cub love," Wallace snickered, "Since we turn into bears. Morgan was about...what, nine?" I nodded. "There was a girl down the road that was two years older than him—"

"One," I interrupted, face still covered, hoping to survive the embarrassment without turning beet red. "She was one year older."

"Alright, one year," Wallace continued. "Anyway, Morgan used to play with her little brother all the time out in their yard. And when Morgan met his friend's sister, he was smitten."

"I wouldn't say smitten," I complained.

"Oh, I think it sounds like you were smitten," Caroline teased, and I turned my head slightly to give her my driest expression. Her grin just widened. "So, what was it that made you fall head over heels? Was it her smile, or her eyes?"

"He said it was her bear form," Wallace explained, and I tried hard to pretend I was invisible. Maybe the whole manifesting your future thing applied to superpowers too.

No dice.

Caroline turned to me; eyebrows raised. "Her *bear form*?"

I thumped my head down on the table, trying to tune out Wallace's annoying laugh.

"He said she came out of the house one day, running toward her brother," he chuckled, "And shifted midstride. Of course, at that age, her bear form was small, but it was impressive to shift that quick. Poor boy was a goner."

"So, what did he do about it?" Caroline asked, sounding much too enthusiastic. "That can't be the only part of the story."

When Wallace replied, there was an evil pleasure to his voice. "Oh, it's not. Morgan figured that he couldn't tell his buddy about his crush, because it would break guy code to be in love with his friend's sister. So instead, this little stinker snuck out of the house in the middle of the night, and left a note taped to her window. I believe it was a poem."

"Nope, just a note," I mumbled against the table. "Just your average, run of the mill, love letter from a nine-year-old boy pouring his tiny little heart out like an idiot."

"Well, she seemed to like it," Wallace snickered, patting my arm. I slapped his hand away. "The next day when he went over to play with his friend, the little girl was raving about this love letter she'd gotten. How many did you leave for her before you confessed? Was it five or six?"

I almost didn't answer. Why further embarrass myself? "Ten." Apparently, I thrived under mortification.

"That's right. In the tenth one he told her it was him and asked her to meet him outside the next night."

"Did she show?" Caroline asked, desperate to know the ending to my adolescent love story.

"Did she Morgan?" Wallace taunted.

I raised my head to scowl at him, but he had that stubborn look on his face that said he would be even more insufferable if I didn't play along and finish the story.

"Yes, she showed up," I said with zero feeling. "She was my first kiss—if you can really call our one peck a kiss. And we dated for exactly one week, meeting in secret, until she said that it was too much stress, and she just couldn't handle it anymore."

Caroline's laughter filtered through the cabin and Wallace wasn't long in joining her. Daisy even poked her head up and thwacked her tail against the back of the wooden chair.

"That's adorable," Care laughed, grinning at me. "I can't believe she didn't think you were worth the stress! Although I guess it depends, did you have beefy forearms then too?"

It didn't escape my notice that Caroline was once again eyeing my forearms the same way she looked at food when she was trying to restrain herself. *Don't restrain yourself on my account, Care.* I felt my ego inflate one or two sizes, and the telltale warmth of pleasure radiated through my body.

"He was a lanky little guy," Wallace somehow found it necessary to say. "Took him until he was twenty before he filled out."

And there goes the ego.

"Aww, I never would have rejected lankly little Morgan with his sweet love letters," Caroline teased, green eyes flashing.

"No?" I challenged. "Even without the forearms?"

She met my gaze head on, studying me in a way that made me think she saw more than I meant to show. "Of course not. That Morgan was *vulnerable,*" she quipped pointedly, reminding me of our earlier conversation about my reputation, "And *honest. Unapologetically himself.* That's all I could ask for."

We stared at each other—more like glared—neither of us willing to bend. When the silence had gone on for a few tense moments, Mr. Wallace coughed. "Well, that escalated quickly."

"Right," I stuttered, shaking my head. "Let's get back on track. Now that we've thoroughly embarrassed me, it's time to talk about the attacks at the Alliance building."

For a moment, I thought Wallace might argue against it and start back in on the embarrassing stories, but to my relief, he rolled his eyes and complied. "Alright, be a buzz kill," he whined. "What did you need from me, Morgan?"

"I was hoping that as the king of gossip, you'd know if anyone might be linked to the break-ins that I'm being framed for."

"I've got lots of gossip," Wallace exclaimed with a little too much enthusiasm to be normal for a full-grown man. "I have it on good authority that Sharyl Danes is dating the Melville kid *and* the Bradly boy at the same time—and that the Bradly boy is five years older than her. It's going to be a big scandal when the mainstream gets ahold of it. I also know that old, widowed Mrs. Lawrence has been spotted bringing a much younger man to her home recently. They were even seen having dinner together—and by younger, I mean she's older than me and the man in question is thirty-seven!"

"Wait, how do you know so much about everyone's business all the way out here in the woods?" Caroline asked, sipping some of her tea—pun intended.

"Most Berserkers live either in the country on their own, or in more secluded neighborhoods," he explained. "That's why Morgan and his ragtag band are the only ones who live in the big house. Bears get together in Sleuths when it's necessary, but we're mostly solitary creatures except for our families. Which means that we all spend a lot of time apart, giving us quiet the appetite for contact via the phone."

Caroline nodded and smirked at me, amused by Wallace's spy network of lonely Berserkers.

"Most people underestimate us old people," he said, his smile devious. "Which is their mistake. They think we're too ancient to understand the current slang. Or that we can't figure out how to take a picture on our phone or see well enough to catch them doing what they shouldn't be doing. Little do they know that we're even on the TikTok. Their doubt makes us very effective spies."

"I'll bet," Care smiled knowingly.

As entertaining as it was to see the two of them bonding, I needed whatever information Wallace was withholding. And he was withholding something alright. He only rambled when he was guilty.

"Wallace, stop stalling," I snapped, earning a glare from my mentor. "Tell me what you heard. I know there's something you're not saying."

"There's nothing—"

"There is!"

"Morgan," Caroline said gently, her hand latching onto my arm.

"What?" I barked, but I should've known better. A glare and a snap would never be enough to scare Caroline away. She simply stared up at me, not cowed by my frustration.

"You're yelling," she said simply, squeezing my arm slightly, "And it's not helping."

Rather than continue to shout at her like I would've done a few days ago, I sighed, watching the steady stubbornness in her eyes. "Fine," I nodded, and she regrettably released my arm.

"Wallace, fess up," she said, her tone gentle and yet brooking no room for argument.

At first, I didn't think Wallace would answer. But then I noticed a pressure beginning to roll out like fog, pressing against him. Confused, I looked over at Caroline. Her attention was focused on the older Berserker.

She's manipulating him. She'd tried to use her magic to manipulate me when we first met. But because of the mate bond, she hadn't been able to achieve it—a fact that she thankfully hadn't yet put together.

I watched with fascination as millimeter by millimeter, Wallace's expression relaxed, and he gave me an apologetic look. *So, this is what it looks like when Care uses her magic.* Very effective.

"I have heard one rumor," he said with a long-suffering sigh. "That someone—I don't know who other than that it was a Berserker—said that if whoever's out there hiring people for these frame jobs keeps upping their price, they'll take the next job."

I felt my muscles tense, and my expression go hard. Anger, defensiveness, judgement, and disgust all fought against each other in my mind. But a deep-rooted disappointment burrowed deep, hitting me harder than all the rest of the emotions.

"How much are they paying?" Caroline asked, not affected by the news like I was.

"Ten grand for each break-in."

I didn't hear what else either one of them said. I was too busy scooting out of my chair so fast that I knocked it over. I managed to mumble a thanks to Wallace before I got to the front door and yanked it open.

I tried to put distance between me and the cabin before I let my emotions take over. It wouldn't stop Care from sensing them, but it would keep me from having to see her reaction. I didn't like these feelings; the personal offense that marked me as the softie I pretended I wasn't.

I knew that my people didn't necessarily have the most faith in me. I mean, I'd been Chief for six years and the council rep for five. Yet I still hadn't managed to shut down even one of the four gambling dens that the Berserkers were responsible for. But for my own people to seriously consider framing me? It had me wondering if I had any business being Chief at all.

Worse, it had me wondering if anyone would ever see me as anything more than rumors. As anything more than the monster I'd never been.

Caroline was right. I hadn't helped my reputation by acting the part of the big boorish bear all these years. But now I was afraid that there wasn't a reputation left to salvage. It wouldn't matter how I acted or what I said—no one was ever going to see me as more than a beast. Not when they were already willing to sell me out.

"Morgan!" Care shouted, and I clenched my eyes shut for a moment, willing myself to outpace her. I was too angry, too hurt, too close to shifting to be around her. There was no telling how little control I'd have if I shifted now with her trying to pry my mind open like she did all the locked doors in her life.

"Go away, Caroline!" I yelled back to her, knowing it wouldn't stop her.

"Mor, just stop for a second." Her voice was gentle as her hands latched onto my arm. She tried to pull me to a stop, but I plowed forward. I wasn't safe right now. *She* wasn't safe right now. "Let's take a breath for a second and talk—"

"No!" I roared, turning abruptly to snarl in her face, holding back a grimace when her eyes widened, and her emotions flashed with hurt. "I don't want to talk, Caroline! And I certainly don't want to talk to you!"

Then I barreled forward, the hurt in her heart following me even as I left her behind.

NINETEEN

Caroline

I didn't see Morgan for the rest of the day—or the next. Last night I could sense him pouting, holed up in his office where he refused to unlock the door. But then this morning he left in a huff, and I was left alone with Logan, Mike and Clint. They evaded my questions about Morgan at every turn, not particularly swayed by my emotional manipulation—though I wasn't trying hard. It felt wrong to manipulate my only friends. So instead, I let them corral me into watching *The Good Place*, which I'd never seen.

I liked the show, but by the time Morgan came home that evening, we'd already made it through two seasons and Mor's absence was grating on me. He didn't speak to any of us when he came in, taking a takeout bag with him to his office and not coming out the rest of the night.

I understood how Morgan was feeling—partly because I could sense his emotions but also because I understood what it was like to have people think less of you than you deserved. But since he wouldn't even let me in the room, I couldn't very well explain my empathy. Which was a shame, because I didn't show it often, so it would've been a gift for him.

"Why are boys so weird?" I asked, my phone pressed against my ear where I lay in bed that night, Daisy sleeping soundly beside me.

"That's a question for God, not your antisocial big sister," Ariel complained from the other end of the line.

"Yeah well, I prayed about it, but God doesn't seem interested in giving me the Morgan Hohlt handbook," I grumbled, sinking deeper into my soft covers.

"Isn't that part of the fun with guys though? Trying to figure them out?"

"Says who?"

"I don't know, I've never even flirted with a man before," Ariel defended, her voice sounding a little garbled.

"Wait, are you eating peanut butter right now?" I demanded. Daisy lifted her head and stared at me, clearly sensing the injustice I was suffering.

Silence resounded from the other end of the phone, and I rolled my eyes at my sister's inability to lie. She'd been like this when we were kids too. If she couldn't answer a question honestly, she'd just stand there and look guilty. A quiet Ariel was a guilty Ariel.

"You're not supposed to do a Jif night without me!" I whined, annoyed when I heard the sound of the spoon scraping against the peanut butter jar.

"You're not here," she said, as if that were reason enough to break our lifelong tradition of wallowing in peanut butter. I rolled my eyes as Daisy went back to sleep. "You're busy being held captive by a smoking hot guy."

"I never told you he was smoking hot," I defended immediately, feeling a little flushed even though I hadn't admitted to anything. Not that there was anything to admit to...other than appreciating nice forearms and sexy face scars just like every other woman on the planet. Hence everyone's obsession with Jason Momoa. *That's what it is! Morgan is just my real-life Jason Momoa.* It wasn't personal, it was purely shallow. I'd feel this way about anyone who looked like that.

"No, but you did tell me his name," Ariel announced triumphantly, "And I Googled him. He's a fox Care!"

"No, technically he's a bear."

She cackled into the phone, and I laughed with her at the dad joke. As annoying as my sister could be, it was nice to have someone so familiar in my life. Someone I could be at ease with. I'd never had a lot of those...and yet somehow, Mike, Clint, Logan and yes, even

Morgan, were slowly becoming those people for me too. Which was terrifying. Because it would only take one screw up, one step too far for them to send me packing.

I was used to being alone, that's what a lifetime of having to distance yourself from people will do to you, but the longer I was here, the more I realized that I didn't really want to be alone anymore...

"Fess up, Care," Ariel said through a mouthful of peanut butter, "You know you think he's gorgeous! So how long do you think it'll take you to kiss him?"

"*Excuse me?*"

"Oh, come on, you talk about him like he's an eight-year-old pulling your pig tails. You're so into him!"

"Uh, no. We can't stand each other. I mean," I sighed, "Yes, I can admit that I find him objectively attractive, as most any woman would. He's all rugged and gruff..." Like Jason Momoa. *Hmm...I wonder what Morgan would look like as Aquaman.* Then—completely out of nowhere and by no fault of my own—I was picturing Morgan as the aquatic superhero. Shirtless, wet, striding around with one eyebrow cocked, a smolder on his face. *Mm mm, they might have to recast the role of Aquaman if Morgan auditions.*

"Care? Did I lose you?"

At the sound of my sister's voice, I shook my head, clearing the confusing daydreams from my mind. "Sorry, just had a hard time finding the right words to describe the insufferableness that is Morgan."

"Right," Ariel scoffed.

"It's true! Sure, he's hot, but we fight constantly, he yells all the time—"

"I thought you said his yelling was more like an old man kind of yelling where the grandkids tell the grandpa that he's yelling, but the grandpa yells that he's not yelling."

I snickered at the description, enjoying both how accurate it was and how much Morgan would hate it.

"Okay yeah, that is true, but still, we don't get along—like at all. Every time we start to have a normal conversation, he finds a way to argue with me," I huffed, feeling one hundred percent justified in my argument.

But when all I heard was silence, my justification suddenly began to shrink.

"What?" I snapped. "Say it Ariel, I know you want to."

"It's just that..." she paused, letting out a loud breath. "You can be really difficult Caroline."

I was so shocked by the brutality of her honesty that I actually sat there, completely at a loss for words for a solid ten seconds.

"Excuse me?" Was all I managed to say once my voice recovered.

"It's true! Remember in high school when Reed Taylor said that based on the way you looked, you'd be a terrible football player? You took it so personally that you took his car keys, strode out to the field next to the school, and chucked them out into the tall grass and said—"

"How's that for a football player?" I finished, smirking at the memory. The guy had not been happy with me. But boy was I satisfied as I flounced away in my ribbons and skirts, knowing I'd proven him wrong. Took him an hour to find his keys. "What's your point?"

"My point, dear sister," she said, a smile in her voice now, "Is that you are an incredibly reactive person. You're great, don't get me wrong. You love fiercely, you're passionate, you're loyal, funny, lively and kind. But you're also ridiculously stubborn. You operate based on your emotions, letting them push you to extreme behaviors quickly, and you're combative."

"Wow, thanks."

Genuinely a little offended, I looked down, picking at a wrinkle in my T shirt. Sure, she was right. I'd always been too determined, too loud, too snarky, too emotional, too reactive and too aggressive, but to hear it all laid out by the person that knew me best...not fun.

"Hold on, I'm not done," she added, but I wasn't sure I wanted to hear the rest. "I love how intense you are, Care. Do you realize how full my life is with you in it? You make me laugh and smile more than anyone I know, and if I'm ever in a pinch, I know I can count on you. You'd threaten anyone who hurt me, and you'd never give up on me or anyone you chose to make a part of your pack. You are the strongest, bravest person I've ever met, and you have the kindest heart though you try to hide it under more snark than Damon Salvatore could muster."

I laughed despite myself, feeling my eyes get a little misty at her words. If I was being honest, I hadn't lacked for positive affirmations growing up—my parents were great at reminding me how special I was or how much they loved me—but the critic in my head was loud, and she only ever remembered the bad.

"I love you, Care. You're an incredible person," Ariel continued, her tone gentler now, "But it sounds like you're not really giving Morgan a fair chance. You're rising to the challenge of pushing his buttons instead of trying to understand the mechanics of why those buttons do what they do. So maybe you could take a beat from the whole antagonistic thing and just try to be friends."

I mulled over her words, not really liking the way they made me feel, all serious and thoughtful, my belly shifting in that weird way that signaled butterflies. Did I want to be friends with Morgan? I wasn't sure.

"You're just saying this because you think he's hot and you're playing matchmaker," I accused. The thought of Morgan and I actually attempting to get along did not settle well in my mind. It made me feel all fidgety and warm and somehow embarrassed.

The whole thing reminded me of when I'd gotten distracted and moony eyed over his forearms the other day in his office. I'd been mortified when I accidentally said my thoughts out loud, telling him that he should wear long sleeve shirts so his forearms wouldn't distract me so much. *Ugh, just thinking about it makes me want to die.*

Morgan had been a little embarrassed too, and annoyingly entertained, but there'd been a different emotion lurking in me when his eyes met mine...

Want. That's what I'd felt. I'd looked at Morgan as a man, and I liked what I saw. Not only that, but I'd actually imagined him holding me. As if I could want such a thing. *Which I don't.* But I couldn't deny that the thought had elicited something deeper in me, some kind of need. And I'd felt it in Morgan too.

What the heck did that mean?

"No, I'm saying it because it sounds like you guys might make a good team if you could stop bickering for five minutes," came Ariel's voice, bringing me back to reality where my daydreams of Morgan bench pressing me came to a screeching halt, "And because you need someone, Care. You need a person who's involved in this world like you are. I'm human, I can't help you spy or have your back in a fight or truly understand your vendetta, but he can."

I didn't know what to do with the whole inconvenient attraction to Morgan thing. Really, it was all superficial, just an outward appreciation for someone's appearance...But then there were the weird feelings in my stomach and the odd desire I had to pull at Morgan's strings until he unraveled enough to come at me, fight me, maybe even latch onto me—*No Caroline!*

I didn't want to think about Morgan as anything *meaningful* in my life, but that last bit Ariel had said about having someone who understood my lifestyle...*That* I could get behind without any confusion.

"Friends," I said, testing out the word. It didn't taste terrible per se. It felt a little wrong to think of Morgan attached to it, but I could maybe get used to the idea.

"Exactly," Ariel exclaimed excitedly. "And if it becomes more, then by all means, put a ring on it and make some babies. Because ya'll's kids would be *adorable.*"

"Oh my gosh Ariel!" I exclaimed, trying hard *not* to picture the image of Morgan and I married, all mushy and content. *Ew.* "I'm hanging up now!"

"I loooove you," Ariel shouted into the phone, and I laughed.

"I love you too, Air. And I promise to never sell you to the circus. Mostly because they'd never take you."

She laughed and we hung up, and then it was just me. Alone with my thoughts.

Was it really that weird for Mor and I to be friends? I mean, I used a nickname for him—a non-derogatory one for a change...And although he ate healthier than anyone I'd ever met in my life—seriously, why are there so many types of quinoa? Who even wants one kind? —he'd helped me pack all my junk food from my house, and not once had he belittled me for my diet. Then there was the fact that he'd killed someone to keep me safe—kind of a big deal—and that he was now calling me 'Care'. Which I hated to admit that I liked.

"We haven't really been enemies for a while now," I said to Daisy, who was sound asleep, snoring. "And calling ourselves antagonistic coworkers is accurate...but is friends really that different from what we are now?"

Maybe it was time to find out...

TWENTY

Caroline

TWENTY MINUTES LATER, I DECIDED TO TEST my sister's theory. After all, how hard could it be to shift from antagonistic coworkers to friends? *Never mind, let's not answer that question.*

"Okay," I announced loudly as I burst into his dimly lit bedroom at one fifteen in the morning, "So I've been thinking, and I decided that we're not doing this whole antagonistic coworkers thing anymore."

"What the—" Morgan roared from the vicinity of a king size bed that sat against the right-hand wall.

"Relax, Bear Man, it's just me."

"Caroline?" He croaked, the light in the bathroom illuminating him just enough for me to tell that he was sitting up and rubbing a hand down his very confused face.

"Yeah, I know it's late," I said, waving my hand dismissively as I marched into the room, "But I was just on the phone with my sister a little bit ago and she made some really good points."

"I'm sorry, are we having a conversation right now?" Morgan's voice was extra gravelly, all heavy with sleep, and the sound did something strange to my body. A weird hum traveled down my spine, and I had a sudden urge to smooth his dark wavy hair from his forehead. *Nope!* I shook my head. *Back on track, Caroline.*

"Yes, because you've been avoiding me for a day and a half now and I'm done with it." I crossed my arms, all business now; completely focused. "I get that you were upset, Mor. After hearing everything Mike said about the chat threads..." I paused, recalling the way people online so casually talked about Morgan like he deserved every bad thing that came his way, "I understand why the idea of one of your own people saying they'd be willing to work against you is such a big deal. *But* what you would have heard me say the other day, if you'd stopped long enough to listen, is that it was *one person*, Morgan."

"Care..."

"No, just listen," I snapped, tired of him resisting all my efforts to be supportive. *Just let me be nice to you, dang it!* "One person out of *hundreds* said that they would frame you in exchange for money. But don't you get it? There are hundreds of Berserkers that *wouldn't* do that."

"I know."

"And I can understand that it's hard—" I paused in my tirade, not sure I'd heard him right. "I'm sorry, did you just agree with me?"

Morgan let out a loud, exasperated sigh and rested his chin on his hand. Poor guy was clearly still groggy and in no place to have a deep conversation. Too bad I wasn't patient enough to wait.

"Don't worry, I won't make a habit of it," he teased dryly, "But yes, I agree with you. I shouldn't have taken the whole thing so personally, and instead of ignoring you, I should have just apologized for reacting so strongly in the first place."

"No."

"I'm sorry?" he asked, eyes squinting in confusion.

"No," I repeated, "As I was saying before, I talked to my sister, and I think we can be friends, you and I, and friends tell each other what's wrong."

"I don't want to do that," he said, deadpan.

I rolled my eyes, but I didn't back down, instead crossing my arms, completely immovable. I was Excalibur in the stone, baby, completely rock solid. *Just try and make me walk away, Morgan Hohlt.* Even with his Berserker strength, he was no match for my defiance.

"Yes, you do," I insisted stubbornly, "For many reasons. For one, you have only men in your life and as great as men are—believe me, I'm a big fan—women offer a different perspective. Plus, you and I can understand each other in ways no one else can," I went on, watching as his brows crinkled, clearly unimpressed with my reasons so far, "We both have issues controlling our emotions sometimes—"

"I've only had that issue since I met you," he argued.

"Rude. And you're wrong. You were good at *hiding* your emotions, but with each other, we don't have to hide. Because we both understand the pressure, the loneliness, the hurt, the anger, all of it—including the stubbornness God seemed to think wise to bestow upon us both. You and I have a foundation in this relationship that we don't have with anyone else. We drive each other crazy, but we also have a deep understanding of each other's motivations. Which means we can understand each other in ways no one else can. So, what do you say? Friends?"

Insecurity choked me into silence as I stood there in the faint yellow light of the bathroom, wondering what the heck I was thinking.Here I was, begging a grown man to be my friend, giving him the sales pitch of my life. *This was a stupid idea.*

I was so swept up in regretting my choices, that I almost didn't hear him when he said, "Okay."

"Wait...okay? Okay as in...Okay, you've put up with me for long enough and it's time for me to go now?" I sputtered, my vulnerability clearly robbing me of all grace, "Or okay, as in, you want to be friends?"

"Okay, as in, we can *try* to be friends." He spoke slower this time, like he was speaking to a child, but I was too excited to be offended.

"Are you sure? Maybe we should celebrate the moment by doing something friend-ish," I teased impishly, grinning wide. "I could teach you how to fishtail braid, or we could make up our own secret handshake. Oh! We should play a game of Mash! I even have my guys picked out already for the husband options! Henry Cavill, Josh Holloway, Viggo Mortensen, and Paul Wesley."

"All of those guys are at least fifteen years older than you," Morgan complained, glaring at me, "And some of them are older than you by a good thirty years or more."

"So? It's my fantasy."

"Your *what?*"

"My fantasy," I said, drawing the word out slowly. "You know, where I picture myself happily married to one of my dream men. It's this daydream where they nuzzle my neck while we're cooking—"

"You don't cook."

"Hush, it's my daydream. They also always come home from work in a dirty white T shirt and kiss me like we're dying in the next ten minutes."

"Oh, Lord," Morgan groaned.

"What? It's a very reasonable fantasy."

"For the love of all that is good and green in the world, please get back on track, Care," he pleaded, and I smiled at how quickly I could unravel him. "How do you and I go about being friends—*besides* playing mash and learning to braid hair?"

"Party pooper," I complained, barely restraining myself from doing my own rendition of the Party Pooper song from *Father of the Bride.* Somehow, I didn't think Morgan would find it funny. "Fine, I'll stay on topic. As friends we'll still be ourselves—we can even argue and banter with each other the same way we always have. Which is good, because I'm pretty sure I can't breathe without being snarky at the same time."

"That checks out."

I, very maturely, chose not to be offended by that comment. See, personal growth happening right before my eyes.

"To be friends," I continued, "You'll also have to use more words to express yourself, and I'll have to use less. We'll both suffer a little, but we'll get used to it."

Morgan didn't agree or disagree, groaning as he stood from his bed and made his way over to me. It was while I was watching his slow approach that I realized how stupid I'd been for coming here in the middle of the night. Because Morgan wasn't wearing traditional pajamas. Instead, he was wearing plaid pajama pants with no socks...and no shirt.

Oh. My.

Morgan Hohlt was a babe on a bad day, and today *certainly* wasn't a bad day. I'd assumed that since he could turn into a bear and had bear level strength, he would be well muscled. Boy was I wrong.

Ladies of the world, he was *very* well muscled. The obvious strength in his shoulders wasn't a surprise since they were always framed nicely in his well-fitted shirts, but his pecs, his abs, his obliques, his necktorals and bipectals were all in *tip* top shape.

Honestly, I wasn't sure how I'd ever be able to see him with a shirt on again. Any time he was fully clothed, I could just pull out this mental image. He'd be like a paper doll in my head. One minute he'd have a shirt on, and then poof, it'd be off.

Okay Caroline, now you're just objectifying him. Maybe so, but he was *objectively* gorgeous. And by the way, who said objectifying someone was such a bad thing? So long as I wasn't thinking of Morgan in any inappropriate scenarios, me finding his physique attractive was a perfectly acceptable thing. *You tell 'em, Care!*

"Careful there, Care Bear," Morgan whispered, stopping only a foot away, "I'm starting to feel like I'm in a zoo."

Caught red handed, I looked around the room for something—anything—other than him to stare at, my face on fire.

"Then again," his voice rumbled, "If this is one of those two-way petting zoos where you pet the animals and they pet you back, I might be interested."

My jaw dropped—and I mean *dropped*—as I stared up at him, completely and totally flabbergasted. Was Morgan...*flirting* with me?

His lopsided smirk was a little devilish and his eyes were full of mischief, a mysterious new warmth emanating through his emotions. *Well, that's new.* And a little confusing.

"You lied," I said, whispering unintentionally—I was working with only twelve braincells thanks to Morgan's hotness frying the rest of them. "You said you've never seen *The Office.*"

"I haven't," he shrugged, lifting a hand to trail down the tail of my black ribbon where it tied off my braid. "Like I said, I just know the references. Why are you wearing all black?"

"Oh!" I glanced down at my black shirt, pants and shoes, remembering the other half of the reason I came here. "Sorry, your chesticles had me distracted for a second. I want to go stakeout the Alliance Building."

"My *what* had you distracted?"

"You know, your chesticle situation, all very manly and a little unexpected."

"*Unexpected?*" he demanded, glancing down at himself. "What part of this is unexpected? Did you think I looked like a sick Victorian boy under here?"

I shrugged, messing with him.

"Mm," I hummed, "More like a nerdy college student. I figured you had big shoulders, but I assumed based on your personality that you'd be pretty...basic underneath."

"*Basic?* You thought I'd be basic—" he growled, and I turned to cover my grin, "And what do you mean 'based on my personality'? I'm a manly man. I'm masculine!"

"Of course, you are," I crooned patronizingly as I opened the door, turning back to give him a pitying expression. "Such a big strong man." I made sure to use a baby voice on those last words. Boy did that get him going.

The light frustration he'd been feeling suddenly faded away into something hotter, and I felt his anger pin itself on me as he took two menacing steps in my direction.

"Caroline!" He shouted, half snarling, but before he could reach me, I slipped into the hall. Then I shut the door in his face.

"You're yelling," I told him calmly.

"I am not," he yelled through the door.

"Yes, you are. Now, we have better things to do than argue. Like getting ready. So please go put on some dark clothes so we can do the stakeout."

"No," came a defiant little shout.

I rolled my eyes. Such a petulant little boy inside the body of such a big man.

"You're still yelling," I reminded him.

A long pause met my ears, and then finally a loud sigh.

"Fine," he grumbled.

I smiled victoriously. "Bear Man, I have a feeling this is the beginning of a beautiful friendship."

TWENTY ONE

Caroline

"Chip?" I said, offering Morgan one of my sour cream and onion Pringles.

He stared at the proffered food like I'd tried to feed him rat poisoning. "No, thank you," he grumbled. Then he turned his eyes back to the Alliance Building like I hadn't just offered him a great honor. I didn't share food with just anybody—he should've been grateful.

We'd been sitting in silence on a downtown street for an hour now, the streets of Shifter Haven mostly quiet at two forty in the morning. All the main lights in the Alliance Building and the surrounding offices were off, but dim security lights illuminated each floor just enough for the security guards on duty to do their rounds.

"You know, insulting my favorite foods with your judgy attitude isn't going to help this friendship," I complained, switching on the radio. 'Come and Get Your Love' by Redbone came through the speakers and I instantly began to shimmy in my seat, wiggling with the beat. "And you're fine and you're mine," I sang, snapping down on another chip, "Ohhh."

The music abruptly stopped. I glared at Morgan—who'd *rudely* switched the radio off.

"Hey, that's a good song," I whined.

"We're here to watch for a criminal, Care, not to do karaoke."

I growled low in my throat and put my feet on the dash, turning my attention to the Alliance Building, the car once again silent. And boring.

"Like you would ever do something as fun as karaoke," I mumbled.

"Now is that what friends say to each other?"

"Yes, friends tell friends when they're being a stick in the mud. And Morgan," I sassed, turning my head to look at him, "You're being a stick in the mud."

"You asked me to come on this stakeout so we could try and see your copycat in the act. That's not supposed to be a fun."

"It always looks fun on TV." I chomped on another chip.

"Don't you do stakeouts before you sneak into a new building?"

I shook my head and reluctantly put the lid on my Pringles, suddenly not in the mood for snack food. "Not really. I usually come during the day and walk around like a tourist. I chat with the homeless people; pretend I need to use the bathroom so I can go inside whichever building and get the lay of the land. Then I look up the floorplans online, and when I do watch for any extended time, I eat and people watch. But there's no people to watch right now."

"Fair point," he sighed.

The streets were dead except for the occasional car driving by, but being a Wednesday, there wasn't a whole lot of that happening. Which meant that this stakeout was *incredibly* boring.

"Oh! I know! Why don't we go inside?" I gasped, taking my feet off the dash and spinning to face him, my elbows on the console and my hands grasped like I was praying.

"What? No," he said quickly, his expression hard and unyielding.

"Come on, Mor. We're not seeing anything this way! Maybe we're at the wrong angle and the person is sneaking in through the back right now. And if we go inside, between your strength and my speed, we could easily catch whoever's framing you."

"Caroline, no," he insisted, his tone leaving no room for argument. "We're not prepared for a fight, let alone to sneak in. We'd need electronic lock picks and camera signal jammer things and—"

He stopped talking as I pulled every single item he listed from my backpack where it lay on the floorboard.

"You planned this." It wasn't a question. "You hoped to wear me down with a stakeout first, and then convince me to go in there."

He was right, but I wouldn't admit it. We were becoming friends, and friends didn't have to admit to things. Or something along those lines. It'd been a really long time since I'd had a friend, so I was a little fuzzy on the rules.

"If we don't catch them, they're just gonna keep doing it," I said instead, hoping his desire for justice was bigger than his annoyance at my manipulation.

When he sighed, loud and irritated, I felt his frustration lessen a little. And I knew I'd won.

"You stay right next to me," he began, glaring at me when I grinned and started bouncing in my seat. "I'm serious, Caroline. The Witch binding keeps you close by me, but not right next to me. So, no running off down the hall by yourself or going into rooms alone. If we go in there, we're a team."

"Yes, Captain," I nodded, trying to bite back my smile. It didn't work.

Morgan shook his head, but he couldn't hide the smirk playing at his lips. "Let's go you little Imp."

We decided to go in through the side of the building, since the front was too well guarded at night and the back seemed like the obvious choice for the amateur attacker who was pretending to be me. With the cameras paused and no longer live thanks to my wireless feed blocker, we made our way down the narrow alley next to the building, completely invisible to the guards watching the security feed inside.

"Hold on," Morgan suddenly growled, his arm shooting out in front of me. I 'oofed' as I stumbled into him and had to grasp his forearm to keep myself upright—such a chore, let me tell you. And no, I absolutely did *not* run my fingers over the veins that spanned from his wrist to his elbow. *I have some self-control.*

"Caroline?" I looked up from my current study of Morgan's arm. *Okay, so maybe not a lot of self-control.*

Up ahead, a man in a well-worn oversized trench coat, a beanie and white sneakers was walking toward us.

"Oh, it's Paul. Hey Paul!" I called out, but when I tried to move forward, Morgan just flipped his hand over and latched it onto my side. Keeping me in place.

There's this classic trope in romance books where the girl talks about how she could feel the heat of the guy's hand through her shirt when he touched her. I've always thought it sounded super corny. Well, not anymore. *I can now verify that the description is accurate.*

In fact, I was a little worried that Morgan's palm might just burn right through my shirt. And wouldn't *that* be embarrassing.

"No, it's okay," I explained, finally able to take my focus away from Morgan's hand thanks to Paul's approach, "This is Paul. He's a friend. He keeps me informed on what's been going on around the building."

"Doing okay Caroline?" Paul asked, a kind smile on his face even as he eyed Morgan with a healthy amount of scrutiny.

Paul was in his early fifties, and I'd learned from our many conversations that he was a former war vet with severe PTSD. He'd been in and out of different shelters, but never stayed long because being around so many other people often exacerbated his issues.

"I'm okay, Paul. Morgan here is a friend too." To prove my point, I smiled up at the Berserker Chief. Morgan sighed heavily but dropped his arm, allowing me to step forward and shake Paul's hand—Paul didn't like hugs. "Oh! And I've got your money. Sorry I didn't get it to your sooner, I was..." I glanced at Morgan, fishing two fifty-dollar bills out of my thin wallet, "Detained."

"You don't have to give me this," Paul insisted, trying to push the money back at me.

"Yes, I do. You're my employee and you need to get paid. Now, speaking of work, have you seen anyone suspicious around here lately? Apparently, someone's been piggy backing off my break-ins and doing some of their own, making it look like my work."

Paul gave me a look that said he knew I was merely relabeling my charity to make him feel better, but he stuffed the cash in his pocket all the same.

"I didn't think it was you doing such a shoddy job in there lately," he said, a proud look on his face. "I've been keeping an eye on the place whenever I'm not sleeping or getting supplies, but I've only seen the usual people. Employees, council members and the occasional delivery service or family member. But no one at night other than security guards. It could be that I'm sleeping through it though. Sorry I don't have better intel for you."

"It's okay, Paul," I assured him, resisting the urge to give him a pat on the shoulder. I was grateful he allowed me to shake his hand and I didn't want to push him. So, instead I did something that I rarely ever did, and I tapped into my magic, tugging his anxiety back toward peace. The magic wrapped itself around him, and then quickly absorbed into his emotions, releasing some of the tension in his body. "I'm just glad I have someone I trust around here," I said, the words genuine.

Paul blushed, a smile crinkling his face.

"You two going in there tonight?" he asked, nodding toward the side door of the building.

"Yeah, I'm hoping we can catch my copycat."

"Good luck! I'll keep a look out while I make my laps."

"Thanks Paul," I smiled. Once Paul had shuffled off to start his usual rounds of self-imposed neighborhood watch, Morgan and I headed for the side door of the Alliance Building.

The main floor was silent as we stepped inside. Thankfully, there were no guards close by; all of them either watching the feed from the security cameras or out patrolling the hallways. The nice thing about sneaking into the Alliance Building at night was that there were less guards on duty. But the downside was that they were actively roaming the building, making it easier to get caught.

"So, you have an employee?" Morgan whispered beside me. To my surprise, I sensed no judgement in him, only respect.

"Yeah, just the one," I replied as we both ducked under the window in the security room door to avoid the eyes of the guards inside.

"How'd you find him?"

Instead of answering Morgan's question, I grabbed him by the wrist and pulled him with me to a door on the right side of the hall. He waited quietly while I used my electronic lock pick to open the door, and then let me drag him into the stairwell—let's be honest, there was no way I could've dragged a Berserker anywhere by force.

"I met him about two years ago," I explained as we began our trek up the stairs. The elevators would have been a more convenient route—especially for the sake of my quads—but since we couldn't be sure if someone would be on the other side of the doors when they opened, the stairs were the safer option. "For the first few months after I came to Shifter Haven, I practiced sneaking into places just to see if I could get in and out unscathed. Once I'd gotten good at it, I started scouting the Alliance Building and that's when I came across Paul."

"He seems like a nice guy," Morgan commented as we turned to go up the next flight of stairs.

"Not what you expected?"

He gave me a guilty look. "Not quite."

"It's okay. Honestly, I think that's how Paul and I bonded. People assume he's a certain way because he's a homeless guy who looks a little weather beaten."

"And there's the trench coat."

"Hey! I got him that for Christmas!"

Mor paused on the third-floor landing and turned to look at me, mystified. It was like he was seeing me for the first time—seeing me *clearly* for the first time.

"I'm ashamed that I didn't see that coming," he said quietly, even though we were the only ones in the stairwell. "Keep proving me wrong, Care, and there might not be any reasons left for me not to like you."

Suddenly, I felt all shy and insecure. "I think you just complimented me."

Then Mor leaned close enough that I could see where the grey in his eyes ended, and the blue began. "I won't tell if you won't."

Not sure what to say other than a quivering 'okay'—which would've made me feel too much like a simpering miss—I chose to nod instead.

"So, you were saying that Paul—like you—understands what it's like to be judged based on appearances," he prompted, and I jumped on the chance to return to a less dangerous topic.

"Yeah, Paul, like a lot of homeless people, just hasn't figured out how to function in a more normal environment. He has pretty severe PTSD from his time in the service, and it makes it hard for him to be around a lot of people, so he chooses to be on his own. I just wish I could help him more..."

"You are helping him," Morgan argued, though I avoided his direct gaze. This conversation was getting a little too emotional to be having in a dark stairwell where everything seemed layered with subtext. "And not just with the money. You're giving him something to do, something to keep him focused. You're giving him the opportunity to work with another person in small intervals. It may not seem like much, but it could do a lot for him in the long run."

"I never thought of it that way." I glanced over at him, feeling like maybe I was seeing him clearly for the first time too. "You know you're not so bad sometimes."

"Gee, thanks." He bumped my shoulder. "You know Care, you were right that I need to use more words when I communicate—particularly with you, but you were also wrong."

I gave him an annoyed look, but he just offered me a kind smile that made him look relaxed. Approachable. *Well, that's a first.*

"You don't need to use less words to communicate," he said, his grey eyes boring into me, and although I kind of wanted to run for the door, I stayed put. This was a big deal for us. A real step toward being real friends. "I don't mind that you talk a lot. I'm not one to monopolize the conversation—"

"You don't say," I teased, needing to break the seriousness of the moment. It worked—he smirked.

"Point is, you little imp, that I'm not an outgoing guy, so for you to do a lot of the talking isn't a bad thing. My issues with you have never been about how much you talk, Care. I don't think you should use less words, I just think you should maybe be more thoughtful about the ones you pick sometimes."

I could've chosen to be offended by the insinuation that I could be callous or rude, but what was the point? He was right. I did have a way of reacting too quickly. Of speaking without thinking. Even my own sister had called me out for my 'difficult' disposition.

"Fair enough." I shrugged, pushing open the door to the floor where the offices for the council members were. "I can be more thoughtful if you'll try to be more verbose."

"Deal. I'll even start now."

Morgan smiled, but with this talk of me needing to be a little more intentional with my words, I wondered if it would ever be fair for me to ask the question that had been burning a hole in my mind.

"What?" he asked, eyeing me curiously.

"Hm?"

"There's something in there that you want to say." He gently tapped my temple.

"Okay," I sighed, "Here's the thing. I'm going to work on using nicer words, but sometimes you might have to let me know if something I said was uncool."

"Meaning that you're afraid whatever it is that you want to say right now is 'uncool'?" he surmised.

"Kinda."

Morgan went quiet for a moment, and I let him be, unsure if it was wise for me to broach this topic at all. We'd made so much progress, and I hated to make us backtrack.

"I guess part of friendship is feeling safe to ask anything," he finally said, glancing over at me as we walked slowly down the dimly lit hall, "And safe to express when something's too raw to discuss. So, go ahead and ask, and I'll let you know if I want to answer or not."

I nodded, and then, figuring it was better to just rip off the band aid, I blurted, "Who's the woman in the picture frame behind your desk?"

Morgan's eyebrows shot up and he blinked, apparently too surprised by my question to speak. We stood there for a moment, and I hoped I hadn't pressed too far, asked him something too personal.

"Walk and talk?" he finally suggested, one hand on the back of his neck like he didn't quite know where to start.

I nodded as he led the way down the hall, making sure to walk slow and keep my eyes roving for any guards on duty.

"The woman in the photo is Genevieve...my wife." His words were heavy, but not with grief like I thought they'd be. Curious, I risked a sideways glance at him. His eyes were firmly ahead, his expression unreadable. But I felt his anxiety, the slight fear that ran through him like an undercurrent. *What is he so afraid of?*

"She passed away four years ago. Cancer," he continued, glancing at me from the corner of his eye, his look a little worried. But then just like that, the expression was gone, and I wasn't sure I'd seen it at all.

"Was she a Berserker too?"

"No, she was human, but she fit right in."

"How'd you meet?" I asked, trying to envision a younger Morgan. One who was falling in love for the first time.

When he smiled, I knew it was the right question. "Mike and Clint were in high school at the time, and although Mr. Wallace was technically raising us, I took on a lot of the responsibility—well, Wallace would say I stole it." Now *that* I could believe. "The boys had gotten into trouble for some stupid prank, so I went down to the school to talk to the principle. But instead of the usual older woman who worked the reception desk, there was this dark-haired beauty that I'd never seen before."

"Did you talk to her?"

Another smile lit Mor's face and he turned to me, shaking his head. "No, I was too nervous. But Mike and Clint could see how interested I was, so the meddling little twirps made sure to get in trouble every day that week until I agreed to talk to her. Any guesses what my opening line was?"

"Hey, I'm Morgan Hohlt," I mocked, doing a terrible impression of his deep voice, "I'm a babe six days a week and a beast on Sunday. Wanna feel my bicep?"

Morgan chuckled quietly. "No. My opening line was, 'Hi, is that an Orange Crush?'."

"You didn't say that to her!"

"Oh, I absolutely did."

"What'd she do?"

"She looked at me like she wasn't sure if I needed help or not," he grinned, and I found myself hypnotized by the sight of it. He didn't grin enough, I decided. If he did, the women of Shifter Haven would run *at* him instead of running away. *On second thought, maybe he shouldn't grin more.* I didn't think I liked the idea of all those women chasing him. *But it's not because I have any personal interest...*

"But then I really impressed her when I went on to explain that I wasn't a fan of Orange Crush, and I preferred Mountain Dew," Morgan continued, completely unaware that I'd been ogling him—thank God. "But of course, orange juice was good too, although I'd never been a fan of Sierra Mist."

"Oh, you poor baby," I teased, using my most patronizing voice.

He rubbed the back of his neck again and I thought I saw his cheeks get pinker, but it was hard to tell for sure in the dim lighting.

"Yeah, it was pretty bad, but she took it in stride," he continued, "We even got into a twenty-minute discussion about our favorite pops, and half an hour later I asked for her number...We got married a year later."

"Was she broody like you?" This question I asked more tentatively, not wanting to push him past his threshold, but desperate to know what kind of woman had held Morgan Hohlt's attention.

"No," he chuckled, flashing me a sweet, reminiscing smile, "She was shy, but she could be chatty when she wanted. She had this sweet, selfless way about her. But boy could she put me in my place when I needed it, and she was always quicker to see the good in people than I was. Genevieve..." he paused, and we both stood still in the hallway as he tried to conjure a description that would fit the woman he loved and lost, "She was gentle and patient. She always fought for me to be more open with people and give them a fair chance, and I loved her more than I knew you could love someone..." he trailed off, and I felt his grief flash a little brighter, "We were married for three years, and in the time that she's been gone, I've realized that the love didn't die with her. It just kept going. I didn't know love could be quite that strong until I lost her."

When he stopped and let out a deep pained sigh, I couldn't stop myself from using my words. Not when his resonated so deeply with me.

"I know what you mean," I treaded carefully, trying not to overstep and upset him. "I never knew my birth parents, but I loved them for what they did for me; the sacrifice they made. And even though they're gone—even though I never got to meet them—the love is still there." Morgan didn't seem offended by my empathy as he turned to fully face me, listening intently. So, I went on. "But I've learned that love is like ribbons," I smiled, picking up the end of the black ribbon that tied off my braid. "It connects us to people, tying us to each other. And it doesn't matter if someone dies, or willingly leaves us, because once the ribbon's tied...it's tied. The love is always there. But the really beautiful part about it all is that there's no end to the ribbon. There's no end to the patterns you can make and the people you can love. I love both my birth parents and my adoptive parents. I didn't have to cut the ribbons to one so I could give them to the other. Love doesn't run out like that, instead you just keep adding more ribbons and the pattern gets bigger and more intricate. Because love can exist without a recipient alive to take it. It just keeps going."

My speech finally finished, I stood and waited, the silence echoing between us. Then Morgan's hand slowly lifted to rub the other end of my ribbon between his fingers, and I barely breathed, afraid I'd scare him off. When his lips tilted up slightly on one side, I felt myself relax, glad that I'd done that. *I'd* made him smile.

"I've never heard it that way," he said, his deep voice breaking the silence. "But it fits. It's like you and your endless hair ribbons. You never run out of them, and even though each one's a little different, they all hold up just as strong."

The moment stretched into something comfortable, a mingling of grief and hope. Something we both understood.

"Morgan..." I whispered, not entirely sure what I was going to say, but wanting him to know that he could talk to me about this kind of stuff. That he could lean on me if he needed to.

"Yeah?"

"I just want you to know that—" But then the muted jangling of keys interrupted the moment. "Shoot! Come here."

Panicked, I pulled Morgan along with me down an adjoining hallway where I yanked us both into the alcove of a drinking fountain. But I made the mistake of tapping into my Nephilim speed, and Morgan stumbled into me, definitely bruising my shoulder.

"Ow!" I hissed quietly, rubbing the spot with one hand while I shoved him deeper into the alcove with the other.

"You're the one who dragged me using super speed," Mor whisper shouted.

"Oh, shut up!" I growled.

Both of us went silent as we waited to hear the security guard's footsteps—and his jingling keys—go past. Unfortunately, we'd chosen a drinking fountain that was close to an elevator. So only a few seconds after the guard passed us, I heard him swipe his keycard, and a quiet ding rang out, a signal that the elevator was on its way up.

'Oh good Lord', I mouthed, rolling my eyes as we waited to hear the elevator arrive.

'What, not as exciting as you were hoping for?' Morgan mouthed back, smirking.

I shoved his shoulder and pouted until *finally* the elevator dinged again, announcing its arrival. We waited another few moments as we waited for the doors to close.

"Finally," I whined quietly, stepping away of the drinking fountain, "That was the longest minute and a half of my life!"

I turned to smile at Morgan but paused when I heard a strange whistling sound close by. Then something hard and cold smacked the back of my head. And the world around me faded.

TWENTY TWO

Caroline

"CARE!"

Morgan's voice echoed strangely around me, the ringing in my ears nearly drowning him out. *Wait, why are my ears ringing?* I moved, trying to get my bearings, but pain ached through the back of my head, urging me to keep still.

"What happened?" I moaned; my body pressed against a hard, cold surface. *The floor. I'm on the floor.* "But why?"

"Caroline!"

"Morgan!" I gasped, opening my eyes—I was so discombobulated that I hadn't realized that they were shut.

I could tell Morgan was standing a few feet away from me, but it took a moment before he fully came into focus. Then I realized that he wasn't standing. He was fighting someone dressed in all black and wearing a ski mask.

Morgan was strong, but whoever he was up against was fighting on defense, always moving just out of Morgan's reach. When I let out an involuntary moan, Mor's eyes flashed to me. Then, with a renewed urgency, he slammed a fist into his attacker's shoulder. I didn't have to hear the bone crack to know Mor had broken something. The attacker let out a muffled cry, clutching their arm. When they spun and ran down the hall, Morgan hesitated, and I knew he was considering going after them. But then he looked at me again.

The ringing in my ears had finally stopped, but my head was killing me, and I shut my eyes to block out the pain. *Please make it stop.*

"Care," Morgan's voice mumbled close by, heavy with worry. It took me a second to realize it, but he was crouched down beside me now, hands running over my body to search for injuries. "Where are you hurt?"

I lifted a hand to feel the back of my head where the sharp, cold pain was radiating from. My fingers came against something slick, and I flinched as I accidentally bumped the wounded spot.

"Am I bleeding?" Sure enough, my fingers were stained crimson.

"They hit you with a heavy-duty flashlight and then you hit the marble floor," Morgan growled, and I was vaguely aware of him moving around me. A few moments later, he helped me sit up and looped an arm behind my back. "Hold onto me."

Before I could ask him what he meant, he lifted me into his arms bridal style. I instinctively latched onto him, and when the ache in my head worsened with my every move, I laid it on his shoulder. Morgan carried me with ease, not burdened in the slightest by my weight. *I clearly haven't appreciated his Berserker strength nearly enough.*

"I suppose it's good that I didn't kill them—even though they deserve it," he hissed, speed walking down the hallway, a man on a mission. "Otherwise, we'd have a body to clean up right now."

"What happened?" I remembered a whistling sound, but nothing else.

"They jumped out from around the corner and hit you in the back of the head." His words came out in short, clipped grunts, and I got the sense that it was as much as he could say without yelling right now. "When you went down, I attacked them. Clearly, they lost. I think they were hoping they could knock us both out and take you. Also, I'm sorry I'm walking so fast, but I don't want to risk a second attack."

"You think there's more of them?"

He shook his head. "I doubt they were working with a partner, but I don't want to risk someone else jumping us. Or a security guard finding us."

I thought about telling him that he could put me down, but given how weak I felt, I'd fall over if I tried to stand. So instead, I held onto him. Not at all enjoying the ride. Okay, so maybe I enjoyed it a little.

Mor was silent the whole way through the building. We went down three flights of stairs, past the guard room and back outside without him saying a single word. As we made our way down the alleyway to the car, I glanced up at his face, his features more in focus than they had been when I first fell. His scowl wasn't a shock to me, I'd grown used to Morgan bearing that expression, but right now he looked angry enough to burn the world down.

If I'd learned anything about Morgan though, it was that he often felt things with much more complexity than he openly showed. So, with my magic a little slow to react thanks to my injury, I focused hard on his emotions to sus out the truth. His feelings were hard to pin down at first, but after a few moments, they sharpened. There was a ton of anger inside of him, but beneath it, there was a pit of panic. Deep, dark, and desperate.

I wrinkled my brow, confused. He couldn't be panicked about us getting caught anymore, we were already almost to the SUV. But what else could have made him so anxious and overcome with worry?

I studied him harder, wishing that I could sense the cause of people's emotions and not just the emotions themselves. If I were a Mermaid, I could just read his thoughts and *know* what was worrying him so much instead of reading into his every move. The way he held me all the way to the car, as if I were made of glass and might shatter at any moment. The way his thumbs kept rubbing my ribs and thigh where his hands held me steady in his arms. The way he kept glancing down as if to assure himself that I was still here, still alive. *Wait...is he worried about* me? No. That level of panic couldn't be for me...right?

"Careful," he whispered as he maneuvered me into the passenger seat of the car, my bum sitting sideways so I still faced him.

"I'm okay, Mor," I assured him, closing my eyes as the ache in my head began to pound a little harder, "I promise."

When he didn't respond, I looked up to find him staring at me. Not moving, just staring. His chest was rising and falling in quick succession, his eyebrows were pinched too close together as wrinkles popped out on his forehead, and his eyes were filled with emotion. The anger had dissipated inside him, and now there was only panic. And it was growing.

"Morgan..." I began, reaching out to touch his hand, hoping to ease the worry away—the worry that was beginning to feel very much like it was about me.

"You could be dead right now," he suddenly erupted, staring down at me with fear blazing in his blue-ringed eyes.

Okay, so that answers that. Clearly, I was the cause of Morgan's anxiety. So why did that make me feel good?

"But I'm not dead. I'm fine, Mor," I tried to assure him, but he wouldn't have it. Instead, he grasped my head and gently forced my chin down so he could inspect my wound.

"Are you still bleeding?" he demanded; his voice too harried, too panicked. "I can't tell with the blood all over your hair!"

"Mor, focus," I said forcefully, trying to stop his panic spiral. "I'm okay. I feel fine except for being a little dizzy, which I gather is common with head injuries." I somehow refrained from explaining that everything I knew about concussions came from watching Dwight's concussion on *The Office*...where the character threw up and ended up in the hospital. *Yeah, he's not gonna find that funny.* "Now tell me, has the bleeding stopped?"

But Morgan didn't answer. He was frozen, completely still as he leaned over me with my chin still pressed to my chest.

"Mor?" I repeated, raising my voice a little.

He didn't move.

So not ready for a giant Berserker to have a panic attack on top of me, I shoved hard at his chest—well, as hard as I could with my body still feeling weak. I realized just how bad his anxiety was when he actually stumbled back a step.

"Morgan Gareth Hohlt," I demanded, grasping his face in my hands, the faint beard along his jaw scratching my fingers, "Look at me!"

He obeyed, his grey eyes locking in on me, still wild but focused now.

"I'm okay," I insisted, saying the words slowly, "I'm not dying. You got us out. We're both okay, Mor."

"But you almost weren't!" he snarled, but I just held him tighter, not letting him tug away.

"Stop being an idiot and look at me! Am I alive?"

His eyes took in every inch of me, all the way from my head to my waist, as if assuring himself that I was still here. Slowly, his expression began to soften, and I felt his panic recede one inch at a time.

"The whole back of your head is covered in blood." He tried to reach for my head again, but I pushed at his face, keeping him at a distance.

"But am I *alive*?" I shouted. It wasn't just that I didn't want him to pass out on me if he had a panic attack. I also just wanted—*needed*—him to be okay, for this worry and anxiety to leave him alone. Because I cared. A lot. *When did that happen?*

"Barely," he growled, glaring at me.

I glared right back, unimpressed.

"Morgan, I'm okay." I made my tone gentler this time, liking the way the fear in his eyes seemed to fade a little. "I'm talking just fine, and I haven't thrown up yet—which is better than I can say for Dwight when he had a concussion—"

"Are you really comparing this to something that happened on *The Office*?"

"You're yelling," I reminded him calmly, letting my thumbs stroke his cheeks, trying to bring him back to the present.

"Am not." This time his words came out more like a pout, and I tried not to find it adorable. Newsflash: it was impossible. Morgan pouting didn't make him less attractive; it just made him more endearing. *Ugh, so annoying!*

"You are. And yes, I am comparing this to *The Office*, because the point is that I'm not throwing up and I'm not having any difficulty talking. I can see you clearly, my ears aren't ringing anymore, and I don't feel any fresh warmth on my head, which makes me suspect that I'm no longer bleeding."

"You're not."

"See? I'm going to be fine, but I need you to calm down."

He let out a loud sigh, and set his hands on my wrists, slowly lowering my arms to my lap.

"I'm sorry," he said—much quieter now—and I felt his worry loosen its grip, "I didn't mean to freak out, I just...It was alarming, seeing you bleeding on the floor like that."

"Did you happen to wipe up the blood?" I asked, only now realizing that we may have left my DNA at the scene.

"Yeah, my sweatshirt is toast now," he replied, untying the black sweatshirt from his waist that he'd apparently shed earlier. The bulk of it was extra dark with the stain of my blood.

"Thanks. I owe you a sweatshirt."

He shrugged and grasped the top of the door frame.

"Don't sweat it. I almost passed out on you, and you did pass out on me. We're even. Although if you do that again, I'm never letting you leave the house," he teased, his emotions finally making their way back down to normal.

"Whatever! Like you can contain me," I scoffed, feeling a little extra sassy for some reason.

"Have you seen you? You're not exactly much of a fighter."

"Rude. You know, if my magic worked on you like it's supposed to, I'd win every fight because I could just mess with your head a little and distract you." As if to prove the point, I tapped his temple with one finger. "I'm still not sure why my magic doesn't work on you though..."

"Shifter magic doesn't work on someone you—" Morgan stopped midsentence, and as his wide eyes locked onto mine, I felt something inside me snap.

Oh no. Did he mean what I thought he meant? Did shifter magic not work on someone you have feelings for? *Why don't I know this?* Probably because I'd spent my whole life in fear of being discovered and therefore had pretty much zero friends. *But shouldn't I have had this happen at some point in life already?*

Well...not if I'd never known anyone well enough to actually develop feelings. I'd had crushes, but they were always from afar, and dating was hard as an adult. Having a vendetta kind of put a damper on my love life. *Wait, but am I even into Morgan?* And much more importantly, could he tell??

"Doesn't work on someone you what?" I demanded, needing to know just how mortified I should be right now. *I* didn't even know if I liked Morgan. It didn't seem fair that *Morgan* should figure it out before I'd even had that conversation with myself! *Maybe this concussion will turn into amnesia, and I won't have to deal with the fallout anyway!* Yes, that could work!

"Shifter magic doesn't work on people in my position," Morgan finally replied, not quite meeting my eyes.

"If that's all it was, then why did you hesitate to tell me?" I asked, narrowing my eyes at him.

Something didn't add up. He was anxious and uncomfortable, which were classic emotions for people who were lying. Except that I wasn't sure he *was* lying. *It's more like he's leaving something out.* And unfortunately, my brain was getting fuzzier and fuzzier by the moment, making it hard for me to think straight.

"Because we don't really share that kind of information with people outside of the Sleuth," Mor shrugged, finally meeting my gaze. "It's a private thing."

Again, there was no lie in his words, but there was something incomplete about the explanation.

I opened my mouth to insist that he explain it to me—maybe later once I was sober—when he took a step closer. His body was so big that he filled up the entire doorway, blocking out the night except for the streetlights. Their light snuck into our corner of darkness, illuminating his face enough for me to notice the earnest look in his eyes and the stubborn set of his strong jaw. *Gosh, he smells delicious.* What was that? Bodywash? Aftershave? It was like manliness in a bottle, with a dash of sweetness just strong enough to make me curious if he tasted the way he smelled. *What?? No! Bad Caroline!*

"What is going on?" I breathed, confused by the unruliness of my own thoughts.

"Care," Morgan whispered, either not hearing my embarrassing question, or not bothered by it, "I know you want me to answer all your questions right this instant, but I can't. Being in my position means that there's certain things I can't share right now, no matter how much I want to. So, for now, please just let me take you home." He paused, studying me intently. "Because for a minute there, I genuinely thought that I'd lost you, and..." He shook his head. "I just want you to be safe, Care. Please, let's go home."

He clearly hadn't noticed my moment of distraction if he seriously thought I was still focused on his explanation of my magic's limitations. *Yeah, like I care about the rules of magic when I've got my own dark-haired hero leaning over me.* Did I mention that he whispered my name and 'please' in the same sentence? Can we say *swoon*?

I had to give him credit though, he was using his words. I just wished they were a little less reasonable—and that there were less of them, because my brain was starting to have difficulty processing.

"You can't share right now?" I clarified, latching onto the fact that he hadn't said 'never', that someday he would explain whatever it was he was holding back. He nodded, and even though it was a vague answer that still left me curious, I gave in.

"Fine, I'll leave it alone," I sighed, attempting to move myself fully into my seat. However, I grossly overestimated my current coordination and almost fell over. *Because I'm graceful like that.*

"Easy," Morgan chuckled, lifting me again to set me facing forward in the seat. Once I was steady, he even buckled my seatbelt for me. Who knew the man could be such a caretaker? *Ten points to Gryffindor for sexy attentiveness.*

"But I'm warning you, Mor," I mumbled, closing my eyes, "I'm going to want answers eventually. I'm a patient woman when I want to be, but I can only do it for so long." Then, to emphasize my words, I pointed a finger in his face. Oops, nope, in his nose.

"Caroline," he complained, but I could hear that he was smiling.

Sure enough, when I opened my eyes again, he was smiling ruefully down at me and shaking his head. Well, I might have been ogling him pretty hard tonight, but there was no danger of him feeling any attraction for me now that I'd picked his nose for him. *Nice job, Care.*

"Sorry, I didn't mean to do that."

"No? Pray tell, what part of me were you aiming for?"

"Your mouth, to shut you up," I complained, pushing him away so I could close the door. But instead, he caught it, holding it open and smirking like the devil.

"Care," he teased; his eyes filled with too much amusement. "If shutting me up was the goal, there are *much* pleasanter ways to do it."

Then, before I could reply, he shut the door in *my* face!

"I hate you." I grumbled, leaning my head back as he climbed into the driver's seat. "Ow! Who hit me?"

"Uh oh, I think the memory loss is starting," Morgan said, chuckling as he grabbed something from the back seat. He then leaned toward me, wadding up a T shirt behind my neck to keep my head away from the seat.

"Leave me alone. I'm groggy and in pain."

"Care," he paused, voice tight with worry, "Should I take you to the hospital? I was going to have a doctor come to the house, but—"

"A doctor is fine, Mor," I assured him, patting his thigh. "But I would like a burger."

Morgan froze, staring down at my hand—which was still on his thigh for some reason—but after a moment, his gaze returned to my face, eyes filled with concern. But he shouldn't have been concerned anymore. Because I was already starting to forget about my pain thanks to the distraction of his muscle beneath my palm. *I should touch him like this more often.*

"You sure you're feeling lucid?" he asked, reaching out to touch my forehead, like that would tell him anything.

"Yes, now please take me to the burgers. Frank's is open twenty-four seven, so you have no excuses!"

"Care, I need to get you home."

"No, you need to feed the monster," I said, giving him an accusatory look. "In fact, if you don't feed this monster ASAP, she's going to eat you and that won't be fun for either of us because I'm pretty sure there are squirrels who'd be a better meal than you."

"Excuse me?" he demanded incredulously.

"You don't have any fat," I explained, rubbing his thigh with my thumb. "You're all muscle, and a good steak has some fat on it. But burgers, on the other hand, are delicious! So please let's go! It's not far and I'll even stay in the car. I promise." To prove myself as the well-behaved woman we both knew I wasn't, I grinned at him. It must not have been convincing though, because he just shook his head, turned the car on and pulled onto the street.

"Fine, but if I get ill because of whatever chemicals they put in the food, you're taking care of me."

I smiled. "Deal. Frank's is over by the dry cleaners."

We drove in silence at first, but as the moments passed, the quiet slowly became less peaceful and more tense. Not sure what was wrong, I reached out with my magic again to get a sense of his feelings. We were both safe, and I wasn't gravely injured. But still, I felt his panic resurfacing. "Hey, I'm okay, Mor," I whispered, squeezing his thigh, "I can tell that you're still worried, but you don't need to be. You'll feed me, we'll go home, the doc will check me out and I'll be fine."

"We don't know that, Care," he growled, his anger coming back in full force. "You could have bleeding on the brain. There could be permanent damage like memory loss..." He squeezed the steering wheel so tight that his knuckles turned white. "I should've killed that guy when I had the chance! I thought if I kept him alive, we could get answers, but it wasn't worth it. No one should get away with hurting you like that!"

"Hey, it's okay," I insisted, sliding my hand down to rub his knee.

"No, it's not! The attacker got away, we're no closer to getting answers, and you were injured. None of it is okay!"

I studied him as the passing streetlights painted yellow streaks across his face, noted the way his eyes zeroed in on the road ahead. The way his shoulders hunched up toward his ears and his muscles clenched beneath my hand on his knee.

This isn't about me. Sure, he might've been genuinely worried to lose me, but he was also drowning in responsibility. Completely overwhelmed with the pressure to not only provide as a leader, but to prove everyone wrong about 'The Chief.' Every fight he didn't win was a failure in his eyes, proof that they were right about him. The entire region thought of him as a man who killed anyone who got in his way, and yet here he was, taking a very loopy, injured girl to get burgers. As far as I was concerned, he had nothing to prove.

"They're wrong, you know," I whispered.

When Morgan removed my hand from his leg, I thought maybe he'd had enough of me poking my way into his business. But then he slid his hand around mine, our palms together, and rested them against his thigh. *Pretty sure this is a milestone moment.* What were the chances that he'd let me take a picture of it?

"Who's wrong?" he asked, parking the car along the street next to Frank's.

I smiled at the humoring tone in his voice, like he was talking to someone innocent and precious, someone too inebriated to be reasonable. *Which is ridiculous, because I feel perfectly in control right now.* In fact, I was seriously considering climbing over the annoying center console and into his lap to take a picture and document this new moment in our friendship...just as soon as I figured out how to unbuckle myself.

"Care? Who's wrong?" Mor asked again, smirking at my very distracted behavior.

"Everyone who doubts you." At these words, his expression shifted from humored to tired, like this topic drained him just by mentioning it. "I'm serious, Mor. I think the real reason people are scared of you is because most people are like cows."

Morgan stared at me like I'd grown another head. "Come again?"

"Listen to me."

"I am," he smiled. "Go ahead, explain the cows."

"Okay, so a lot of people are like cows. They don't think about where they're going, they just follow the herd. If someone walks into a crowd and that crowd starts clapping, most people will join in even if they don't understand what's happening. But then there are people like you and me." I paused, trying to remind myself where I was going with this analogy. I wasn't so loopy that I'd forgotten what I was going to say, but the way Morgan rubbed the back of my hand with his thumb was really throwing me off.

"People like you and me?" Mor prompted, realizing I'd lost my train of thought.

"Right, yeah," I shook my head, smiling sheepishly. "People like us—people who question things. You don't just start clapping because everyone in the room is clapping—you want to know what you're clapping for. You see things most don't, and that makes you a great leader, but it also means that the people you lead are often kinda stupid. Like cows. So don't take it personally when they doubt you, because they're just doing what cows do: going where they're herded."

Morgan was silent for a few moments, and I became quickly distracted by his touch again, because now *both* his hands were holding mine, rubbing my skin like I was precious. But I might as well have been kindling for how my whole being caught fire.

"I was wrong about you, Caroline," he whispered, snapping me out of my head dive. "Maybe I'll keep you afterall."

TWENTY THREE

Morgan

I SIGHED AS I SETTLED INTO THE CHAIR behind my desk, trying to untangle all the emotions that were still raging inside me after last night.

Immediately after declaring that I wanted to 'keep' Caroline, I'd fled into the burger place, both from her and from the confusing feelings that she'd invoked in me.

Frank had been very suspicious of my identity and when I said I was there to get food for Caroline—he was convinced I was a stalker. No sir, just a kidnapper.

To convince Frank that I wasn't a psycho, I brought him outside and rolled down the window so he could talk to Caroline. He immediately noticed her very loopy behavior and we sold him a story about her banging her head when she'd fallen on the street. It wasn't far from the truth and Frank was appeased. And even though the detour ended up being much longer than I'd planned, I had to admit that I was happy Caroline had some people in her life who cared about her safety.

We ate in the car at Care's insistence, and I had to grudgingly admit that the food was good. So good in fact, that I'd ordered it in from DoorDash this morning. I made sure to dispose of the bag in the outside trash can though. I wasn't about to let anyone know just how much sway Caroline—or Frank's food—had over me.

Caroline had fallen asleep on the way home from Frank's and I hadn't wanted to wake her, instead carrying her up to her room. It wasn't until I'd laid her in her bed that she woke up, mumbling, "Would it be presumptuous of me to propose to your biceps?" She then fell back asleep before I could manage to shut my gaping mouth and respond. Which was for the best, because at the time, with her looking so peaceful and innocent, I probably would have said something stupid. Like 'I'm your mate and I think maybe I'm not as angry about it as I thought I was.' Which would've been a terrible mistake. If I ever did tell Caroline that we were mated, I definitely wouldn't say it like that. Although doing it while she wasn't totally coherent wasn't a bad idea. That way she couldn't attack me.

The doctor I'd called arrived twenty minutes after we did. Caroline woke up for the exam but fell asleep soon after the doctor gave her pain medication. He assured me that while she had a concussion, and she would have some tenderness for a few weeks, there was no serious damage. I, however, wasn't convinced. Which was why I kept checking on her every half hour.

"Thank God, she hasn't caught me yet," I said to myself as I turned on my computer.

Every time I'd gone upstairs to see how she was doing, she'd been asleep and therefore blissfully unaware of my Edward Cullen level stalking. Except that Edward was the hero in *Twilight*...so maybe this variety of stalking was okay? I shook my head. Regardless, I didn't want to find out Caroline's opinion.

I could sense her now, her peaceful emotions assuring me that she was still asleep—Caroline was never that calm when she was awake. Daisy Mae had barely left her side since we came home, and I was comforted in knowing that someone was there watching her. Someone who was *allowed* to be watching her. Because as her secret mate who didn't want to be mates, I had no right to worry at her bedside.

So instead, I worried in my office.

I glanced through my emails, skimming documents sent to me by the council for next week's meeting. Truthfully though, I didn't really see any of them. No matter how hard I tried to focus, my thoughts were upstairs. With Caroline.

Which was both incredibly annoying after how hard I'd fought against my innate desire to know her, and terrifying because as I'd learned, loving meant losing. I cringed as the image of Caroline hitting the marble floor flitted through my mind for the hundredth time. Her blood smearing the ground, her eyes sliding shut, the sound of her pained groan echoing in my ears. I hadn't felt my heart drop out of my chest like that in four years, and I never wanted to feel it again. *But it's Caroline we're talking about.* She was absolutely going to put herself in dangerous positions again. *This is just the beginning.*

And after Gen, I certainly didn't want a mate that I was always afraid of losing.

Turning in my chair, I stared at the photo behind my desk. Genevieve smiled from the safety of my arms in the photo, but that safety hadn't been enough. I hadn't been able to protect her from cancer. Hadn't been able to keep her, no matter how hard I tried.

I remembered seeing the mate bond in Gen's eyes that first day at the high school. I'd been so terrified to see the bond in a stranger, to look at someone I didn't know, and be fully aware that this was the person God wanted me to be with. It made it all the more terrifying to talk to her. But on our first date, she asked me about the blue rings around my irises, and because I had no motivation other than embarrassment to lie to her, I explained the bond. It had been strange at first, to know that someone was 'the one' without really knowing them first. But within three dates, we were inseparable. By the time we got married, I'd realized just how powerful the bond was—not the magic itself, but the love we built out of it.

Which meant that I knew the potential that Caroline and I had together. I'd experienced true love before, and if given time, effort, and tender cultivation, that's what we could build...But I also knew what it felt like when that all came tumbling down. *I can't go through that again.* So instead, I would swallow my emotions, resist the bond, and never speak of it so she'd never feel pressured to choose me. But the one thing I couldn't do—wouldn't do—was lose my mate.

And if I was being honest, it wasn't even just because I'd already lost one mate. Because when I thought of Caroline—of her stubbornness, her fire, her cleverness, her whit, her loyalty, and bravery...I realized that something more important than the mate bond had developed between us: respect. I respected Caroline and her choices, and I even enjoyed her company sometimes. *Emphasis on sometimes.* Other times she just annoyed the crap out of me. But still. We'd made big progress in a short amount of time.

"Knockity knock."

I jumped at the sound of Logan's voice—not having heard him come in—and spun so quickly in my desk chair that I fell out of it. Yep. I, a grown man, fell *out* of my chair and onto my backside. *Perfect! Just do more stuff like that and Care won't want you anyway.* Mate bond problem solved.

"What did I catch you doing that you're not supposed to be doing?" Logan laughed, doubling over as he shut the door behind him. "And can you please do an encore of that performance so I can get it on video? It'll do wonders for your reputation."

And it probably would. The murderous Berserker Chief who fell out of his desk chair would definitely loose street cred as a bad guy.

"Shut up," I grumbled, pulling myself up off the floor like the schmuck I was. "You just startled me."

"Yeah, but the question is what were you doing that you were scared of being caught?" he teased, finally ceasing his laughter long enough to sit on the couch. With a cocky smile on his face, he folded his arms behind his head and raised an eyebrow. Silently daring me to lie to him.

"Keep looking at me like that and I'm going to rip your stupid blonde eyebrows from your stupid baby Chris Hemsworth face," I threatened, sitting back in my chair with a petulant pout. He was right. I had been doing something I didn't want anyone to know I was doing. Claiming Caroline as my mate. At least in the safety of my head.

"You think I look like Chris Hemsworth? Maybe I should dress up like Thor for Halloween this year. I might be able to double my quota of women's phone numbers from last year."

"I said you look like a *baby* Chris Hemsworth," I reminded him, though I wasn't genuinely concerned about his ego. Logan acted like a playboy sometimes, but he was all smoke and mirrors. "And why would you want to get more girls' phone numbers? You never call them back anyway."

Logan fidget on the couch, suddenly uncomfortable. *Good. It's about time someone besides me was uncomfortable talking about women.*

"What, no snarky comebacks now?" I teased, smirking because I for once had the upper hand.

"No secrets about a certain redhead you want to share?" Logan retorted.

I shut my mouth. So much for the upper hand.

"I don't have any secrets," I insisted, turning my eyes back to the computer screen where I stared blindly at my emails.

"Morgan Gareth Hohlt," he complained, and even though I wasn't looking at him—I was going to look at those emails until my eyes crossed—I could still feel him watching me, "I am your best friend and your oldest friend. In all these years, we've never had secrets. You know that I can't do my own laundry to save my life, which is why you always do mine along with yours. You know that I love it when my mom babies me and that my favorite character on *The Good Place* is Eleanor because every time she has a breakthrough, it makes me cry. And you know that I never call the women who give me their numbers because they secretly terrify me just as much as they intrigue me." Through his speech I remained silent, knowing where this was going and knowing that he was right. Dang best friends. "And I know when you're lying to me. So, tell me the truth Morgan. What's going on with you?"

I considered telling him that it was Chief business that had me so strung out, but telling him an outright lie just felt wrong. He was right, we'd never lied to each other. The benefit of Logan not being my brother was that I didn't have to be a positive influence on him or worry about his decisions. I didn't feel responsible for him in the same way. Which meant that I was often more straightforward with him. Until Caroline...

"I just...I'm a little worried about her," I said, shoving the words out one syllable at a time.

"Caroline?" I nodded. Logan was quiet for a moment, and I finally turned to gauge his reaction.

His blue eyes were scrutinizing me in a way that was more curious than critical, but I still squirmed under the weight of it. I wasn't even sure what my feelings toward Caroline were, and I certainly didn't want Logan to know the extent of them. Especially after last night.

All of Care's blatant flirting and familiar touches on my leg had completely messed with my mind. In fact, it was her fault that I was no longer at war with the mate bond and instead holding a truce. If she hadn't looked at me with so much appreciation, and if I hadn't been able to sense her fierce attraction, it would have been easier to pretend that our connection didn't exist. But all my lies about not feeling anything for her had shattered the moment she stroked my knee and told me that everyone who doubted me was wrong. If I thought there was a shot in hell that she'd say yes, I would've proposed right there in the car. *Stupid mate bond.*

"How is she?" Logan asked, breaking me out of my traitorous memories.

"Fine. The doctor said she has a concussion and should take it easy for a few days, but he couldn't find any lasting damage."

"Hm," Logan hummed, "How's she feeling this morning?"

I instinctively pulled the information from the mate bond, Care's emotions always right there with me in the back of my mind. She was still content, peaceful and calm, though there was a little joy in there too, and I wondered what she was dreaming about. *Hope she's dreaming about you?* My mind taunted me. *No...yes.*

"She's doing fine," I said aloud, calmly deleting a spam email and silently telling myself to *stop thinking confusingly romantic-ish things about Caroline.* "Sleeping so far this morning."

"How can you be sure she hasn't woken up since you last checked on her?"

"Because I'd sense if she—"

I froze, eyes wide and heart suddenly pounding. Slowly, centimeter by centimeter, I looked over at Logan. Who was staring at me with a big dopey grin on his face.

"I mean—"

"You're mated??" he exclaimed, and I waved a hand at him to lower his voice. He waved me off. "Dude, this room is soundproof."

"I don't care! I can't let anyone hear this."

"Then why are you shouting?" he whispered dramatically, again quirking an eyebrow at me. Mental note: wax them off in his sleep tonight. *Let's just see how many phone numbers he gets with no eyebrows.*

"I'm not shouting," I grumbled, wiping a hand across my face, "And if you keep looking at me like that, I'm going to break your nose *and* rip off your eyebrows."

"You and the eyebrows," Logan scoffed, "And I am not giving you any kind of look."

"And I don't yell." I rolled my eyes, unimpressed.

"Alright fine, I'm giving you a look. But it's just because I'm happy for you!"

At first, I wasn't sure what to say, so I just sat there, staring at him. Deadpan.

"Happy?" I demanded incredulously once the shock wore off. "Have you *seen* me and Caroline? We're oil and water, matches and gasoline, peanut butter and anchovies. We do *not* go together."

"Uh, the chemistry in the room says differently," Logan argued, smirking at me. "It practically explodes every time you two are together."

"It does not—"

"It does, and what I don't get is why you're so unhappy about it."

When he crossed his arms, scrutinizing me, I sighed. Letting my shoulders drop and the mask I'd been failing to seal over my emotions fade away.

"I don't want a second mate," I explained, the quietness of my voice giving away the weight of my words. "I didn't want to lose my first."

"So, this is about Gen?"

"It's about not having to grieve two mates in one lifetime."

"Ah." That was it. Just one little sigh of understanding and then Logan went silent.

I didn't like this silence. It was too thoughtful, too empathetic. Logan had known me for twenty years. He'd seen me as a young kid that all the other students either feared or pitied, then as an adult who was learning how to live outside of people's expectations. He saw me fall in love, saw me become the most feared Berserker Chief in the history of the western region of the U.S....and he saw me grieve when I lost Gen. He knew what I was trying to avoid by resisting the mate bond with Caroline. The question was whether or not he thought it was a stupid idea.

"Can't grieve something if you never have it," he nodded finally, "But you can't celebrate it either."

Somehow, I knew he'd make that argument.

"Yeah, yeah. If you keep out pain, you keep out love. I get it." Not moved by the sentiment, I went back to deleting emails.

"And what of Caroline? Even if you resist her forever, the mate bond won't go away. She'll never be mated to anyone but you, and no matter who she marries, it's your emotions she'll have in her head."

"With enough distance and time—"

"You know just as well as I do that it's an old wives' tale that mate bonds can fade," Logan argued, serious now. "You and Caroline are bound to each other. Shifters with mate bonds don't marry the wrong people when they've already met their mate. It would be suicide. You'd both be miserable forever."

He was right. And I hated it.

"I wish she'd married someone before she met me. Then we'd never know we were mates." The mate bond only manifested between unmarried people. So, if Caroline had married someone else before she met me, then our mate bond wouldn't have started. I wouldn't have seen the blue in her eyes, and she wouldn't have seen it in mine. We wouldn't sense each other's emotions...*But everything else would still be there.* The attraction. The curiosity. The protectiveness. It was why Berserkers almost never married without being mates. Because it was a miserable life to marry someone, always wondering who 'the one' really was. *I'd never wish that on either of us.*

"No, you don't," Logan said, his words free of judgement.

I sighed, pushing away from the computer. "No, I don't."

"So, Caroline's your mate, whether you like it or not, and if you don't let yourself fall in love with her, you're both doomed to miserable, single lives where you're always secretly into each other, but unwillingly to let yourselves be happy."

"Why are you and I friends?" I complained, glaring at him.

"Because I always tell you the truth," he said with a grin.

"Now that, I can agree with."

Apparently sensing that I was at my limit for pushing the bounds of my emotional decision making for the moment, Logan slid his arms back behind his head, putting on the charmer attitude for my benefit.

"Alright, let me cheer you up with something funny," he said.

"Is this actually going to be something funny, or are you just going to tell me another story about your mom's book club?"

"Hey, those ladies are a good time!"

He defended them so genuinely that I actually chuckled.

"Alright, tell me whatever it is that'll lighten my mood."

"So, you know how we love a good bet around here," he smiled, bouncing with amusement. Meanwhile, I was already groaning. It was never good when my family started making bets. Because half the time I was the one they were betting about. "Mike and Clint and I have all taken bets to see how long until you and Caroline kiss. Don't worry though, only Grey and I betted on how long before you get married. We didn't even mention it to your brothers. Figured their tactless ribbing would just slow the process, and I've got a hundred bucks on September."

"Is that seriously supposed to cheer me up?" I mumbled, slamming my forehead against the desk. "Ow."

"Well, it should cheer you up! Because if I win the bet, I'll split the profit with you."

"You're a regular philanthropist, Logan. Seriously, Bill Gates has nothing on you."

"You know you love me," he teased, but then went silent as a knock resounded through the door office door.

Oh no. I'd been so preoccupied with Logan's realization that Caroline and I were mates that I hadn't been paying as close attention to her emotions. Which I could now tell were just outside the office doors.

"It's her. Don't say a word," I threatened, lifting my head and pointing a finger at him.

He gave me a botched attempt at a Boys Scout salute, then opened the door with a smile. "Hi Caroline." Care stepped into the room, her demeanor just a tad timid. *Odd.* "How are you feeling?"

Care glanced first at Logan and then at me, still seeming slightly unsure. She was dressed in different clothes now, a pair of basketball shorts and a T shirt that was about four sizes too big. It hung to her knees, and a pair of fluffy socks clung to her calves, some fuzzy pink slippers on her feet. Her face was free of makeup today, all fresh and freckled and sweet, her hair up in a messy bun that revealed the elegant curve of her neck. Triggered by the sight, my mind teased me with daydreams of her lying next to me on the couch, my fingers trailing circles along her neck and toying with the hairs that fell out of her updo.

Immediately, I flashed my eyes up back to hers, trying to smother my flare of attraction. Knowing that if I didn't kill it now, she'd sense it. *Yeah, good luck finding an aspect of her that* doesn't *have you daydreaming like a sap.* Her too big shirt made me want to see her in *my* shirt, her fuzzy socks made me want to have a contest to see which of us could slide down the hall the fastest—which would of course lead to us falling over in a tangled heap. Which had me thinking about her neck again...and touching it...*Crap.*

"I'm doing good," she said answering Logan's question, her eyes focused on me. Reading me. "Why wouldn't I be?" When Logan gave her a curious look at her obvious defensiveness, she sighed, stepping further into the room. "Sorry, I just don't like—"

"Feeling weak?" I supplied, shooting her a teasing smirk that I hoped would make her smile. "Yeah, I noticed."

As planned, she tilted her head, a sassy look in her eyes and a rueful smile on her pink lips. Alright, I had to admit that seeing the expression felt pretty good. *Really good.*

"Don't listen to him," Logan teased, slinging an arm around Care's shoulder, and squeezing her in a side hug. I had to bite my lip to keep myself from insisting that he be gentle with her. *She's not glass, Hohlt. Calm down.* "He's just grouchy this morning. It's completely understandable that you're a little defensive about being hurt. We'll do our best not to coddle you."

"I think you speak for everyone but Morgan when you say that," she scoffed.

"I do *not* coddle you," I argued, trying not to think about the fourteen times I'd checked on her in the last seven hours. Those didn't count. "I just can't have you getting any lasting injuries on my watch. You might sue me."

"Don't give me any ideas." Her smile tugged up further, challenging me.

"Like you need my help coming up with ways to mess with me." It was just a miracle she hadn't yet figured out how much her very presence messed with me. How much it unraveled me to see her all small and innocent looking right now, making me want to wrap her up and protect her. *She'd be lethal if she figured that out.*

"Well, I'll give you two a moment," Logan said, winking at me before he gave Caroline one last hug. "See you later Care Bear. Don't yell at him too much or you'll worsen your concussion."

Caroline smacked his arm playfully and he left the room with a grin. Then it was just me and Care. She stood in front of my desk, arms dangling at her sides and fingers playing with the hem of her shirt.

"So..." she hummed, looking vastly uncomfortable. "Is it just me, or does it smell like burgers in here?"

I stiffened, willing my guilt to disappear so she wouldn't feel it. I'd almost prefer for her to sense my attraction instead. Being attracted to her wouldn't make her mad, but if she found out I liked Frank's after I'd given her a bad time about her junk food? She'd never let me live it down.

"I'm afraid I'm not familiar enough with the smell of poisonous foods to really say," I shrugged, hoping I looked successfully unconcerned. "What is it that brought you down here, Care? You seem like you have something on your mind."

At first, I thought she might question me further about the food. Her eyes homed in on me, a wrinkle forming between her brows.

"How are you doing today?" she asked instead, stepping forward to take a pencil from the cup on my desk, and rotating it in her hands as she was prone to do.

"I'm fine, why?" I knew perfectly well why she was asking—I remembered with perfect clarity how I'd panicked last night. I was just determined to be obtuse about it.

"It's just that..." she paused, her scrutiny softening to concern. "You were pretty panicked last night."

Determined to feign ignorance, I shrugged and turned my gaze to my computer screen, probably deleting important emails—I'd dig them out of the trash file later.

"I'm fine," I lied.

Almost before I finished getting the words out, small fingers covered my wrist, and I went perfectly still. Despite my every intention to resist her, every molecule in my body and ounce of dopamine in my brain sung to have her touch me so willingly, so gently. Once again, she was treating me like I was soft. *Me.*

"Morgan, you don't have to pretend with me," she whispered, and I was held prisoner by her stubborn green eyes. "Last night was a big deal. Head injuries bleed a lot, and I was clearly getting a little loopy. It was very possible that my concussion could have been something much worse. I don't think you overreacted or that your panic was unreasonable. Especially..." she hesitated, then steeled herself to continue, "Especially given what you've been through. I can only imagine how sensitive you'd be to loss after losing so much. Even if that loss is someone like me who probably gives you five new grey hairs a day."

I couldn't help it; I smiled.

"Ten," I corrected, part of me wanting to lean into the softness of the moment, but the other part terrified of what might happen if I did.

She chuckled and removed her hand from my wrist, and I immediately missed the contact. 'Come back', I wanted to beg. But I held the words in, knowing that giving into Caroline wouldn't be something I could do in small bits. No, this girl would swallow me whole. And I'd let her.

Yet even though I wasn't willing to give into the mate bond like a sliver of me wanted to, I also wasn't willing to let her doubt me. Not when I recalled that night in the living room when she was attacked for the first time. 'We both value each other's lives more than we've led the other to believe,' she'd said. I never wanted her to feel that way again. To wonder if I had any attachment to her. *Because I do Caroline.* Big time.

"Care?" I said as she sat in one of the armchairs.

"Hm?"

"I wasn't just worried about you," I admitted, holding her surprised gaze. "I was terrified. When I saw you hit the floor, I wasn't sure if you were even alive, and then when you started bleeding...I panicked. You drive me nuts, and my life was a lot quieter before you." At that she laughed, and I found myself smiling—really smiling. "But I'm getting kind of fond of the way it is now...The thought that you might not make it out alive last night, it broke me. Because although we may not always get along, you're worming your way in around here, and the world would be just a little too peaceful without you making trouble in it."

There, I'd admitted that the idea of her death upset me, while also establishing that she needed to remain in the world—but not necessarily mine. *Nicely done, Hohlt.* Now if only *I* believed there was nothing more to it.

"Thanks, Mor," Care smiled, and I sensed her appreciation, the way my words sank in and made her feel all the sentimental things she normally never felt in my presence. "Okay, now that we got the mushy stuff over with, let's talk about my plan."

"Oh no."

"Oh, come on!" she complained as I sunk back into my chair. "This is a good plan."

"Does it involve you leaving the house?"

She didn't reply, simply giving me a puppy dog look that I'm ashamed to say almost worked. Almost.

"Then no." I shook my head, standing from the chair, ready to die on this hill. I almost lost her last night. I wasn't risking her a second time.

"Morgan, stop being a butthead and just listen for a second," she begged, blocking my path as I headed for the door.

"What did we say about choosing your words?"

She smirked. "I did choose them. Very carefully. Remember five minutes ago when you said that you don't coddle me?"

I sighed, already annoyed at myself and my weak will. "Fine, you have one minute."

"Oh, that's plenty of time," she said, waving her hand. "Look, I know we got caught last night, which isn't great, but the good thing is that now we know we're right! The culprit is sneaking in at night, and now they'll be expecting us!"

"I'm not sure what part of that is supposed to be good," I complained, crossing my arms.

Caroline shook her head, grabbing hold of my biceps as she continued to excitedly explain herself. I had half a mind to remind her of her proposal of marriage to them last night, just to see if I could make her blush. But she spoke before I could get another word out.

"Listen, Bear Man. The point is that the bad guy is now expecting us to show up at night to try and catch him again, which means that we can almost guarantee they'll be there again at night. So, all we have to do is stakeout the place—no, Morgan, listen," she begged as I began to shake my head. "Come on! We won't even leave the car this time! We'll just watch to see what kind of car the person is driving, what entrance they use—maybe we can even follow them and get a lead on who they are. But that's it! And you know what? Even though I'm willing to bet that I could get a decent way away from you before the Witch binding stopped me, I'm willingly swearing that I won't leave the vehicle this time."

I scowled, unmoved.

"Not even to pee," she added.

My scowl deepened.

"You can even handcuff me to the door."

I sighed and rolled my neck, wondering, if I had a chance to go back to a life pre-Caroline—a peaceful, quiet, life as the beast everyone avoided—would I do it? *No*. I was too addicted to the constant craziness that followed my mate like a shadow. *Pathetic.*

"I can't handcuff you to the door," I said, already regretting the words, "Just in case someone attacks us there. But I will cuff you to me—"

"Thank you!" she squealed, though she immediately grimaced. "Oh! Squealing is not pleasant when you have a concussion."

"No, I'd imagine not."

"Shut up, you grumpy old man."

I raised an eyebrow.

"I mean, thank you, you beautiful, wonderful grumpy old man," she winked.

Oh Lord. *What have I done?*

TWENTY FOUR

Caroline

Morgan may have ended up agreeing to my request for another stakeout, but he also insisted that I spend one full day resting first. He might as well have tortured me.

Especially because according to the doctor, I wasn't supposed to watch TV or use a computer until I was fully recovered. And according to Morgan, whatever I did, I had to be laying down. So, between all the rules and Morgan's motley crew not leaving me alone for more than five minutes, my options were severely limited.

Fortunately—or unfortunately, depending on who you ask—Mike, Clint, and Logan had my entertainment covered. They pulled out a giant stack of old boardgames, ordered me to lie down on the couch, and then made us play every single game. We played Life, Sorry, Uno, Scrabble and pretty much every other game you can imagine. Although, the fun was kind of sucked out of it for me when the guys insisted on moving my game pieces for me so I wouldn't have to 'get up'—AKA, lean forward. I swear I would've killed them if I didn't still have a headache.

But since me remaining reclined for the entire day was one of Morgan's stipulations, I grudgingly allowed the three—surprisingly diligent—babysitters to move my game pieces and hand me cards from the draw pile. Honestly, it was more like I was watching them play games than actually participating.

"You owe me for making me go through that yesterday," I whined, glaring over at Morgan, who sat in the driver's seat of his SUV.

"Hey, I let you bring double the snacks this time, and I even stopped at that gas station so you could get more toxic goodies," he reminded me, pointing a carrot stick in my face.

I scowled at the vegetable, minorly offended that he brought such a thing on a stakeout.

"Have you never seen a movie?" I complained from the passenger seat. "You're supposed to eat donuts and chips and drink warm drinks. No one eats carrots at a stakeout."

"I'm eating them," he argued, and I could tell by the set of his mouth that he was only arguing to rile me. It was working.

"Yes, but we've already established that something is wrong with you since you haven't seen *The Office*."

"I've seen scenes."

"So not the same thing!" I exclaimed, using my hands to help explain the level of offense I was feeling—it was big, let me tell you. "You can't just see memes of *The Office* and think you understand it. You have to experience it from start to finish. Let me introduce you to it! We'll start with the first two seasons—because the first season isn't the best and you have to at least experience season two before you can make an opinion. Although, honestly, I think you're going to love it. We'll probably make it to season nine in three months."

"Caroline, I'll let you force me into binging whatever shows you want if you stop moving that arm," Mor complained, glaring at our wrists. Which were conjoined by a pair of zip ties.

"You will regret those words," I promised with a smirk. "Were the zip ties really necessary though?"

"Is watching two whole seasons of a comedy show necessary?"

"Yes! Because the first season is super short—six episodes—and not super great, but you need to see it to establish some of the dynamics. The second season, now that's gold!"

Morgan chomped on another carrot, watching me. The streetlight ahead of us illuminated him just enough that I could make out his features—and see the boredom in his expression.

"You're too attached to this show."

"No," I argued, grabbing a container from my snack bag, "You're too attached to the word no—especially when used in my direction."

"You make it more fun to say no than to say yes. Your reactions, your fault," he smirked, then scrutinized the tin of chips in my hand. "Did you really bring Pringles again?"

"What's your beef with Pringles? They're a staple snack food in any American, chemically processed diet."

"Exactly. They're terrible for you. They—along with everything else in your snack bags—deteriorate your quality of life."

"Yeah, but so do you, and I'm still here, aren't I?"

He rolled his eyes, unable to hold back the short chuckle that escaped him like a scoff. But I wasn't fooled. *I'm breaking you down, Morgan Hohlt. One well-placed one-liner at a time.* And here my eighth-grade teacher Mr. Phillips had said that my snarky attitude would never get me anywhere in life. *Look at me now, Mr. Phillips.*

"Touché..." Morgan nodded, pausing to study me. "What's your last name?"

"Is that your second question?" I retorted, referring to the two questions we'd promised to answer for each other. So far, I'd used both of mine, but he'd only used one.

I had asked him about his blue ringed eyes—something I still wasn't totally convinced he'd been fully honest about. However, since the other night when he said that there were certain things he couldn't tell me 'right now', I decided to give him a little more time before I interrogated him again. I'd also asked him about his deceased wife, which he'd seemed much more willing to tell me about than I'd anticipated. Morgan had only used one question to ask about my family, leaving him with one question left.

"No, I'm not wasting that on a name."

"Then I'm not saying."

"Please?" he asked, batting his eyes like a little girl. I couldn't stop myself from laughing, wishing I'd been fast enough to get his look on camera.

"Is that the expression you used on your friend's sister before she told you it was too complicated to keep dating in secret?" I teased, referring to the story Mr. Wallace had told me about Morgan's 'first love'. Whom he'd written love letters to, confessing his feelings. It sounded like the romance of the century. Until she dumped him because it was too stressful. I started snickering just thinking about it—and more importantly, how embarrassed Morgan had been when Mr. Wallace told it.

"Ha ha," he said dryly, but I saw the glimmer of amusement in his eyes—sensed it leaking out of him against his will. "Very funny."

"Tell you what, this is boring waiting here with nothing to do, and I'm always down for a good story. So, I'll tell you my full name and it won't count as your second question *if* you answer one more question of mine."

He stared at me for a moment, considering. But ultimately, he shook his head. "Not worth it."

"Oh, come on! You know you want answers," I taunted, waving a chip in front of his face.

He batted it away. Not one to waste snack food—or any food—I picked it up off the floor and ate it anyway. To his credit, Mor didn't seem fazed by this.

"Tell me the question first, then I'll decide if I want to make the deal," he bargained, eating another carrot. Ew.

"If I tell you, you'll say no."

And he would. I'd been wanting to ask him this particular question for a while now. Initially, I hadn't asked because I wasn't sure how true the rumors about him were. But the more I got to know him, the more convinced I'd become that the 'Mr. Hohlt' in the news was *not* the real Morgan. And now, knowing him like I did, I felt like this one question—this one story—was the missing piece in Morgan's puzzle. A puzzle that I *desperately* needed to solve. Because as much as we annoyed each other, he was my friend, and knowing him on this level felt important because...*Because reasons!* Ones I really didn't feel like trying to understand just now.

"Then maybe you should pick a different question," Mor taunted, taking a swig from his water bottle.

"But I want this answer. Bad."

"Then tell me the question."

I pouted for a moment. Then stared off into the night. Ate a few more chips. Shifted in my seat. Shifted again. Just how badly did I want to know the answer to this question?

I glanced at Mor, looking deep into the eyes of the man who no one seemed to fully understand. And for some reason—a reason that I did *not* want to consider in case it grew legs and ran right out of my mouth like so many of my thoughts seemed to—I needed to be the one to do it. To finally know him; see him. My eyes followed the line of his faint scar and the jagged path it cut across his left eyebrow and right cheek. This was the last of the big Morgan mysteries, and I needed to solve it.

Morgan must have noticed where my gaze had been drawn, because he went suddenly stiff. His expression impassive. But I felt everything he wasn't showing. The discomfort, fear and stubbornness that held him back, made him wonder if I would look at him differently after this.

But when I cautiously set my hand on his wrist, to silently reassure him that this odd, fiery, combustible friendship we'd formed wasn't going anywhere, I felt him relax. *He trusts me.* At least enough for this.

"What's your name?" He asked, his voice deep and raspy in the silence, reminding me of the way his stubble had scraped against my palm the other night. I could listen to that sound—feel his jaw in my hand—over and over and never grow tired of it.

Answering him wasn't an option, it was an instinct. I doubted I could resist him no matter the question when he used that tone. "Caroline Felicity Birch."

"Caroline Felicity," he hummed, the rumbling in his chest skating over me, causing a strange hum to vibrate through my body, "I like it."

"My birth parents chose the middle name, but my adoptive parents chose the first."

"Your birth parents clearly wanted you to be happy. They could've gone with Hope or Harmony for a middle name, but they picked a word that means happiness."

"Intense happiness," I corrected with a thoughtful smile. "Which is why I'm pretty sure they'd hate what I do now."

"Not possible," he shook his head, rotating his hand in the zip tie so he could clasp my hand. It was an awkward angle, only allowing him to hold the side of my hand, but it still felt achingly intimate and comforting. "You're giving up everything to help other people. Instead of being angry at the world for all you suffered, all the relationships you had to sacrifice pursuing, all the loneliness I know you went through even if you don't like talking about it, you're fighting in the shadows. Not getting any recognition, only hoping to save other people the suffering you've endured. You're a hero, Care. I can say with absolute certainty that your birth parents would be proud of you. I know I am."

That hit me like a punch to the gut, making my voice come out small and insecure. "You are?"

Morgan squeezed my hand. "I am."

I bit the inside of my cheek to keep from grinning—it felt like a bad idea to let him see just how much his praise meant to me. Mostly because I was pretty sure it meant more than it should've. My own parents could have said the same words, and I wasn't sure they would've carried the same weight that Morgan's did.

"I'm not sure you can call me a hero though," I argued, mostly because I didn't quite know what to do with his praise. *Hi, I'm an adult who doesn't know how to accept a compliment. Oh look! There's an entire generation of us, I feel better.* "It's not like I'm Oliver Queen and my birth parents left me some legacy to uphold. I was just a teenager who saw a group of people being wronged, people who were suffering in so many of the ways that I had—only worse. So, when I turned eighteen and my parents told me that my birth parents had set aside some money for me, I used it to relocate into the city and fund my new pastime."

The car went quiet again, and I regretted speaking. Why hadn't I just taken his compliment and shut my mouth? Why did I have to explain myself and ruin his beautiful sentiment?

"Say something," I begged, nervously reaching up to tug on the ribbon that I'd tied around my high ponytail.

"I'm just..." Morgan paused, giving me a gentle smile. "I'm glad I was right about this."

"About what?"

"You. That you aren't just some vengeful spy who lives off the suffering of others. I know that's what you wanted me to believe at first."

"What made you doubt it? Was it the ribbons or the florals that gave me away?"

"It was the empathy."

My eyes flashed up to meet his, surprise overwhelming me. Not only was he *proud* of me, but he'd also proven that he wasn't like everyone else. He hadn't underestimated me because of my appearance, instead he saw through it altogether.

"Thank you," I squeaked, reaching for another chip, and hoping he didn't notice the way my fingers trembled. "I...Those were good words."

As I'd hoped, he smiled in that 'what am I going to do with you' way of his that I was growing somewhat attached to.

"Alright, fair is fair, ask your question," he sighed, closing the bag of carrots with one hand and tossing them unceremoniously into a cup holder.

"Oh, um..." I said inelegantly, "I don't have to—"

"Ask." The word wasn't abrupt so much as it was pleading. Whether he was desperate to get it over with, or desperate to get the words out, I didn't know.

"What happened to give you that scar?"

"Another Berserker."

This much I knew. The rumors of The Chief had circulated to me quickly when I moved to Shifter Haven three years ago. The problem was that now that I knew Morgan, I wasn't sure which parts of the rumors were true. I knew he hadn't killed any of the gambling den members in the news, but the rest of it? The man he supposedly killed when he was a child? That part I wasn't so sure I knew the full story about.

"My dad was…" he paused, searching for words as he stared down at our conjoined wrists. I sensed him closing himself off, nervous and afraid, but I wasn't willing to lose the ground we'd covered together. So, I flipped my hand over and grabbed his instead. *You're not hiding from me, Mor.* Not now.

Morgan froze for a moment, but then he met my eyes again, stubbornness overcoming the nerves. "He wasn't the best," he continued, bolstered for the moment, "He was an alcoholic and although he was never abusive, he had a serious gambling problem. His tab with a gambling den on the west side of town was high—much higher than he could ever pay. Eventually, they came to collect. My dad wasn't home, probably off losing more money he didn't have."

There was a bite to Morgan's words, and I wished more than ever that my magic worked on him so I could ease some of his hurt. For all the sadness I felt over not knowing my birth parents, I'd won the lottery with my adoptive ones. My mom and dad didn't always understand my current lifestyle, but they adored me and my sister. Either one of them would give up anything to make us happy. And I desperately wished that Morgan had been so lucky.

"Mike and Clint were only two and three at the time, and I was ten. My mom tried to explain to the men who came to the house that my dad wasn't home. They didn't care, they wanted the money. But my mom didn't have it—Dad owed three times what our house was worth. When it became clear that my dad didn't have two nickels to rub together, the leader of the gambling den decided that taking his debtor's wife as collateral would get my dad to somehow produce the money…" Morgan took a deep breath, and I rubbed the side of his hand, wishing that there wasn't a console between us so I could hold him. But since I couldn't do that, I covered his arm with my free hand, letting my thumb skate over his skin, my grip firm but tender. He could be big and strong and immovable tomorrow, but today, he needed me.

"Take your time, Mor," I whispered, not trying to cloak my emotions behind snarky expressions this time. He needed my vulnerability, and he could have it. "I'm not going anywhere."

He nodded, and I didn't have to use magic to know the grief that he was feeling. It was clear in his grey eyes. What had this poor man suffered the past two decades serving time as a feared monster to the public, when he had his own grief to deal with? It made me sick to think that no one had given him the space to just be instead of perform. That he hadn't been allowed to sort through his feelings; instead, always worried about an audience that hated him.

"When my mom fought back, they attacked her," he continued, his gaze holding mine like I was a lifeline; the lighthouse keeping him from floating out into a sea of grief. *Talk about pressure*. But I was happy to bear it. For him. "I reacted, shifting faster than I'd ever done before. They weren't prepared for it, and I was able to maul two of them bad enough that they ran away, but the ringleader wasn't going to let it go. He shifted too, and even though he was a heck of a lot bigger than me, I fought him. Mike was able to get himself and Clint under the coffee table and out of the way, but my mom...She tried to intervene and protect me, but she was already too badly injured. She went down, but the leader wasn't satisfied, he came at me again. Thanks to him, I ended up in the hospital for a week."

Mor shifted in his seat, turning his back to me. With his free hand he grasped the hem of his Henley and pulled it up high, revealing three jagged scars that went from the bottom of his neck all the way down to his right hip. I had a sudden desire to run my fingertips over the old wounds, to let him know that they didn't mar him. Didn't change my view of him. But I held myself back, knowing he wouldn't appreciate that kind of breach in physical boundaries. Holding hands was probably his limit.

"I'm so sorry," I breathed, overcome with grief on his behalf.

He turned back around, uncomfortable and insecure. "I know," he nodded.

But he didn't know. He didn't know just how much my heart broke for him and his ten-year-old self who'd endured so much.

"No," I insisted gently, shaking my head, "You don't. But that's okay. Because I'm gonna prove it by sitting right here, and not letting go."

When I caught the slightest bit of glossiness in his eyes, I knew I'd said the right thing.

"Thank..." he began, stopping when his voice cracked with emotion.

"You don't have to," I insisted, squeezing his arm. "I know."

He nodded, studying me for a few silent moments, gathering himself to continue.

"Um...Even though I was injured, I kept fighting. He was too cocky, thought his hit had killed me. So he didn't see me go for his throat...Once he was dead, I checked on my mom, but she was already—" he broke off, and I nodded to let him know that I knew. He didn't have to say it out loud for me. "Thankfully, Mike and Clint were okay. Their memories of it are hazy and faded, but I know they still remember enough to feel the trauma. And my dad...after that he just drank more and more. His debt had been ignored thanks to my disposal of his creditor, but he didn't gamble again, just worked enough to pay for his liquor, then drank the money away. About six months after Mom passed, Mr. Wallace took us in. Dad didn't even fight him on it. I think he knew that we were better off with Wallace."

"Is he still—"

"He's passed away. Liver cancer about ten years ago. We kept in touch, but not enough for me to miss him now."

I opened my mouth to apologize again or offer assurance or do pretty much anything other than just sit there and stare, but he spoke before I had the chance.

"Distract me?" he pleaded, the desperation in his voice toying with my empathy. "What about your adoptive parents? Where are they?"

"Uh," I stuttered, trying to get my brain to switch gears. "They still live in the same town—the same house even—that we grew up in. About two hours from here. My mom works as a fifth-grade teacher and my dad is a mechanic. It's quiet and peaceful and they love it. Um...Ariel and I visit them at holidays, and I usually call them once a week or so, though I haven't called them since some crazy guy kidnapped me." I flashed him a smirk, and a little of the tension in his shoulders seemed to ease. "They don't love what I'm doing here, mostly because they worry. They come to visit sometimes, but usually Ariel and I go to them. I think it's hard for my mom to see me here, knowing that I'm putting myself in danger all the time. She doesn't like the reminder."

"Moms are protective," he nodded.

"Very. The only reason she doesn't try and pack me up and move me back home is because Ariel lives here too. She figures we're safer together."

"Makes sense. Though I don't think I'd ever label you as safe," he teased, turning to look out the windshield, "You have a penchant for finding troub..."

Morgan trailed off, his eyes going wide, and I followed his gaze out into the night. The side street we'd parked on was connected to a dimly lit alley behind the Alliance Building. Where someone seemed to be running.

"Wait, is that..." I said, squinting to get a better look.

"Our perp."

Morgan swung his door open but froze as he glanced down at our zip-tied wrists. He gave me one long look of indecision, then pulled a pocketknife from his jeans. "You stay here," he growled, sawing the plastic off. "I'm giving the Witch binding a little slack so I can get the perp—but no matter what happens, you will keep the doors locked and stay in the car."

"But I can help!" I complained as he stepped outside. "I'm faster than you!"

"I don't have to chase them, Care," he said with an arrogant smirk, "I just have to cut them off."

Then he slammed the door and took off running into the night. I let out a huff, snapping the lid on my Pringles. Although I had the urge to throw them on the floor, I set them calmly in my cupholder. I wasn't going to destroy perfectly good chips over this.

"This is stupid," I complained after a few moments of waiting, my legs jiggling with impatience.

Morgan was never going to catch the person and we both knew it. He was strong, not fast. I wasn't even sure he owned a treadmill in his fancy gym at the house. *I wonder what his cardio routine is like...*

Suddenly, images of Morgan doing burpees and kickboxing came to mind. The man had to burn his calories somehow, and all my imaginings just so happened to include him doing it without a shirt on. Not because I liked him or anything. I could dislike red velvet cake and still think it looked yummy. *And boy does Morgan look yummy.*

"Maybe I should start working out so I have an excuse to watch—for research purposes of course," I mused aloud to myself. It was a valid idea, although it would mean that I'd have to actually work out. *Not a fan of that.*

I sat there for a few more moments, trying to distract myself with thoughts of Morgan in the gym. But finally, I couldn't stand it anymore. "He's not fast enough, and I am." Plus, the doctor had said that concussions don't last for more than a day or two, so I wasn't in danger of hurting myself.

"Let's go."

Making sure to take Morgan's keys with me and lock the car, I took off down the street at a jog. And by jog, I mean that I could have kept up with Usain Bolt, and if I would have put my full effort into it, I could almost lap him.

With my juiced-up Nephilim powers, I was able to cover the distance to the ally in no time. The path was dark and quiet, with less streetlights here. I paused next to a dumpster, not sure if the person had run down a connecting alley or kept going straight. Then I heard footsteps up ahead and I took off running again.

At the speed I was going, it didn't take long for me to catch up to the person. They ran just ahead of me, dressed in black just like last time. Before they could make it to the next alley to turn though, someone came skidding out from the connecting path and cut them off.

Morgan.

He sauntered forward, his face cast in shadows, and his emotions tangling between confidence, anger and worry. I gathered that the latter two were directed at me. *I might have underestimated how mad he's going to be at me.*

"You're trapped," Mor called out, his deep voice echoing in the dark. The runner froze, looking from me to Morgan, realizing there was nowhere to run. "Give up and I won't hurt you."

I sensed the moment the culprit made their decision. A clever determination flooded through them, and suddenly they spun. Running straight for me.

It was a smart move. Morgan was strong enough to take them out with no problem, but me? I could only run.

Except that I didn't get the chance, because suddenly the person in black was throwing something at the ground. Before I could turn and flee, the alley filled with smoke.

Grey clouds rolled around me, filling my vision until it was all I could see. Blind and panicked, I reached out with my magic to try and sense my attacker by their emotions. But I was a few moments too late.

Arms came around me from behind, pinning my arms to my sides and dragging me backwards. Morgan wasn't going to have to berate me for leaving the car once this was over, because I was berating myself plenty right now.

"I can't believe I have to tell him he was right!" I shouted, hoping Morgan could find me by my voice in all this smoke. The attacker's arms didn't release no matter how much I thrashed, but I kept at it anyway. I pounded my feet against their shins, threw my head back into their face, and even dropped like dead weight, but they refused to drop me. I could sense their stubbornness, their determination to take me out of here and knew they weren't going to give up.

I can work with that. I unleashed my magic, and instead of tugging at the attacker's emotions, it yanked them right where I wanted them. One moment they were determined, and the next, with just a burst of my magic, they were terrified. As the horror flooded them, they dropped me on the pavement—headfirst—and ran off.

I wanted to go after them, to herd them back to Morgan, but the smoke had only just begun to fade, and I still couldn't see clearly. Although now I was wondering if part of that had to do with the ringing in my ears and the ache in the back of my head.

"Care!" Came Mors' worried voice from within the cloud of smoke.

"Over here!" I called out, wincing at the way it made my head pound.

A moment later, Morgan broke through the smog, his panic strong as he knelt beside me on the ground.

"Are you hurt?" he demanded in that low, threatening tone he'd used on the attacker.

Before I could even answer him, he was pushing aside my bedraggled ponytail to assess my head. I wasn't bleeding this time, and I could see Morgan clearly, so I didn't think this hit was as serious as the last.

"I didn't hit as hard this time," I assured him, though he continued to inspect me like he'd find a gaping wound at any moment. "And they didn't hit me in the head. I just bonked the pavement."

"*Just?*" he demanded—loudly.

"Ow! No yelling please," I whispered, closing my eyes against the headache.

I felt some of Mor's worry abate, replaced with anger and something softer—maybe an affectionate kind of concern? It was more like a desire to take care of someone who's sick rather than a full-blown panic that they were dying. *Progress.*

"Sorry," Mor said, much quieter now as he helped me sit up, "It's just that this is the second time you've been hurt like this, and I..."

"I know, Mor," I assured him, smiling to let him know I understood. "Sorry I scared you again."

He shook his head but couldn't quite hide the way his lips tilted up at the corners. Not a smile, but not a frown. "You have nothing to be sorry for. Just hold on and let me coddle you for a little bit."

I wanted to protest, but he was too quick and suddenly I was lifted into his arms, pressed against his solid chest. Of course, with nothing else to do, it made sense for me to wrap my arm around his neck—couldn't have me falling over. Then, simply because I needed to make sure he wasn't panicking again, I rested my other hand against his chest, feeling his heartbeat beneath it. Could I have just paid attention to his emotions? Sure. But what would be the fun in that?

When Morgan's non-smile became a full smirk, I wondered if I'd said my thoughts out loud.

"Did I say something?" I asked, watching his face, sensing a bit of pleasure in him.

"No, why?" His tone betrayed nothing.

I watched him as we made our way back to the car—on the main street this time instead of through the dark alleys. The streetlights painted harsh shadows on his face, his scar seeming all the more menacing in the dark. Now that I knew the story behind it though, his scar seemed less scary and more a testament to the person he was. The loyalty and devotion he had for those he loved. Knowing this story—the story of his mom's death—had cracked open a door between Morgan and me. It felt like there was an entire wing in him that I hadn't known existed. There were so many rooms to explore and understand, and I was realizing that despite our differences, I wanted to understand all of them.

"You didn't shift," I said carefully, not wanting to fracture this tenuous trust we'd built, but curious enough to risk it. "Last time we were attacked, I thought maybe you chose not to shift into bear form because you didn't want to leave evidence in the building by clawing up the floors or leaving fur behind. But you didn't shift tonight either, even though could've run faster in bear form..."

Mor didn't reply, but his shoulders went tense beneath my arm, and his heartrate picked up speed under my palm.

"How long has it been since you shifted, Mor?"

It took him a moment to answer, his feelings slowly sliding from fear into something warmer—trust. It was like I could hear him unlocking a new door for me in his mind. Letting me into a deeper place.

"I shift frequently," he replied, his words careful, "Just like my brothers and Logan. I just don't shift around other people. Not around Mike or Clint or Logan...not around anyone."

"Why?" I understood that his refusal to shift around others was connected to 'that night', but was it out of guilt? Fear?

"Because ever since...shifting makes me feel out of control. I hadn't really meant to kill that man, and yet I did. So now...I don't trust myself not to hurt someone, so I don't shift unless I'm alone."

Ah. Now it made sense. Ten-year-old Morgan had acted in anger and protectiveness and not only had his mom still died, but he'd killed someone himself. I could only imagine the baggage cart he'd been carrying around all these years because of it. *The Berserker Chief who locks everyone out with an evil reputation.* And me, the lone Elf who built herself a fortress out of purpose and resentment. A fortress that not only protected me but alienated me. I wondered, if Mor and I had known each other as suffering teenagers, could we have helped each other heal? Learned to live without these coping skills that seemed to hurt as much as they protected?

I opened my mouth, knowing my words would mean little, if anything at all, but determined to say them, nonetheless.

"You may not trust you, Mor, but I do," I mumbled, and he looked down at me, a cross between wonder and shock lining his features. "Whatever form you're in, I trust you."

Then the world went dark.

TWENTY FIVE

Morgan

Caroline was light in my arms; a stark reminder that she wasn't a hardened warrior, she was a spy. She was clever and sly, but she was also breakable, and so easily taken from me. No one could mistake my mate for being fragile—I'd seen WWE wrestlers that weren't as terrifying as she was when she was angry—but she wasn't a fighter. She had speed and manipulation, but as seen tonight, those things couldn't save her.

I tried to be gentle as I carried her into the house from the garage even though my instinct was to hold her so tight that she could never get away. Never be in danger again. But one didn't suppress Caroline. She'd kill me if I tried.

I was on my way up the stairs when I heard Logan call out to me. "What happened?" he demanded as he stood from where he'd been sitting on the couch in the living room. Daisy Mae jumped up from her spot beside him as his Kindle clattered to the floor. When she saw me, she came trotting to the stairs.

"Care was right, the copycat showed up," I answered grimly, my fingers flexing against her back, needing her closer; safer. "They used a smoke grenade to confuse us and tried to take her. When she got them to let her go, they dropped her on her head."

"Oh my gosh," Logan hissed, pulling his phone from his sweatpants. "Want me to call the doctor? It'll probably take him a little while to get here, but—"

"No, I called him on the way home—paid him double to get here immediately."

Logan nodded, but his concerned expression didn't soften. "They tried to take her?"

"Yeah...Again." I knew what he was thinking—it was the same thing I'd been thinking the whole ride home. When someone broke into the house and tried to take Caroline, we assumed it was an isolated incident. That one of her victims was out for revenge...but then at the Alliance Building the other day, the attacker didn't seem to want me. Just her. And tonight, it wasn't me the copycat had tried to take, it was Caroline.

"I don't know if she's just leverage against me, or if this is just as much about her as it is me," I admitted, terrified that I'd somehow put Caroline in danger. That this copycat was only after her because of me.

"She could be leverage," Logan agreed, and I watched Daisy hop up to put her front paws on my thigh, sniffing Caroline with great concern.

"Or?"

"Or this could be about more than just the Berserkers. That attacker who came to the house wasn't here for you. And Caroline had only been here a few days, so there was no reason for anyone to assume that she mattered to you." Logan sighed as he glanced at Care, his expression sad. "She's an extinct species who's been making a lot of waves by extorting Shifter Alliance employees. I think it's possible that someone wants you out of their way, as well as her in a cage. Why, I don't know, but—"

"It's something we should investigate," I agreed reluctantly.

To think of someone wanting to put *my* Caroline in a cage—I shook my head, trying to rid myself of the rage the thought caused. If I marinated on it, I'd end up shifting out of pure protectiveness, and that certainly wouldn't help Care.

"I'll make some tea?" Logan suggested, "I assume we'll both be up for a while."

I nodded and thanked him before continuing upstairs to Caroline's room. Daisy followed me the whole way, antsy and underfoot as I flipped down the covers on the bed. But it wasn't until I laid Caroline down and tugged the covers up around her shoulders that Daisy calmed down. She immediately crawled over to her mom and gave her cheek a good lick before curling up beside her.

"We just won't tell her you did that," I whispered, unsure which thing Caroline would be angrier about. Daisy's contaminated kiss or my watching over her like a helicopter mom.

"She said not to coddle her, but she doesn't know how hard that is to accomplish." I sat on the edge of the bed, pretending to brush invisible strands of hair from her face as I trailed my fingers over her forehead.

Seeing her like this, her auburn hair splayed out beneath her, her dark eyelashes brushing the tops of her freckled cheeks, she looked so innocent. So young and fragile and sweet. It made all my primal instinct scream at me to permanently set up camp on the floor beside her bed and rip apart anyone who tried to touch her. *That would definitely tick her off.*

Although for all of Caroline's bluster, I was willing to bet that having someone near, someone willing to do anything to keep her safe, would comfort her. Because even though I knew she'd experienced enough hardship to make her just as gruff and thick skinned as I was, I also knew that below the snarky exterior, there was a softer Caroline. A more vulnerable one. One who wanted to be protected and cared for just as much as she wanted to be respected as an equal.

Which made it all the harder to push her away and resist the connection we had. But I had to resist. Because even if she was starting to grow on me, I couldn't risk caring for someone so deeply again. Couldn't risk the loss. Being tethered to me would only bring her trouble. She was too good, and I was too calloused. And yet...*she trusts me.*

Before she passed out, she'd said that she trusted me in any form. Even after all the ugly things she'd heard about me—the rumors that I murdered gambling den workers by tearing them apart and blackmailed the DA in order to get away with it, and after hearing from my own mouth that I'd killed a man when I was ten—she somehow still trusted me. *She isn't afraid.* She didn't shy away from my touch or look at me warily. Instead, she leaned *into* me like I was a haven to her.

Which was all I wanted to be. I didn't want to be mates, to dirty her by being tied to me, to risk falling in love and losing again. But I did want to be her support, to be her friend, her confidant. I wanted us to truly see all of each other and not run away. Something I hadn't had since Gen.

It had been different with Genevieve though. Because with Gen, the fall, the vulnerability, the joy had all been so simple. We met, we dated, we fell in love and got married. End of story. But with Caroline...everything was a struggle and a battle of wills. Yet I couldn't seem to get enough of it.

I care. I cared about Caroline, and not just in a grudging, reluctant way. I cared about her like a man cares about a woman he wants to know, wants to have close.

A smile tugged at my lips as I stared down at her, fondly remembering the way her cheeks turned crimson when she blushed, and the way she always narrowed her green eyes at me when she was annoyed—unaware that it was sexy instead of intimidating. My attraction to Caroline had never been a question—even when I wanted to pretend otherwise. And although the instinct to keep her safe was largely motivated by my ability to sense her emotions through the mate bond, there was something else. Something deeper, something beyond choice.

I was beginning to realize, as I watched her chest rise and fall with steady breaths and sensed her peace, knowing she wasn't currently in pain, that even if we hadn't been bonded—even if there was no reason for me to keep her around and no magical guiding light telling me she was the one—I would've grown to care about her anyway.

Just because she was stubborn, feisty, secretly gentle Caroline. And that scared me more than any attack ever could.

TWENTY SIX

Morgan

The marble lobby of the Shifter Alliance Building echoed with my loud stomps and people stopped to watch—warily—as I passed. I didn't even bother to try and appear less murderous—because I *was* murderous.

The doctor had arrived at the house only twenty minutes after I'd laid Caroline in her bed. He had assured me that she was fine since she didn't hit her head as hard this time, but that if she had a third incident, she'd require close monitoring in case it caused brain damage. Once she woke up, she tried to persuade me that she was fine, but the moment she accepted the pain pills the doctor prescribed, I knew she was in severe pain. Caroline never admitted to weakness.

So now I was feeling vengeful.

I'd left Care with my brothers and Logan, having sent Grey out to do some investigating on my behalf. I was exhausted, my eyes were sunken, my head ached with the lack of sleep, and I felt my muscles begging me for rest, but I didn't care. I was going to find some answers.

Logan and I had spent all night last night pouring through the public records of every Shifter Alliance employee that had been terminated for undisclosed reasons during the last three years. The mayor didn't always share who Caroline's victims were, which meant that we had to go searching for them. But even after all that searching, we'd come up empty.

None of Caroline's former victims seemed to have any open vendettas against her, and most of them had left the area altogether after being sacked. Which meant that we were right back to square one, wondering how Caroline fit into the plans of the copycat spy.

Except that today I had the opportunity to speak with an entire room full of people with shady histories and the means to pull a frame job/kidnapping. It was council meeting day, and I intended to put the fear of God into everyone in that room.

"Mr. Hohlt," the elderly guard at the heavy metal door to the council room said as I walked up, "Looking to make the Firebird wet his pants with that scowl on your face?"

"Among other things," I answered brusquely, sliding my key card over the lock on the door after typing in my passcode.

"What I wouldn't give for a picture of that." The guard gave me a mischievous smile.

"I'll see what I can do." I gave him a nod and his smile widened as I slipped into the council room.

The bustle of conversation ceased at my entry, and every set of eyes turned to me. I'd purposefully arrived late, knowing it would irritate some of the council members and unnerve others. Right now, at least half of them looked ready to do just as the guard had said and wet their pants. The other half looked on edge, wondering what 'The Chief' might do.

"Sorry I'm late," I called out with a cheeky smile, "I didn't want to come. Got a lot on my plate right now, and a weasel to hunt down."

The scrape of metal on stone echoed in the room as I pulled out my chair at the ring-shaped table. My fellow council members traded looks, many of them looking to Mayor Fitz like they hoped he could keep me on a leash. *As if.*

"You think your plate is full now?" Chloe the Mermaid rep asked in that annoyingly superior way of hers. "Just wait until we get to item number four on the itinerary for today."

"Why wait?" I said jovially, clapping my hands against the table as I sat. "Let's go ahead and get to the meat of the meeting. What do you say Mr. Mayor? Should we get the gossip over with so people won't be so distracted during the rundowns?"

Mayor Fitz watched me silently from the other side of the table, his expression inscrutable, but his blue eyes concerned. Whether he was concerned for my wellbeing or about what I might do, I wasn't sure. The man didn't really show favoritism or even fondness for anyone in particular—although I often caught the shadow of a smirk when someone put one of the more sour representatives in their place.

"Are you sure, Chief Hohlt?" he finally asked, already looking down at his stack of papers.

"Go for it."

"Alright then. Item number four on the agenda, the break-ins. Today we have Agent Johnson here to brief us on the progress they've made with the case. Agent Johnson is the head of the Shifter Unit and I expect us all to treat him with respect as he shares his report."

Right on cue, a large man stood from the audience seating off to the side of the room. Since he'd been sitting a few rows back in the fold down chairs, I hadn't noticed him at first. Now looking at him, I was shocked that I hadn't seen him immediately. Agent Johnson was a huge black man—and when I say huge, I mean *huge.* He was probably almost seven feet tall and double the size of the average man, his bulk made of pure muscle.

"Agent Johnson," Mayor Fitz greeted as the man came up to the table. "Thank you for joining us today."

There wasn't a single person in the room who wasn't rightfully intimidated by the man. Drew the Firebird rep shrunk down so low in his seat that I wondered how his ego survived giving up so much attention. Fitch the interim Pixie rep cowered in his seat, visibly terrified. But Gerard the Hunter rep sat up straighter. I wondered if he was trying to appear strong because of our visitor, or because of the story about his affair that the copycat spy had leaked to the press. Although the story had died down a little thanks to the statements his wife made, saying that he'd come clean about the affair four years ago and had been faithful to her ever since. She also told the media to go jump off a cliff—among other things—which seemed to garner both him and her some favor with the public. Myself included.

"It's my pleasure," Agent Johnson nodded to the group. "Although it'd be nice to be here under better circumstances."

"I'll come up with something less ominous next time," Mayor Fitz smiled—a genuine one for once.

Agent Johnson nodded and took a folder out from under his arm, flipping through the pages. "As for the investigation, we have no evidence from the security cameras as they were all jammed during the time of the heist—which fits the MO of the vigilante."

"I'm sorry Agent Johnson," Eileen the Dragon rep interrupted, "Did you just call the person who's been getting people fired a 'vigilante'?"

Eileen the Dragon Queen was an...interesting old lady. From her perfectly coifed grey hair to her coordinated pantsuits—not to mention the way her mouth always puckered like she swallowed a lemon—she was a regular miss congeniality. Seriously, Sandra Bullock had nothing on her. Mostly because Sandra Bullock was actually nice, and Eileen was so selfish it shriveled her dark heart every time she spoke.

"Yes, that's generally what you call someone who betters the world despite not having any legal authority," Agent Johnson replied, not at all intimidated or rattled by her interruption.

"Betters the world? But this vigilante cost my uncle his position," Fitch the Pixie rep timidly pointed out, still trembling and half sunken in his seat.

"I have here a list of all the Shifter Alliance employees we know for certain were let go based on the findings of the Vigilante," Agent Johnson said, turning his attention back to his folder. "Drake Thompson worked in the Shifter Intake department and was fired for selling the names, addresses and species of over two hundred Shifters. Some of whom were later liberated after having been sold to the black market where they were caged, had their blood drawn regularly for the creation of illegal magic, and given drugs to make them compliant so that they would perform their respective kind of magic on cue." Without pausing, Agent Johnson went right into the next example. "Isabel Flores was fired after the vigilante revealed that she had been taking bribes from different shifters to shut off certain power grids in the city so that the Shifters who lived in those areas would make for easy theft targets. From what we can tell, this caused over a million dollars in stolen property, three million in damages to people's homes, and eleven people were killed while defending themselves against intruders."

Agent Johnson paused, looking up from his file to stare Eileen down. "Shall I go on, or has my point been made?"

Preach it, I wanted to yell. Because that vigilante who'd been single handedly saving the city was *my* mate! I'd been such a jerk when we first met, questioning Caroline's right to her vendetta, but I'd known for a while now that she was a spy with a heart of gold. And Agent Johnson had just proven it. Caroline had been fighting this huge battle all by herself for three years. Righting wrongs and fighting injustices for those who couldn't fight for themselves. We should be spending our time planning her a parade and giving her a salary, not arguing about whether or not she had a right to be called a hero.

"I think they get it now," Mayor Fitz interjected, giving us all his no-nonsense look. "The goal here isn't to catch a vigilante, it's to find out who's behind this new tactic of outing people to the news. Because our current theory is that the most recent heists weren't carried out by our vigilante, but by a copycat."

"Yes sir," Agent Johnson smiled, clearly in agreement that the vigilante—AKA Caroline—wasn't the problem. *I knew I liked this guy.* "As I was saying, we don't have any video footage of the break-ins. However, we do know that the methods and motivations have changed. Previously, the vigilante always pulled their heists during the day, but these last few jobs have been done at night. Also, in the past, employee's offices were often searched, and their computers hacked before their damning evidence made its way to the administration. But now, that information is being leaked straight to the news."

"You had mentioned having some more concrete leads when we last spoke," Mayor Fitz prompted.

When Agent Johnson went quiet, seeming to look at every council member but me, I felt my stomach drop. I knew exactly where this was going.

"Yes..." the Agent hesitated, "We had found some DNA at one of the crime scenes, but it was unfortunately destroyed during processing. So, it's not much of a lead now."

This, unfortunately, didn't seem to appease anyone. And as if on cue, both the seemingly innocent and the notoriously guilty looked to me, a mixture of judgment, curiosity, fear and pity in their eyes. But I didn't look away, instead taking note of their reactions, wondering who in the room might be tied to the attacker who'd hurt Caroline.

Brooks the Fenrir seemed mostly empathetic and almost annoyed on my behalf, and I made a mental note to pay more attention to him in the future. He was young—younger than me—with a mess of light brown hair and a lopsided grin. Evidence of his friendly, easy-going demeanor that wasn't completely unbearable.

Asher the Wyvern King was impossible to read and almost more intimidating than me with his dark hair, dark eyes and short beard. Lawrence the Pride of the Sphinxes wasn't much easier to get a grasp on, sitting silently in his chair, a baseball cap shading his face. He wasn't unkind per se, but he was difficult to read since he rarely commented except to tell someone to shut up. For that, I liked him immensely. Parker the nineteen-year-old Harpy rep gave me a supportive smile and stuck out her tongue at Francine the Minotaur.

For someone with the face of a cherub and the blonde hair of a princess, she had quite the sassy streak. Which was exactly why we got along.

"I heard they got a positive ID on the DNA before it was corrupted," Francine the Minotaur said, shooting a haughty look first to Parker and then to me.

"We test all DNA three times before we trust the results," Agent Johnson replied immediately, his tone brooking no room for argument. "This DNA only survived one test. Therefore, its results are a moot point."

But Francine loved to disagree.

"So, it doesn't matter that the first test identified the DNA as Berserker DNA—before it was so conveniently destroyed?" She taunted, daring me to explode.

"What are you implying Francine?" I growled, purposefully not using her proper title.

"I'm not implying anything," she shrugged innocently. It was an act that Caroline used often, but the difference was that Caroline's act was actually believable. "I'm merely stating the facts. You should be grateful I'm so well informed, considering that you're—how did you put it—hunting a weasel."

I was about to knock over my chair, grip her by the throat and demand to know if she was the one who'd sent someone to take *my* mate, when my phone buzzed in my pocket. I considered ignoring it, but my anger was already triggering my magic, twining with my adrenaline and begging me to shift into bear form. *I* can't. *Not here.* So instead, I pulled my phone from my pocket and found a text waiting for me.

Caroline: Are you okay? Cus it feels like you're about to rip the head off of a council member.

I sighed, letting some of the tension in my shoulders ease. Part of me hated that the simple act of her reaching out was enough to calm me down. But the other part was enjoying having this kind of connection to someone again. The kind where they got it—got me.

Me: Actually I am about to rip someone's head off. You're interrupting.

Caroline: If you go through with it, do you know what that would mean?

Fully aware that Francine was waiting for me to reengage and pleased that it would annoy her if I continued to text instead, I typed away.

Me: That I would be incarcerated?

Caroline: That their capa would be detated from their head.

Me: Is that a quote from *The Office?*

Caroline: *GIF of Michael Scott saying 'his capa was detated from his head'*

I smiled, an expression that would've been shocking if I'd done it for anyone else.

Me: So I have your permission to decapitate Francine then?

Caroline: Oh, this is about Francine?? Double win! The wicked beast goes down AND I have an excuse to use an *Office* quote that I'll never get to use otherwise! *dancing emoji*

I rolled my eyes but texted her back, telling her not to do any actual dancing until her week of caution—via my decree—was over. She was unimpressed and sent me a GIF of Stanley from *The Office* rolling his eyes.

I was just about to turn my attention back to the meeting when she texted again.

Caroline: BTW, why can I sense your emotions even though you're all the way across town? That's never happened with anyone else.

Immediately, my heart started racing and my palms began to sweat. I knew she'd figure out the mate bond eventually, but I'd hoped to keep her off the scent a bit longer. Just until I figured out what to do about it.

What do I say? I couldn't exactly tell her the truth, that I was her mate, and that I hadn't told her about the bond because I was trying to find a way out of it. She'd immediately set out to make my life miserable as retribution for keeping it from her.

But then I remembered that night we snuck into the Alliance Building. She'd asked me why she couldn't use her magic on me, and while I'd been floundering for an answer, she'd gone quiet, embarrassed. *Why?* I thought back to that night, remembering how touchy feely she'd been on the drive home and how much she blushed. She was attracted to me; I knew that much. And now I was wondering if she'd initially assumed that the reason she couldn't use magic on me was because of that attraction. *I can use that.*

Unsure if I was about to open a can of worms or close one, I texted her back.

Me: Do you really want me to answer that?

It was dangerous to play this card. I could be wrong. She might not be fazed by her attraction to me. To her it might not be anything to be embarrassed about—in which case, she'd make me tell her point blank why she could sense me over a distance. And I didn't know if I could manage an outright lie to her. She was my mate, unwanted or not, and if this whole thing ever came out, I wanted to be able to tell her that I never outright lied to her. *Just lots of lies by omission...*

Caroline: Never mind.

Caroline: Can you bring me a milkshake on your way home?

Caroline: I want to celebrate this epic *Office* quote I'm going to make today when we bail you out of jail and the warden asks me what you did.

Well, that was effective. It seemed that Caroline's attraction made her just embarrassed enough that she bought my insinuation. *Yet another half lie.* I face palmed, wondering how many I'd end up burying myself in. I hoped that when Care eventually found out about all of it, she'd leave my upper body unscathed enough that I could still have an open casket funeral after she killed me.

"That's enough conjecture Commander Stewart," Mayor Fitz exclaimed, the ice in his voice bringing me back to the discussion. Apparently, Francine had continued with her insinuations even while I was too distracted to give her the reaction she wanted. "The DNA was corrupted, end of story. Based on what I just saw, and the two examples of the vigilante's victims that Agent Johnson read—a list of which there are *dozens* just like them—we have a problem in Shifter Haven. And it starts in this room."

Everyone went silent, fully chastised by the mayor with the normally calm disposition.

"Frankly, catching the person behind these new heists isn't my greatest concern right now. You all are," he said, shooting a disappointed look at each one of us. "Because it's clear that the number one problem in this city is crimes against Shifters by other Shifters. Does it not bother any of you that it was a Shifter employee who sold Shifter information to people who put those Shifters in *cages?* Does it not bother you that it was a Shifter employee who took bribes to shut down power grids in primarily Shifter neighborhoods? Your own people turn against each other at the slightest provocation, as shown by your willingness to blame a fellow council member without evidence or cause. And yet none of you seem bothered by this."

My eyebrows shot up so high that they just about joined my hairline. Never had I heard the mayor so impassioned, so...on point. I wanted to clap but was afraid it'd be seen as sarcastic.

"Get your stuff together, all of you." His stern expression hardened into a glare, and we all sunk a little further in our seats. "The problem starts in this room. And it'll end in this room. So, grow up and stop blaming each other without reason. We have much bigger fish to fry than your personal vendettas."

Though everyone at the table nodded like a bunch of chastised children, it was hard to tell whose compliance was genuine and whose was only a placation while they planned to misbehave in secret. *Because someone here is planning something.* I was sure of it.

TWENTY SEVEN

Caroline

"Are you sure this is smart?" I asked, turning in the passenger seat to watch Morgan and his two brothers clip weapons onto their hips in the backseat.

"We've snuck in once already, what's a second time?" Morgan replied, shooting me an encouraging smile. Which just proved my point that this was dangerous—Morgan rarely ever smiled.

"May I remind you that I was attacked last time."

"Exactly, *you* were attacked. But now I've removed the liability." Then he *tapped* my *nose*. "So instead of our copycat finding you when we go in there, they're going to find three Berserkers."

"You do realize that you just called me a liability," I snapped, reaching back to smack his knee.

But Morgan snatched hold of my wrist and leaned forward until our faces were close enough that I could see where the grey in his eyes ended, and the blue ring began.

"Do you know what a liability is Care? It's someone who's likely to be in danger or get hurt." His voice was soft, his hold on my wrist gentle, and something deep inside me seemed to almost purr. "But you're a double liability, because you're not just a random bystander."

"No, I'm the ever-present thorn in that very nice backside of yours," I snarked, trying to cloak the nerves that had begun to churn inside me with humor. My specialty.

Morgan smirked and glanced back over his shoulder, pretending to check out his derriere. "It is pretty nice."

"Shut up," I complained, rolling my eyes.

"Care," he said, his tone less teasing now as he turned his attention back to me, "You're my friend, and I'd be pretty freaking bugged if something bad happened to you."

It wasn't a declaration of deep meaningful friendship. He didn't say his life would lose meaning without me...And yet, I knew by the look in his eyes that if something happened to me—again—he'd be wrecked. I had three past experiences with him to prove it.

"Well how am I supposed to argue with that?" I wined, pouting as I crossed one arm—Mor still held the other one—over my stomach.

"That's kind of the point," Morgan teased, squeezing my wrist once before letting me go.

I tried to smack him, but he'd already retreated to the backseat, and I hit the leather upholstery of the driver's seat instead.

"We just want to keep you safe, Caroline," Mike chirped, and I had to turn in my seat to see him where he sat behind me. He had a black beanie over his dark hair to match his all-black outfit, and judging by his excitement, I was pretty sure he was pretending that he was in *Mission Impossible.*

"Yeah, we can't lose our Care Bear," Clint added from Morgan's other side. "Who else would binge watch comedy shows with us?"

I rolled my eyes again but conceded.

"Fine," I sighed, flopping dramatically back against my seat, "I'll stay in the car."

"Good girl," Morgan teased. This time when I smacked him, I made contact. "Ow!"

"If you want to talk to a dog, go home and talk to Daisy."

Mor rolled his eyes, rubbing his knee where I'd hit him. Big wussy.

"Alright, time to get moving," Logan announced from the very back row. "Now remember the drill. You get in, you let yourselves get attacked, you capture your attacker, and you get out."

"Very elaborate plan you have there," Grey said drily, sitting in the driver's seat—clip-board-free for once.

"Yes, very well thought out," I nodded. "One problem though; how am I supposed to stay in the car?"

Morgan studied me for a minute, confused and thoughtful. Then he leaned over the console and reached around me, tugging on my seatbelt.

"It's pretty easy, but I'm sure Grey or Logan can remind you if you forget," he began, his tone patronizing. "You see, all you do is keep your seatbelt on, and don't lift that well-toned butt from the cushion."

"I mean," I hissed, glaring up at him, "How am I supposed to be separated from you with the bond?"

Morgan froze, one hand on the console and the other still on my seatbelt, shock and panic roaring to life inside him. "What?" he rasped.

"I mean, with the Witch binding," I stammered, admittedly drawn to the way his grey eyes locked in on me, his body heat warming the space between us in a matter of seconds. "How can I stay in the car if I'm bound to be close to you when we're away from the house?"

"Oh," Morgan sighed, seeming oddly relieved—and yet somehow disappointed. "I, uh...I ended it. No more Witch binding."

"What? When?"

"About an hour ago," he shrugged shyly. "Friends don't bind friends."

He wouldn't meet my eyes, but I stared up at him anyway, a little bemused. Morgan had been different lately—Morgan and *I* had been different lately. We were gentler with each other, more thoughtful...closer. But part of me wondered now that he'd released me from the binding, if he was hoping I'd go away...or hoping I'd stick around.

"So, am I evicted from the house now?" I asked quietly, dimly aware that everyone in the car sat listening to our somehow intimate conversation.

Morgan's grey eyes flashed to me then, and the blue ring around the irises seemed brighter somehow; hotter.

"No," he shook his head, his gravelly voice skating across my skin, leaving goosebumps in its wake. "That wasn't the point of releasing you. The point was to give you the freedom to leave if you wanted...But if it were up to me, I'd have you stay."

"Yeah?"

"Yeah."

"Okay then."

"Okay?" he asked, eyebrows raised and a hopeful look in his eyes.

"I'll stay, but I expect to be reimbursed for my cooperative attitude."

"You want me to watch *The Office*, don't you?"

I grinned and he rolled his eyes.

"Deal. Now if you'll excuse us, we have to go catch a bad guy." He smirked at me, but before he could go far, I slipped my arms around him. Then, because apparently I was a masochist and thrived on mortification, I *pressed* my *face* into his *neck*.

He stiffened beneath my touch, reasonably confused by the contact. And I wondered if the doctors would be able to tell from my autopsy that I'd died of humiliation. With any luck, they'd just assume it was from brain damage caused by my repeated concussions.

"Be careful, okay?" I mumbled, squeezing him once more before releasing him.

Mor was silent for a moment, and I feigned interest in the seam of my jeans, praying that my death would be swift. But instead of responding, Mor leaned forward and pressed his lips against my temple. "I'll be back," he whispered, his warm breath brushing my cheek.

Then, without another word, he ushered his brothers out of the SUV and into the night. I watched them through my window long after they'd faded into the shadows—avoiding the two sets of eyes burning a hole into my head.

"So..." Logan said, drawing the word out tauntingly, "That was interesting."

No, it was terrifying, strange, awkward...and a little thrilling. But it was *not* interesting.

Thankfully, I was saved from having to defend myself when my phone began to ring. I eagerly pulled it from my pocket, then sighed seeing an incoming facetime from my sister. *Out of the frying pan and into the fire.*

"Hey sis, what's up?" I said cheerily as I answered the facetime.

"*What's up*?" Ariel parroted incredulously. Her curly blonde hair was soft and fluffy around her shoulders, but her blue eyes glaring daggers at me through her glasses. "You were attacked *three* times; you have head trauma and yet you're going to start this conversation with 'what's up'?"

I sighed and rubbed the spot between my eyebrows where a headache was starting to form. *Oh, what a shock.*

"I didn't tell you those things so you could use them against me," I complained.

"No, *you* didn't tell me at all. Your hot warden did when he texted me from your phone."

I felt a blush heat not only my cheeks but the tops of my ears. Mortified, I sent a glance at Grey and Logan, who were both watching with mischievous smirks.

"He's not hot," I defended weakly—but the truth was that Morgan *was* hot. I just wasn't going to admit it in front of Logan and Grey. "And he texted you without my permission while I was unconscious, which automatically deducts ten brownie points from his score."

"And yet he's still a perfect ten! And if he hadn't texted me, I wouldn't know about the attacks at all," she said, her light blue eyes flashing with anger.

"I didn't want to worry you when I don't have any answers."

"Caroline Felicity, that is not how family works, and you know it! We tell each other everything, because at the very least I could be praying for you. Not to mention, you know how I hate being out of the loop!"

I cringed at her shout, turning down the volume on my phone before she blew all our eardrums. "I know, it was wrong. I'm sorry. I will keep you properly updated from now on."

"So then why haven't I heard from you since the day before yesterday?"

"You want daily check ins?"

"Wouldn't you?"

Well, that wasn't fair. I growled, wishing I was far away on a beach somewhere, being handed a plate of nachos by a handsome man. *Wait, why does the man in my fantasy have a scar on his face? Did he just call me an adorable pain in the backside?* Horrified by the liberties my own imagination was taking, I shook my head and focused back on reality.

"Fine, I'll check in daily," I sighed. "But I'm only promising text messages and *occasional* phone calls. I am not calling you every day."

"I also want updates on the Morgan front while you're at it," Ariel teased, wagging her eyebrows. "Now that you're friends-ish, your chemistry is going to be off the charts! And in honor of my wisdom being the thing that got the ball rolling, I want at least one niece or nephew named after me."

"Ariel!" I snapped, glancing at Grey and Logan. "I will call you tomorrow if you stop talking right now."

I was shifting uncomfortably in my seat when Ariel's eyes suddenly went wide. Confused, I looked at the view finder on my screen, but didn't see anything odd—*oh.* Except for the big blonde Berserker sitting in the background.

An evil smile twitched my lips as I watched Ariel's reaction to Logan. Her cheeks turned pink, her eyes shifting to look anywhere but at the screen. *This'll be fun.*

"Problem, Ariel?" I asked innocently, shifting in my seat to make sure she had the best view of Logan.

She smiled, her teeth clenched and her eyes practically shooting fire at me. "Not at all. Talk to you tomorrow baby sis! Oh, and she totally did tell me she thinks Morgan is hot!"

In a rush of embarrassment, I tried to end the call but ended up dropping the phone on the floor. Ariel's loud cackles echoed as I fumbled around. When I finally found the phone, not only did I end the call, but I turned off the phone altogether. I was not about to have these guys catch a glimpse of whatever inappropriate text messages she decided to send me as retribution.

Sighing, I slowly let my eyes drift first to Grey, then to Logan in the backseat.

"So..." Logan began, fiddling with a headrest in front of him, "That's your sister."

Oh, thank God. He was too interested in fishing for information about Ariel to bother ribbing me about my attraction to Morgan. *Works for me!*

"Uh huh," I smiled. "Her name is Ariel."

"Hm," Logan hummed, popping his lips—as if I would ever believe he was merely bored, "She seems interesting."

"Interesting?"

"Not interesting as in odd," he quickly clarified, and I struggled to hold back a grin. "Just interesting as in..."

"Interesting?" I suggested and he nodded.

"Yeah, exactly."

When I looked over at Grey, the lines around his eyes were crinkling—his version of a smile. Grey was a stoic man, one of few words and simple emotions, but even he found Logan's flustered behavior amusing.

"She's single, by the way," I teased, glancing back at Logan. Just as I'd anticipated, his emotions flashed with nervous excitement. "She's not really a people person, but she's a good time once you get to know her."

"She sounds perfect," he said dreamily. Then, catching himself, he began to stutter. "Uh, I mean—not that I'm particularly invested or anything."

I hummed, barely suppressing a grin. *Their kids are going to be the cutest, blushing little nerds.*

"I'm curious about something," Grey spoke up, eyes on the alleyway ahead of us. "Did you describe Morgan using the term 'hot' or was that your sister's own way of describing your attraction?"

And just like that, my fun teasing Logan was over. *That's it. Ariel is going to pay.* Starting tomorrow, all those pictures of her in cosplay that she'd made me promise to never show anyone were getting airdropped to the smitten Berserker in the backseat. That photo of Ariel with Princess Leia's side buns? Getting sent. The one of her dressed up as a male dwarf? Getting sent. *Revenge will be sweet.*

"I never called him hot," I insisted, turning a glare on Grey, who just shrugged, unconvinced. "That was all Ariel."

"But you clearly called him something complimentary if your sister assumes you have an attraction to him—or is she lying?"

I stared him down, red faced and mortified. I knew he was pushing my buttons on purpose, phrasing the question so that my denial would seem like a question against my sister's character.

"Oh, come on Caroline," Logan teased, his smile annoyingly wide. "It's okay to admit that you like the way he looks. We won't judge."

"It seemed probable, given how much the two of you argue," Grey droned in his monotone voice, "That you had an interest in each other."

"Wait, hold up! I *never* said I had an interest in Morgan! And even if I were attracted to him—which I'm not—attraction is not the same as interest. Attraction is very passive, it's not something you do, it just happens. Interest though, that's very active, something you decide to pursue. I did *not* say that I was even remotely interested in Morgan!"

The two men were quiet for a moment, but I didn't trust the silence. There was a calculating glint in Logan's eyes and amusement rolled off him in waves.

"What do you think Grey?" he asked coyly.

Grey gave me a blank stare even as the beginnings of a tiny sly smile touched his lips. "Me think the lady doth protest too much."

"Well, you're both wrong," I pouted, pointing a finger at each of them. "But if either of you breathes a word of this conversation to anyone, I'll tell everyone that you," I said, glaring at Grey, "Watch *The Bachelor* when you're alone. And that you," I continued, swinging my glare to Logan—who was busy laughing at Grey's guilty pleasure, "Have a new crush you need to be ridiculed about."

And just like that, Logan's mouth snapped shut. I smiled as the joy slid from his face like ice cream off a popsicle stick.

"I don't have a crush," he argued lamely.

"I could introduce you to her, you know," I suggested, extending an olive branch.

"Yeah?"

"If you keep your mouth shut about this."

"Deal." And his smirk was back.

"*The Bachelor* is respectable reality TV," Grey frowned beside me, still hung up on his own blackmail. "There's nothing wrong with me finding entertainment in a bunch of young people all trying to find love...even if they're mostly idiots."

I smiled and patted Grey's arm, glad to finally know that he was human. "No there's nothing wrong with it; I watch it too. But if you tell, I tell."

"Deal," he sighed. "What'd you think about Jake sending Halley home?"

"Such a mistake!"

"I thought so too," Grey agreed, nodding emphatically. "They were so good together."

"The chemistry!"

"Oh, the chemistry," he groaned, shaking his head.

Our mutual love for *The Bachelor* was interrupted as the two-way radio began blaring where it sat in a cup holder.

Mike's voice was the first to come through the small speaker. "Alright, radios are on. Can everyone hear me?"

"We hear you," Grey replied quickly, pressing the button on the radio.

"We're on the third floor," Morgan's voice came through with a scratch of static. "So hopefully if the copycat is here, they'll gravitate toward the council member's offices."

We didn't actually know which floors the copycat would be on. But since they'd been coming after council members specifically, it seemed like a decent bet that they'd choose the third floor.

Grey, Logan and I all waited with bated breath, leaning forward in our seats. I wasn't sure what would be a worse outcome for this mission, that the copycat never showed, and we had to go home empty handed. Or that they did make an appearance...and one of our guys potentially got hurt.

"Did you hear that?" Clint whispered through the radio. "It sounded like footsteps."

"Go to the left," Morgan replied urgently. "Stay close to the walls. It could just be a guard."

The trio went quiet but for the sounds of their breaths. And even though my anxiety spiked as we waited, Morgan was calm. His emotions even and focused.

"They'll be okay," Grey assured me, even as a bit of panic rose inside him. "They have to be."

I didn't get a chance to respond before grunts were filtering through the radio. I lurched forward in my seat and turned up the volume as high as it would go. The sounds of a fight flooded through the car, and I heard the impact of fists and feet and—was that a knife?

"Morgan?" Grey shouted calmly, pressing the speaker button on the radio. "Mike? Clint? Do you need assistance?"

When no answer came, I began to panic. Morgan was angry, I could sense it, and when his stress suddenly skyrocketed, so did mine.

"Morgan?" I demanded, taking the radio from the cup holder. "Answer me!"

But all I got in response was more grunting, and the sound of Morgan hissing in pain. Instinct flooded me and I reached to undo my seatbelt, but Grey stopped me with a tight hand on my arm.

"You can't leave the car," he insisted, "I promised Morgan that I wouldn't let you."

"He's hurt, Grey!" I snarled, trying to rip my arm free.

"And it could be a trap to lure you out," Logan pointed out, but his logic did nothing but bounce off me. All I could feel was Morgan's pain—probably fueled by whatever life-threatening injury he had. All my brain could picture was him bleeding out on the floor.

"I'm too fast to be caught." I once again fought to free my arm and failed. "I'll be fine."

When a loud pained groan echoed through the speakers, we all froze. Was that from one of our guys, or someone else?

"We're okay," Mike gasped, and though Grey and Logan both seemed relieved, I wasn't placated in the least.

"Where's Morgan?" I snapped, ready to bite Grey's hand off if I had to.

But then I heard Morgan's voice. "I'm here. I'm fine. We got him."

I sighed and let my head fall back against the headrest. My heart was pounding, and my eyes burned with the random urge to cry, but I fought the tears back. Clint and Mike narrated their return down the building—probably trying to keep me from screaming in their earpieces.

I listened silently as I unbuckled my seatbelt, coiled and tense. Ready to pounce. *Is this how Morgan felt when I was hurt?* I'd sensed his panic when I was injured, but to be deep in that feeling myself...I didn't like it. But no matter how hard I tried to calm down, nothing soothed me. And I had a feeling that nothing would. Not until he was here, tangible, and safe.

"There they are!" Logan exclaimed, popping the trunk open so he could scramble out through the back. Grey and I followed suit, stepping out onto the pavement as four shapes made their way through the dimness toward us. Clint and Mike carried an unconscious person dressed in black between them, while Morgan brought up the rear, limping.

That need I felt to have him near and safe pulsed harder, moving me to action. Shoving away from the car, I stomped across the pavement, ignoring the unconscious captive. Morgan sighed as I neared him, probably preparing himself for a shouting match. But I didn't want to yell.

I just wanted to hold him.

"They tried to run, so it took us a minute, but—oof!" He stumbled slightly as I plowed into him, surprised enough for me to actually move him. Unconcerned with his shock, I wrapped my arms around his middle and nuzzled myself against him.

"You're hurt," I snapped, not releasing him even though his arms dangled like a rag doll.

His shock seemed to last a few moments longer before his arms came around me. "I'm okay, Care."

"But you so easily might not have been okay. I could have lost you."

Morgan went quiet for a moment, hesitant. "*Can* you lose me?"

Confused, I pulled my face from where I'd burrowed into his shirt and stared up at him. His grey eyes were hard to make out in the dim reach of the streetlights, but I sensed his cautious hope.

"What do you mean?"

"I mean that losing someone is personal. It implies that you had them...that they were so important to you, that their absence would alter you, leave you scarred," he whispered, his gruff features painted with insecurity.

Oh Morgan. The man had no idea just how deeply he'd marked me. From the first time he glared at me, I knew he would have an impact. Of course, at the time, I thought he'd only be a giant roadblock. Turns out that this hulking roadblock was really a safe haven—*my* safe haven. A few weeks ago, I might've thought that I'd be grateful to be separated from him.

But now...

"I can absolutely lose you, Mor," I whispered, allowing myself to be vulnerable—for him. "Those scars would be bone deep."

Mor's eyes bored into me, his hands flexing on my back, and I felt something snap between us; a canyon bridged, a river crossed, a boundary erased. We were no longer two separate places at war, but a united front.

"And I could lose you," he whispered back. "I'd never be the same."

And neither would I.

TWENTY EIGHT

Morgan

"WAIT, YOU HAVE A DUNGEON?" CAROLINE grinned beside me as we walked down the stairs to the basement.

"No, I have a basement that's been fortified to deal with dangerous people," I corrected. "Not a dungeon."

"Hm…brick walls, fluorescent lights, no windows…if it looks like a dungeon and it quacks like a dungeon."

I glared down at her, but she just shot me a cheeky smirk. The little imp was never intimidated by anything I did. *Why do I like that so much?*

When she hugged me last night, her emotions fraught with worry, I wasn't sure what to think. I'd known for a while now that losing her would mark me, change me. But to hear her say that she'd be changed if she lost *me*…it wrecked me in a way I didn't fully understand.

Without my permission and despite my desires to deny our mate bond, Caroline had become a safe space for me. She was the one person that I didn't have to modify myself for. She wasn't fazed by my growl or shouts. She didn't care about my reputation, and she didn't buy the emotionless alpha male attitude. I didn't have to try to convince her of who I was or water myself down to be acceptable, because somehow, she knew who I was. And for whatever reason, she didn't hate it. *That alone makes her the most valuable person in my life.*

"It's not a dungeon," I argued, opening the heavy steel door at the bottom of the stairs, and motioning her through ahead of me, "But if you keep arguing with me, I'm definitely locking you in the dungeon."

Care spun on the heal of her pink Converse and smirked up at me. Her auburn hair was loose and curled today, with a ribbon tied around her head like a headband. I tried my best to glare in spite of her adorable freckles and mesmerizing green eyes, but based on her amusement, I failed miserably.

"No, you like me too much to put me down here," she teased. Then, as seamlessly as if we'd been doing this forever, she stepped up beside me and slipped her arm through mine. I tried not to let my bafflement show as we walked to the end of the short hallway. But it was hard when she clung to me like I was a storybook hero.

"So you think," I teased her, liking the way she narrowed her eyes, all gloaty and defiant.

"So I *know.*"

The light feeling in my chest that came from Caroline's general presence began to fade as we stopped in front of a second metal door. Even her natural light couldn't break through the dark anger that took over at the knowledge that her attacker was in the next room.

Visions of Caroline on the floor of the Alliance Building flooded my mind. Blood pooling around her head, her whimpers of pain. Seeing her collapsed on the pavement, her passing out in my arms.

Whoever was behind this door, I was going to kill them.

"Let's go," I growled.

"Whoa there, what's got you so prickly Bear Man?"

"Whoever's behind that door hurt you!"

Care's expression immediately softened. "Mor..."

"You almost died, Caroline!" I snapped—even I could admit that I was yelling—but Care wasn't scared. She just held my arm tighter. "Whoever's behind this, I want to rip their head from their body and play a game of golf with it. I want to sever limbs with my claws and show everyone what awaits them should they try to hurt you! I just..." I trembled as magic buzzed under my skin, *begging* me to shift.

"You're afraid you won't be able to control yourself," Caroline whispered, her words free of judgement. I nodded, the urge to shift too strong to speak.

"Okay, let's try something." She turned, setting her hands on my shoulders. "Focus on your rage, on the way it tightens your chest, makes you feel like you might explode—"

"How will this help?" I gritted out, my vision going red with fury.

"Because now I want you to think about the fact that I can feel your rage. I can feel the way it rises higher and higher until you feel like you're drowning. I can feel the way it twines with your magic, buzzing like it needs to be set free. I can't manipulate you into feeling calm, but I can feel exactly what you're feeling. So, take comfort in knowing that someone gets it. That you're not feeling it alone."

I did as she asked, but instead of just knowing that Care could sense my feelings, I latched onto her feelings. Her patience, her acceptance, and her glowing support. *I'm not doing it alone.* Thanks to the bond, I'd never be alone again.

"That's..." I sighed, studying the thoughtful look in her eyes, unsure if I was grateful that she was so amazing, or annoyed that she wasn't easier to walk away from, "Actually really helpful."

"Don't sound so surprised! I've been known to have a good, non-reckless idea every once in a blue moon."

I rolled my eyes. "Meaning that you're not due for another one for another six months now."

"Give or take a few weeks," she smiled. Then she stepped back over to my side, linking our arms again. "Now shall we go interrogate a kidnapper?"

"Let's."

The dungeon—because Care was right, and I just liked to be difficult—was one big room with concrete floors and brick walls that had six feet of concrete behind them. It was a state-of-the-art facility, with floors that were polished smooth and shiny, and fluorescent lights hanging from the ceiling in neat rows.

On the left side of the room, two large cells were set against the wall. The right side of the room held a metal table where Grey and Mike were already seated and waiting. A laptop, a small stack of folders, and Grey's trusty clipboard sat on the table in front of them.

On the other side of the table, a young woman sat in a metal chair, her ankles cuffed and chained to the floor, and her wrists tied to the arms of the chair.

"Alright, let's get started. What do we know about the house guest?" I asked, nodding to Clint and Logan, who both stood a few feet from our prisoner, ready to intervene should she get loose. Was I being a helicopter mom, having five Berserkers ready to stop one human? Yes. But my mate was here—my mate who'd already been injured *twice*. My logic had left me the moment I saw her bleeding on the floor.

I watched our prisoner warily, hating the way her gaze continued to flick to Caroline. Sure, the woman was strapped to a chair, there wasn't much chance of her getting free. But some primal part of me wanted—needed—Care as far from harm as possible.

Caroline sighed heavily beside me, and I looked down just in time to see her roll her eyes. "Just this once, I'll appease you," she whispered. Then she squeezed my arm, went over to the table and took the empty chair beside Mike.

'Thank you', I mouthed, grateful that she understood. I wasn't trying to control her—only an idiot would try to control Caroline—but my inner bear needed very little motivation to come out today. So, anything I could do to keep Caroline just a little safer would help.

"Alright," Grey began, reading from his notes, "Shelly Mercer is a human who lives at 279 Front St. She has no spouse, no kids, no roommate. And it's stated on her lease agreement that she works for a finance company."

For a human, she was a bulky young woman. The muscles in her arms and shoulders were big enough to be visible through her long-sleeved black shirt. It wasn't uncommon for humans to commit crimes against Shifters, but those humans were usually specially trained and willing to face extreme punishments should they be caught. She fit the bill.

"A finance company that doesn't exist," Mike added, as he scrolled through his computer. "It's a shell company. And yet Miss. Mercer has fairly consistent deposits in her bank account of varying amounts, with nothing over ten thousand dollars. Sounds like your classic hitman slash kidnapper."

Turning to the woman in the chair, I crossed my arms and scrutinized her. Her blonde hair was frizzy and tangled around her shoulders. And despite the fact that we were talking about her, she just stared straight ahead. She was a somewhat severe looking person with a face built for frowning. She couldn't have been much younger than me, but there was a hardness to her that aged her, made her seem cruel.

"Who hired you?" I asked, watching her for signs that she was lying.

"I don't know." She practically spit the words out.

"You don't know?"

"All of my employers hire me anonymously. It's kind of the point."

Convenient but true. "What were you hired for?"

The woman's gaze finally wavered, flicking over to Caroline. "To break into the Alliance Building."

Not buying it for a second, I turned toward Caroline, who was watching our captive with narrowed eyes. I raised an eyebrow at her in silent question, and she subtly shook her head. *So, the girl* is *lying.* With Care's ability to sense emotions, she'd be able to tell.

When Care sent me a look that sought my permission, I nodded and took a step back from the woman in the chair.

"Why don't we try that last question again," Care suggested innocently. But the magic uncurling in the air betrayed her. Luckily, thanks to the mate bond, I was the only one who could sense her magic. "Who hired you, and why?" Slowly, the woman's harsh expression softened a little, the lines on her face easing slightly—but it wasn't enough. She still wasn't talking.

So, I let my leadership magic slip out and assist Caroline's manipulation. Much like Care, I only ever used my magic when it was necessary. As Chief, my powers were slightly enhanced, but I despised taking advantage of people without cause. This time though, I felt justified.

"Answer her," I said gently, urging my magic to coax her into trusting me.

"I..." she began, slightly confused, but mostly relaxed, "I was hired through a Craigslist ad. It's how most hitmen or thieves are hired."

"How?"

The woman glanced at me, and Caroline and I's combined magic must've been enough, because she answered.

"If someone wants a job done, they post an ad. There are certain phrases you use to convey the type of job you want. I was supposed to do a simple frame job and a kidnapping. They wanted *her*."

All eyes turned to Caroline, whose expression was hardening with every passing moment. But I could sense the worry building inside her. She'd gone twenty-two years completely undetected as a Nephilim, and now she was being hunted.

Not for long. I'd do whatever I had to in order to keep her and her secret safe.

"Was this your first time working with that employer?" Clint asked, his slightly lither appearance misleading where he stood with his arms crossed. He wasn't quite as strong as Mike, but he was a fierce fighter. The woman seemed to remember that he was the one who'd knocked her unconscious, because she stiffened in her chair.

"I can't say for sure," she answered in spite of her reaction to him. "The employers and employees are anonymous. I don't know them, and they don't know me. They paid in cash and left it at an agreed-upon location so I never saw them. I was supposed to get the other half of the money once I'd caught the girl and transferred her to someone else a few streets away."

"Was hurting her part of your job then?" I barked, my words coming out harsher than I meant them to. I didn't like the way this woman talked about Caroline like she was a package passed between bike messengers. It made my grip on the anger in my chest begin to slip, allowing the feeling to scorch through me.

The woman avoided my gaze, but I wasn't interested in playing nice. Two people—two separate attackers including the one I'd killed here at the house—had harmed Caroline. *My mate*. I wasn't about to just let that go.

"Answer me," I hissed, leaning down so my face was level with hers. "What were the terms of her capture?"

"I was only told that she needed to be captured alive—not unharmed."

My control snapped, and the protectiveness I felt for Caroline blurred together with my affection, pushing me into action. I'd just begun to clench my fists when Caroline shouted.

"Morgan!"

I could've been hit with a steam roller, and I wouldn't have been deterred. But one word from Caroline and I froze. When I turned to look at her and saw the blue rings around her green eyes, I was reminded that she could sense my feelings right now. That she knew how I felt. She understood.

Mentally reaching out for her, I grasped for her feelings of concern and affection, letting them ground me. "I'm okay," I promised, my eyes not leaving hers.

Her eyebrows furrowed and she tilted her head. "You sure?" And even though I knew it was just going to encourage my idiot family to make more embarrassing bets about Care and I, I stepped up to the table and set my hand over hers, giving it a gentle squeeze.

"I'm sure."

She nodded, still skeptical but more relaxed.

"Do you think you can find the ad, Mike?" I asked, walking around the table, and setting both my hands on the back of Caroline's chair. When my knuckles brushed her hair, it was a struggle to keep myself from playing with it.

"Yeah," Mike nodded, glancing between Care and I with a mischievous look, "If I know her username."

I looked over at the prisoner, who seemed grouchier now that I'd stopped using my magic. "What is it?"

The woman didn't answer, and I was tempted to threaten her with force this time. But when Caroline reached up and covered my fingers with her own, my frustration faded. Her magic rolled out again, and our prisoner faltered long enough to reveal her email address.

"So..." Mike hummed as he worked, his screen showing a bunch of letters and numbers that were beyond my understanding, "It looks like the employer who posted the job requested a kidnapping by asking for a cat to catch a mouse. And they also posted one previous ad almost a month ago. Which I would assume was accepted by the attacker that came to the house."

"So, this isn't just about us," Clint mused, him and Logan both stepping up to the table. "Someone wants to bag a—" he paused, looking over his shoulder at the woman, "A Caroline, and—"

"And have me removed as Chief," I sighed, completing his thought.

Caroline looked up at me, the same worry I felt reflected on her face. There was no longer a question about why someone was after us. They wanted me gone...and to catch the only living Elf.

We'll see about that.

TWENTY NINE

Morgan

"MR. HOHLT, CAN YOU EXPLAIN HOW THE body of yet another gambling den worker has been discovered with the same neck wounds that are known to be your MO."

I scowled at the news reporter who'd stuck her microphone in my face. Usually, the press wasn't this brave. Whenever another body turned up with my 'signature' kill method, they'd just speculate from the safety of their newsrooms. I hadn't had someone try to interview me personally since my mom's death over twenty years ago. They were all too scared.

"Can you please move?" I growled. "My friend is waiting." *There, I used my words just like Caroline told me to.* She'd probably gloat about it later.

"What does your friend think of your reputation?" The reporter continued to hound me. If she really believed I was a heartless murderer, then she'd be wise to get that microphone out of my face before I found other things to do with it.

"I'm not going to comment on anything, so can you—"

A blood-curdling scream cut me off, sending goosebumps across my arms. The reporter—*finally* scared—stepped back, revealing a crowd gathered on the sidewalk. They'd all turned to stare down at something, and when they saw me, they parted.

Confused, I walked over to them, but when I saw what they'd been staring at, my heart stopped beating. Lying on the ground, with blood pooled around her auburn hair, was Caroline. Her eyes staring lifelessly up at me.

"No," I breathed, dropping to my knees beside her. This couldn't be real...But there was no pulse in her neck, no breath moving her chest. She laid perfectly still.

"Who did this?" I screamed, my voice breaking along with my sanity.

But when I looked up, the crowd stared me down, unrepentant.

"You deserve it," someone shouted, and then they all began to nod, shouting various insults at me. Blaming me for this.

Anger fell over me like a mask, covering up the grief until only rage remained. Then magic swooped in, buzzing in my veins and urging me to shift. *And why not give in?* The only person I would've been scared to hurt was already dead.

She was gone and the pain was too much, too big. So, I let the transition begin.

"Morgan," came a worried voice. *Her* voice.

Blinking and confused, I looked down, but Care was still dead. Her eyes still empty and lifeless.

"Caroline," I pleaded, waiting to see her eyelids flutter or her chest rise. Anything to show she was alive.

"Morgan, wake up." I could have sworn it was her voice, but when I began to study her more closely, someone shoved me. Just before I fell forward, I woke up.

There were no reporters, no evil crowds or dead mates to be found as I looked around my bedroom. Instead, there was just Caroline standing above me, bathed in the yellow glow of the bathroom light.

"Care?" I rasped; my voice raw as if I'd actually been screaming.

"I felt your panic," she quickly explained, her brows puckered, and her eyes filled with worry. Her hair was loose, spilling across one shoulder as she leaned over. She had on a giant T shirt that went nearly to her knees, and one hand was still pressed against my shoulder. Like she didn't quite know if she should let go yet or not. "At first I thought you were being attacked, but then I realized you were having a nightmare."

A nightmare...I sighed, looking up into Caroline's face, and studying her hungrily. The way her green eyes searched me, the freckles on her cheeks, the warmth of her hand on my skin. *It wasn't real. She's here.* She was safe.

"Morgan, are you—"

Overcome with relief, I swept my arms around her, and lifted her onto my lap. I pressed her against my chest, resting my chin on the top of her head. My body trembled as I clutched her like a lifeline.

"Morgan?" she whispered. She was frozen for a moment, but then ever so slowly, she reached her arms around me. When her hands found the scars on my back, her soft fingers traced them gently, and I sunk into her. "You're okay, Mor. You're okay."

"I lost you," I explained, my voice breaking over the words. "You were dead, and it was my fault."

At first, she was shocked, full of disbelief. But the longer I held her, the more those feelings seemed to fade. Affection began to bloom instead, filling her with a warmth that reflected the one in my chest. An affection I'd tried and failed to put off.

From the moment I'd met Caroline, I'd been determined to refuse the mate bond. Because I couldn't risk finding that kind of love again only to lose it. But of course, in true Caroline fashion, she'd gone and weaseled her way into my heart without my permission. It was like she said, love was like ribbons. And although I'd resisted it—refused it and planned against it—I'd tied a string to Caroline.

She was challenging, and frustrating. She was fiery when I was ice cold, chaotic when I grasped for control, and she was gas for my fire ninety percent of the time...But as I'd come to discover, she was more than just the snarky, fierce, tough exterior she put on. Because the facade she'd built of this sweet, innocent, soft woman in order to trick people wasn't such a facade. Caroline *was* soft, she was innocent, she was good and sweet and thoughtful and gentle. She just needed to feel safe enough to show it. And somehow, I gave her that. I saw Caroline for who she was, and at some point, I'd taken a nosedive off the cliff for her. Even though I knew I might crash.

There's no going back though. Not now. I was in too deep. Because whether or not she ever returned my feelings, I'd already jumped. So, whether it was Caroline's arms that met me at the bottom or unending pain, I was falling.

"What happened to being antagonistic friends?" she whispered, a bit of insecurity poking holes in her affection.

"You grew on me," I said, trailing my fingers through her hair, my body practically singing to have her so close. "Like a fungus."

She laughed, a sweet light sound that went straight to my soul. "Sounds about right." A few more moments of peaceful quiet passed, but I wasn't bothered. I knew she wasn't scared or offended. Just thoughtful. "You've grown on me too," she admitted timidly.

"I couldn't tell by the way you threw yourself at me the other night."

She pinched my side for teasing her. "So, what does this mean? Now that we officially don't hate each other."

"Hmm...I guess it makes us actual friends." For now. Eventually, I'd have to man up and make a move—because Caroline as *just* a friend was never going to be enough. Oh, and I'd also have to tell her about the mate bond. *Hopefully I survive.*

"No," she hummed, pushing away from me just enough to sit up. She was still sitting in my lap as she tucked her hair behind her ear. I had to bite back a grin at the blush staining her cheeks. *I did that.* And I wanted to do it again and again. "What about safe friends?"

I was *not* a sappy person. In fact, I considered myself allergic to sap. But hearing Caroline call me her safe friend? That had me feeling all kinds of sentimental.

"Safe friends?" I nodded thoughtfully.

"I just mean that we're a safe space for each other," she stuttered, blushing brighter, her embarrassment rising with every word. "We can throw relentless barbs at each other just because it's entertaining, and argue like cats and dogs when we don't agree—which is often...And we can have vulnerable conversations like this..."

"I like it, Care," I assured her, reaching out to squeeze her hand. "No more antagonistic friends. From now on, we're safe friends."

She smiled at me for a few moments before she seemed to realize she was still sitting in my lap. Her Nephilim abilities were on full display as she launched from the bed at top speed. "You gonna be able to sleep now?" she babbled nervously.

"Actually," I said, standing and stretching my arms with a yawn, "What would you say to staying up with me? We can watch *The Office* downstairs?"

When Caroline failed to answer at first, it took me a moment to realize why she was distracted. Her attraction blared through the mate bond as her eyes lingered on...well, all of me. First my shoulders, then my chest, my abs, my arms; she was looking her fill—and I didn't mind. I may have had a long way to go to get her to love me, but at least the attraction was already there.

"As long as you agree to put on a shirt," she managed to say as her eyes finally made their way back to my face.

I didn't bother to fight the grin that spread across my lips, which had Care rolling her eyes and heading for the door.

"Don't go getting cocky Bear Man. I'm adult enough to admit that I like what I see. Doesn't mean I don't like other men I see too," she challenged, smirking at me over her shoulder.

"What other shirtless men are you ogling?" I demanded, grabbing a shirt from my dresser before racing after her.

The way she shrugged one shoulder, her basketball shorts *barely* visible under her oversized shirt, had me shoving every possessive, caveman instinct to the back of my mind. What was worse was that she didn't have any idea what she was putting me through. *I can only imagine how evil she'll be once she realizes that I'm so much more than* just *attracted to her.*

Heaven help me.

"Well, I haven't seen him shirtless," she said, giving me that innocent look she had so perfectly practiced, "But I imagine Logan isn't too shabby to look at."

"*Excuse me??*"

THIRTY

Caroline

Twenty minutes later, we were sprawled out on a couch in the enormous living room downstairs, with Daisy Mae snoring in front of the fireplace, soaking up the heat like a salamander. *Speaking of heat*...I shifted under my blanket, acutely aware of Morgan sitting beside me. I'd been a little disappointed when he handed me my own blanket—part of me had been daydreaming about a little friendly cuddling. *Friends cuddle, right?*

Well, apparently, *we* didn't. So instead, I daydreamed about it. Imagining what it would be like to curl up against him. Maybe rest my hand on his firm chest...

Unable to stop myself, I glanced at him from the corner of my eye. He sat close beside me, his face adorably scrunched up as he watched the second episode of *The Office*. Like many of us, he wasn't quite sold on it at first.

It seemed like a trick, that this man with the scars and the unnerving grey eyes and the dangerous reputation was sitting here watching *The Office* with me. Everything about this moment was so sweet, from the way he watched so studiously to the fact that he kept checking on me every few minutes as if to assure himself that I was still here. Still safe. This version of him was so different than the one that the rumors painted him to be.

Because contrary to what the world believed, Morgan Hohlt wasn't scary or cruel or evil. Instead, he was the kind of man who panicked when I was injured. Who bought me milkshakes and fries, no matter how poisonous he thought they were. He was the kind of man who fought hard for those he cared about and spent all his energy pretending that others' opinions of him didn't matter.

But I'd heard what people said about him. The rumors, the cruel nicknames, the horrible stories of the evil Berserker Chief. And I knew the pain it caused him; the weight he carried, trying to prove them all wrong and yet knowing that it would never be enough. I knew who Morgan Gareth Hohlt was, and it wasn't at all who I'd judged him to be.

"You told me I didn't have to like the first season," he said, giving me a side eyed look. "So, you can't judge me for not loving the show on the first episode."

"I'm not judging you."

"Then why are you staring? I'm wearing a shirt now, so I know my muscles can't be distracting you," he teased, his eyes light and happy. Such a contrast to how distraught he'd been when he woke up. "Unless you're still thinking about it. Should I take the shirt back off so you can see them again? Maybe you want to take a picture."

He reached for the hem of his T shirt, and even though I knew he was joking, I shoved his arm down. The last thing I needed was a second showing. *I'd like to keep my foot* outside *my mouth, thank you.* And seeing him in all his shirtless glory again would make me all kinds of stupid.

"Oh, get a grip! I'm not hot and bothered, I'm just bothered." It was a lie, but there was no way I was about to inflate his ego by admitting the truth.

"About?"

Good question. "Um...I was just thinking about...what the hitwoman said." *Yeah, that'll work.* "How she was sent to frame you and capture me—which we kind of already suspected...But what I can't figure out is how anyone knew I even existed—or that I was staying here."

All joy fled from Morgan's face, and I immediately regretted my words. He so rarely looked happy and carefree. I hated to see it fade.

"My bet is on the council," he said with a frustrated sigh. "I just don't know who..."

"But how would they have found out about me?"

"We probably won't know until we find them."

The annoying thing was that he was right. Someone was out there, plotting ways to ruin Morgan's life and take me captive. And I had a feeling that this time, my captor wouldn't be like Morgan. They weren't going to buy me milkshakes and respect my personal boundaries. Instead, I would become someone's dancing monkey. I'd be drugged and coaxed into committing crimes on their behalf. They'd prick me with needles, selling my blood to make illegal potions. I would become a trophy, a lion in a cage.

"Only the worst kind of people want an Elf for a pet," I mumbled quietly, unable to hide my fear.

I was very aware of Morgan's eyes on me, but I couldn't bring myself to meet his gaze. I didn't want him to see me like this; weak and afraid. But when he reached over and covered my hand with his, all I felt was comfort.

"I'll die before I let anyone put you in a cage Care," he whispered angrily, his calloused fingers gentle as they stroked mine. "I swear it."

And I believed him. But I couldn't understand why he'd risk *so* much for me. Why my safety and freedom were important enough to die for. *Maybe this is just what friendship is.* Other than Ariel, I'd never had a friend that knew all my secrets, that I really believed would stick around. Morgan was my first.

"Thank you..." I stared at our hands for a moment before meeting his gaze. "Although maybe don't die. I'd be kinda bummed about it."

Mor grinned, and just like that, happiness flooded my chest. Who knew his smiles could be so powerful. But before either one of us could fully enjoy the moment, Morgan's phone began to buzz beside him. He barely glanced at the screen before showing it to me. Merida was calling.

"Hey Merida," he answered, putting the phone on speaker, "What's up?"

"Okay, so you know how I have contacts on the black market?" she asked, her voice a little hurried.

I raised an eyebrow at Morgan, and he smirked.

"I did, but Caroline didn't," he replied cheekily.

"Oh..." Merida went quiet for a few moments, and I wondered if she was bothered to have me there listening. But when she spoke again, it wasn't with dislike so much as discomfort. "Hi Caroline, I'm glad you're here for this...I just wish it was under better circumstances."

Morgan's tightened on mine, and his expression hardened. "Merida? What's wrong?"

"One of my contacts from the black market told me that there's going to be an auction in two days...for the vigilante."

At first, I wasn't sure I heard her right. First of all, unless we were talking about a bachelorette auction—and I was positive we weren't—people weren't supposed to auction off other people. And second of all, you can't auction off what you don't have.

While I considered this new information silently, Morgan opted to express himself more vocally. By shouting. "*Excuse me?*"

"Mor, you're yelling," I pointed out, covering our conjoined hands with my free one.

"Am not!"

"Yes, you are," Merida and I said in unison.

Morgan glared at me, but I wasn't moved by the expression. Especially when he leaned closer, as if he needed the close proximity in order to calm down.

"Did you find out anything else about the auction?" I asked, trying to fit all the pieces together.

"I don't know who'll be attending," Merida replied without hesitation, "But I do know that it'll be at the Treasury Hotel."

Well, that had Morgan's anger revving its engine again. "Eileen the Dragon Queen is behind it?" he demanded.

"As far as I know, she isn't officially the seller, but given that it's at her hotel, I'm assuming she is."

Morgan and I shared a look, and I knew we were thinking the same thing. It wasn't a coincidence that Merida just so happened to hear about this auction. Nor did it make sense that the location of the auction was public knowledge on the black market. Things like this were always linked to public locations, where bidders would be vetted by a bouncer before being given the real address. I'd gotten enough Shifter Alliance employees sacked for going to illegal magic auctions in the last three years to know how the process worked.

"It's a setup," Morgan said, his concern melding with his anger. "Eileen wanted the information to get back to us."

"Yeah...but I'll bet you she has all kinds of information in that penthouse suite of hers," I pointed out, stroking the back of his hand with my thumb. "She probably even has evidence of her frame job against you, and information on how she found out about me. All we have to do is go get it."

"Care, she's expecting us." He wasn't wrong, but he was forgetting that the Shifter Alliance had been expecting me to break into the Alliance Building every day for three years. Yet I'd never been caught. *Well, not by them anyway.*

"Are you forgetting the very reason you kidnapped me? I'm good at what I do, Mor. We won't get caught."

He didn't seem convinced, giving me that 'don't make me risk losing you' face that I was really beginning to hate. It made it almost impossible for me to be mad at him. Thankfully, Merida was immune.

"Oh, if you're pulling a heist, can I help?" she begged excitedly, and I realized that I should've befriended her a long time ago. Especially if she could help me wear down Morgan.

"No," Mor growled, "You've already put yourself in enough danger for me. You can be ground support, but you can't break in."

"So..." I smiled, "Does that mean that *we're* breaking in?"

Morgan sighed and rubbed his forehead. Poor guy had probably sprouted three new grey hairs in the last five minutes.

"I hate this idea so much. I hate that it puts you in danger, I hate that things could so easily go wrong." He paused, shaking his head. "But I can't seem to say no to you."

Merida and I both squealed and I launched myself at Morgan, squeezing him in a tight hug.

"I'm saying yes," he whispered in my ear so Merida couldn't hear, "But so help me, Care, I'm not losing you. I don't care what I have to do or who I have to eliminate. We go in together, we come out together."

Goosebumps prickled down my spine and I held him tighter. Now that I knew what it felt like to not only be this important to someone, but to have them be so vital to me, I wasn't losing that. I wasn't losing *him*. No matter what.

THIRTY ONE

Caroline

The next day—technically a few hours later—we all sat gathered in Morgan's office, planning our heist.

"So, we're just going to...break in?" Clint asked from an armchair.

"Yep." I scooted further back on Morgan's desk, mentally preparing a speech to convince the gang to go along with my plans. I hadn't imposed magical manipulation on any of them yet. But I might if they tried to stop me. Because not only would Eileen the Dragon Queen have information on who'd discovered me, but there could also be evidence to clear Morgan's name.

"To the Treasury Hotel?" Mike asked incredulously.

I smiled at the group. "Yep."

Morgan grumbled under his breath about the lack of intelligence required to conceive a plan like this. I chose not to be offended. Sure, the Treasury Hotel was the home base for the Dragons in Shifter Haven. But only Eileen and a handful of her most trusted people lived in the hotel...A large handful.

"Certainty of death," Mike shrugged, turning to Clint, "Small chance of success..."

Clint grinned. "What are we waiting for?"

"Wait, did you just quote *The Lord of The Rings*?" I asked, smiling at their excitement.

"Why do you sound so surprised? Because we're too cool to be nerdy? Too strong and manly to appreciate an epic fantasy?" Clint sassed, flexing his bicep.

I shrugged and tossed my hair over my shoulder. "No, I'm just surprised you had the attention span to watch it."

Both men pretended to be offended, gasping dramatically. They were clutching their chests as if wounded when Morgan slammed a fist against his desk. "Enough joking," he growled. "This isn't some fun little adventure. What we're doing is dangerous. The Treasury Hotel is filled with people who turn into *Dragons*."

"Not full-sized ones," Logan pointed out, reclining lazily on the couch. When Morgan glared at him, he just smirked. "What? I'm just pointing out that yes, they turn into Dragons, but they're not much bigger than a Berserker in bear form. Plus, we're stronger."

Morgan wasn't impressed.

He stared unblinking at his best friend, and I felt his frustrations skyrocketing. What Logan and the rest of the group didn't understand was that Mor wasn't being a wet blanket just to be one. He was worried. Desperately terrified. And I knew that his fear extended not just to me but to his family too. So many things could go wrong with this plan, and I wasn't ignorant of the risk we were all taking.

"Aside from the general size of Dragons," Grey interrupted, diffusing the tension that had sprung up between the men, "They also have extreme loyalty on their side."

"Forced loyalty," Mike scoffed. "They're essentially a dictatorship."

"But since they still obey human laws, no one cares how the leadership in their faction functions," Grey shrugged, unbothered. "The point though is that not only do they turn into large Dragons, but they'll also blindly follow their leader's rule. No matter the cost. So, if the goal is to catch Caroline, then they'll stop at nothing to ensure it. There are, however, many places in the hotel where it won't be possible for them to shift."

"Yes," I nodded, taking the map of the hotel from Morgan's desk. "The only floors they have sufficient space to shift in—particularly if more than one tries to shift at a time—are the conference center on the third floor, the ballroom on the eighth floor, the pool on the fifth floor, the main lobby, and the penthouse way up on the fifteenth floor."

"Which is where we expect not only the dragon representative to be," Morgan added, his anxiety softening now that we were focused on making a plan, "But also any information she has on Caroline. The goal is to get safely in and out of the building, *and* to recover everything Eileen has on Caroline, as well as proof that she's been framing us."

"Sure, because that won't be difficult at all," Logan said dryly, leaning back on the couch.

I didn't have to look at Morgan to know that he was glaring. But Logan was unfazed, smiling at the grumpy Berserker behind me.

"So, what are we—"

Mike's question was interrupted by a knock at the office door. I jumped at the sound, wondering who would be knocking since we were all here.

"It's just Wallace," Mor assured me, setting a hand on my back as he stood. "He texted to let me know he was coming." Then—because apparently, he couldn't tell that his touch was frying my braincells—he ran his hand up to my shoulder and gave it a squeeze before heading to the door. *Well that's...unexpected.*

"Why am I hearing about an auction to *buy* the vigilante?" Mr. Wallace demanded the second Morgan opened the door.

"Hi Mr. Wallace," I greeted him with a wave and a smile.

"Good afternoon, Caroline." Mr. Wallace smiled, but his lips turned right back down into a frown when he looked at Morgan. "That sweet girl is apparently being auctioned off like a cow. How? Why? What are you doing about it?"

Morgan sighed and ushered Mr. Wallace out into the hall. But Morgan paused and turned back to look at me. Meeting my eyes, he gave me a sweet, reassuring smile. Then he *winked* and shut the door.

This—this was what had me feeling all kinds of strange today. From the way he'd held me in his bed after his nightmare this morning, to holding my hand when Merida called, Morgan was acting different. And although I didn't have a lot of experience with friends, and I really wanted to believe otherwise so we could cuddle, I didn't think they touched each other *this* much. Yet Mor was being so attentive. Touching me in ways that weren't inappropriate or unwanted, but not totally necessary—like touching my back just now. He was still Morgan, still grouchy and bristly, but there was something softer there too. His affection for me felt stronger, brighter. But since he also felt affection toward his brothers and Grey and Logan, I didn't really know what that meant for me...

"Well, that was telling," Grey hummed, writing something on his clipboard.

"What was?" I narrowed my eyes first at him and then the rest of the group. Every last one of them was filled to the brim with amusement.

"Just the general tenderness of big brother Hohlt," Clint grinned, setting his hands behind his neck.

Mike, a little less cheeky than his brother, smiled at me. "It's interesting to watch him with you."

Interesting wasn't the word I would've used. Confusing was more like it. Because I wasn't blind, I knew Morgan treated me differently than the rest of the group. He was gentler, more attentive, more concerned. But the really confusing part was how it made me *feel. How* does *it make me feel?*

Thankfully, I was saved from having to think about it as my phone started ringing. I excused myself and slipped into the hall. Since Morgan and Mr. Wallace were nowhere to be found, I shut the office door and leaned back against the wall.

"Hey sis." I pressed the phone to my ear; thankful it wasn't a facetime. I didn't particularly want to see my sister's expression for this conversation.

"Hey sis?" she parroted, already annoyed. "That's all you have to say to me? You leave me a voicemail saying that you're going to be off the grid for a while and that you can't tell me any details, and now all you have to say is 'hey sis'?"

I winced at her screech. "Ow, Ariel! You don't have to yell at me. I'd like to maintain full hearing in both ears, thank you."

"Oh, but I do have to yell at you! Because clearly, you've forgotten the rules of sisterhood!"

I hadn't. The rules we wrote down when we were fourteen were emblazoned on my brain. Mostly because Ariel liked to repeat them to me anytime I did something to make her angry. Which was often. I also knew that she still had the original rules framed in her house—she was nothing if not sentimental.

Essentially, the rules demanded that we not keep secrets from each other, not call the police if either of us committed murder—and also help bury the bodies—and never marry Zac Efron since we couldn't both have him. Like I said, the rules were made by fourteen-year-olds.

"You do know that some of those rules no longer make sense, right? Because if Zac Efron suddenly slides into my DMs, I'm not turning him down," I joked dryly, only partly serious.

"I'll fight you for him. And I might be small, but I can take you." And she probably could. "Now tell me what the heck is going on. What's this plan you so vaguely mentioned?"

And just like that, all the snark fled my body, leaving behind only raging anxiety. I'd called her right after Mor and I got off the phone with Merida to let her know that I was going on a heist. But I'd purposefully called in the middle of the night so I could just leave a voicemail and *not* have this conversation...

"Someone knows what I am." When Ariel didn't immediately reply, I barreled forward, needing to get it all out. "The copycat was hired to frame Morgan, and to take me alive. We think whoever's behind it knows that I'm an Elf. And we just found out that there's an auction going down tomorrow at the Treasury Hotel to buy the vigilante."

"*Excuse me?*"

"It's not a real auction. It's a trap."

Ariel didn't say anything at first, but I could hear the gears turning in her head. And I could almost hear the moment she realized why I'd called her. "You're going to spring it."

"Yes...and even if Morgan and I are able to stop the Dragon Queen, it's possible that she learned about me from someone else. I'd like to think that this mission will give us all the answers..."

"But it might not, and you need me and Mom and Dad to keep our distance." There was no judgement in Ariel's voice, no anger. Because she understood what was at stake. She knew that if any of my family were in danger, it would put me in danger too. Ariel might not have always understood why I did what I did, but she did understand that.

"Yeah," I nodded, pausing when I felt tears burn the backs of my eyes. I liked to be all bravado and sass, and most of the time I felt pretty in control...But the truth was that I was scared. Scared that we wouldn't stop whoever was behind this. Scared that despite Morgan's promises, I would end up in a cage. Scared that he'd die trying to save me. Scared that my family would be used against me. I was a big ball of fear, and I *hated* it. "I'm sorry to put this on you. I just—"

"Caroline Felicity Birch, don't you dare apologize to me! You *never* have to apologize to me for this. I know you think I don't get it, and yeah, there are parts of your life as an Elf that I'll never quite understand because I'm not one. But you're my sister and I love you. I support you. Do I hate that your job puts you in danger? Heck yes. But I'm so proud of you, Care. You're helping people, no matter the cost to you. How could I not support that? I just hate that I can't help to keep you safe."

My poor sentimental heart ached at her sincerity. She would totally fight off kidnappers for me if I let her. "I know, but if it makes you feel any better, I've got five Berserkers that won't leave me alone."

"It does make me feel better actually. Especially since I know one of those Berserkers is Morgan the sexy—"

"I will pay you anything," I begged, cutting her off, "If you just *please* stop talking!"

"Fine, buzzkill," she sighed, and I could practically hear her rolling her eyes. "But you owe me."

"You know, you're kind of annoying," I laughed, grateful for the distraction from my tears. "But I don't know what I'd do without you."

"Combust like a dying star, obviously."

"True—then you could go after Zac Efron without having to fight me for him."

She laughed and after I promised to call her the minute the heist was over, we hung up. And I was left standing there in the hallway. Just me and all the feelings I'd repressed.

Fear, pain, loneliness, exhaustion and endless tears all came at me like a massive wave. One after the other they crashed over me. Unable to stand under the weight of it, I crumpled to the floor and let myself cry. The hiccup sobs were just starting when I heard footsteps thundering from the other end of the house.

"Caroline?" Morgan yelled. But this time, he wasn't annoyed or grouchy. This time, he was *terrified*.

"Here," I gasped through another sob. When Mor came running down the hallway, I was so drenched in salt water and snot that I could hardly see him. He dropped to his knees, and I felt his hands flutter around me, checking me for injuries. "I'm not hurt."

"What's wrong?" he demanded, his low voice laced with worry.

"I'm just..." I paused, taking a shaky breath, and rubbing the tears from my eyes. Morgan was watching me so intently, like he was looking for something he could fix. A problem he could solve. He wanted to slay the boogieman for me and save my day. But I wasn't sure my day could be saved. "I'm so tired Mor. I'm tired of being scared, and yet never letting myself *be* scared because it makes me feel weak. I'm tired of being alone, of carrying so much all by myself. I'm tired of holding myself together with snark and clever plans because the truth is that it's not really working. I'm falling apart and I just...I don't want to be hunted, and I don't want to be afraid of it alone anymore."

Before I could even finish my speech, Morgan was there. On the floor right beside me. Tugging me into his arms.

I went easily onto his lap, clutching him like a security blanket. And despite the panic and fear and anger I felt inside him, he held me so gently. One hand combed through my hair, gently grazing against my scalp. The other pressed against my back, his arm cocooning me against his chest.

"Shatter, Care," he whispered, "Break, unravel. And when it's over, when all the tears are out and the frustrations have been vented, I'll be here. *We'll* be here. We'll be scared together, and fight together, and carry it all together. I know you've been alone for a long time, and you're more than capable of taking care of yourself, but..." he paused, and I sniffed back my snot, looking up into his grey eyes. His affection was strong, but I sensed the nerves beneath it, the hesitation.

"But what?" I breathed, desperate to know what he was holding back.

He took a deep breath, pulling me a tad closer. "I know that you can take care of yourself, but there are going to be times when you can't. When it gets to be too much. And I want to fill the gap for you, Care. I want to lift the burdens when you can't and be the safe space you go to when you're scared. I don't want you to hide from the ugly things or shove them aside. I want you to let yourself feel them. And while you're breaking and weak, I'll hold you up. Because weakness isn't bad, Care. It's an opportunity for grace, and an opportunity for those who care about you to be there for you."

Okay, so as it turns out, crying happens both when you're scared *and* when you're feeling super sappy. *How stupid is that??*

"I think," I sniffled, burying my face back in his shirt so he wouldn't have to see my ugly cry, "I'm going to keep you."

"You sure?" he murmured, a smile in his voice. "Because there's a no returns policy."

"Don't need one. Just a lifetime warranty."

"Lifetime, huh?"

I nuzzled myself further against him, wedging my head beneath his chin. "You object?"

"No." He sighed, turning to rest his cheek on my hair. "But I want one too."

"A lifetime warranty?"

"A lifetime warranty."

I smiled, surprised that I could feel so happy after feeling so broken. "Deal."

THIRTY TWO

Morgan

Was I wearing a noose? A bandana maybe? A choker necklace or a dog collar? Because I could've sworn that I felt something strangling me. *Oh, that's right. It's just my immense panic, casually choking me to death.*

In my defense, we were currently standing in a bookstore across from the Treasury Hotel. The very hotel we planned to break into. Tonight. Hence my panic.

"Stop it," Care whispered, nudging me with her elbow.

Startled out of my brooding, I glanced down at her. Her auburn hair was swept to the side in a low, loose ponytail. A blue ribbon was tied around it, matching her blue jacket. She'd wanted to wear all black, but the point of this mission was to be inconspicuous.

Clint, however, was already failing at it. He was pretending to read a book as he winked at a pair of young women who walked by. The women giggled and pointed at Clint as they walked away. It was only then that my baby brother realized he'd been holding a book about IBS.

Shaking my head, I turned my attention back to Caroline. "Stop what?" I asked, trying to appear nonchalant. Which was pretty much impossible when my brothers, my best friend, my second in command and my *bond mate* were all about to risk their lives in less than three minutes.

"Really? You're going to try to lie to me? I'm an Elf, genius. I can feel you freaking out right now."

"I love it when you say sweet nothings to me."

She rolled her eyes but couldn't keep her lips from tipping up on one side.

"She's right," Logan agreed, pretending to peruse the shelves beside Care. "You're like those nervous dogs. The ones where you're not sure if they're going to bite you or pee themselves."

I scowled at him but didn't bother commenting. I'd only get us kicked out for yelling. "Alright, it's time. Is everyone clear on what they're supposed to do?"

Grey nodded. He was clipboard free tonight, and I wondered if he was suffering from separation anxiety. The man never left the house without it. "Yes, Mike and I will rob the bank next door to the hotel."

"Okay, let's not announce that part so loudly," I warned, motioning for him to be quieter.

"We'll *pretend* to rob the bank," Mike corrected, shooting a nervous look around the store. "Which should draw the majority of the Dragons away from the building while you guys do your thing."

Pretending to rob the bank was risky. It was owned and run by the Dragons, and a good chunk of their net worth was wrapped up in it. So, while it was dangerous to rob it, it was also a surefire way to get some of the Dragons out of the hotel.

"And you're sure you can do that other thing?" I asked, looking at Logan. His part of the plan was the riskiest besides Caroline and I's.

Logan nodded; all traces of teasing gone. "They won't see me coming."

"And I'll take care of the power with Mike's help via earpiece," Clint added, finally paying attention to us instead of the new woman he'd been making eyes at.

"Alright, then we're ready," I sighed, saying the words but not really meaning them. With everyone prepared and ready to go, there was no reason to delay...Except that every single important person in my life was about to be in danger. And that didn't sit well with me.

"We'll all be okay." Care set a hand on my arm, drawing me out of my worry. "Let's just get it done."

I wanted to argue with her, because she didn't *know* that we'd all be okay, but instead I nodded. We had to do this. "Okay, everyone be careful, and remember, no part of this mission is worth your life. We can always back out and try another way, but only if we all come out alive. No hero moments, no risky decisions. Just stick to the plan and bail if you have to."

Everyone silently nodded, feeling the gravity of what we were about to do.

"Logan, you be careful." I stepped forward and we clapped each other on the shoulder.

"Just this once." He smirked, heading for the door of the bookstore. "But after this is over, I'm back to being reckless."

After he stepped outside, I turned my attention to my brothers. "Whatever you do, don't get caught."

"We'll come back," Mike said as the three of us touched our foreheads together.

"We promise," Clint added.

The silly tradition of sticking our heads together like this started back when we lived with Mr. Wallace. Mike had pretty severe nightmares about our mom's death at the time, and when he woke up screaming, it would scare Clint. So, to calm us all down, we'd all press our heads together and pray. It was our way of reminding each other that even if we were all we had, it was enough.

"Now go before I get all sappy and try to stop you," I coughed—an attempt to cover the emotion welling up inside me. Both boys smiled and nodded before they too slipped out the door.

Three down, one to go.

I turned to Grey, and he smiled at me in that fatherly way of his. Grey had been my second in command since I'd first taken the job of Chief six years ago. He, more than anymore, knew how scared I'd been to do this job.

"We'll be fine," he said, giving me a nod—his version of a hug. "You two watch your backs in there. We're all going home tonight."

I just silently returned his nod, too emotional to say goodbye. Once he left the store, it was just me and Caroline.

"Ready?" she asked, smiling up at me. I had no choice but to smile back; she was contagious like that. "Because things are about to get weird."

Then, without warning, her dainty features began to shift, and her hair changed from auburn to blonde. It was like a ripple flowing over her body. First her hair changed, then her eyes grew dark. Her features became harsher, the line of her jaw and the shape of her nose all shifting to appear a little more stocky. By the time she was done, she was still pretty. But not nearly as beautiful as the real Caroline.

"Wow," I breathed, staring at a complete stranger, "That's...insane."

"Pretty cool, huh?" She grinned, fluffing her now blonde ponytail. "You wouldn't even know it was me."

I knew we needed to go, to get the plan moving so the rest of the team could do their parts...But first I needed a proper goodbye with my mate. Just in case.

"I'd still know," I said, tugging on a strand of blonde hair. "Even if this face doesn't blush like yours does. Even if it doesn't have your freckles or your green eyes that always look a little bit gold in the right light. Even if I passed you on the street tomorrow and you didn't look like you, I'd still know you, Care. Always."

Caroline stared mutely up at me. Her eyes were wide with a little bit of wonder, the ring of blue around the center still there. Because no matter what face she was wearing, she was still my mate.

"Can you," I stuttered, my emotions rising up in my throat, "Can you switch back for a second?"

She nodded, and in a matter of moments she was Caroline again—my Caroline. Without saying a word, I stepped closer and tenderly took her face in my hands. Her cheeks were smooth beneath my thumbs where they brushed her freckles. All the while, Care stood silently. Confusion, nerves and *hope* flowed from her through the mate bond.

"I need to tell you something," I whispered, knowing that I couldn't go into the hotel and do this heist without telling her what she was to me. "You're not just my safe friend anymore, Care. You're my *best friend*. You're the place I feel safest, most understood. You were a parasite at first." At this, she laughed, and I felt myself smile. "But now you're the person I need most. You're the one I'm most worried about tonight. Because I can't go home without you. I won't."

Okay, so it wasn't a confession of romantic feelings. But in my defense, I couldn't tell if Caroline was romantically interested in me just yet. And the last thing I wanted to do was scare her away. So instead of being brutally honest, I was partially honest. Baby steps. *Someday she'll be ready to hear all of it.* Hopefully.

Care just watched me for a few moments, saying nothing. I tried to get a read on her feelings, but they were too confusing as they all tumbled together. Then, with a determined look, she flung herself against my chest. "You're my best friend too, you big flea ridden Bear Man," she grumbled against me.

I laughed, immediately wrapping my arms around her. "You and your sweet nothings."

"Shut up, I'm not done," she complained, and I complied, happy to rest my cheek on her hair while she talked into my shirt. "You annoy the crap out of me sometimes, and if someone had told me six months ago that you'd be my best friend, I would have died laughing...But you are, Mor. You're the one person that makes me feel safest, most known, most...precious. And now that I've got you, I refuse to lose you. You hear me Bear Man? We're both coming out of this fight tonight!"

"Deal," I whispered, breathing in the scent of her: sweet and cozy. "We're a team, you and me. We come out together or not at all."

"Together or not at all," she echoed.

We stood like that for a few more moments, just drinking up the comfort of having each other close. Of having each other safe.

Then I finally released her. "Ready?" I held up my arm, and with a cheeky smile, she stepped under it.

"Ready."

We left the bookstore, making our way across the street. It was late, but business signs and quaint little streetlights illuminated the area. Caroline and I both made sure to stumble as we walked over to the half circle driveway in front of the hotel. She leaned heavily into my side, and I slurred a greeting to the doorman as Caroline laughed loudly. Though the doorman looked less than pleased with our fake drunkenness, he opened the door for us.

The moment we stepped inside—giggling and stumbling—everyone in the marble lobby looked our way with varying sneers and judging side eyes. But we ignored them all as we strode—haphazardly—straight back to the elevators. Thankfully, the doors opened quickly. We wanted to get attention, but we weren't quite ready to be caught just yet.

"So far so good," I whispered close to Caroline's ear as the elevator doors closed. Hopefully to the cameras it would look like I was being flirty.

"You think those will be enough?" Care asked glancing down at the knives holstered to my sides beneath my jacket.

"Between them and my super strength, I hope so."

"Well, hopefully my disguise and emotional manipulation will help since I can't really fight."

"I can teach you, you know," I suggested, letting my thumb rub her shoulder. For the cameras. Obviously.

"With knives?" She eyed the weapons at my sides like they might bite.

"Eventually, yeah. We'd start with fists first though. No way am I giving you a sharp weapon right off the bat."

She glared and pinched my hip. I was just starting to tickle her in retaliation when the elevator doors opened. Panicked, I turned us around and pressed Care into the back corner. Resting my hands on the wall on either side of her head, I blocked her from view as eight Dragon shifters piled in behind us. All Shifters looked human when not using magic to shift, but the Dragon Queen was notorious for requiring those in her inner circle to wear dark suits and pins with her emblem on them.

"Not ready to be caught with me?" Care teased, setting her hands on my chest. I knew it was part of the act. We wanted to get caught, but on our terms. Which meant that right now, we needed to make people too uncomfortable to look our way. But with her palm over my racing heart and her body so close, *my* body was having a hard time separating reality from fantasy.

"Not quite, sweetheart." I tried to make the comment teasing, but it was hard to hide my nerves when she could sense them.

"Listen, I know it's...a little different for us to act like this," she whispered, grabbing hold of my jacket, and tugging me closer. But I'd already been standing toe to toe with her. So now, we were chest to chest, and I could feel her breath on my face. Terror sliced through me as my attraction skyrocketed. *Surely, she can feel that.* But she didn't seem uncomfortable. Instead, her eyes were darting around me toward the Dragon Shifters. "But we have to sell this whole drunk lovers thing if we want to appear inconspicuous," Care went on—I'd forgotten that she'd been speaking. *I blame her lips. Or her eyes.* They were both distracting. "So, I need you to pretend to kiss me."

"*What?*"

Care immediately pressed a finger to my lips to quiet me, and my insides trembled. *Shutting up now.* "Follow my lead," she whispered. Then she grasped my face and pulled it to her neck. *Lord, help me.*

My face was pressed against my mate's neck. My mate, who didn't know she was my mate. My mate, whom I was very much into. My mate who *didn't know* that I was into her. *Lord, beer me strength.*

When Care huffed a laugh, I realized I'd said that particular *The Office* quote out loud. And then an idea hit. I was not about to actually kiss Caroline's neck. No way was our first romantic interaction going to be fake. But all we needed to sell the necking was a little laughing and smiling.

So, I moved my head subtly up and down her neck—*without* touching it—and then started telling jokes.

"So, is this the start of the two-way petting zoo?" I whispered.

It worked. Caroline chuckled. When her hands drifted into my hair—part of our cover, I reminded myself—I kept the jokes flowing to distract myself.

"You didn't even use it right," she complained quietly after I'd made a 'that's what she said' joke.

I grinned. "That's what she said."

This time, Care's laugh was a little louder, and I could *feel* all eyes in the elevator turn to us. A little nervous at the attention, I lifted my face and pressed my forehead to hers.

"Don't worry, they only looked for about a second before my love drunk smile made them uncomfortable," she assured me. "They're not looking now."

That was good, I gathered. Problem was, staring down at Caroline, I was a little lost. This was a dangerous mission and a part of me *was* focused on that. Focused on my friends and family who were risking their lives for this. On the danger that Care and I were in right now...But another part of me—a big part of me—was wholly focused on Caroline. Because despite logic and danger, all that seemed to matter was her.

Weak and desperately obsessed with her, I gave in. The mate bond would have sung with joy if it could've as I rested my nose against hers. Our breaths mingled together, and my heart just wanted her closer. *Closer.*

"Care..." My voice came out raspy and dry. As if my entire body knew just how much I wanted her. Needed her. Not to have or use, but just to hold. To protect. To support.

"Yeah?" she replied, barely more than a breath. Her emotions were still a jumble, but her affection stood out. Strong and vibrant.

This close, I couldn't see the differences between this face and her real one. To me she was Caroline. The blue ring in her eyes still tied us together, binding us. And her voice still brushed against me like it knew me, calling me home. And suddenly, the secret of our bond just felt like too much. Too heavy. How could we have a good start if she didn't know where we were starting from?

"There's something I haven't told you..." I said plowing forward even though I *knew* it was the wrong place for this conversation. All I could seem to focus on was the emotional space between Care and I, and my brain's *need* to eliminate all space. "I—"

The elevator cut me off, dinging to announce our arrival on the fourteenth floor. "Shoot, this is us," I growled, hating that this moment had been interrupted. Yet some part of me was grateful that it hadn't happened here with an audience watching our backs.

Still pretending to be drunkenly in love, Care latched onto my arm, and we squeezed our way out of the elevator. A large group of Dragon Shifters rushed past us to get on, and I tugged Care closer.

"Grey and Mike's side of things must be working," Care whispered as the Dragons piled onto the elevator and immediately began slamming fingers against the elevator buttons. When the doors finally closed, we both let out a breath of relief.

Well, I *was* relieved...until Care turned her eyes up at me. I could see the question in them before she even spoke it, and all the tension came flooding back into my body.

"What were you gonna say back in the elevator?"

Here in the hall, the shimmery intensity from our close proximity in the elevator was gone, leaving my sense of logic enough room to wiggle back to the forefront of my mind. And now, as I watched her waiting for an answer, I couldn't give it. To her, I was a friend with news to share. She had no idea that my news was to announce that we were destined to be romantic partners. Because it hadn't occurred to her to associate me with romance. Care had been alone for practically her whole life. Carrying all her burdens by herself. Yet here she was, letting me support her. *As a friend.* And I knew that she wasn't ready yet to let me take up more space in her life. At least not as her mate.

She was already giving a lot by letting me be her best friend, letting me into her vulnerable space. If I added in the news that we were mates, I was certain she'd run. So, for now, I'd keep my mouth shut and give her time to trust me; trust *us*.

"That Merida has a friend keeping watch over Ariel's house." The lie tasted like ash on my tongue. It was true that Merida did have a friend watching Ariel's house just in case Eileen had something else up her sleeve, but I was still lying by omission. And I hated it. "I meant to tell you earlier, but I forgot."

"Oh! I didn't even think about having someone watch out for Ariel!" Care exclaimed, and I sensed her guilt, probably thinking that she wasn't a good sister. And there was my proof that she wasn't ready to hear about the mate bond. She bought my lie, without ever considering that I would have something romantic to say. *She needs time.* "Thank you for looking out for her, Mor," she said, her body full of relief and gratitude.

"Anything for you." At least in that I could be honest.

Her eyes brightened and she gave me a soft smile that did sappy things to my brain. "Ditto, Mor," she said, leaning against my arm.

"Ready for phase two?" I asked, leading us toward the stairwell.

"Absolutely I am."

I smiled at her reference to *The Office* and then pressed against my earpiece to talk to the rest of the team. "Alright guys, we're ready."

"Distraction number two coming right up," Clint responded into both Caroline and I's earpieces—sounding way too enthused to be doing this.

A moment later, the power went out, and everything went dark.

THIRTY THREE

Morgan

AT FIRST, I HADN'T BEEN CONVINCED THAT we could pull this off. To be honest, I *still* wasn't convinced. We were at the top of the stairs on the fifteenth floor now. The door in front of us was the emergency exit for the penthouse, where we were supposed to begin the next phase of the plan. But honestly, I was seriously considering throwing Caroline over my shoulder and running all the way home.

"Don't you go freaking out on me." I glanced over at Care, who now resembled Merida instead of the blonde from earlier.

"I'm not freaking out," I growled, stretching my neck. I was one hundred percent freaking out.

Caroline just sighed and grabbed my hand, tugging me toward the door. "We don't have time for panicking. The longer we stand here, the greater the danger. Now are you ready to do this?"

I scowled but nodded. Care had opted to utilize Merida's appearance in the hopes that it would confuse Eileen the Dragon Queen. This was the last of our distractions, and we needed it to work. *It has to work.*

I tugged Caroline a little closer—there was no way I was going to let her get separated from me—and reached for the metal door. Care had already used her electronic lockpick on it, so it swung open without issue when I turned the handle. The penthouse inside was dark thanks to Clint, and we crept in silently. I knew from studying the floorplans that the emergency exit was in a hallway, and if we went left, it would lead to a large office that connected to a living room.

"This way," I whispered, pulling Care along with me toward the office, my hand trailing along the wall to guide us.

We'd barely stepped out of the hall when all the lights suddenly flashed on. And standing around the perimeter of the room, blocking the cased opening to the living room, were twenty Dragon Shifters. All armed. And to add insult to injury, four more Dragons came sauntering down the hall, making a retreat to the stairwell impossible.

"I expected better," came a bitter, wilted voice.

Eileen stepped forward from the throng, her grey hair perfectly coifed, her matching blazer and pencil skirt perfectly pressed, and her wrinkled face perfectly miserable. She was a cruel old woman whose cranky attitude had only aged her.

"Evening you old bat," I said with a dry smile. "Isn't it a little dangerous for you to be up without your walker?"

"You've always been an arrogant brute," she sneered, unimpressed as her cold eyes swept over me. "It still astounds me that someone with a murderous reputation like yours doesn't have more common sense."

Rage roared to life in my chest at the mention of my so called 'reputation'. People often whispered about me and gossiped behind my back, but no one was dumb enough to accuse me to my face. But then Caroline squeezed my hand and pressed herself closer to me. I breathed deep, sensing her protectiveness, her support, and her affection. *I'm not alone.*

"Alright, get to the point Midol," I barked, pushing back my anger for the moment. Now wasn't the time to fight. Not yet.

"Excuse me?" Eileen scoffed, confused.

"Midol," I repeated carelessly, "As in the laxative brand. Because listening to you talk is like taking a laxative: painful, ugly to listen to, and sometimes vomit inducing."

"Why you—"

Thankfully, Caroline interrupted the Dragon Queen before I could be provoked into ripping her wrinkly head from her body. "Get to the point, Eileen."

Eileen took a deep breath, her features contorted into an ugly glare. She was already a somewhat unattractive woman, but the severity of her expression certainly didn't help. "You know, I have to give you credit, Morgan," she said, a patronizing sweetness to her voice. "You managed to get in here without getting caught first. However, you've proven my point that you lack common sense. Because you've forgotten that you still need to get *out*."

"I'm sorry, I'm still waiting for the point," Caroline sassed, but it was Merida's voice coming from her mouth since she still hadn't shifted back to herself. "Or are you so senile that you forgot it already?"

"You're a feisty little thing, aren't you?" Eileen's smile was every bit as ugly as her glare. And there was a calculating edge to it that I didn't like one bit. The old woman took a step closer to us, and I released Care's hand, instead wrapping my arm around her shoulders. "I'm sure your new owner will find that entertaining at least."

When I snarled at her, Eileen took a step back. And even though she laughed, there was fear in her eyes. She was afraid of me. *Good, she should be.*

"You didn't think the rumor about an auction here tonight was *completely* fake, did you?" she sneered, and I could see her trying to regain her composure as she pulled on her skirt. "There's no auction, sure. But that's because you've already been bought and paid for, dear. And it's my job to get you to your new home."

I was about to let go of Care and shut Eileen up via my hands on her throat when Caroline squeezed my hand. "Is that all you get out of this whole thing? Money?" she asked, redirecting the conversation.

"Money is more than enough as a motivator," Eileen shrugged, the guards around the room shifting, waiting for her cue to pounce. "But it's not my only motivation. You see, I needed to draw you out," she said, nodding at Caroline, "And it just so happened that the two of you were somewhat of a package deal. Framing the Berserkers for the break-ins was an easy way to kill two birds with one stone. I get the vigilante out of my hair so that my own transgressions won't be revealed, and I also get to eliminate my biggest enemy on the council."

"Enemy, really? Isn't that a little extreme?" I complained. "What have I ever done to you other than point out the holes in your ideas?"

"Those *ideas* would have had a major impact on the Dragons had they not been shot down."

"More like they would've impacted your pocketbook," Care mumbled under her breath. I laughed, but Eileen just glared harder.

She stomped forward, pointing a finger toward my face, staying just far enough away that I'd have to step forward to reach her. "When I wanted to expand my holdings and open new hotels, *you* got the rest of the council to shut me down. And when I tried to pass a law that outlined better protections for Dragons, you got everyone to vote against me."

"Because you hid a bunch of things in your proposal that would've required all Dragons to swear fealty to you." I remembered the hidden items in her proposal. She'd laid it all out like she was offering asylum to any Dragons who needed it. But really it was a way to strongarm those who eluded her control into being her slaves. "It was a sneaky way to get control of any Dragons that don't kiss the ground you walk on. Not to mention the new taxation you hid in there too. And as for the hotels, you already have two properties in this city as well as multiple other businesses. The last thing any Shifter community needs is a monopoly. It's dangerous."

Eileen's nostrils flared and if her eyes could shoot fire, I'd be ashes right now. As some of her guards began to unholster their weapons, I wondered how much time we had left to milk this distraction. *Just a few more minutes...*

"You know what else is dangerous?" Eileen taunted, eyes swinging to Caroline. "Having something so valuable be so poorly protected."

"I'm not a *thing*," Caroline hissed, and I was sure if Eileen came any closer, Care would bite her fingers off.

But Eileen was oblivious to the danger of Caroline. Like so many others, she assumed that based on her appearance, my mate wasn't capable of much. I couldn't wait to see the look on her face when she realized how wrong she was.

"You're a weapon," Eileen argued, crossing her arms, "And I'm going to use you to get a confession from Morgan. He'll take the fall for the heists, I'll give you to your new owner, and then I'll go to sleep tonight knowing that I got what I wanted."

"And how do you expect to make me confess?" I didn't particularly care what her plans were—I didn't intend to let her go through with it—but I needed to keep the conversation going.

Eileen tapped her chin, pretending to think it through. "Well, forgive me if I'm wrong, but I do believe that Nephilim can change faces. All I need is one recorded confession..."

Care wouldn't do it. And not because we were mates, but because she was Caroline. And no one forced her to do anything she didn't want to. *I pity the person who tries to make her.*

"What makes you think she'll do it?" I asked, my fingers itching to grab my knives.

"I can be very convincing."

"Not convincing enough," Caroline growled. "Hell could freeze over, and I wouldn't help you. Pigs could fly, it could snow in July, lightning could strike me twice, and you could find five needles in a haystack, but I still wouldn't help you. Did I miss any?" Care turned an innocent look up at me, and I silently applauded her performance.

"Hm, what about 'it could be the first day of never and you still wouldn't help her'?" I suggested, matching her snarky tone.

Caroline giggled, but Eileen was done listening. "Enough!" she shouted, finally losing her control. "You'll get me that confession, because if you don't, I'll begin hurting people. Starting with your sister."

Care's temper flared like lightning and mine jumped up to match it. My body begged to move into action, but I told myself to wait. *Just a few more moments...*

"Not so snarky now, are you?" Eileen smiled, but I wasn't bothered. I could sense Caroline's victory. *Time's up.* I didn't have to listen to Eileen gloat anymore. Knowing what came next, I let my lips kick up into a wicked smile.

"You're forgetting," I said, lazily pulling a knife from its sheath, "What Caroline is best at."

Eileen scoffed, but her eyes latched onto my blade, and she swallowed. "What's that?"

"Sneaking."

The Dragon Queen's face pinched with confusion. Her eyes darted between Care and I, clearly unimpressed since we stood surrounded by her guards. Except that we weren't *all* surrounded by guards...

"Fun fact," came a man's voice from the throng of Dragon Shifters, and the crowd parted to reveal a tall, burly looking man standing behind the computer desk, "Nephilim are notorious for their insubordination. Even started a war over it."

Then the man shifted, and Caroline appeared in his place.

THIRTY FOUR

Caroline

Flashback to fifteen minutes ago...

The stairwell was dark as we stepped inside. I took out my phone and turned on the flashlight. "You guys in here?" I called out.

A moment later, another light came on and Mor and I both turned to see Logan holding a flashlight. And Merida standing beside him.

She wore the exact same outfit as me—thanks to a quick shopping trip earlier today. Her hair was also pulled over in the same side ponytail as mine, hers longer and darker. It wasn't technically necessary for us to be dressed and styled alike since I could shift my entire appearance. But the similarities would help sell our distraction.

"Any problems?" Morgan asked as Logan and Merida stepped over to us.

"You know I'm too good to get caught," Logan teased, lifting a shoulder as he winked.

Mor rolled his eyes, but I saw the smile he tried to hide and felt the bit of relief and amusement that sparked inside him. "Okay, calm down Ethan Hunt. We still have the exit phase of the plan to get through. AKA the really dangerous part."

"You okay? You seem extra tense." Merida nodded at Morgan, and I looked up at him, studying the wrinkles in his forehead. The fierce look in his eyes. He *was* tense, the question was whether or not it was because of the mission or...me.

Our little charade in the elevator had been...intimate. It certainly hadn't been a chore by any means. Morgan—as my sister had said—was a fox, and I my attraction certainly had no problems having him close. I did wonder though how much of a chore it had been for him. I knew he was attracted to me, and that he felt affection for me, but that affection could've been brotherly, friendly, or...*Nope. That's it. Those are the only options.* Mor and I had a good thing going right now—something I'd never had before. We were friends, best friends, and any thoughts about what *more* we could be would only ruin what we already had. *And I'm not losing this.* I didn't think I'd survive it.

"I'm about to take you into a den of Dragons," Mor said, deadpan, "So that my best friend can search for incriminating documents. A plan that only works if we can successfully take on probably over a dozen Dragon Shifters. So yes, I'm tense."

Merida looked over at me and I shrugged. Morgan was always extra cantankerous when he was stressed. "Okay, fair enough," she said, raising her hands in defeat. "But if it helps, the second you give Logan the all-clear sign, we'll call my guy on the Response Team. He'll help you with clean up. So, all you have to do is—"

"Stay alive? Yeah, no problem. Just us against an army," Mor snarked with a tight smile, batting his eyes. *Wow, he's strung up tight right now.*

"Okayyyy," I said, looping my arm through his, hoping that somehow it would help calm him down. "How about you Merida? You ready to do this?"

"Very ready," Merida smiled. And this wasn't a demure, sweet smile. No, this was a ready for battle, excited for bloodshed kind of smile.

"Remember, you can't fight," Logan reminded her. She immediately scowled at him.

"Don't you start with me! I've put up with a lot from you, but I'm not against finally giving you the slap you deserved." Merida pointed a finger in Logan's face, and he sighed, rolling his eyes.

"Seriously? It was years ago."

"Yes, seriously. You were an idiot."

He shook his head but didn't argue, and I immediately wondered what kind of history these two could have.

"Merida, you can't do magic tonight," Morgan insisted, giving the Witch his most intimidating look. "There's a Witch Hunter on the Response Team, and if you use magic, they can trace it back to you. The last thing you need is to be accused of something. So, I know you hate it, but no magic." Merida pouted but said nothing. "Promise me?"

Merida glared at him, but eventually huffed and nodded. "Fine, I promise."

"Now was that so hard—ow!" Logan exclaimed quietly, reaching down to clutch his shin.

Merida smiled. "Don't patronize me and I won't kick you."

"I like you," I nodded, for the first time truly appreciating the Witch's snarky personality. Now that I wasn't viewing her as a threat—just going to completely ignore the fact that I felt threatened over Morgan; my *friend*—I could see just how cool she was.

"Thank you." She smiled at me, but the expression seemed to wane as she looked at Morgan. He was staring down at my arm where it looped through his. His brows were pinched together, and anxiety rolled off him so thick I almost couldn't breathe. "Logan, I think you should escort me up to the fifteenth floor now."

"But I—ow! Again, with the kicking!" Logan grimaced but led Merida to the stairs, leaving Morgan and I alone.

I waited until all I could see of Logan and Merida was the faint glow of Logan's flashlight before I turned to Morgan. Taking my arm out of his, I stepped in front of him. He met my eyes easily, but they were stormy; afraid.

"Are you sure you want to do this?" I asked, setting my hands on his arms.

Morgan was risking so much for me with this heist. His entire family was in danger tonight—for *me*. That was no small thing. Because they didn't really need this heist like I did. Sure, I was going to get evidence to clear Morgan as a suspect for *my* heists as well as find documentation on how Eileen found me, but Morgan didn't really need the evidence. Merida had already shared her concerns with the mayor, and he hadn't been convinced with the accusations against Mor anyway. So, at the end of the day, this whole thing was for *me*. Yet Morgan had signed up, no questions asked.

But instead of answering my question, he asked his own, his voice quiet and his words vulnerable. "Do you trust me?"

I lifted my hands to his face, his five o'clock shadow tickling my palms. Careful to answer his question in both words and actions, I lifted a hand to trace it over his scar. Letting him know that I saw it—that I saw his past—and I wasn't scared.

"In any form," I whispered, promising him my trust, my loyalty, my affection. No matter what.

Morgan said nothing as his eyes grew misty. Seconds passed in silence.

And then he was crushing me to him, holding me like I might be ripped away at any moment. I sighed deep and content as I wrapped my arms around his waist. Burying my face in his shirt, I breathed in the scent of him like it was my last chance. It wasn't. We were both going to survive this. And yet I couldn't let him go. I wanted to stay like this, melded to him and the safety he made me feel, for the rest of my life.

We stood like that for a few more moments, just silently breathing each other in. Committing this moment to memory. But eventually, it was time to let go. We said nothing as we parted and walked hand in hand up to the fifteenth floor. There were no words for the anxiety we both felt on each other's behalf.

"Ready to go?" Merida asked as we joined her and Logan on the landing.

"Yeah," I nodded, offering her a friendly smile. "But first, I'd like to apologize. For being such a monstrous child when you showed up at Morgan's house that first day—though in my defense, you did put me under house arrest."

She laughed, unoffended by my words. "Fair enough. I'd have acted pretty similarly in your situation."

I nodded, but felt the need to add, "Also, I'm sorry for hating you out of jealousy." Without waiting for her to respond, I took the electronic lock pick from my purse and attached it to the keypad on the metal door. "Even though you didn't know about it."

"Uh..." Merida mumbled, confused. "That's okay?"

Meanwhile, Morgan was coughing, and I could sense his embarrassment. Though I couldn't figure out what he'd have to be embarrassed about. He'd always found it funny that I got jealous of his friendship with Merida.

"Anyway," he announced, turning to Logan, "You need to go get in position."

"I know, I know." Logan rolled his eyes, reaching out to slap Morgan on the shoulder in one of those guy non-hug things that I never understood the point of. *Just hug, you big pansies.* "But you be careful in there, okay? I am *not* prepared to raise your brothers by myself."

Mor laughed and clapped him on the shoulder. "We're all coming home tonight. End of story. Now get out of here."

Logan wished us all luck before heading back down the stairs, taking his flashlight with him.

"Remember," Morgan reminded me, his voice taking on that authoritative quality that would've annoyed me if I didn't know how stressed he was, "You get in, get the info, and erase the hard drive. No tricks, Care."

"But I like tricks," I teased, giving him my most innocent look. He wasn't impressed. "Okay fine, no more jokes until you're not so tense. There will be no tricks...other than the one where I fool everyone into believing that I'm a man. That is a pretty big trick."

"Caroline," Mor sighed, closing his eyes. Four new grey hairs were probably sprouting somewhere on his head at this very moment.

"Shall we?" Merida put a hand on the door handle, smiling at Mor and I like she found the whole thing entertaining. *Ugh, I should've befriended her sooner.*

Morgan nodded and released my hand, readying himself for action. Silently, Merida opened the door, blocking herself from view. Mor stepped through into a dark hallway and I followed, the flashlight on my phone pointed down to give us just enough light to move by.

"Feel anyone?" Morgan whispered, standing a few feet away from me in the hallway.

I let my magic unfurl, and it reached out around us. "Two," I breathed, sensing two distinct sets of emotions close by. Both of them on edge and annoyed. I turned to my right, unsure which exact direction they were coming from. Then grunts erupted behind me and I jumped.

Turning around, I pointed my flashlight at Morgan. And the unconscious man he was lowering to the ground. "Nice," I nodded. "That was fast."

"Yeah well—"

But I spun around before he could finish, hearing a quiet shuffling behind me. Sure enough, a large burly man stood in front of me, my light casting harsh shadows on his already intimidating face. *Shoot.*

"Finally. We've been waiting for you," he complained in a deep, rough tone.

But as he reached out to grab me, I yanked on my magic. Working quickly, I latched onto his feeling of irritation, and pushed him into rage. He blinked, confused, so I funneled more magic at him. His anger built higher and higher until he was frozen with it, his chest pumping and his breaths coming fast.

"What did you—ah." He gasped as Morgan's arm went around his neck, having been too distracted by his anger to notice Mor slip around me. The man was out in a matter of seconds, and Morgan dragged him back toward the door with the guidance of my light.

"Well, that was fast," Merida commented as we piled both unconscious men out on the landing.

"If you think that's impressive, what till you see this," I smirked, pulling the chord on my abilities and letting the change ripple through me. From my hair down to my shoes, every bit of me changed to match the man who'd tried to attack me. In some ways, it was strange to shift, strange to look like someone else. But I still felt like me. Still felt like I was in my body, because technically, I was. It just appeared different right now.

"So," I said, popping my hips out one after the other like a model, "How do I look?"

Morgan and Merida both stared at me with a mixture of wonder and curiosity. And a little bit of horror.

"You look..." Morgan started, and then he sighed. "I can't say I'm a fan."

"Yes, but do I look like *him*?" I pointed my light down at the man who lay unconscious.

"I can't even tell the difference between you," Merida smiled, not as fazed by my appearance as Morgan apparently was. "Except for the voice. Can you do voices?"

"I don't know," I smirked, shifting my voice into the one I'd heard from the man, "Can I?"

Merida grinned, impressed. Morgan glared, concerned.

"I'll be fine," I insisted, grasping hold of his arm. "It's you who needs to be careful in there."

"I just..." he paused, staring *up* at me for once. Then he shuddered. "I can't do this with you looking like that. It feels wrong."

Merida and I snickered as Morgan scowled at us.

"Okay, I'm going in now," I said, turning for the door.

But Morgan stopped me with a hand on my much-broader-than-normal shoulder. "Be careful, Care," he whispered, his worry blending with affection, both of them making my heart squeeze. "Remember, we come out together or not at all."

"Together or not at all," I promised.

Appeased but still worried, he let me go.

I wasted no time as I slipped into the hall, knowing that if I stayed in Morgan's presence too long, I wouldn't be able to leave him. And I had a job to do. So, with my phone off and in my pocket, I made my way silently down the hall to the office.

The Dragon Shifters were there, so focused on waiting for Morgan and Merida to appear that they said nothing as I joined them. After all, why would they suspect a fellow colleague of being the Elf they were waiting for?

And when the lights went on a few moments later as Morgan and Merida entered the room, I slipped behind the line of Dragon Shifters toward Eileen's desk. Completely unnoticed.

THIRTY FIVE

Caroline

Currently...

As expected, the room went silent with the shock of my announcement. I grinned, glad to see that I hadn't lost my touch. Meanwhile, Eileen the cranky Dragon Queen stared at me, then at Merida, then at me again.

"Well, you may have fooled me into thinking she was you," the old woman snarled, "But you're still outnumbered, and let's not forget that you've been paid for. You aren't leaving this room a free woman. And now all you've done is given me leverage."

Then she tried to reach for Merida. Big mistake. Huge. Morgan had his knives whipped out so fast that Eileen almost lost a hand before realizing that Morgan was armed.

"I don't think so," he hissed. Merida pressed closer to his side, pulling a dagger from inside her jacket. I knew she didn't know how to fight with it, but I admired the way she bared her teeth at the Dragon Queen anyway.

Time for a distraction. "Hey Eileen." She and her lackeys turned to look at me as I shouted at them. Then, giving my best impression of Katherine Pierce from *The Vampire Diaries*, I said, "Ba-boom." Then I pulled the pins on the two smoke grenades I'd been hiding in my jacket pockets. And with a wicked smirk that would've made Damon

Salvatore proud, I tossed them over the Dragon Shifters' heads. And smoke began to fill the room.

While they were confused and distracted, yelling at each other—idiots—I slipped around them. I stumbled a little, tripping over someone's foot and then the rug, but finally made it over to Morgan and Merida.

"Take this and get the heck out of here," I whispered, not wanting to make it easier for the Dragon Shifters to find us. Then I blindly shoved the USB drive into Merida's hands, struggling to see her clearly through the smoke.

"I hate leaving you guys to fight alone," she complained, and I didn't have to see her clearly to know that she had that determined look on her face. This was a girl who *wanted* to do battle.

"Psht. I've got a Berserker on my side; we'll be just fine." I gave Merida an assuring smile even as nerves flared inside me. And when Morgan's hand brushed against my wrist before finally finding my fingers, I knew he understood. It was about to be the two of us against twenty-four Dragon Shifters. And despite my bravado, I was genuinely terrified that I could lose Morgan tonight.

But when he twined his fingers with mine and gave me a gentle squeeze, I chose to believe that we would be okay. Because any other outcome just wasn't acceptable.

"We're fine, but you need to go," Mor insisted, leading us all back toward the emergency exit. It was hard to navigate in the smoke, but luckily, we were already right outside the hall. "I already radioed Logan and he's waiting at the landing."

Merida's petulant sigh was so loud that I could hear it even with the Dragon's still shouting at each other. "Fine, but I'm going to get some fight training so I don't have to leave next time all the fun starts."

"Me too sister," I nodded. Then I turned my attention to my magic. I knew a few guards had blocked Morgan and Merida in when they'd arrived. Now I just needed to find them.

Their feelings were close, and I manipulated them one after the other. The first guy was annoyed, so I tugged on that annoyance and pushed all his focus into it. When he finally came into view, he was so busy batting his hands through the air like he was fighting off the smoke that he didn't even notice Morgan take a swing at him.

The guy went down immediately, and Morgan even managed to keep hold of my hand the whole time. The other three guards were similarly easy, leaving us a clear path to the emergency exit. Mor knocked on the door, and a second later it swung open to reveal Logan.

"Long time no see," he grinned. Merida and I laughed, but Morgan just growled about needing to move the bodies we'd left on the stairwell into the penthouse so the Shifter Unit could find them later.

Once all the bodies were back in the hall, Morgan pinned Logan with a glare. "Now you two get to safety and stay there," he commanded.

Logan saluted his Chief, smirking all the while. "Will do, captain."

Morgan opened his mouth, presumably to yell at his best friend, but Logan had already started leading Merida down the stairs.

"He's an idiot," Morgan grumbled as we slipped back into the hall, the smoke now mostly diluted.

"But he's *your* idiot," I pointed out, smiling as Mor whipped out both knives again.

"No, *you're* my idiot." I wasn't sure if I should be flattered or insulted by the comment, but Morgan started speaking again before I could decide. "Now you focus on manipulating while I take them down."

I nodded, although I *hated* hiding behind him while he did all the fighting. So, I resolved to start fight training first thing tomorrow. Next time we were being attacked, *I* was going to save *his* nicely toned backside.

When we got back to the end of the hall, Eileen was shouting at her minions, and I could see her aged face turning red with rage. "Stop standing around and get them! But I need her *alive*."

Hm... That could work...

"Change of plans Bear Man," I said, slipping in front of Morgan. "I'll manipulate them and then when they're close enough, I'll move so you can strike."

"Caroli—"

"Morgan, they have guns. If you stand here, they're going to shoot you. But you heard Eileen, they're not going to shoot at me. I'm too valuable."

"I'm not concerned with your logic; I'm concerned that they're stupid enough to shoot at you anyway."

He had a point. I also hoped they weren't stupid enough to risk burning down their own building by using their fire magic. *Guess we'll find out.*

I stood my ground in front of Morgan, waiting to see who would be brave enough to strike first. Finally, a few arrogant Dragon Shifters strode toward us, eyeing me like I was easy prey. Unfortunately for them, I *loved* proving people wrong.

Showing them a saccharine smile, I played on their confidence, dialing it up as high as I could. Their bodies immediately relaxed as wide smiles split across their faces. Then, when they were within range, I squatted to the floor.

Morgan didn't miss a beat. Leaning over me, he grabbed the two men by their hair and smashed their skulls together. They went down like those inflatable tube men that they used to advertise at car lots. I could even hear the breath whooshing out of them as they slumped to the floor.

"Nice," I grinned, holding up my hand so my palm faced him. Meanwhile, the rest of my body faced forward, and I focused my magic on our next round of attackers.

"What are you doing?" Morgan grumbled behind me.

I ignored him for the moment, instead focusing on the furthest of the next five attackers. At least they had the intelligence to attack as a group this time. But the one that was furthest away seemed to be harboring a lot of jealousy and competitiveness. *Someone wants to be line leader.* I could work with that.

"I'm waiting for you to high five me," I said to Morgan, wiggling my fingers. Then I let my magic tinker around in the furthest attacker's emotions, dousing him with as much competitiveness as I could manage.

"Are you serious right now?" I didn't think Mor was really looking for an answer, so I just wiggled my hand at him.

Meanwhile, the jealousy inside the man I was manipulating rose so high that he started fighting with his four teammates. He pulled one down to the ground and punched another in the face. Soon the entire room was involved, and we had an all-out brawl on our hands. "Wow, nice job," Mor mumbled as we watched the pandemonium ensue.

One of the Dragon Shifters broke free of the throng and ambled toward me. This one had the wherewithal to hold a knife in my direction. But when I ducked and he looked at Morgan, his fear spiked. Understandable, since Mor looked pretty murderous at the moment. I barely had to tug on the man's fear to make him freeze. And he was so terrified that all Morgan had to do was grasp the front of his shirt and toss him against the wall. Where he fell to the floor. Unconscious.

"We are on a roll! Now come on Jimbo, don't leave Pam hanging," I said as I stood, *still* holding my palm toward him.

"*The Office*? Really? You're going to reference it *now*?" I just nodded and Morgan rolled his eyes. But with a very dramatic sigh, he appeased me and gave me an air high five.

"Thank you! See, was that so hard?"

Mor grumbled something about the cheekiness of Elves. But before I could call him out on it, we were fending off more attackers.

They started coming in twos, breaking away from the back in quick darting movements. I had to hand it to them, at least they were changing up their tactics. But since they still had to face Morgan, it really didn't matter how they came at us. He defeated them all anyway.

"Hi!" I said brightly to one woman who ran at me. Clearly, she'd expected me to duck like I'd been doing, because she paused for just a moment, confused. Which gave me just enough time to reach back and steal a knife from Morgan's hand. He gave it up without a fight, and I used my super speed to stab the woman in the forearm.

The woman cried out, clutching her arm. And now that she was in pain, I played off of it, intensifying it as I moved to the side. Morgan smoothly stepped in and knocked her unconscious while she was too distracted by her pain to notice. And just because he was that good, he also took out the second attacker without missing a beat.

And then it was done. Every Dragon Shifter was now lying unconscious on the floor. Most were piled around us, but a few were strewn about the middle of the room from the brawl they'd gotten into. Finally, it was over.

"Well, you know what they say about teamwork," I smiled, stepping into the office since no one was left awake to attack.

Morgan just stared at me.

"Oh, come on, don't be such a sourpuss. What do they say about teamwork, Morgan Gareth Hohlt?" I crossed my arms and tapped my foot, waiting for him to cave.

It took him exactly four seconds. "That it makes the dream work," he said, completely unenthused. But I wasn't fooled; I felt his joy, his relief, and his amusement. We won and it felt *good*. "Now if you're done teasing me, I need to tell Merida to call her conta—"

"Getting a little ahead of yourselves, aren't you?" came a familiar voice. And as if in sync, Morgan and I both turned toward the living room.

Standing there in the middle of the room, with glistening red scales and enormous wings tucked into its side, was a Dragon. Eileen the Dragon Queen was taller than me in her Dragon form, her head looming a good foot higher than mine. She was much prettier as a Dragon too, her red scales shimmering with flecks of gold. Of course, she was also much more intimidating like this, her long scaled tail wrapping itself around her clawed feet.

"I forgot about her," I said, whispering for no reason.

"Me too."

"Come and fight me little bear," Eileen taunted, her voice exactly the same, even in this form. "You win, you both go free. I win, and you're both mine. And if you're as tough as they say you are, then you've got nothing to lose."

Then, like he thought he was Thorin Oakenshield fighting the pale orc or Aragorn running into battle at the black gate—*Ariel's made me watch way too much fantasy*—he strutted toward the living room.

"Wait just a minute there, bucko," I said, grabbing his arm. "Where do you think you're going?"

Morgan stopped and looked back at me. Then, with a serious expression, he turned and set his hands on my shoulders. "Care—"

"No. Not happening." I shook my head. There was no way I was going to let him fight a *Dragon* by himself—because that's exactly what would happen. For whatever reason, it was almost impossible for me to manipulate someone when they shifted. Meaning that I would be useless to help Morgan against Eileen.

"You said you trusted me," he whispered, and I sighed.

"That's not fair," I pouted. "I just don't want to lose you."

"And I don't want to lose you either. But I need you to trust me."

I blocked out Eileen's impatient growls and my own fear, instead focusing only on Morgan. On the bright spot of affection inside him, on the blue ring around his irises, and on the pressure of his hands on my shoulders. If my trust would help him survive, then he had it.

"I do trust you," I promised, reaching up to press my palm over his heart, "In any form."

Mor smiled softly, then pressed a tender kiss to my forehead. My eyes fluttered closed at his touch and I drank up the moment. The way he held me so gently, the determination that mingled with his affection, and the hope that we would come out of this together.

But all too soon, he squeezed my shoulders and stepped away. "Good," he said, and I opened my eyes to find a stubborn look on his face, "Because that trust is about to be tested."

Whether his kiss had affected the oxygen in my brain, or the adrenaline of the fight had dumbed down my senses, it took me too long to figure out what he meant. By the time it clicked, he was already halfway to Eileen.

I wanted to shout at him and call him back but stopped myself. I couldn't question him—not with this. He needed me to trust him, to remind him to trust himself. I just hoped it was enough. Because I refused to leave here without him.

Morgan stopped a few yards from Eileen and turned to face me. Then he began to shift.

His body stretched, growing taller until he towered above the dragon. His shoulders widened as his features began to morph, and fur sprouted across his body. With a hoarse roar he fell onto all four feet, the most impressive bear I'd ever seen.

His head stood a full foot above mine, his body bigger than his brothers had been in their bear forms. Long silver fur fluffed out along his entire form, glistening like metal. But while his fur was silver, all four of his legs and his face were brushed with a cool beige color. And even with his bear eyes so different than his human ones, I could still see that blue ring around the irises. Reminding me that he was still Morgan.

"Hey Mor," I called out as he turned to face Eileen. He paused, his big bear head swinging over his shoulder to look back at me. "Remember, you're still you."

He nodded at me, and his lips curled into the bear version of a smile. But that smile turned into a snarl as he faced off against the Dragon.

Eileen was technically larger than Morgan if I included her tail and wingspan, but since the ceilings were only ten feet high, she didn't bother to open them. She was honestly a beautiful Dragon even if she was the only one I'd seen in real life. *Too bad she sucks.*

"Now we'll see how true the rumors really are," Eileen taunted, her long scaled tail whipping out behind her. "Are you as vicious as they say? Or is it all talk?"

Morgan didn't respond, but I could feel his emotions swirling around inside him like a hurricane. Fear, anger, determination, protectiveness, panic—they were all present, all screaming for attention. And when he roared, it was so loud that it made my chest vibrate. *Let the battle begin.*

Morgan lunged toward Eileen, and I watched, Morgan's pain almost becoming my own as she swiped a clawed foot at his head. His snout snapped to the side, and I let out a squeal, afraid she'd snapped his neck. But I should've known better. Morgan wasn't injured—he was angry.

He dove toward her, driving his entire body into her chest. A loud huff escaped her scaled lips and she fell back onto her side. But just as Morgan was about to take a bite out of her hide, she reached a clawed foot up and gouged his side.

"Morgan!" My body shivered at the sound of his whimper. Unsure what to do but unwilling to just stand there and watch, I snatched a heavy paperweight from Eileen's desk. Then I threw it at her.

She let out a very cat like yowl when the metal paperweight hit her in the snout. And when she turned her glistening eyes to me, Morgan bit into her shoulder.

Eileen roared and tried to throw him off, but he wouldn't let go. So she dragged her claws down his side, and he let out a pained growl. Tearing himself from her grasp, he didn't retreat, instead lumbering over to her tail.

As Eileen struggled to get herself standing again, Morgan grasped her tail in his mouth. Then he flicked his head—*hard*—and I heard a crunch as the bones cracked.

Eileen screamed, the sound piercing through the air with an ungodly tone. Pressing my hands to my ears, I watched as she finally stood. And just as I began to wonder if she'd shift back and admit defeat, she spun around...

...her broken tail sweeping Morgan's feet out from under him. My shout was swallowed by her roar as he fell to the ground on his side. Then, striking like a snake, she darted toward his unprotected belly. Razor sharp teeth rushed toward him, and I was frozen, desperate to help but utterly useless.

Just as her teeth brushed his fur, Morgan suddenly flipped all the way onto his back and donkey kicked her with all four legs. Eileen went sliding across the wood floors, sprawled out on her back.

Without a moment of hesitation, Morgan jumped up. Limping over to where she now lay, he stood up on his back feet. Then, with an ear-shattering roar, he slammed his paws down against her head, knocking her unconscious.

My attention went immediately to Morgan, who had blood staining his silver fur. He was panting heavily, his entire body moving with the effort it took to breathe. He didn't move his eyes away from Eileen, his rage strong, only fueled by the panic that had welled up higher.

"Morgan?" I called out, taking a step toward him.

His head snapped up with a snarl, his eyes not quite focusing on me. Only then did I realize there was drool hanging from his snout. *Oh, Morgan.* I could only imagine the memories going through his mind. Memories that were probably holding him hostage.

Determined to help, I took a few steps forward, but stopped when he began to growl. "Mor," I crooned gently, "It's me. It's Caroline."

He huffed, his nostrils flaring. "It's over now," I promised him. "You're okay. *We're* okay." I wasn't afraid of Morgan—even like this. But I *was* afraid that if I approached this wrong, it would only solidify the judgements he'd had of himself for so long. Judgements that I knew weren't true. So when his growl softened, I moved closer.

"Morgan Gareth Hohlt," I said, walking around the unconscious Dragon to reach him, "I am *not* leaving. So, you might as well stop trying to warn me away with your big bad bear act. Because I'm not buying it."

Not willing to give him a chance to run, I threw myself at him. My arms wound around his big hairy neck, and I pressed my face into his fur.

"I trust you in any form," I whispered. "And I refuse to leave you. You're not alone now."

Because he had been alone—we both had. For years we'd both fought our battles by ourselves, with no one to truly get it. Sure, he had his family and I had mine, but we relied on ourselves. Never sharing our burdens or letting anyone in. Fears, pains, hopes, and everything in between had been held so privately. Until now.

Because finally, I didn't want to hold back. I didn't want to carry it all alone. Instead, I found myself wanting to invite Morgan into the safe space where I hid all my bruised, battered and innocent things. Because I trusted him. In a way I'd never trusted anyone, I trusted *him*. And I felt it deep in his bones that he trusted me too.

"I do," his voice rasped, and I slowly realized that human arms were now holding me close. Somehow, I'd been so deep in my own realization that I hadn't even felt him shift. "I do trust you, Care. Always."

Apparently, I'd said that last part out loud, but I didn't care. Morgan was here; that was all that mattered.

THIRTY SIX

Caroline

WE STOOD LIKE THAT FOR A FEW MINUTES, just reveling in the peace of having each other near. Of having each other safe. I could've stayed that way for days, completely content to be held by him. All I needed was some food and I'd have everything I needed for the rest of my life. *Well, and maybe a couch. And Daisy Mae. And a change of clothes.* But the sentiment was there.

"Thank you," Morgan said, pulling back just far enough to look at me. "I wasn't...For a minute it felt like I was back there. Like my mom was dying all over again and I couldn't stop it. But then reality and memory merged and instead of Eileen on the ground, it was you. You were dying and it was my fault..." He paused, lifting a hand to run his fingers down my cheek. "I almost lost it Care, but *you* brought me back. My first time shifting around another person in twenty-two years, and you got me through it."

My heart ached at the unshed tears in his eyes, and I was struck with the overwhelming need to comfort him. So, I threw my arms around his neck and hugged him hard. He readily returned the embrace, pressing his face into my neck. When he began to cry, I combed my fingers through his hair to sooth him.

"It's okay, Mor. Cry, whimper, scream; I've got you." I closed my eyes as he held me tighter, drinking up the opportunity to support him.

The moment was interrupted, however, when a new voice called out. "Am I in the right place?"

Morgan and I released each other, turning to see a man in his mid-twenties with brown hair and a friendly smile. He stood at the entrance to a wide hallway beside the living room, the doors to an elevator closing a little ways behind him.

"Who sent you?" Morgan growled, slinging his arm around my shoulders. I squinted up at him, a little surprised, but he was too busy staring down the newcomer to notice.

"Merida," the young man smiled, eyes tracking the way Morgan's arm pulled me closer. "I'm Ace. And you must be Morgan and Caroline. Nice to meet you."

Morgan and I both relaxed—though I noticed that Mor didn't release me. Ace's arrival meant that the Shifter Unit was on its way, so we probably had very little time to clean up our mess before they arrived.

"Nice to meet you too," I smiled, then nodded at the room full of unconscious bodies. Some of which were starting to groan. "So, what's the plan? Merida didn't explain how you could help, only that you would."

"And I will." Ace pulled a handful of zip ties from his back pocket and handed a chunk of them to us.

"Not zip ties," I whined.

Morgan smirked, squeezing my shoulder. "She usually stays away from them because they get her so excited. But I love to see her all riled up." Then he had the nerve to wink at me.

"I *will* bite you," I threatened, shoving his arm off, and moving to the nearest Dragon Shifter.

"Promises, promises," Morgan mumbled, still smiling.

"You two are...interesting," Ace hummed, walking into the office to begin tying up more Dragon Shifters. "Merida mentioned that I should be careful not to show any interest in Caroline, but now I get it."

Confused, I looked between Morgan—who was now glaring at Ace—and the young man who apparently knew something I didn't. "What are you talking abo—"

"So, I assume you have some kind of plan to either wipe these guys' memories or keep them quiet?" I glared at Morgan's interruption, but he ignored me as he started zip tying people. *Hmm...*

"Yeah, I'll take care of erasing a few things from their memories. What specifically do you want them to forget?"

Morgan turned to me, and I shrugged. By now, Mike had already erased the security footage in the hotel. So really all we needed was to ensure that we appeared as victims and Eileen appeared guilty.

"I guess we need them to forget why we we're here," I said, tying another person's wrists behind their back. "Instead of us having snuck in, it'd be great if they all believed we'd been kidnapped. Also, they need to forget what I am..." I paused, looking warily over at Ace.

It took him a moment to notice my discomfort, but when he did, he just smiled. "Hey, I don't need to know anything you don't want me to. I understand secrets and I'm good at keeping them—just ask Merida. I have no interest in sussing out the skeletons in your closet when I've got plenty in my own. All I need to know is what you want them to remember. That's it."

I studied Ace, prodding around his emotions, trying to get a sense of how trustworthy he was. When Morgan lifted his eyebrows at me in a silent question, I nodded. Ace wasn't going to betray us. *I hope.* My ability to sense emotions wasn't foolproof. I could misinterpret those emotions, but I didn't think I was this time.

"Alright, we just need them to believe that we were brought here as captives," Morgan announced, pulling out another zip tie. "That Eileen had plotted to frame me and used Caroline as leverage. But as far as they know, she's just my friend and nothing more. There's nothing special about her and Eileen didn't know anything about her other than that she was a pressure point for me. We fought back and won. End of story."

Ace nodded, not asking any questions about which parts of the story were and weren't true. And thankfully, since I'd erased the hard drive of Eileen's computer, the Shifter Unit wouldn't find anything on me when they got here.

"So, what exactly are you?" I asked a few minutes later, all the Dragon Shifters now tied up.

Morgan and I watched as Ace leaned over a man. He didn't wake the man up to talk to him or give him any potions to mess with his memories. Instead, he hovered his hands in the air over the man's head, pulling his fingers this way and that. Not unlike the way Witches wove spells...

"Officially, I'm a Sphinx Hunter," Ace replied, not looking away from his task. He worked fast, moving from person to person. But if he was a Sphinx Hunter, then none of what he was doing made sense. There was a species of Hunter for every species of Shifter. And each type of Hunter had the opposite abilities of their respective Shifter. So, while Sphinxes could bind people to a secret, Sphinx Hunters could unbind secrets. And *only* Witches and Witch Hunters could see spells and weave them. Which was what I suspected he was doing right now.

"And unofficially?" Mor asked, arms crossed as he watched Ace finish his work up on the last of the Dragon Shifters—Eileen.

Ace stood and smiled. "My unofficial species is one of the skeletons in my closet."

Ah. If we didn't ask, he wouldn't either. "Fair enough," I agreed. "So can't these guys all just start shifting into Dragon form once they wake up?"

"No, these zip ties are charmed, so—"

"Ace!"

I jumped at the shout, and we all turned toward the elevator in the hallway. Where a man about the same age as Ace stood, pointing at the Sphinx Hunter. The newcomer was a little dorky looking, with large wire rimmed glasses, and a button-down shirt and tie under his black Shifter Unit jacket. "You did that on purpose!" he shouted again.

"Did what?" Ace asked, and I had to give him credit. The innocent look he gave the newcomer was very convincing.

Slowly, a few other people began to trail out of the elevator, all dressed in the same black jackets. Although the dorky guy was the only one with a dress shirt and tie underneath.

"You *stole* the elevator and ignored me when I asked you to hold it," the dorky guy exclaimed, stomping further into the room. "Then, you pressed every single button after you got off, so that even when I pushed the fifteenth floor, we had to go all the way down to the first floor and back up!"

"Hm...doesn't sound like me." Ace hummed noncommittally.

One glance at the rest of the group—all patiently waiting and completely unfazed—told me that this was the duo's normal behavior.

"They're like a mythical version of Dwight and Jim," I whispered excitedly to Morgan.

"Who do you think the Michael Scott is?" Morgan whispered back.

"Hmm...I don't know. Maybe the older guy who's smiling about the whole thing? It's a very Michael Scott kind of behavior to find this entertaining."

We watched the group as a young woman got between the two guys and tried to get the group on task. Meanwhile, the older guy I'd pointed out started making *really* bad elevator jokes that I was pretty sure he was telling wrong.

"So, are they going to question us now?" I asked, leaning into Mor when he again wrapped his arm around my shoulder. This time the move felt more supportive than possessive.

"Yeah, but since Ace did...whatever he did, the Dragon Shifters will remember us as victims. So, the questioning shouldn't take long. And the gang is already waiting downstairs to take us home. We'll go through the stairwell to avoid any press."

"How's your side?" His face was already a tiny bit bruised, but he didn't seem to be bleeding or in any major pain since shifting. Still, I wouldn't put him past it to be putting on a brave face to placate me.

"Flesh wound," he shrugged. But I paid close attention to his emotions to make sure he wasn't lying.

"It doesn't feel like you're lying..."

He smiled at me, and it *looked* genuine. "That's because I'm not. It'll probably need stitches, but I'll be fine."

"So does that mean I can coddle you like you did with me and my concussions?"

"No. Because unlike you with your concussions, *I* can still stand, and *I'm* not delirious."

*Hm...*He had a point.

"Fine. You win, but we're gonna have the doctor meet us at the house." Then, before he could argue with me, I went on. "Also, can we get Frank's on the way home?" I begged excitedly, turning my best approximation of puppy dog eyes up at him.

"No," he shook his head, "I cannot knowingly get you food that will someday kill you."

"But then you'd be rid of me, and all your problems would disappear. See? Win, win."

Instead of laughing or smiling, Morgan grew serious. He curled his arm further around me, pressing me into his chest. I went willingly, letting my head rest against him. "What if I don't want to be rid of you?"

"Then you'd better buy me the food," I sighed, though there was no snark behind the words. Just contentment. "Otherwise, I'll make you wish you had gotten rid of me."

"Deal. I give you food, and you don't leave."

I smiled and snuggled a little closer. "Now you're getting it, Bear Man."

THIRTY SEVEN

Caroline

It hadn't been long since I'd first been brought to Morgan's house. But sitting here now on the edge of my bed in the room that had once been my prison, that seemed like a lifetime ago. I remembered how much I hated Morgan at the time. How badly I wanted to get away. Yet now...I didn't want to leave. A different me had entered this house than the one that might be leaving it now. *If he doesn't want me to stay...*

"Now why do you look so sad?"

I turned at the sound of Morgan's voice. He stood in the doorway, hands in the pockets of his jeans and a zip up hoodie hanging open over a fitted T shirt. He looked the same as the Morgan that had thrown me over his shoulder and kidnapped me. And yet he was somehow different. Lighter maybe. He still looked intimidating with his white scar, unnerving grey eyes and impressive physique, but there was something sweeter about him now. Maybe it was the look in his eyes or the affection I felt brimming inside him. And the fact that it was directed at me.

"You haven't brought me any food today," I teased, but I couldn't quite muster up a smile. I was too anxious, wondering if I'd be moving back to my house by the end of this conversation. I didn't *think* Morgan wanted me to go, but I wasn't sure if he wanted me to stay either.

Mor cocked his head, studying me. I wondered what all he could see when he looked at me like that. What secrets he could discern. Then, pushing off the doorframe, he strode over to the bed and sat beside me. His thigh brushed against mine, our arms pressing together. I felt him watching me, but I kept my eyes on Daisy Mae who was lying in a patch of sunlight on the floor.

"What's wrong Care?" Morgan finally asked. "You seem worried, but I can't tell why. Eileen is in Niffleheim now, I've been cleared of all charges, and no one from the hotel remembers that you're an Elf. Sure, Eileen still has a trial to get through, but we both know she's not getting out of prison. So, what is it that's bothering you?"

He was right. I wasn't stressed about Eileen or her charges. The evidence against her was too compelling to get her out of Niffleheim prison. And I had no fears that the charges against Morgan would resurface. I wasn't even worried about myself—at least not right this second. No, my problem was entirely Morgan centered, and I had no idea how to voice it.

The truth was that I wanted this; the ability to sit next to him and talk at any time of day. I wanted to see Mike and Clint and Logan every morning at breakfast. I wanted to watch *The Bachelor* with Grey...And I more than anything, I wanted to be near Morgan. This place, this house, had become a home for me. And as much as I loved my house across the street from Mr. Finch, it had always been a place holder. A hideout, a base of operations, but not a *home*. This, sitting here with Morgan right now, was home.

But I can't tell him that. Telling him that he was my best friend was one thing. But asking him if I could move in was a totally different story. *Nope, not happening.*

"Why are you shaking your head?" he asked, eyebrows scrunching as he watched me.

Embarrassed at my inability to keep my thoughts on the *inside*, I closed my eyes and rubbed my forehead. "I'm not shaking my head."

"You are, and you're doing it again."

I opened my eyes and glared at him. "I am not."

"You are," he insisted, taking my chin between his fingers to stop the head shaking that I was apparently *still* doing. "Now *please* tell me what's wrong."

I sighed, letting his hand support the weight of my head as I gave into a petulant pout. "I don't know where I belong."

Somehow, he seemed almost offended by this statement. “What do you mean? You belong here.”

“Do I though? I’m not a Berserker.”

Morgan stilled. I could almost feel the words banging on his lips, trying to get out. Yet he hesitated, grey eyes bouncing between mine with indecision.

“No, you’re not a berserker,” he finally agreed with a whisper. “You’re something far more important.”

“What’s that?”

He paused, weighing his words. “You’re my best friend. My safe space. You belong here, Care. I need you.”

“You need me?” I parroted dumbly, a little in awe. Not too long ago he’d hated me, and now he...didn’t.

Morgan shrugged, suddenly shy as he dropped his hand from my chin.

“Mor?” I prompted, only continuing once he met my eyes. “I need you too.”

He smiled, and I felt his pleasure waft around us like a scent on the air; sweet and intangible. Then, without giving me a chance to think, he pulled me into his arms. Somehow, this hug felt bigger than all the others. Like we were marking a moment. I couldn’t help it as tears stung my eyes. For the first time, I had a place *and* a person that felt like home.

“Hey, you okay?” Mor whispered, and I realized too late that I’d unleashed my tears onto his shirt.

“I’m sorry, I didn’t mean to cry on you.” I pulled myself from his arms, patting at his T shirt like I could dry it through touch. Of course, when I really thought about the chiseled firmness of his pecs beneath my fingers, I blushed hot enough that I probably *could’ve* dried it through touch. The man was a *specimen.*

“I’m not worried about my shirt, Care,” he said, smirking at my blush. “I *am*, however,” he added, swiping his thumb gently under my eyes, “Worried about you. Are you okay?”

I nodded, trying to focus on calming my heart rate. *Dang pecs.* “Yeah, I’m okay. I just...thank you. For everything.”

“Caroline Birch, thanking me?” Morgan feigned shock, laying his fingers dramatically on his chest. “I think I’d better document this moment. Let me go grab a camera.”

“Shut up,” I laughed, shoving his arm. “So, since you *need* me in your life, does this mean you’ll help me move all my things here?”

His smile slipped. “Define all of your things.”

"Do you want me to move in, or don't you?"

"I do."

"Then I need my things."

"...all of it?" he exclaimed; eyes wide. "You mean even your furniture?"

"Yeah. I mean don't get me wrong, I love it here," I said, glancing around the bedroom. "But this place wasn't exactly designed with me in mind."

His eyebrows lowered, and his mouth turned down into a ridiculous frown. But the moment he sighed, I knew he would humor me.

"Caroline Felicity Birch, you are going to give me a run for my money, aren't you?" he complained, his voice warm and affectionate as he wrapped an arm around my shoulders.

"You have no idea, Morgan Gareth Hohlt," I replied, settling into his side. "I'm just getting started."

THIRTY EIGHT

Caroline

"TRY NOT TO SCRATCH THE LEGS," I shouted as Mike and Clint easily carted my faded periwinkle couch out the front door of my house.

"We're professionals Caroline," Clint called back. "Give us some credit...Oof, hold on, I'm slipping."

I probably would've followed them out to make sure they didn't break anything, but I heard Mr. Finch's voice shouting something about lazy workers and figured he had it covered. I was thankful that Morgan and the guys were helping me move so I didn't have to hire anyone. But if they busted up my stuff, I was fully prepared to make them regret it.

"Don't worry, Care Bear," Logan said, stepping up beside me, a ridiculously large sandwich in his hand. "I'm supervising, so I'll keep them in line."

"Oh, I feel my faith restored." I smiled snidely at him.

"Hey now, I'm a good supervisor."

And as if on cue, there was a crash outside. I just raised my eyebrows at Logan. "Really? How's the supervising going then?"

Logan opened his mouth and then closed it. "Right, sorry about that. But don't worry, I'll take care of it!" Then he took off out the front door. It really wasn't necessary though because I could already hear Mr. Finch shouting at them all. *He's got it covered.*

Assured that I didn't want to know how things were going outside—otherwise I'd probably turn violent—I headed for my office. I'd been using the second bedroom as a workspace since I'd moved in. It was a nice room, with a big window and a built-in. But honestly, I was excited to move into Morgan's instead.

When he'd initially invited me to move into their Berserker frat house, I worried that he was doing it out of pity or responsibility. But when I told him he didn't have to move me or my stuff into his house, he went and rented a moving truck. He said if I had no objections, he was going to kidnap me permanently. *I have absolutely zero objections.*

"None at all," I mumbled to myself as I entered the office. Most of the stuff in the room had already been boxed up, but my desk and laptop remained. I'd already gone through most of Eileen's files while Logan and Morgan had argued over the best way to get my bed out of the house earlier. There hadn't been anything surprising in them so far, but I still had a few left.

I walked around my faded grey green desk, admiring its bronzed edges and accents that had been my one and only successful DIY project. I'd definitely have to supervise the boys myself when they took it out to the van. Sitting in the soft pink desk chair, I unlocked my computer.

The last three remaining files stared at me from the screen, and I quickly scanned through them. The information in the first two was similar to what I'd already read in previous files. So far, I'd discovered files documenting Eileen's payments to the attackers she'd hired, notes she'd made on framing Morgan—which I'd gladly gotten into the hands of the mayor—and a background check she'd run on me. I'd also come across a few incriminating pieces that detailed her plans to force all Dragons to treat her like a dictator rather than a monarch. Those I also passed on to Mayor Fitz.

Not expecting to find anything new, I clicked on the last file. I'd been hoping to find information on who Eileen had 'sold' me to, but so far, no dice.

"Wait," I mumbled, skimming over the file. It was a dossier on me—which wasn't exactly unexpected—except that this one had information I hadn't seen before. "Parents, Shannon and Marcus Birch," I read aloud, "Birthday, January fifth...Wait, what?"

I froze, the mouse hovering over the words that I couldn't quite grasp. Shaking my head, I read it again. Then again. And again.

"Care?" Morgan called from down the hall.

I didn't respond. I wasn't sure I could pull my eyes from the screen, let alone speak.

"Care—hey, are you okay?" I didn't look at him, but it didn't matter. Within seconds, he was crouching beside me, his hands gently turning my face to look at him. "Talk to me. What's wrong?"

"Everything," I breathed, surprised that I could find my voice.

"Care, you're scaring me. What's going on?"

I pointed to the screen, and Morgan watched me for another few moments before he began reading.

"Eileen apparently had some serious connections," I said numbly, filling him in even as he read it for himself. "Whoever she hired found a safety deposit box under my name. It had my records in it. My real ones, from birth parents. Their names...my real last name, my real date of birth, it's all there."

"Your birth parents' names were William and Irene Ljosalfar," Morgan read, his voice holding the same bemusement I felt. "Wait, Ljosalfar as in...the royal family?"

"The *Alfar* royal family," I added when he turned back to me. "It doesn't make sense, Mor. According to this, not only were my birth parents *not* Nephilim, but they were also descended from the royal family. What the heck does that make me?"

He shrugged. "Queen."

"Of what? Myself? I'm the only Elf left. There's nothing to be queen of." I paused, rubbing my forehead as I felt an incoming headache. "Do you know what this means?"

Morgan nodded and grasped my hands. His fingers were warm around mine, his comfort sweet. But it wasn't enough to make this go away. It couldn't stop the dominos from falling now that they'd begun.

"I'm an Alfar—or at least part Alfar," I whispered, the words sounding just as ridiculous as they had in my head. "And I'm descended from the royal Elf family that lost the civil war over seven hundred years ago. Eileen found this information with help. *And* she sold me to someone that we still don't have a lead on. Morgan, I just went from rare and desirable, to completely *mythical*. If word of this gets out, there won't be anywhere for me to hide."

Morgan shook his head, pulling at my hands until they rested on his chest. His heart pounded beneath my fingers, and his determination and stubborn affection wrapped around me like armor.

"You feel this? So long as this heart is still beating, I'll be fighting for you," he insisted, grey eyes stormy. "I just got you, Care. I'll fight through Hell before I lose you."

I went willingly into his arms when he hugged me, burrowing myself against him. But no matter how safe Morgan made me feel, I knew he couldn't protect me from this. *But he won't have to.* Because I was going to find answers. Whoever it was that had tried to buy me—*own me* like an animal—they were about to find out what kind of queen I could be.

The End...For Now.

Want to be the first to know when book two comes out? Make sure to subscribe to my newsletter (and also get a free eBook) at my website (reswriterchick.com) or at my Instagram (res_writer_chick).

Book 2 ***A Tale of Ribbons & Claws: Bond-Mate*** *coming* very *soon!*

Other Books By R.E.S.

Contemporary

The Grinch Next Door

Fantasy

Legends of Avalon: Merlin

Legends of Avalon: Arthur

Acknowledgments

Okay, time to thank my village. Because like raising a child, raising a book takes a village. And I wouldn't have survived without mine.

First of all, thank You God for always providing, Whether it be in strength, rest, support, or just the *idea* for this story that you blessed me with. You always have my back. Through the hills and valleys, You're here.

Thank you to my momma, my best friend and my Lorelai. You're always in my corner and I would be so lost (and so broke) without you and your constant support. Whether it was childhood dreams of being a figure skater, or now pursuing being an author, you're always here for me. Thank you for letting me *still* bunk at home, and thank you for always lifting me up.

To all my online friends, I'm eternally grateful for you! Who knew that so many soul sisters would be found thanks to Instagram? Distance has no impact on us, and I'm so glad I know you all. Bethany, Melody, Jennie, Penny, Austin, Leigh, you guys make my life feel full.

And speaking of friends, thank you Leigh for being a fantastic beta reader! This story is 100 times better thanks to you and your insight! Thank you so much for reading my terrible rough draft and seeing the diamond under all that rough.

A shout out to my brother and sister-in-law. You guys are always stellar cheerleaders and even though you aren't close enough to take me to ice cream every time I need you (boo distance), you always show up for me. Love you guys.

And of course, thank you to the joys of my life, my dogs. Daisy Mae, you finally got your own book, and Marshall Moose, I promise to get working on your story again soon. My two fur babies, you are the bright spots of every day, and you really are my favorite part of life.

And last but certainly not least, thank YOU reader for reading this book (and reading the acknowledgements. Wow, you rock). This book wouldn't be here if not for you, because I would have given up on the career path of my dreams if not for you *wanting* to keep reading. So thank you for reading, for reviewing and rating, AND for sending me DMs and emails about how much you love these stories! Your support really does keep me going, and I appreciate you more than I can say.

I'm a blessed girl, and I'm so grateful.

About the Author

Rachel (R.E.S.) is an author of both contemporary and fantasy stories. She's a *The Office* enthusiast, a *The Lord of the Rings* superfan, and a sucker for all things geek. She reads anything with some clean romance—bonus points if there's some snarky MCs, funny side characters, and a happy ending. But if there's a poorly used miscommunication trope, she's probably throwing that book across the room. Rachel is dog obsessed, and two of her series even include her dogs (Daisy Mae appears in *A Tale of Ribbons & Claws* and Marshall is in *Legends of Avalon*). This hobbit author and her dogs spend lots of time writing, walking, and of course, watching *The Office* and *The Lord of the Rings.*

Where to Find Me

Website: reswriterchick.com

Instagram: @res_writer_chick

Facebook Group: The PPC R.E.S.' Reader Group

Newsletter (keep up on upcoming releases): sign up on my website

Podcasts: Good On Paper (available wherever you get your podcasts)

Made in the USA
Monee, IL
16 July 2023

39375513R00164